elementary, my dear watkins

mindy starns clark

HARVEST HOUSE PUBLISHERS

EUGENE, OREGON

Cover by Terry Dugan Design, Minneapolis, Minnesota

Cover photo © Christopher Wilhelm / Photodisc Red / Getty Images

ELEMENTARY, MY DEAR WATKINS
Copyright © 2007 by Mindy Starns Clark
Published by Harvest House Publishers
Eugene, Oregon 97402
www.harvesthousepublishers.com

Library of Congress Cataloging-in-Publication Data
Clark, Mindy Starns.
Elementary, my dear Watkins / Mindy Starns Clark.
  p. cm.
ISBN-13: 978-0-7369-1487-1
ISBN-10: 0-7369-1487-0
1. Tulip, Jo (Fictitious character)—Fiction. 2. Westchester County (N.Y.)—Fiction. I. Title.
PS3603.L366E44 2007
813.'54—dc22   2006028635

Printed in the United States of America

07 08 09 10 11 12 13 14 / BP-CF / 10 9 8 7 6 5 4 3 2

This book is dedicated to
Kim Moore,
Christlike example of love and service,
editor extraordinaire,
and dear friend.
You are such a blessing in my life!

ACKNOWLEDGMENTS

Many, many thanks to:

John Clark, for everything.

Emily and Lauren Clark, my precious daughters, who really had to go the extra mile for this one.

Jackie Starns, my mom and friend and the best cheerleader going.

My trusted staff of "medical advisors": Robert M. Starns, MD, J.K. Wolf, MD, and D.P. Lyle, MD.

Fran Severn, for Chewie. I hope he enjoyed the ride!

The lovely folks at Harvest House Publishers, who are always living examples of the One we serve.

My small groups at FVCN, both of which contain some mighty prayer warriors.

Those who bless me with their hospitality just when I need it most: Larry and Bebe Hebling, Ned and Marie Scannell, and the Teske-White Family.

Some great brainstormers and idea people, including Sharon Pontillas, DiAnn Mills, Josh Himes, and Sharon Wildwind.

Miriam Stein, Siri Mitchell, and Tim and Peggy Wright, for sharing their areas of expertise.

The brilliant minds of DorothyL, especially Colleen Barnett, Wendy Bartlett, Sarah Bewley, BA Bolton, Carl Brookins, Alafair Burke, Tony Burton, Lee Carper, Tammy Cravit, Carola Dunn, Ellen H. Ehrig, Sarah Fisher, Sara Hoskinson Frommer, Anne M Jones, Clyde Linsley, Kay Martinez, Shelley McKibbon, Meredith Phillips, Jeanna Schilling, Triss Stein, Cathy Strasser, Shannon Surly, and Cindy Williams.

Chi Libris, for being there in so many ways. Truly, I couldn't do this without you!

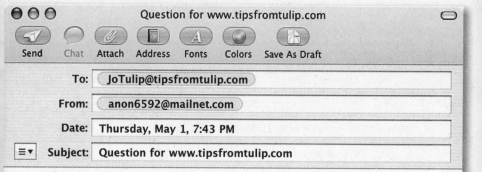

Dear Tulip,

If someone's life was in danger and I knew about it, how could I tell them without having to get involved myself? Also, what's the best way to clean a really dirty toaster oven?

Sincerely,

Trying To Stay Out Of It

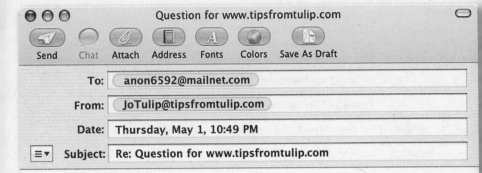

To: anon6592@mailnet.com

From: JoTulip@tipsfromtulip.com

Date: Thursday, May 1, 10:49 PM

Subject: Re: Question for www.tipsfromtulip.com

Dear Trying,

I hate to tell you this, but if someone's life is in danger and you know about it, you're already involved. Go to the person who is in danger *immediately* and let them know. Contact the police as well. This is no simple matter, and if you withhold information that could prevent someone from being harmed, then you might be implicated in a crime.

May I help in some way? Perhaps act as a go-between with the authorities? Please write back as soon as possible.

To answer your other question, in my experience the single best way to clean a really dirty toaster oven is to give it away and buy a new one.

Jo Tulip

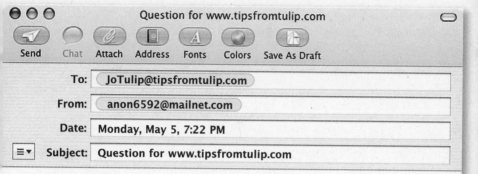

To: JoTulip@tipsfromtulip.com

From: anon6592@mailnet.com

Date: Monday, May 5, 7:22 PM

Subject: Question for www.tipsfromtulip.com

Dear Tulip,

Sorry it took so long to reply. I've been busy. Thanks for writing back, but I've got to ask you why you think I should be implicated in a crime if I have nothing to do with it? I'm just trying to be a good citizen.

Look, this thing is going to happen very soon. Like in a day or two. I feel bad, but I've had a few run-ins with the law myself and I really can't get involved. What do I do?

Signed,

Trying To Stay Out Of It

P.S. Thanks for the advice about the toaster oven. I think you're right. It's probably time to toss it and start over. Are there any features in particular you'd recommend?

1

Jo Tulip sat across from the detective, trying not to be distracted by his tie. It was obviously silk, but it was flat and dull and very much in need of freshening. She wondered if it would seem intrusive if she advised him to turn his iron on the highest setting, wrap a damp cloth over the soleplate of the iron, and run it back and forth directly over the fabric, almost but not quite touching it. The steam would bring the tie back to life nicely, for sure.

"That's as close as we gonna get to this person, unless we stake out the library," the detective was saying in a thick Bronx accent. "And that's not gonna happen. So I guess it ends here, least 'til something further develops. But thanks for bringing the situation to our attention."

Jo took her gaze from the man's tie and met his eyes. He was in his mid-forties, chubby and red cheeked, with a collar too tight for his thick neck.

"Until something further develops," she repeated. "You mean like when somebody gets hurt? Or even killed?"

He glanced at his watch.

"I'm sorry, but at this point, we can't justify the manpower for a stakeout if there's been no real crime."

"But look at his second e-mail. It says something's going to happen 'in a day or two.' He wrote that one on Monday—and it's already Wednesday!"

"So maybe whatever he was talking about is over and done with by now. Like I said, there's really nothing we can do about it anyway."

Jo sighed heavily, wishing Chief Cooper had come with her. His official cop presence might have carried more weight with this guy than she obviously did. Harvey Cooper, who was both a friend and the local

police chief for her hometown, had helped trace the source of the strange
e-mail Jo had received at her "Tips from Tulip" website, a trail which led
to a library in Kreston, New York. The police there hadn't responded
with much interest to the chief's report or Jo's subsequent phone calls,
so she had decided to stop by the Kreston station today in person, since
she had to come up to nearby Manhattan for an appointment with an
orthopedic specialist anyway.

Now that Jo was there in person, however, she was still hitting a very
frustrating dead end. The detective who had agreed to meet with her
had contacted the library, but they said that since a library card was
not required for using the computers, there was no way to check their
records to learn the real identity of the person who had been online at
the time the e-mails were sent.

"Chances are, the person with that e-mail address will be back again,"
Jo said to the reticent detective. "I believe you can put some sort of elec-
tronic alert system on the computers in the library. Then if this person
logs on again, you'll be notified and can move in and apprehend them."

"No can do."

"At the very least, couldn't you stake out the library between seven
and eight each night? He sent the first one at 7:43 last Thursday and the
second one at 7:22 on Monday. Obviously, he has some sort of routine.
Can't you at least try?"

The detective shook his head.

"Again, kind of hard to apprehend someone who ain't done nothing
wrong. There's been no real crime here. He just says he knows someone
whose life is in danger. That could mean a lot of things. Maybe his wife's
brake cables are nearly shot or his brother keeps playing golf in a thun-
derstorm or his diabetic mother won't stop eating ice cream. We got no
way of knowing."

"But—"

"Or it could be a woman," he continued, clearly on a roll, "maybe worried that her husband's been drinking too much or that her best friend
joined a motorcycle gang. Whatever. There just isn't enough information
here for us to act on."

Jo shook her head. Surely, that's not what this person—man or
woman—meant.

"He, or she, whatever, called what's going to happen a *crime*," she
argued. "They said they can't get involved because in the past they've had
their own mix-ups with the law. It sounds very serious to me."

The detective looked at her with what seemed to be a cross between scorn and pity, as if he were sorry she was quite so dumb.

"Miss Tulip," he said, patting his tie and tucking it into his jacket, "as a celebrity, surely you know there are nuts of all kinds out there, and some of them love nothin' more than to play with the heads of good folks like you."

"I'm not exactly a celebrity. I just write a newspaper column."

"Yeah, a nationwide newspaper column, which makes you a lot more well-known than the average person. I mean, we appreciate what you've done to track this down and all, but I think you're gonna have to write this one off as a prank. You've written back, urging this person to contact the authorities. I think that's the most you can do."

Jo watched as the man slipped the papers she had brought into a manila folder and then placed the folder on top of a filing cabinet behind him. She felt sure that the moment she walked out of the door that folder would somehow find its way into the trash. But what else could she do?

Actually, she knew exactly what she could do—and it didn't involve trying to convince this guy with logic or reason. It was time to pull some strings over his head.

"Well, I appreciate your time," she said, standing. "If you're not going to follow up, may I have my paperwork back, please?"

"Uh, sure," he said, handing her the file.

"Thanks," Jo said, adding the words *for nothing* in her mind.

"No prob," he replied, standing as well.

As Jo limped toward the door, trying to keep her weight off her injured foot, she started to turn around to tell him about the benefits of using steam on silk. But then she decided she wouldn't.

A man with that kind of attitude deserved to walk around with an unfreshened tie.

Danny skipped down the steps of the *Métro*, relieved to see a crowd waiting at the platform and his train just coming to a stop. He had cut it so close, he was afraid he might have missed it.

The doors opened with a *whoosh* and he climbed aboard with the others, taking a seat on the gray plastic bench along the wall. As he did, he glanced at his watch and calculated the time back home in the States.

It was 6:28 in the evening, Paris time, which meant 12:28 in the afternoon in Pennsylvania. For some reason, the longer he and Jo were apart, the more frequently he felt the need to calculate the time difference and think about her and picture what she might be doing at that moment. Right now, she was probably also on a train, heading from Kreston, in the Bronx, to Manhattan, where she would meet up with her grandmother and go see some world-renowned medical specialist.

Danny was interested to hear what the doctor would have to say about Jo's ankle, of course, but he was also eager to learn about her visit to the police department in Kreston, where she had gone to report some creepy e-mails she had received last week through her Tips from Tulip website. Danny knew that Jo's life was complicated enough as it was; she surely didn't need to be hassled by some nut with an anonymous e-mail account and a dirty toaster oven.

In the past year, Jo had been instrumental in solving several high-profile murders, so now apparently someone had decided she must be the go-to gal not just for cleaning questions, but for police-related matters as well. Six weeks ago Jo had been caught up in an investigation that ended with a bang, literally, landing her in the hospital after being caught in an explosion. Since then she had had a lot to adjust to: injuries from that explosion, her home in ashes, a temporary residence, and her best-friend-turned-boyfriend moving to Europe to take a three-month magazine internship. At this point the poor thing needed a break, not more crime-related complications. Danny's hope was that the Kreston police would take matters into their own hands and leave Jo free to concentrate on her recovery, her work, and her housing situation. The last thing she needed was another mystery on her hands.

"*Vas-y, vas-y,*" a mother said to her young son as they squeezed on board. The train car had filled up fast, so Danny gave his seat to the woman and reached for a handle in the middle instead. Once they were moving, he held on tightly as the walls outside of the windows turned to a blur.

He waited for the third stop and then got off and walked up the steps. He was still two blocks from the restaurant, so he started sprinting, covering the distance as quickly as possible, weaving in and among the more slow-moving pedestrians. He hated being an ugly American, rude and pushy and in a hurry, but this dinner was at the invitation and expense of his friend and coworker Luc, and Danny thought it would be even ruder to show up late to a free meal.

At least it felt good to be able to move so fast. Coincidentally, Danny had broken his foot a few days before Jo had—though his injury had come from pure stupidity, slipping on a rock while trying to help Jo's dog, Chewie, scamper out of a pond. Danny's cast had come off last week, but, unlike Jo, he'd had no further complications and was already almost back to normal. The doctor said he recovered so fast because he was in such good shape to begin with, but Jo was in better shape than he was, so the delay in her recovery really wasn't fair. Besides, it was a relief to be on two good feet, and it made him sad that Jo wasn't also able to enjoy that feeling yet.

He reached the restaurant and stepped inside, pausing in the foyer to catch his breath and run a hand over his messy brown hair. From what he could see, the place was definitely swanky and oh-so-French, with several low-lit crystal chandeliers hanging from the ceiling, lots of pinched-lipped waiters, and tiny servings on fancy plates. Stepping into the dining room, Danny spotted Luc discreetly waving him over from a corner table, where he was sitting with an older man dressed in a suit and sipping a glass of red wine. Danny hadn't realized anyone else would be joining them, but considering the way the guy was dressed, he was glad he'd thought to throw on a jacket and tie at the last moment. Crossing the room, Danny reached the table and was introduced to Chester Parks.

"Nice to meet you," Chester said, shaking Danny's hand.

"Sounds like a good ol' American accent to me," Danny replied with a smile, taking his seat. "Where are you from?"

"New York."

"Chester's with *Haute Couture* magazine," Luc added, one eyebrow high.

Danny simply nodded, immediately reassessing the situation. Luc was quite ambitious, with aspirations more cosmopolitan than the nature photography of *Scene It* magazine, where he and Danny both currently worked. Danny realized that Luc must be angling for a position with *Haute Couture,* and his hope was that Danny would make him look good.

Danny could do that. He liked Luc well enough, and the guy was a decent photographer, if a bit of a cold fish. He and *Haute Couture* might be a perfect fit, especially blue-tinted shots with unsmiling models draped stiffly around stark sets. That wasn't Danny's cup of tea, but if that's what Luc wanted, he'd be happy to help out.

"*Haute Couture?* Impressive," Danny said. "What brings you to France?"

"I had some business in our Paris office," the man replied. "Tonight, however, you might say I'm on a recruiting mission. But enough of that for now. What will you have? I recommend the *coq-au-vin*. In fact, may I order for all of us?"

That sounded good to Danny. His French was still a bit rudimentary, and the descriptive phrases in the menu were mostly over his head.

"Please do," Danny said, closing the menu and handing it to the tuxedoed waiter. "I'm game for anything except *escargot*—a mistake I won't make twice."

Chester placed their orders in fluent-but-American-accented French, and once the waiter was gone the conversation turned to New York. Knowing that's where Jo was right now, Danny felt a sudden, painful surge of loneliness. After being apart for nearly five weeks, the separation was getting harder and harder to take. In the beginning, his job had absorbed so much of his time and energy that he was able to put thoughts of Jo out of his mind for most of the day. Lately, however, that was getting more and more difficult to do. He couldn't imagine how he was going to get through two more months without her.

Chester was waxing poetic about the city, and as he went on, Danny kept picturing Jo, striding—well, limping, maybe—through stately Penn Station, meeting up with her grandmother's limo for the ride to the doctor, peering out of the vehicle's sunroof at the tall buildings that flanked the busy Manhattan streets.

Danny especially missed Jo tonight because he'd had such a busy day that he never had time to go online and check his e-mail. She usually wrote to him throughout the afternoon, either from her home computer or from her handheld digital assistant if she was out and about, and the near-constant communication kept him feeling connected to her despite the distance that separated them. Though he would enjoy this dinner, the highlight of his day was going to be when he got home to his computer and had a chance to go online and read about Jo's day.

"Earth to Danny," Luc said, and Danny glanced over to see his friend staring at him. "Are you—how do you say—zoning out on us, *mon ami?* The food *est arrivé.*"

Startled, Danny looked up to see the waiter placing a small plate in front of him. The first course featured a long, thin slice of cucumber wrapped around a dollop of what looked like crab salad. Called an *amuse-bouche,* the small but tasty serving was supposed to wake up the appetite and whet it for all that would come next.

"Sorry," Danny said, forcing a smile as he picked up his fork. "It's been a long day." Sure enough, just the sight and smell of the food in front of him made him realize how hungry he was.

The men began to eat, resuming their conversation between bites. As they talked, Danny asked a discreet and silent grace first, asking God to bless the food and please, please bless Jo as she navigated the complicated waters of that disturbing e-mail that had sent her to the police in Kreston—not to mention the even deeper, more turbulent waters of having to spend time with her grandmother.

Jo's grandmother, Eleanor Bosworth, sat stiffly in the limo, shaking her head. The diamonds in her earrings caught the sunlight as she did so, casting a shower of tiny sparkles around the elegant interior of the vehicle.

"You've been reckless, Jo," Eleanor said. "For such a sensible person, I must say I'm surprised at your cavalier attitude about your health. "

Jo sighed heavily, regretting ever telling her grandmother about the complication with her ankle. This was so like the woman to step in after the fact and try to run the show—when she'd never even bothered to show up once when Jo was in the hospital or in the weeks of her recovery since.

"I've not been cavalier, Gran. The doctors have signed off on every one of my injuries except for the foot. And at this point, they say it's simply a matter of time."

"Tell me again what your little doctor told you," Eleanor said with a flippant wave of her heavily bejeweled hand.

"She's not a 'little doctor,'" Jo said. "She's a highly qualified surgeon."

"In Mulberry Glen, Pennsylvania. I'm sure."

Jo ignored the biting comment and explained that her doctor had X-rayed her foot again once the cast was off, and that she was perfectly satisfied with the healing of the bones.

"The pain I'm having now is not from the break but from the sprain, which is taking longer to heal," Jo explained. "She recommended ice packs and anti-inflammatories. At this point, it just seems like overkill to consult one of the nation's preeminent orthopedists for a mere sprained ankle."

"Darling, you're only twenty-seven years old. A bad healing at this point in your young life could prove to be disastrous down the line. Trust me in this. It's worth the risk of a little overkill if it saves you from foot problems when you're older."

The woman had a point there. Jo didn't even know why she was still arguing with her. She was here, wasn't she, en route to the doctor's office? Argument or not, her grandmother had already won this particular battle.

Besides, Jo had something more important to discuss anyway. As they inched their way through heavy traffic, she opened her bag and pulled out the printouts of the e-mails and the report from Chief Cooper that she had brought to the police.

"On a different matter," Jo said, glancing down at the papers, "I was wondering if you might know anyone of influence in the Bronx."

"The Bronx? Yes, I suppose, but why?"

"I need you to pull some strings in Kreston, if possible."

"Kreston?" her grandmother asked with a sneer. "Why on earth would you want to have anything to do with Kreston?"

Jo didn't share the sneer. She had thought the blue-collar town had been quaint, if a little rough around the edges, and certainly nothing at which to turn up her nose.

"Don't be a snob, Gran."

"Snob, schnob. What do you want me to do?"

Danny sipped a hot cup of decaf as Luc and Chester enjoyed an after-dinner drink called a *digestif*. The meal had been delicious but slow, dragged out through nine courses, and Danny was ready to call it a night and take off. Unfortunately, Chester pulled out a cigar, which probably meant he was just settling in.

Since coming to France, Danny had learned that the evening meal often continued late into the night, way past dessert. Sometimes that was fine, but tonight he was exhausted, having spent the day helping to prepare for an upcoming international photo shoot. There had been many details to handle, with no room for error, and because Danny had been in charge of packing up the film, equipment, and other supplies for the photographer, the pressure had been intense. Now, on top of his physical exhaustion, the heavy meal was making him sleepy. He decided to make a pitch for Luc as best he could and then hit the road.

"So, Chester," Danny said as the man lit a match, held it to the tip of the cigar, and puffed furiously. "You say you're here tonight on a recruiting mission? I think that's very exciting. Luc is a highly skilled photographer, and I know he would be an asset to your magazine."

Chester and Luc exchanged glances as Chester continued to puff his cigar. Once it caught, he flipped his hand to put out the flame and then pulled the stogie from his mouth.

"It's not Luc I'm here to recruit," Chester replied, blinking from the smoke. "It's you."

Danny hesitated, wondering if he had heard the man correctly.

"Me?"

"Yes. Your work has come to my attention, and I'm interested to see if you might consider a move to New York and the world of high fashion photography."

Danny was dumbfounded. He looked at Luc, who merely smiled and shrugged. Luc didn't seem disappointed, so he must have known all along that this wasn't about him.

"Thank you, but that's not the type of photography I do—or want to do," Danny said. "I'm a *Scene It* kind of guy all the way."

"*Scene It*, bah," Chester scoffed with a flip of his cigar. "What's the challenge there? Snap a few close-ups of some big cats in a zoo and call it an African safari?"

"No, they—"

"You want to see fangs and claws? Try putting three models in Prada bathing suits and tell them the best-looking one gets the cover shot."

Luc laughed, but Danny was deeply offended. There was nothing fake or engineered about the photography for *Scene It*. The zoo? Get real. Their photo shoots were some of the most notoriously ambitious and authentic in the industry.

"Even if *Scene It* is your type of place," Chester continued, "surely you can't be enjoying the piddling little internship salary they're currently paying you. What have they got you doing, anyway? Running the fax machine? Making coffee?"

"Mostly rights clearance and color corrections," Danny replied, listing jobs that were a step up from making coffee—though not by much. "But it's not about the money right now or my specific duties. I'm learning the ropes. I'm seeing the magazine business from the inside out. I've been able to work with some of the top nature photographers in the world. Just today I met Kalunga Bashiri and helped prepare for his next photo shoot to Switzerland and then Africa." Danny smiled at the thought of the tiny man with the big lens, a legend and a hero to nature photographers around the world.

"I know your background, son," Chester said, shaking his head. "Before you landed this internship, you were nothing but a backwoods portrait photographer with some stock photo sales on the side. Small potatoes."

"That's not exactly true," Danny said defensively. "One of my stock photos was recently bought by Twentieth Century Fox for background in a movie poster. I wouldn't call that small potatoes."

"Perhaps. But how many times can lightning strike? Come work for *Haute Couture,* and we'll make you much more than the underpaid color monkey you are here. You'll be a contract photographer doing studio product shots."

"Thank you so much, sir, but I'm afraid I'm not interested. Not my kind of photos and not my kind of magazine. No offense."

Chester took a puff on his cigar, the smoke hovering around his lips like a tiny gray cloud.

"I can offer you a retainer of one seventy-five plus bonuses and expenses. Effective immediately."

Danny blinked, momentarily speechless.

A hundred and seventy-five thousand dollars plus bonuses and expenses? Even though Danny had absolutely no interest in working for a fashion magazine, the thought of that much money made the *coq-au-vin* turn a flip in his stomach.

He swallowed hard, wondering what he'd done to deserve such an offer.

In the end, one of the top orthopedic surgeons in the country told Jo that her pain was coming from a sprained ankle, and he would suggest ice packs and anti-inflammatories.

"But you were right to bring me here anyway," Jo admitted humbly to her grandmother as she climbed back into the waiting limo. "He also gave me a removable cast and an order for physical therapy."

Jo settled onto the deep leather seat and held out her leg to show off the black removable cast. After the doctor's thorough poking and prodding, the bad foot felt worse than before, and Jo found the support and security of the cast to be an absolute relief. She was glad she had come.

"So your doctor was right too," her grandmother conceded. "Just not as aggressive in her treatment."

"Correct."

Both women smiled. With Jo's grandmother as stubborn as she was, a draw was usually the best outcome to their arguments. As the driver pulled away from the curb, Eleanor surprised Jo by inviting her to come and stay at her estate for the duration of the physical therapy.

"The timing couldn't be better," Jo's grandmother said, directing the driver to head toward Westchester County. "After I had the stroke last year, we converted the carriage house into an on-site medical facility. There's a whirlpool in there and all sorts of machines. The physical therapist already comes every other day. It's ridiculous for you not to take advantage of it as well. We'll pick up a few clothes and toiletries to tide you over tonight and then you can send for your things tomorrow."

"That's very kind, Gran," Jo said, surprised that her grandmother was still getting so much therapy this long after her stroke. It had been more than a year, and she seemed almost completely recovered other than tiring more easily and needing the wheelchair for longer excursions. "I didn't realize you were still under treatment."

"Oh, the therapy's not for me these days. We have a young guest at the house—but that's a long story. I'm sure you'd find her delightful, and I know she'd welcome a new face around there, particularly someone younger."

"What about Chewie?" Jo asked, knowing that her grandmother would never allow Jo's rambunctious chocolate Lab to roam the hallowed halls of her home. Six weeks ago, when Jo was first injured and in the hospital and her own house had burned to the ground, her grandmother had offered Jo the use of her vacation home in the Poconos until she got back on her feet. Jo had accepted her offer, but when she learned that Chewie was not a part of the bargain, she had turned her grandmother down and made other arrangements.

"Darling, that's what kennels are for," Eleanor answered, smoothing her skirt across her knees as she repeated the sentiment she had expressed the last time.

"Yes, well, like the last time, that doesn't work for me," Jo said, instructing the driver to take her to the Times Square Marriott instead. "But thanks for the offer." Forsaking her precious pet for the sake of a little convenience and pampering was out of the question.

As they drove, Jo's grandmother was quiet, seeming to be vaguely offended by Jo's refusal. Jo tried to make conversation, asking more about her grandmother's young houseguest, whoever she was, but the subject was closed. Finally, tired of the cold shoulder, Jo decided to change course and toss out something that was sure to get the woman's attention.

"I guess you're wondering why I want to be dropped at Times Square rather than back at Penn Station," Jo said matter-of-factly.

Her grandmother shrugged, still staring out the window. "I suppose you're going to the theater."

"No, I'm going to meet with Bradford," Jo said, referring to the man who had jilted her at the altar last fall, ducking out of their wedding without excuse or explanation. Since then, she and Bradford had barely spoken, except for several irritating phone calls and one bizarre moment when he showed up in her hospital room six weeks ago, begging her for another chance at a relationship. Shocked and vulnerable, Jo had called for a nurse and had him removed from the premises.

"Bradford?" Eleanor replied, turning to Jo, her eyes wide. "Last I heard, you were having him escorted out of your room by hospital security."

"Well, he deserved it," Jo said. "Waltzing in there without warning and me lying there injured and helpless. The last thing I felt like doing was dealing with him."

"But you're willing to see him now."

"We're finally going to talk. He's called a few times since then, asking me to meet with him, so I finally gave in. I think I need to find some closure. I suppose one meeting with him won't kill me, and maybe it'll help me put the whole relationship to rest once and for all. I still don't know why Bradford dumped me then, or what he wants to tell me now."

"No chance of a reconciliation?" her grandmother asked. She had always been partial to Bradford, most likely because he was from a wealthy family and at one time had been a real up-and-comer in the family business, Bosworth Industries. Bradford used to work directly for

Jo's father, who was the CEO of the company. Since the whole wedding fiasco, however, Jo had no idea if he even worked there anymore or not. She and her parents didn't talk about him, and she'd had no extended communication with him herself.

"A reconciliation?" Jo asked, thinking of what her friend Marie would say: *Not for all the pumps in the DSW Shoe Warehouse.* Putting it in terms her grandmother would understand, Jo amended the saying: "Not for all the blue boxes in Tiffany's, Gran. Trust me, the only shred of emotion I have left for that man is sheer contempt."

"Ah, Jo," her grandmother said, sighing and shaking her head. "You always have been far too influenced by your emotions. He still would be a good, logical choice for a husband whether you truly care for him or not."

Jo bit her lip to stop her own reply. She knew her grandmother well enough to know that there was nothing she could say to convince her otherwise.

"Then again," Eleanor added, "your Danny is a nice boy too. From what I hear, he's turning in an impressive appearance with the powers that be at *Scene It.*"

"I'm sure he is," Jo replied, simultaneously glad that her grandmother approved but irritated that she was keeping tabs.

They reached Times Square, and the driver pulled through the drop-off lane of the Marriott and came to a stop. A hotel doorman opened the door, and as Jo gathered her purse and tote bag, her grandmother reiterated her invitation to come and stay at her house, insisting that her door was open in case Jo changed her mind.

"Thanks, Gran. That means a lot," Jo said, leaning over to kiss her on the cheek. The woman, in turn, flinched from the kiss and then dismissed Jo with the wave of her hand.

"Love you," Jo said softly.

"Very well," her grandmother replied. "Keep us posted on the foot, won't you?"

Feeling oddly rejected, Jo stood and watched as the limo pulled away. Then, walking awkwardly in the new cast, she thanked the doorman and made her way into the vast hotel. It was times like this that Jo most missed her other grandmother, who had passed away a little over a year ago. Jo's Grandmother Tulip had been everything that Grandmother Bosworth was not: warm, nurturing, and incredibly kind. Truly, if not for her paternal grandparents, Jo might have grown up without any real love at all.

"Except for Danny," she amended to herself, smiling, as she stepped onto the escalator. Danny had always been there, in Jo's life and in her heart. Now that they had moved from friendship-love to love-love, it was as though a missing puzzle piece had finally fallen into place. That's probably why she was now able to face Bradford and wrap up all of those loose ends and unanswered questions. Once Jo talked with him and heard what he had to say, she could finally move forward with her life.

Jo took a whole series of switch-back escalators to get to the hotel's main lobby on the eighth floor. Though she wasn't willing to share a meal with Bradford, there was a nice public area with plenty of comfortable seating where they could sit and have coffee and talk in relative privacy.

She glanced at her watch, glad she was early. She wanted to choose the seating herself, not to mention collect her thoughts, put together an ice pack, and check her e-mail. Last night, just before going to bed, she had thought about e-mailing Danny to tell him about this visit with Bradford. But in the end, she had decided against it. News like that was better given over the phone, so she would tell him the next time they talked instead.

In theory, Danny wanted Jo to have one final, wrap-up conversation with Bradford so that she could finally put all of her questions to rest. But in reality she knew that the idea of her getting together with her former fiancé while Danny was an ocean away was probably a bit unnerving. She just hoped he wasn't worrying too much. There was nothing for him to worry about.

Danny had her heart hook, line, and sinker, and he always would.

Jo found the perfect spot, isolated yet public. She ordered a soda and an extra cup of ice and made herself comfortable, discreetly propping up her foot on the wide, low table in front of her. Once her drink came, Jo pulled a small plastic bag from her purse, poured the extra ice into the bag, sealed it, and propped it on her foot, against her sock, under one of the Velcro straps. When she was all set, she pulled out her handheld digital assistant and checked her e-mail. There was nothing from Danny yet, much to Jo's disappointment.

There was, however, a new message from anon6592@mailnet.com, her anonymous library correspondent. Heart pounding, Jo scrolled down and pressed the button that would bring the e-mail up on the tiny screen.

The sender had copied back part of Jo's last e-mail: <<*May I help in some way? Perhaps act as a go-between with the authorities?*>>

The reply, which followed underneath, took Jo's breath away.

Dear Jo Tulip, I don't need you to be a go-between because the person in danger is YOU.

There, I told you. Please don't try to find me. I got nothing to do with this, I just heard about it and thought you deserved to know. I've seen you on your website and in the newspaper, and you seem like a nice person and I don't think this is right.

Be careful and watch your back.

The note was signed, as before, by *Trying To Stay Out of It.* Underneath was a PS: *One of the toaster ovens I'm looking at has a Teflon interior. What do you think? Would a nonstick coating be worth the extra cost?*

"Hello, beautiful."

Jo looked up, startled.

There, in front of her, was Bradford, smiling and holding out a dozen roses.

2

Flustered, Jo found the button that would save the e-mail, quickly exited the program, and closed the device. She didn't know how to process any of it: the e-mail telling her she was in danger or the fact that Bradford was standing here in front of her. The last time she'd seen him, she was flat on her back in the hospital, terribly injured, and he had barged into her room without warning, hidden behind a giant bouquet of flowers. Funny, but she almost felt as helpless now as she had then.

"I guess the roses are a little over the top, huh?" he said, the smile fading from his face. He let his arm fall down by his side. "Sorry about that. Here I go again, trying too hard. I can tell I've upset you."

Jo tried to pull herself together, her mind still racing from the e-mail. Maybe this toaster oven guy really was just some nut out for kicks, like the Kreston detective had said. Forcing herself to focus, Jo tucked away her PDA and turned her full attention on Bradford. She would deal with the e-mail later, after he was gone.

Bradford stood there in front of her, a little weathered but still movie-star handsome, with blond hair and blue eyes and a chiseled jaw straight out of *GQ* magazine. Truly, he was so gorgeous that Jo wouldn't have been surprised to look out of the window onto Times Square and see his face on a billboard. She didn't know why it had never crossed her mind before that he was better looking than she was. In a world that favored equal-beauty dating, somehow she had bagged one slightly beyond her limit—physically speaking, that is. She wasn't unattractive, but she was more cute than pretty, kind of like her surname, a tulip, sitting there looking up at a rare orchid.

Correction. Not a rare orchid, that was too lovely. Bradford is more like a carrion flower—beautiful on the outside, putrid on the inside.

"Have a seat," Jo said, finally finding her voice.

Bradford set the roses on the coffee table and took the chair that was at an angle to hers, his knees coming to rest against her thigh. Back when they were dating, he had been a very physical guy, always standing close, sitting even closer, brushing his legs against hers or running his hands lightly along her back. Back then, she'd thought it was sexy, if sometimes a little forward.

Now it seemed almost threatening.

Jo sat up straight, visibly pulling her leg a few inches away so that they were no longer touching.

"You said you were completely recovered," he told her, spotting her foot propped up in the cast. "That doesn't look good."

"Just a sprain, taking its time to heal. It'll be fine soon."

"Good. Otherwise, you look great. You look beautiful, Jo. But then, you always do. With all your injuries in that explosion, you're so lucky you didn't have any cuts to your face."

He flashed her what she'd always thought of as his million-watt smile. She studied it as if it were some sort of artifact. How that smile used to captivate her. Now it only seemed foreign and somehow artificial. Jo wondered what it was like to be so perfect—and if he expected his loved ones also to be perfect. If so, would cuts to her face and the resultant facial scarring have disqualified her from his affections? She felt nauseous at the thought that she had almost married this man.

"You wanted to talk, Bradford. So talk."

He glanced away, seeming nervous. Wringing his hands in his lap, he looked furtively around the room and then back at her.

"Just hear me out," he said, his voice suddenly very low. "Because you're going to have trouble believing what I have to tell you."

Oh, please. Here we go with the drama.

"Bradford, why did you walk out on our wedding?" Jo asked, not bothering to lower her voice. That was the question she'd been wanting to ask for months. It was high time he answered it.

"Because..." he said, nervously tugging at the back of his hair, "because I realized I was falling in love with you."

Jo just stared at him, wondering what *Twilight Zone* episode she had wandered into. She thought she was beyond caring about this, but suddenly she could feel her chest fill with an emotion she couldn't name. Hurt? Righteous indignation? She supposed that *rage* was the best word for it. She was furious.

"Isn't love supposed to be part of a wedding?" she asked, trying to hold her temper. "Kind of a big part?"

He nodded, his expression grave.

"Yes, but when you came walking up the aisle, and I looked into your beautiful green eyes, I knew I couldn't do it, not that way. I was in love with you. You deserved better than that."

"Better than a fiancé who says 'I don't' rather than 'I do' and then runs away?"

"Jo, I—"

"Better than a groom who cashes in the two coach-class honeymoon tickets to Bermuda for one in first class and takes the trip without the bride?"

"I had to get away," he pleaded. "I had to think."

"I hope you enjoyed the honeymoon suite."

"I was miserable. I never expected love to enter into it. But you deserved better than to be the victim of a hoax."

Jo squinted at him, trying to understand.

"You're calling our wedding a *hoax?*" she cried. "Funny, but I seem to recall paying actual money for the wedding gown, not to mention the cake and the flowers and everything else. I certainly used real friends as my bridesmaids, and my own, actual father walked me down the aisle. Even the pastor at the front of the room was a bona fide, ordained minister. I know that for a fact. If he had pronounced us husband and wife, it would've actually stuck. Yeah, sure sounds like a hoax to me."

Jo didn't like the sarcastic bitterness in her own voice, but she was unable to stop herself. Until that moment, she hadn't realized how much anger she still carried about the whole incident. Obviously, she still had a ways to go in the forgiveness department.

"Look," Bradford said softly, "when I first walked out, I tried to figure out how I could tell you the truth about what had been going on without losing you. But I knew that could never happen. You were lost to me forever."

"Hey, *you* ran out on *me!*"

He nodded miserably.

"And I knew that if you found out the truth, you'd never take me back. Finally, I just tried to get over you. Tried to forget about you. Tried to go on with my life."

"Good. I've certainly gotten over you."

"But it hasn't worked for me because somewhere in all of that pretense, I really fell for you. I fell hard, Jo. Finally I decided the only chance I might have of winning you back was to come completely clean. That's why I showed up at the hospital and why I'm here now. I want to tell you everything, and in spite of it, I want you to consider giving our relationship a second chance."

Jo ran a hand through her hair. She wouldn't get back with him if they were the last two beings on earth and her only choice for companionship was between him and a potted plant. At least the potted plant would be exactly what it was, not something else it only pretended to be.

The image of Danny suddenly filled her mind, and she felt a deep, silent gratefulness that God in His infinite wisdom had sent Bradford running out at the last moment, saving her from making the mistake of a lifetime. But even if Danny weren't in the picture, which he most absolutely was, Bradford was *so* over, so been-there-done-that, so finished. Their relationship was as done as done could get. He had hurt her beyond belief, and even though in the end his rejection had turned out to be a tremendous blessing in disguise, it had still been a hard pill to swallow.

"Bradford, please get to the point. What sham? What hoax?"

"Our relationship. It was all fake."

Jo's eyes widened.

"Fake?"

"From the very beginning. The courtship, the engagement, even the engagement ring."

"That's not true. That diamond was no fake and you know it."

Before the wedding, Jo had had the ring appraised for insurance purposes—and she'd been shocked to learn that it was worth almost $25,000. Given that, once everything fell apart, she had shipped the ring back to Bradford heavily insured, along with a note kindly suggesting he get a refund and use it to sponsor the national budget for a small country.

"Yes, the ring was real. But what I mean is, I'm not the one who paid for it."

Jo's eyes suddenly filled with tears.

"My feelings were real," she said softly, irritated that she was crying. But the tears weren't for Bradford—they were for her hurt, her shame, her humiliation. Sometimes she wondered if she'd ever get over the shock of what he'd done to her. Now it seemed as if there would be even more to get over.

"Jo, listen," he said, leaning toward her, elbows on his knees. He leaned so far forward that his face was only inches from hers. Her heart pounding, she wondered if he was the danger to her, if he, in fact, was the one that the Kreston e-mailer had warned her about. In her gut Jo didn't think so, but she couldn't be sure. At the very least, she was glad they were in a public place.

"From the moment we met," he continued, "our entire relationship was...engineered."

"Engineered?"

"I don't know any other way to tell you this: I was *paid*. I was paid to make you fall in love with me."

"What?"

"Jo, I was paid to marry you."

"This makes no sense," Danny said finally, shaking his head. He wasn't worth $175,000 to anyone yet. He was good, but not that good, especially in a studio. "I'm sorry, but my field of study, my focus, my *art* is in nature."

"So pose the perfume bottles around a waterfall or something," Luc quipped, and Chester laughed, nodding.

"You're an outstanding photographer," the older man said, "and we want the artistic perspective you bring to the table. If that includes getting out of the studio and into nature, we might be able to make that happen. I know talent when I see it, son, and I see it in you."

"Thank you, sir," Danny replied humbly, his mind spinning.

"And don't forget," Chester added, "you'd be working with some of the most beautiful models in the world."

Danny studied the man in front of him, fully aware of the most obvious question: *Why me?* Most of his photos hadn't received enough exposure yet to merit this kind of attention—and the few that had were all landscape shots, not fashion spreads.

Something seemed fishy about the whole deal, and he didn't just mean the crabmeat in the appetizers.

"Have you seen the models in *Haute Couture*, Danny?" Chester continued, lowering his voice and winking. "A good-looking fellow like you could find plenty of, uh, side benefits in that situation, if you know what I mean."

Chester and Luc both chuckled, but Danny wasn't smiling.

"Sorry," Danny replied, "but I have a little trouble thinking of beautiful women as being mere 'side benefits.' They're people, not perks."

Chester and Luc laughed in surprise.

"I forget to tell you, *monsieur*," Luc said to Chester, "that our Danny is a man of morals."

"Morals, eh?" Chester asked, eyeing Danny with a bemused expression. "Now there's something you don't see every day."

"Not to mention he already has a girlfriend, soon to be a fiancé, I think. The models would not tempt him, *pas de tout*."

"Yeah, I'm going to take a pass on the job," Danny said, setting his napkin on the table, trying to keep the interview off the personal level, "but thank you very much for the offer."

Chester's expression didn't change. He merely tapped his smelly cigar against the ashtray and then seemed to try a different approach.

"A girlfriend," he said. "Is she here in Paris with you?"

Danny shook his head slightly.

"She's back home. In Pennsylvania."

"And you're from…what's it called? Mulberry Bush?"

"Mulberry Glen, just south of Moore City."

"Moore City? Why, that's just a few hours from New York. If you scheduled your shootings efficiently, you could practically commute."

For a flicker of an instant, Danny was tempted: great salary, close to Jo, working as a photographer for one of the most prestigious magazines in the world...

But it wasn't his dream, not even close. Why should he have sacrificed so much to come this far, only to compromise in the end?

He took a deep breath and searched for the words that would convince this man that he should look elsewhere.

"Sir, I am flattered by your persistence, and believe me, your offer is more than generous. But I'm not a fashion photographer; I'm a nature photographer. My ultimate goal is to use the knowledge and experience and connections I'm gaining here in Paris and parlay them into a full-time career back home in Pennsylvania as a contract photographer for one of the major nature photography markets. No offense, but I have zero interest in living in New York City and working for *Haute Couture* magazine."

"Zero?" the man asked skeptically, still looking as if he weren't getting the point. Danny had a feeling that offers like this weren't made every day—much less rejected, particularly by a nobody like him.

"Yes," Danny said, his mind's eye seeing $175,000 slipping through his fingers. "Less than zero."

"It's true," Bradford said to Jo earnestly. "Before we ever met, I was given lists, long lists, of everything about you. Favorite food, favorite movies, favorite pastimes. I memorized them and pretended they were my favorites, too. Didn't it ever occur to you how strange it was that we had so very much in common? Practically from the night we met, we seemed like soulmates."

Jo looked down at her neatly manicured nails, remembering that night. She'd been visiting with her parents in the city, and they had all but forced her to go on a blind date with a young man who worked at the family company.

"You'll just *love* Bradford," Jo's mother had gushed. "He's simply perfect for you."

Jo had agreed to the date only to get her mother off her back, but after spending the evening with Bradford, Jo had been shocked to find that what her mother had said was true. Bradford was handsome, smart, funny, sensitive—and they had so much in common. By the end of the evening, they were already making plans to get together the next day. Within two months, they were engaged.

"So what you're telling me," Jo said, "is that the Bradford I thought I knew doesn't exist?"

He shrugged.

"You knew me, Jo," he said. "For the most part. You knew my personality and how we got along. You just weren't clear on certain things about my life or my preferences. Or my plans for the future."

"And what are those plans?"

"I was paid all through the engagement, but our wedding was supposed to guarantee me one huge final financial payoff, plus a Fifth Avenue condo, a big promotion at work, and a raise. I would also be put on the fast track toward the ultimate position of CEO of Bosworth Industries, stepping into your father's shoes upon his retirement, if I proved myself worthy between now and then."

"And history would repeat itself," Jo said quietly to herself. "Just as my father married into my mother's family business and eventually took over from my grandfather, you would do the same through me."

"It worked out well for your parents and the company, didn't it?"

"That's only because my father is brilliant at business. And he worked his way up legitimately—unless you're telling me that someone paid my father to marry my mother too."

"No, not that I know of," Bradford replied, shaking his head. "Just that the dynamic would be the same, yet again a son-in-law working his way up to the helm. It seemed perfect to everyone involved. They really want to keep things in the family."

"So who is 'everyone involved'? And why did they do this? Did my grandmother pay you to marry me?"

"Your grandmother? No, I don't believe she knows anything about it."

"Who, then? My father? My mother? The company? Was this just about locking in a good CEO through marriage?"

"No, of course not. It's so much more complicated than that. The fact that our marriage would keep the business in the family was simply a nice side benefit. The fact is, they needed you to marry someone, *anyone*. They just liked the choice of me because they knew I could make it happen fast—"

"Boy, did you ever."

"—and they knew I was a nice guy, great at business, and loyal to Bosworth Industries. I was the perfect choice."

"Especially because you were just amoral enough to do what they wanted."

Bradford's eyes were pleading as he gazed at her.

"Jo, you have no idea the amounts of money they were throwing my way. Anyone could've been swayed."

Not me. Not Danny.

"Again, who paid you to marry me, Bradford? Who was behind this? And why were they in such a hurry? What difference does it make to anyone if I'm married or not?"

Bradford opened his mouth to speak, but then his head jerked up, turning toward some movement Jo had also spotted from the corner of her eye. She glanced in that direction as well but didn't see anything unusual.

"We can't stay here," Bradford whispered. "Is there somewhere we could go?"

Jo felt the hairs on the back of her neck stand on end.

"Why?"

"Because you're in danger. Please. It's too public. It's not safe for you."

Here was someone else telling her she was in danger! Was Bradford the one who sent the e-mail? Or was he the danger the e-mail had been talking about?

"Do you know anyone in Kreston?" Jo asked suspiciously.

"Kreston, out in the Bronx? What are you talking about? We've got to get you out of here, to somewhere close by. Quickly."

Bradford's eyes met hers, and she could see the panic and urgency there. His expression seemed sincere. Of course, he'd just admitted to her that their entire relationship had been a lie, so how was she to know if this was also an act or not? Maybe he was crazy, off the deep end. Or maybe he thought if he cooked up some sort of over-the-top drama, she would fall into his arms for protection and love—and they could ride off into the sunset together and live happily ever after.

"Why am I in danger?" Jo insisted. "I'm not moving from this spot until you give me an explanation."

He sucked in a sharp breath, put both hands on her shoulders, and leaned forward until she could feel his lips at her ear.

"According to my sources," he whispered sharply, "there's something big going on at your family's company. Rumor has it that you're going to be...eliminated."

"Eliminated?" Jo scoffed. "Like, fired from Bosworth Industries? How can they fire me? I don't even work there."

"No, *eliminated*, Jo. Like... killed."

Jo felt dizzy, her view of the elegant surroundings suddenly dimming around the edges. Truly, Bradford had gone insane.

"What do you mean?" she asked, an incredulous laugh escaping her lips. "Why?"

"It's not funny, Jo. Your life is in jeopardy. That's all I can say right now. Let's go somewhere safe and private, and I'll tell you everything I know."

Bradford gripped Jo's upper arm and practically dragged her to a standing position. With her bad foot, she nearly fell back down, but his hold was strong. Suddenly, the situation had gone from absurd to frightening.

"I'm going to get us a room in the hotel," he said intensely, glancing toward the eighth floor check-in area. "I think that's the best option we have right now. I know you think I'm crazy or I'm kidding, but I'm not. Trust me on this, Jo."

Trust me? The man who supposedly took money to marry her, courted her under false pretenses, and walked out of their wedding was asking her to trust him? Jo blinked, clearing her vision and clearing her mind. At this point she didn't trust anyone—least of all him.

"No hotel room," she said sternly, pulling her arm free from his grip.

He seemed surprised by her reaction, and then understanding crossed his features.

"I won't try anything, Jo, I promise. You know I'm a gentleman. Thanks to your stupid Christian rules, I controlled myself for six months while dating you. I think I can handle sitting across from you in a private room for a few hours. I just want to talk. Considering the information I have, I would think you'd want to hear what I have to say."

Your stupid Christian rules? So even his faith had been a sham, yet one more way he had pretended to be someone he was not, all for the sake of getting her to the altar. She felt like such an idiot. Danny had said all along that he didn't think Bradford was sincere in his faith, and that if Jo married him they would be unevenly yoked. To say the least! If only she had listened to Danny from the beginning. How had she been so blind?

"Please, Jo. Come on."

"Fine," she said finally, gathering her things. "Get us a room. I'll meet you at the elevators."

"I think we should stay together."

"I have to go to the ladies' room," she said sharply, pointing across the bustling lobby to the restroom doorway. "Unless you want to come in there with me, I'll meet you at the elevators."

"Can't you wait until you get to the room? "

"No, I can't. The line at check-in is way too long."

He looked across the lobby and then back at her.

"All right, let's go," he said, glancing in all directions as he escorted her toward the restroom. "You can wait there for me, and I'll be back as soon as I have a room key."

"Fine."

Jo's mind raced as they walked. She really did want to hear more of what he had come to tell her, just not in a private place where he might be able to do her harm. The look in his eyes was growing more intense, almost crazed, and that was scaring her as much as the things he'd been saying. Considering the limited choices available to her at the moment, Jo decided her safest option was to get away from Bradford for now and get to her father as quickly as possible. Kent Tulip was a cold and calculating businessman, yes, but Jo also knew that he would never, ever physically harm her or allow harm to come to her. It was possible that he had a lot of explaining to do, but at least she knew she would be safe with him. Fortunately, his office was also in Manhattan, only about ten or fifteen blocks away. From there, perhaps she and her father could talk to Bradford together, maybe even over the phone, and hear the rest of his claims.

At least then Bradford wouldn't be in a position to harm her.

Once they reached the bathroom doorway, Bradford nodded at Jo, pulled out his wallet, and headed for the front desk. She went into the restroom, turned back, and peeked out to watch him walk away. She waited until her view of him was blocked by the elevator bank.

Then she hobbled as fast as she could to the escalator, wishing she could throw off the cast and simply run.

Danny waited in the *Métro* station for his train, though the place was much more quiet and empty than before. He was still trying to wrap his brain around what had just happened. A contract photography position with *Haute Couture*? For $175,000? For an unknown? It made no sense.

In the end, Chester wouldn't take Danny's no for an answer. He said merely that he'd give Danny a few days to think about it—and that he would call him before he headed back to the States. Danny didn't care how long the guy gave him to make up his mind. No meant no. Danny wasn't even going to consider it. Maybe.

"*Attend!* Danny! *Attend!*"

Danny looked up to see Luc quickly coming down the *Métro* stairs toward him. From his heavy breathing it appeared as if he'd been running, cell phone clutched tightly in one hand.

"I was hoping your train hadn't come yet," Luc said, coming to a stop in front of him and holding out the phone. "Georgette called, looking for you. She said it was urgent."

A cell phone was a luxury Danny had given up when he moved to Paris. He couldn't afford the monthly fee, and even if he could, cell phone rates for international long distance were prohibitive, and he didn't know that many people locally who might be calling him anyway.

"Georgette?" he asked, taking the proffered phone from Luc. "Why?"

"She didn't say. I told her to give me five minutes and I would try to catch up with you."

Georgette Tatou was their boss, a smart and efficient woman who helmed the photo department at the Paris office of *Scene It*. She rarely worked past six o'clock, but tonight she was probably still busy making final arrangements with the photographer or the magazine's liaison for the photo shoot. Danny just hoped that nothing had gone wrong with any of the details that had been left to him. He'd been so careful about everything. His stomach clenched at the thought of having made a mistake.

"Just press there and then there," Luc instructed, pointing to the buttons that would return the last incoming call. Danny did as Luc instructed, another thought suddenly occurring to him as soon as it started ringing.

"Does she know about Chester and *Haute Couture?*" Danny whispered to Luc, his thumb over the speaker holes, feeling slightly guilty even though he had done nothing wrong.

"Not from me," Luc replied, shaking his head. "But she knew we were dining together tonight. She figured calling me to find you was, how do you say, 'worth a shot'?"

Danny heard a click and then the voice of his boss.

"Luc? Did you find him?"

"Georgette? It's Danny. Luc told me you were looking for me."

"*Bon soir,* Danny," Georgette replied, pronouncing it—as most Parisians did—Dah-nee. "I'm sorry to call all over town and track you down like this."

"That's fine. What's up?"

"*J'ai une question:* How quickly can you pack and get to *Gare de l'Est*?"

"The train station? Why?" he asked urgently, hoping beyond hope that her question meant what he thought it meant.

"Because Rémi's wife went into labor three weeks early. Congratulations, Dah-nee, you will have to take his place as liaison on the photo shoot."

3

Fifty-seventh and Madison," Jo told the driver as she slipped into the backseat of a taxi. She was going straight to her father's office to get herself to safety—and to have the truth spelled out for her once and for all. This whole thing was ridiculous.

The cabdriver flipped on the meter, slid a baseball cap onto his shiny brown head, and pulled away from the hotel. As he did, Jo scooted down low in the seat and watched out of the back window. Other cabs were also pulling away from the Marriott, so she had no way to know if she was being followed or not.

The drive to Bosworth Industries was quick and uneventful, thank goodness. Jo paid the driver, glancing backward to make sure no other cabs or cars were also pulling to the curb. She didn't see any, so she climbed out and moved as quickly as possible into the massive building.

The lobby was busy, though she didn't notice anyone who seemed particularly threatening. She made her way to front desk security. It had been so long since she had been there that she didn't recognize either of the men behind the desk.

"Help you?"

"I need to see Kent Tulip."

"Do you have an appointment?"

"I'm his daughter. I don't need an appointment."

The man reached for the phone, no expression on his face.

"Just a moment, Ms. Tulip. I'll let them know you're here."

He spoke into the phone, and it didn't sound good. Finally, he held out the receiver toward Jo. It was her father's secretary, who said that he was out of the office today at a ribbon-cutting ceremony in nearby North Ulton, but that he should be back around 5:00 PM.

"You're welcome to wait for him up here," the woman said. "Our employee lounge is quite comfortable."

Jo told her no thanks and instead asked for the specifics about where her father was, exactly, knowing that if there were a train leaving from Grand Central soon, she could probably be at North Ulton within half an hour at the most. Jo thanked the woman and then handed the receiver back to the guard. Back at the door, the coast seemed clear, but as she stepped outside, she gasped. Bradford was just climbing out of a cab, and he spotted her before she could turn and run.

Danny rolled up a T-shirt and crammed it into his duffel bag, glad that he was an expert in packing light. With all of the camera equipment they were bringing, there wouldn't be much room for clothes and toiletries. Fortunately, Danny had no qualms about getting grungy or wearing the same gear for days in a row. He had a feeling that the great photographer Kalunga Bashiri was more concerned with the quality of his work than the cleanliness of his clothes anyway, at least once they got to Africa and set to work on the main part of the story.

Tentatively titled "Refuge of Hope," the article they were photographing focused on a successful group of European doctors who temporarily turned their backs on their cushy lives in order to donate months at a time working in third world refugee camps. Mr. Bashiri had already traveled to Bangladesh with a project team from Doctors Without Borders, and he had come back with some compelling photos of the work they were doing there in caring for the displaced peoples of Myanmar. Now, the plan was to go with a group from a similar organization, Global Mobile Medical, or GMM for short, down to a much larger camp in the Democratic Republic of Congo in Africa.

First stop, however, was to spend a few days at GMM's headquarters in Zurich, Switzerland, to show all of the preparations that went into such a trip—not to mention photograph a few of the doctors in their fancy offices and expensive homes for a neat juxtaposition of environments. Danny knew he might need to dress professionally for all of that, so he begrudgingly added a sports jacket, one dress shirt, three ties, and a pair of loafers to his bag. Thank goodness he had worked with Rémi, the liaison he was replacing, on creating the itinerary. Danny was aware of each stop they'd be making.

His only regret was that he wished he were back at home in the States right then, so he could go down into his basement and grab some old issues of *Scene It* for the plane ride, to study more closely some of Mr. Bashiri's past work. Bashiri was one of Danny's all-time favorite photographers, a master of the 4 x 5-inch view camera, known primarily for his photos in and around Africa. Now that Rémi's wife was in labor and Danny was taking his place on this trip as the magazine's liaison, he realized that getting some one-on-one time with one of the most talented photographers in the world was the opportunity of a lifetime, not to mention a real God thing.

"You were reinforcing my decision with *Haute Couture*, weren't You?" Danny prayed out loud, grinning, as he rolled up another T-shirt. "You sure don't waste any time!"

Sometimes God's will was difficult to discern—and sometimes it might as well come with flashing lights and big horns. Danny had no doubt that his fate was securely in God's hands and that the big money he'd been offered today was a temptation he'd needed to resist in order to find his way to more God-ordained opportunities. Working as a liaison between *Scene It* and Kalunga Bashiri, Danny was probably going to learn more about photography in the next two weeks than he had in four years of college. Somehow, that had to be worth way more than a salaried position at a fashion mag.

Eager to share his exciting news with Jo, Danny glanced at the computer on the desk in the corner. He didn't have time to go online—or even to call her, for that matter, to give her his big news. He decided he would try to phone from the train station if he had the chance, no matter the cost of the long distance. Pinching pennies was one thing, but telling Jo about this amazing opportunity was something that shouldn't have to wait.

In the meantime, he was going to be lucky if he made the station on time. It depended on the traffic, not to mention the nerve of the driver the magazine sent over. As if in answer to his thoughts, a horn sounded outside, and he peeked out the window to see a small Volvo waiting at the curb.

Pulse surging, Danny tossed in a few granola bars and then grabbed his own Nikon DX1 for personal use. No doubt, he'd be too busy coordinating details to take many photos himself, but he wanted to be ready and able, just in case. He then locked up his flat, raced down the steps, and waved at the Volvo, surprised to see Luc sitting behind the wheel.

"*Bon soir,* Danny," he said with a grin when Danny opened the door. "Guess what? Georgette has decided that I am to go on the trip as well."

"Really?"

Danny tossed his duffel bag onto the backseat next to Luc's neat leather suitcase and climbed in the front. As soon as he shut the door, Luc took off, squealing away from the curb at top speed. Maybe they would make it to the train in time after all.

Danny was surprised that Luc was coming along, mostly because it seemed like such a duplication of effort. They essentially held the same position at the magazine; why did both of them need to go? He asked the question as tactfully as he could.

"Georgette is concerned about the language barrier in Switzerland," Luc explained as he turned onto the main road and sped through the night at top speed. "I speak German, so I will be on the first leg of the journey to translate. After that, though, you and Bashiri will be heading to Africa without me, assuming your visa can be expedited in time." He flashed a smile and added, "Your poorly accented American French should be passable enough for the Congo."

"Gee, thanks. But, really, why don't you just make the whole trip instead of me? I hadn't even thought about the language issue. If you speak all these different languages, wouldn't it make more sense for you to be the liaison? Especially since the doctors that are going probably all speak German?"

Luc shrugged, easing around another car and shifting into fifth gear before replying, "You are right. That would make more sense. But most of the doctors are probably multilingual. If they don't know English, they will at least know French. You will survive." He blasted the horn at a slow-moving truck and then swerved around it.

"Besides, Georgette said that Bashiri asked for you specifically."

"He did?" Danny asked, his eyes wide. "Me? Specifically?" Unbelievable. Had Bashiri seen Danny's work? Did he sense a fellow artiste? Did he recognize the burning ambition in Danny's soul, the raw talent that yearned for recognition? "How do you know?"

"Georgette told me that Bashiri said he had never seen anyone pack a set of lenses with such care. He was also impressed with the amount of weight you were lifting while loading the truck. They are calling you a liaison, but I have the feeling that 'pack animal' is more like it. Get ready to feel like a burro, *mon ami*."

Luc laughed, but Danny didn't know whether to laugh or cry. He realized that this evening's offer from Chester Parks had pumped up his ego to the point where he was ready to believe that even someone like Kalunga Bashiri could be impressed with his talent. Instead, this dream opportunity had come about only because Danny had a few muscles and knew how to handle good equipment.

It figured.

"What's the problem, Danny? Do you not want to go?"

"Of course I do. In fact, I want this more than I've wanted anything since I've been in Paris."

"Certainly more than a high-paying job at *Haute Couture,* eh?"

Danny felt a flush of embarrassment. How could he explain to Luc his reasons for turning that down? More than likely, it was Luc's dream job, and considering that he was the one who set up the meeting between Danny and Chester Parks in the first place, he was probably more shocked about the outcome than Chester had been. Danny realized that maybe an apology was in order.

"Listen, man, I'm really sorry about how that all turned out. The whole thing sort of blindsided me, you know? I never saw that job offer coming."

"You followed your heart and not your wallet, *mon ami.* That's to be admired, I suppose."

"How about you, Luc? You'd be great for *Haute Couture.* If you know the guy, why not pitch yourself for the same position he offered me?"

"I did, after you left. Chester said he would consider it. I know what that means, 'Thanks but no thanks.' Then Georgette called, looking for you, and I had to make a quick exit. Perhaps Chester will reconsider later."

"Is he familiar with your work? How do you know him, anyway?"

Luc rode aggressively close to the bumper of the car in front of him, forcing it to pull into the slow lane before speeding past.

"I do not know him well. We met the other night at the *Gallerie du Monde.* He was very taken by the picture you have on display there, and Georgette was bragging that you were one of her interns. She even started telling him about your movie poster and your other stock photo sales—just bragging, I am sure, not knowing he was listening very carefully, planning to steal you out from under her."

Danny flinched as they reached their exit and Luc raced to pass a car on the single-lane exit ramp. Danny had skipped the gallery event on purpose, fearing yet another boring, drawn-out cocktail party where everybody got drunk on the free booze and spent the whole evening name-dropping, one-upping, and pretending they were art experts.

"This morning I got a call from Chester, asking me to arrange an introduction to you. I suggested dinner and that was that."

"But why didn't you tell me the real reason for the dinner? I just thought you wanted company at the restaurant."

"Georgette was nearby at the time. As was Kalunga Bashiri. What would you have had me say? 'Come to dinner with me tonight, Danny, where you are going to be wooed by the competition'?"

Danny gripped the armrest as Luc floored the accelerator to make it through a light that had already been yellow for several long seconds. It was red when they reached the intersection, so he simply pressed down the horn and kept going.

"It would be nice to make it to the station alive," Danny gasped as they narrowly missed a car coming at them from the side.

"*Eh bein,* we will make it, do not worry. I grew up in a racing family. My uncle drove in the Grand Prix."

"Wow. How'd he do?"

Luc slammed on the brakes, clipping a rubber traffic cone before swerving to miss an open manhole.

"He lived to tell about it," he replied. "As will we."

"I had a feeling I might find you here," Bradford said, stepping toward Jo. "If you're going upstairs to talk to your dad, I'd like to come too. He's been refusing my calls for the last few weeks, but if I'm with you, he'll have to see me and listen to me. Between the three of us, maybe we can figure out what's really going on."

Jo swallowed hard, searching Bradford's face for signs of malice or anger or insanity. Instead, all she could see was an eager sort of desperation. Was he to be believed about anything?

"He's at a ribbon-cutting ceremony," she said finally. "I'm going there."

"Fine. We can take my cab."

"It's out in North Ulton. I'm going by train."

"I'll come too. We can talk on the way." Bradford stepped closer to her and lowered his voice. "I know you don't really trust me right now Jo, but you need someone with you, to protect you."

"Hey, buddy," the cabbie called. "Your fare?"

"Just a second," Bradford said, holding out one hand. "Jo, let me finish telling you what I have to say on the train ride out there. When we get to North Ulton, we can talk to your father together."

"I don't know," she whispered.

"Come on. You seem almost frightened of me. Believe me, Jo, I'm the one person right now you *don't* need to be frightened of."

He gestured again toward the cab. Jo looked at the driver, who was watching their exchange warily, as though he was afraid Bradford might bolt without paying.

"What could happen in a cab or on a train, Jo? Once we get there and talk to your father, I'll say goodbye and promise to leave you alone forever if that's what you want."

Jo squinted at him, feeling suspicious and skeptical but also frightened. What if Bradford really was telling the truth and she truly was in danger?

"This all seems like a stupid joke, Bradford, but right now I'm trying to give you the benefit of the doubt. If someone really wants me dead, then tell me who it is, and why."

"It's complicated, Jo. I'll try to explain as much as I know on the way."

"Then at least tell me who paid you to marry me. Who signed the checks or made the bank transfers or whatever? Was it my father?"

Bradford hesitated.

"Give me a name and I'll go with you."

Bradford looked around and then back at her, lowering his voice even more.

"I know what they did was wrong, Jo, but they do love you in their own weird way. I'm sure once they find out that your life is in danger, they'll move heaven and earth to protect you. They've got the knowledge and the resources to figure out who's behind this—and hopefully to stop it."

"Who is 'they,' Bradford? Are you talking about my parents? Tell me straight out. Did my father pay you to marry me?"

"Yes, he did," Bradford whispered sharply. "Along with your mother. They did a dumb thing, but right now I think they're the only ones who can help."

Heart pounding, Jo didn't even reply. She simply stood there and considered her options, and then she walked to the cab and climbed inside.

"Grand Central Station," Bradford told the driver, slipping in beside her.

Jo stared straight ahead, silently burning all the way to the train station. Even if Bradford was nuts or was lying about most of this, something in Jo's gut told her that her father still had some big explaining to do.

By the time they reached the train station, Danny was ready to jump out and kiss the ground. Instead, he simply climbed from the car, grabbed his bag, and ran with Luc from the parking lot to the station. Rémi was waiting for them at the door, a plastic bag in one hand and a fistful of papers in other, pacing wildly, a look of immense relief covering his face when he saw them.

"Rémi!" Danny said, his heart plummeting. "What are you doing here? I thought Sabine was in labor!"

Rémi gestured for both men to follow him, and he spoke as they dashed down the long hallways of the expansive train station.

"She is, but we are not supposed to go to the hospital until the pains are five minutes apart. Right now, they are between ten and fifteen and she is at her mother's. I just wanted to make sure everything is taken care of here. Quickly, quickly. Mr. Bashiri is waiting for us at track six."

They dashed through a series of long halls and down a wide stairway, finally emerging into the open, cavernous part of the station where they would board. As they approached track six, they saw that the train was already there, a shiny and sleek high speed TGV that looked like something out of a science fiction movie. Danny saw that the other passengers had already gotten on, save for one very short, very dark-skinned man dressed in his usual garb of a multi-pocketed khaki jacket and slacks, a neat cotton hat upon his head and a small, tidy camera bag hanging from his shoulder. On the ground nearby was a well-worn black leather suitcase.

"You said they would make it and they did," Mr. Bashiri told Rémi calmly with a soft, African lilt. Then, with a nod to Danny and Luc, he stepped aboard the train.

"Go with him," Rémi instructed Danny, thrusting the plastic bag he'd been carrying into Danny's hands. "I'll give the paperwork and final instructions to Luc. Grab Bashiri's suitcase, would you?"

Immediately, Rémi redirected his attention to Luc, switching to their native French language and speaking so quickly that Danny only caught a little bit of it, something about baggage and customs and tickets. Danny picked up the black bag and stepped aboard, looking up the narrow hallway of the train just in time to see Mr. Bashiri step from the hallway into a room. Danny quickly sprinted up the hall and joined him, knocking first and then stepping inside to see a small-but-impressive first-class sleeper compartment.

On the far wall was a large window, flanked on each side by gray velvet seats that faced each other. Above each seat, set into the walls, were folded-up berths. To the right of the door was the private bathroom, which included a toilet, a shower head, and a small, stainless steel sink adorned with several crisp white towels and a freshly-wrapped soap. To the left was a small closet.

Trying not to look flustered or breathe heavily from all of the running, Danny put his bags on the floor beside the door and then set Mr. Bashiri's suitcase inside the closet.

"Would you like for me to hang up any of your things?" Danny asked, gesturing toward the suitcase.

Mr. Bashiri, a man of few words, simply held out the strap of his camera case. Danny carefully took it from him and put it in the closet as well. Mr. Bashiri settled in the forward-facing seat next to the window, and when Danny asked if he could get him anything, the man asked for a cold bottle of water.

"Of course," Danny said, suddenly wondering how he thought he was going to pull all of this off.

Liaison? What a joke! Except for a few weekend jaunts to more rural parts of France, Danny had never been on a European train in his life. He didn't know where to get water. Did they have a club car? A water cooler? Some sort of cabin steward?

Danny hesitated, glancing at Mr. Bashiri, who smiled bemusedly and then gestured toward the plastic bag on the floor, the one Rémi had handed Danny at the last minute. Danny reached for it, picked it up, and looked inside to see two wrapped sandwiches and three bottles of water, foggy with condensation. Smiling, Danny handed one to Mr. Bashiri.

"Here you go," Danny said, closing the bag and setting it neatly on the floor next to him. "There's more in there if you need it. Will there be anything else?"

Mr. Bashiri took a long sip of the water, wiped his mouth with a crisply folded cloth handkerchief, and then replied, "Not right now, thank you."

The train slowly began to move. Leaving his bag on the floor, Danny excused himself to look for Luc. Fortunately, the confident Frenchman was just coming up the hallway, a wide grin on his face.

"Whew! We did it," Luc said enthusiastically.

Reading the numbers on the doors, he stopped at the one just prior to Mr. Bashiri's, said *"Voici,"* opened it, and tossed his luggage inside.

Then he brushed past Danny and stepped next door into Mr. Bashiri's compartment, stepping over Danny's suitcase and taking the other window seat, across from Mr. Bashiri. Danny was a bit startled at Luc's aggressiveness, but he had come to learn that it was par for the course with him.

"Eh bien, monsieur," Luc said, flipping through the papers in his hand. "I will just take a moment to tell you all you need to know. First of all, Danny and I are in the sleeper right next door. If you need anything, you can just knock on the wall. *Comme ça.*" To demonstrate, he tapped lightly on the wall beside the seat. "It's too late for any meals tonight, but Rémi provided you with some sandwiches. Breakfast will show up between six and six thirty, and we'll reach Zurich at seven twenty-four. We have asked the *préposé* to turn down your bed in about an hour."

The train began to pick up speed, and Danny realized that he ought to put his own stuff away. As Luc continued to tell Mr. Bashiri about the arrangements in Zurich, Danny moved his duffel bag into the other room, taking out his camera first and then setting the bag safely on the floor of the closet. He still couldn't believe he'd been given this opportunity.

Danny moved back to the doorway of Bashiri's room and stood there for another moment, observing his conversing travel companions. According to what Rémi had told him back at the office, though most successful photographers worked alone, Mr. Bashiri no longer did. With his advancing age and a bad back, he couldn't handle the weight of his equipment, and he didn't like the logistics of preparing an itinerary or driving in unfamiliar locations once he got there. Being semiretired, Mr. Bashiri could pick and choose his work more carefully these days, and one of his stipulations was that whatever magazine hired him for a job must provide what he called a "liaison"—but was actually just someone to do the footwork, the gruntwork, and the navigating.

Of course, Mr. Bashiri's loss was Danny's gain, as he had never expected to work so closely with such an icon in his field. Pushing down an anxious surge of nervousness and excitement, Danny said a prayer of thanks for the opportunity, asking God to help him do a good job and to be with them all on their journey.

Bradford held Jo's arm as they made their way through the train station.

"Start talking," Jo said softly, still feeling doubtful but also strangely nervous. "Tell me everything that has happened and everything you know."

He put an arm around her, pulled her close, and placed his cheek against her hair as they walked, so that his lips were near her ear. She didn't like his proximity—or familiarity—but right now she didn't see that she had much choice in the matter.

"It all started with a Jaguar," he said softly. "A little more than a year ago, your dad invited me to the company house out in the Hamptons for a weekend. I was thrilled to go and glad to have a quiet time of relaxing and getting to know each other better. Your mom came too. She made a fabulous rack of lamb and spent most of the dinner talking about you, about how great you are."

Jo didn't comment, but inside her stomach was clenching. Her mother always made rack of lamb when she wanted to impress someone—or butter them up to do something she wanted.

"The next morning, your dad invited me out to the garage. In it was a brand-new Jaguar XJ8, indigo blue exterior with a champagne interior. I was in love."

Jo felt bile rising in her stomach, remembering all the times she had ridden in that car with Bradford. Was she really ready to hear this?

"I thought it was his new car, but then he said, 'I bought this for you, Bradford, and there's a lot more where that came from. I've got a proposition for you, and if you're interested, you'll never want for anything again.'"

Jo's heart was pounding, and she felt sure that everyone who passed them by could see her emotions flashing clearly across her face. She was scared, angry, frustrated, and most of all anxious to hear what else he had to say. So far, knowing her parents as she did, everything Bradford was saying rang strangely true. Her father had pulled the same thing on her once with a red Porsche when she was fresh out of college and he was trying to get her to forget all about being a household hints expert and come to work for him at Bosworth Industries instead. Jo had been secretly flattered by his gesture, but the world of big business held no appeal for her at all. She had turned down the Porsche and the big salary, saying she was quite happy living with her grandparents in Mulberry Glen, thank you, and learning everything she needed to know to take over the "Tips from Tulip" newspaper column from her grandmother. Jo had never regretted that decision, especially when one after the other her sweet grandparents died and she was left to carry on the legacy alone.

"Oh, man, I forgot it was rush hour," Bradford said. "It's so crowded here."

The station grew even more crowded as they neared the boarding area. Jo realized he would have to finish talking once they were on the train and couldn't be overheard quite so easily. She allowed Bradford to keep his arm around her anyway, partly because she didn't want to lose him in the shuffle, partly because she needed the support for all this walking in her cast, and partly because she was starting to feel downright scared. Next to her, she could feel that Bradford's body was tense and on alert, his eyes darting constantly around the corridor. Jo found herself doing the same, though she wasn't sure what she expected to see. Finally, she couldn't keep quiet any longer.

"Bradford, what are we watching for? Who is it that you think wants me 'eliminated'? Is it someone I know? Someone in the company? Someone in my family?"

"Jo, all I know is that your life is in danger," he whispered in return, "and that it has to do with something big that's going on at Bosworth Industries. Otherwise, I'm as clueless as you are."

Jo swallowed hard. If by some wild chance Bradford really was telling her the truth, then her life could be in serious jeopardy right now.

"But *why?*" Jo demanded. "I have nothing at all to do with Bosworth Industries. I don't work there, and I don't have any dealings with them. I own a couple of measly shares of stock, certainly not enough to be killed over. I don't participate in any of the votes. When the stockholder's report comes in the mail, I usually toss it in the trash. I'm telling you, before today I hadn't even set foot the Bosworth building in several years."

"Look, all I know is that something's cooking at Bosworth, and for some reason you present a problem. I've tried everything I can to get more information, but once I started sniffing around with some of my old contacts and former fellow employees, it's like they closed ranks. Nobody's talking."

They separated to take the narrow escalator and head downward. Jo stepped on after Bradford so that she could lean forward and whisper in his ear.

"Who told you all of this?" she asked, halfway between skepticism and terror. Could he really be telling the truth? Or was he just working some strange sort of ploy, the motives of which she had yet to learn?

Holding onto the rail, Bradford turned his head to whisper in return.

"Let's just say that I heard it from a friend who was in a position to know."

"Oh, good grief, Bradford, stop being so cryptic and just say what you came here to say. Lay it out on the table."

He lowered his voice even more and whispered, "Just wait. I'll tell you everything I can once we're on the train. In the end, you'll probably want to skip your father completely and go strait to see your grandmother instead. She's really the only one who might be able to help."

They reached the bottom of the escalator platform, and because of the proximity of crowds, they once again had to stop talking. Bradford stood closely by her side, this time with both hands clutching her arm at the elbow, holding on tightly as a throng of people closed in around them. Jo's senses were on hyperalert, picking up the smells and sounds of the throng: garlic, curry, cheap perfume, aftershave, body odor, sneezing, coughing, chattering, one-sided cell-phone conversations. For someone who no longer lived in the city, it was overwhelming. A sense of light-headedness briefly threatened, but she took a deep breath and inched as close as she could to the yellow line at the edge of the platform, relieved when a train whistle sounded in the distance.

As the train drew closer, Jo's mind swirled with doubt, confusion, and fear. She thought about the questions she would ask Bradford once they were on board, and how she could figure out what was truly going on. Was she really targeted to be killed? If so, why—and how did Bradford know? What did her father have to do with any of it? Did he really want her to be married so badly that he had gone so far as to buy her husband? And how did that tie in with this supposed threat on her life?

Another whistle sounded and then the train rounded the bend and began to roar closer toward them. By now the platform was completely full, and Jo could feel the crowd pressing in from every side.

Suddenly, Jo felt the distinct pressure of a hand on her back. The hand pushed and Jo lost her balance, falling forward, directly toward the path of the oncoming train.

She screamed. Bradford was still holding her arm with both hands, and as she started to fall, he jerked backward, hard, turning at the same time, trying to twist her around and back into balance. As he did, she managed to find her footing and recover. But their movements caused him to lose *his* balance.

Before she could scream again, Bradford fell from the platform—right against the hard, steel side of the speeding train.

4

Alexa quietly shut the door and slid the lock into place. She had been given a lot of things since she moved on to the estate, but privacy wasn't one of them. She knew it wouldn't be long before someone started banging on the door, asking why it was locked, insisting that it be opened. At least the old lady wasn't around today. She had gone into the city for a meeting and then to take her granddaughter to the doctor. But for everybody else around here, it was business as usual.

Alexa knew she had better move fast.

Quickly, she tiptoed across the study to the shelves that held the oversized part of the collection. When she had been in the room that morning, working on a research paper with her tutor, she had spotted what looked like a bunch of blueprints up on a high shelf. But this was the first chance all day that Alexa had had to come back alone and take a look. Her desperate hope was that she'd find a drawing of the entire Bosworth compound, one that included the outbuildings and the perimeter of the old stone wall that surrounded the place.

Nervously, she stood on a step stool and reached high, grabbing from the pile, retrieving a cardboard tube about three feet long and capped with white plastic. Climbing down from the stool, she pulled off the lid and then tilted the tube so that the contents slid out onto the nearby table. Trying not to make much noise, she unrolled the large paper and took a look.

As her Uncle Rick liked to say, *Close, but no cigar.*

It was a blueprint, all right, but just of one building. From the looks of it, it was the gardener's cottage or the carriage house. She rolled it up, managed to get it back into the tube, and then climbed up on the stool, put it away, and tried again. Her physical therapist wouldn't have been happy to see her up there balancing on the stool as she went through the tubes, but Alexa wasn't worried about getting hurt; if she did fall, her biggest concern was that the crash would be so noisy it would alert everyone in the house to what she was doing.

There were ten cardboard rolls, and Alexa went through them one by one, still hoping for a master plan, one that showed everything. To her mind, it could be the key to her freedom—not that she was being held prisoner here in the compound, exactly. But getting away still wasn't a simple matter, at least not if she wanted to go alone and unobserved. If she had the blueprints, her hope was that she could find a better way to come and go, all on her own, despite the high stone wall and the security guards.

She'd already escaped twice. The first time went off without a hitch, but the second time she'd been caught on her way back in by a security guard. That had earned her a stern lecture from Dr. Stebbins, a loving reprimand from his wife, Nicole, and a cold warning from the old lady. They all kept saying the same thing, that Alexa was free to leave, but not like that, not at night, not when she would be putting herself in danger. Of course, Alexa didn't really want to leave—or, at least, she didn't want to *stay* away.

She just wanted some freedom, some air. A night to visit the old neighborhood and maybe meet up with some friends at the Grave Cave. A few hours to chill with her girls where no one was studying her or teaching her or examining her.

A chance to be a normal 14-year-old again.

They kept saying they would take her wherever she wanted to go, which wasn't exactly true because no way would they take her to the Grave Cave—not if they knew what went on there. But even if they did, if they gave her permission, drove her somewhere, and then waited for her, where was the freedom in that? She wanted out of here *on her own,* even if it meant going to a lot of trouble and putting herself in a little danger.

"Yes!" Alexa whispered now, peeking inside the second-to-last tube. "Sweet!"

Alexa's right arm and leg were starting to feel tired and shaky. She carefully climbed down from the stool, finished pulling the paper all the way out of the tube, and spread it open on the table.

She had found what she was looking for, a map of the whole joint.

Quickly, she traced her finger around the stone wall, searching for hidden gates or openings she hadn't been able to find simply by strolling around and looking.

There had to be a way to get out of there somehow.

Everything was a blur—of impressions, of sounds, of movements. Jo wasn't even sure how much time was passing. Mostly, there were hands, lots of hands, pulling Bradford to safety, gripping his lifeless wrist for a pulse, guiding Jo to a nearby bench to sit. Cell phones, there were cell phones, and she could hear someone calling for the police and ambulance. Jo took that as a good sign, that an ambulance was called.

That must mean that Bradford was still alive.

The noise got very loud for a while as more people gathered, as the paramedics came, worked on Bradford, and carted him away. Then the noise grew more quiet until Jo realized that the area had been cordoned off, with only a few cops inside the yellow tape line. One of those cops was sitting on the bench beside her, trying to talk to her, but Jo couldn't really understand what the woman was saying.

Jo blinked, forcing herself to focus, not surprised when the policewoman waved over another paramedic, who began taking Jo's vital signs. Maybe she was in shock. No, that wasn't it, she hadn't lost any bodily fluids or anything. She wasn't in shock.

She was just shocked.

Luc snored.

Several feet away, in his own berth, Danny tried to block the noise by holding his pillow over his ears, but it didn't help. He felt as though he were standing on the runway at the Moore City airport, airplanes taking off over his head at the rate of about one every five seconds.

Danny had already poked Luc once and asked him to turn over, but that had only helped for a short while. Danny did it again now, clutching the metal side of his bunk and leaning across the space between them to jab his friend on the shoulder. Without truly awaking, Luc grumbled something and flipped so that he was facing the wall. For the moment, at least, the noise stopped.

Thank goodness.

Danny was glad Luc had come along on the trip for logistical and language reasons, but he would almost be glad when it was time to move on to Africa and send Luc back to Paris. The young Frenchman was helpful, sure, but he was also aggressive and impertinent, like asking Mr. Bashiri if he could have one of his sandwiches because he "might want a midnight snack" or flirting shamelessly in the hallway with an attractive Dutch woman who was staying in the end compartment.

It wasn't that Luc was uncouth, really. He just didn't seem to sense the need for calmness and decorum or pick up on the very quiet and reserved nature of Mr. Bashiri. Danny was mortified, but the famous photographer seemed, if anything, amused. He didn't say much, but his eyes sparkled at Luc's antics, and when Luc actually scored a date for later in Zurich with the Dutch woman, Mr. Bashiri had merely shaken his head in quiet disbelief.

Danny fiddled now with the air vent over his head, feeling hot and restless despite the cool air pouring over his face. The train itself was nice, the bed comfortable, the ride much smoother than he had expected, considering how fast they were going. Maybe what was bothering him was just that he had never had the chance to speak directly with Jo and tell her what was up.

Earlier, when Luc was getting ready for bed, Danny had given him ten euro and borrowed his cell phone to make that call. Pacing out in the hallway, Danny's heart had raced with excitement to talk to Jo and tell her his good news, but all he had gotten was her voice mail, first on her cell and then at her home. He had left a rambling message on the machine at the house, giving her his big news that way, sorry that he hadn't been able to tell her in person. Something just felt weird and kind of wrong not to have actually talked to her. For no good reason at all, Danny felt unsettled—almost worried—about her.

In any event, that was no reason to lose sleep now; he could always catch up with her tomorrow. He turned over on his other side and tried to force himself to relax, wanting to seize whatever snore-free moments he had to cross over into slumber before the racket started up again.

Danny actually was almost asleep when he heard it, a steady tap-tap-tapping on the wall. For a moment, he was confused, and then he realized that the sound was coming from Mr. Bashiri's room. Quickly,

Danny rolled from the bunk to the floor, pulled pants on over his shorts, and stepped out into the hall, smoothing down his T-shirt.

He knocked, noting a sliver of light coming from under the door. After a moment of quiet, a soft voice said, "Come."

Danny opened the door to see Mr. Bashiri sitting in the chair opposite the folded-down bed, wearing beige cotton pajamas and holding a tobacco pipe.

"Yes?"

"I'm sorry," Danny said, smoothing his hair. "I thought heard you knocking. Did you need something?"

It took a moment and then understanding crossed Mr. Bashiri's shiny, dark features. He glanced down at the pipe and then back at Danny.

"Oh, my young friend, it is I who should be sorry. I was only packing the tobacco. It makes for a better smoke. I completely forgot about the signal."

He did it again now for demonstration, tapping the pipe against the metal armrest of the chair. Danny exhaled slowly, glad there was nothing wrong. He couldn't imagine why the man had been knocking in the middle of the night.

"I feel so bad. Did I wake you up?"

"Not really," Danny replied gamely. "For some reason, I'm kind of wired up tonight anyway."

Mr. Bashiri nodded.

"As am I. Perhaps we could pass some time together. Would you like to come in?"

Danny hesitated, wondering if he should.

"I do not bite, you know," Mr. Bashiri added. "In fact, I am a mere mortal, just like you."

Surprised, Danny inhaled sharply. Then he smiled. He supposed he *had* been a bit intimidated, not to mention a tad obsequious.

"Please. Fold up the berth and join me."

Danny tried to relax, stepping into the room, putting up the bed, and taking a seat opposite the man whose work had appeared in everything from *Life* magazine decades ago to *National Geographic* last month. He was a legend, an icon, with a lifelong career of hopping the globe and documenting it in pictures. By Danny's calculations, Mr. Bashiri had to be almost 80 years old, but it wasn't obvious by looking at him. His body movements were those of an older man, yes, but his dark features were almost youthful, and his closely shaven hair was deep black without a hint of gray. Only his hands belied his age; they were gnarled and wrinkled and told of years spent out in the sun, exploring and photographing.

"So tell me why you treat me like I am made of glass. Did Ms. Tatou instruct you to be so helpful and polite? Or is that just the sort of man you are?"

Mr. Bashiri posed his question and then let it sit there as he continued fooling with his pipe, stuffing in more tobacco and tapping it down some more.

Danny wasn't sure how to answer. What could he say? That the man sitting here in his cotton pajamas was Danny's hero, his professional example?

"I guess it's because you are everything I want to be," Danny said finally, hoping he didn't sound too stupid. "I've been dreaming of success like yours for many years. I never thought I'd be in such close proximity to it."

Mr. Bashiri nodded, tucking away his pouch of tobacco and then striking a match and holding it to the pipe, sucking deeply on the stem. Danny had a feeling that pipe smoking wasn't allowed on the train—but he sure wasn't going to be the one to stop him.

"Success comes at a price, you know," Mr. Bashiri said finally, a puff of smoke swirling from his lips. "I did not just wake up one day and snap my fingers and make it happen. I sacrificed much. I worked hard. I have…" he hesitated, pipe poised in the air, eyes distant. Then he zeroed in on Danny, looking directly at him with eyes black and deep, the irises the same color as the pupils. "…regrets. I have regrets."

Danny shook his head enthusiastically.

"But you've accomplished so much! Your career is unrivaled."

Mr. Bashiri finally got the pipe to light and a gray haze filled the tiny room. He spoke in vague generalities about the cost of fame, but Danny didn't need to hear this. It was the standard be-careful-what-you-wish-for-because-you-just-might-get-it speech that wizened old professionals always tried to toss the way of aspiring hopefuls. He'd heard it all before and had a feeling that most of it was bunk anyway.

"What I am saying," the man continued, "is that sometimes we cannot undo what has been done. Success does not come cheap, my friend, and it is not always worth the price paid."

"I'm not worried about any of that," Danny said, settling back into the seat, eager to change the subject. "And I'm no stranger to hard work.

But I'd love to hear some stories from the road. Tell me about your most exciting photo shoot."

Mr. Bashiri smoked several long puffs before he answered, seeming to accept the change of subject and moving in the conversational direction of Danny's choice.

"There have been many, too many to choose," Mr. Bashiri said, resting the hand that held his pipe on his knee, "but there was this one time in the Sudan…"

Alexa carefully folded the blueprint and slid it down the front of her shirt. Then she put the cap back on the empty tube, climbed up on the stool, and put it back where she had found it.

What was it her tutor was always telling her? Knowledge is power? *You bet, baby.*

With this map, she had everything she needed to make her escape. Now she just had to get it back to her room without being spotted, hide it somewhere safe, and go over it again more carefully tonight. From just a quick glance, she had found several possible routes. Right now, she was more happy and excited than she'd been in weeks. She was going to get some freedom after all.

She crossed to the door, listened for a long moment, and carefully unlocked it without a click. Holding her breath, she pulled it open and peeked out into the hall. No one was there.

So far, so good.

If only it weren't so far back to her bedroom. Sometimes this house felt bigger than the Newark train station. Alexa crossed her arms in front of her chest, nervous about the crinkling noise the blueprints made, and headed off. She tried to walk casually, as if nothing were wrong, as if she hadn't just stolen a map of the whole estate and tucked it into her shirt.

She passed two of the part-time maids in the hallway, but they were chatting with each other and barely noticed her. Alexa kept going. She still had to get all the way upstairs and down the hall without running into Consuela, the full-time cook and housekeeper. Consuela was nice and all, but she was always too much in Alexa's business, always asking how she felt and if she missed her mother.

"Señoritas need their mamacitas," Consuela liked to say. "They belong together."

Alexa had overheard a conversation once between Consuela and the physical therapist, Yasmine. Consuela kept saying how wrong it was to remove a girl from her mother's home and plunk her down in a mansion without any parents at all, even if it was for the sake of science. Yasmine just parroted Dr. Stebbins, saying that Alexa was a "medical miracle" and an "astounding prodigy" and that living here gave her opportunities far beyond anything her mother could ever provide.

"Don't kid yourself," Consuela had responded sharply, taking her anger out on Yasmine, even though she had nothing to do with it. "I think Mrs. Bosworth is getting a lot more than she's giving with this arrangment. Or at least she will once Dr. Stebbins brings home his Nobel prize."

Alexa had slipped away at that point, choosing not to hear the rest of their conversation. She didn't like it when people talked about her that way—as though she was the sum of all those tests and examinations they were always doing, rather than a real person with feelings. Consuela's intentions were good, but she had been wrong about one thing: Taking Alexa out of her mother's home and plunking her down *anywhere* was the nicest thing anyone could have done for her. At least now Alexa didn't lie awake at night worrying that her mother's freebasing would catch the house on fire, or wake up the next morning to find yet another "uncle" in her kitchen, making breakfast. To be honest, her mom had never been much of a mother.

Sometimes, Alexa didn't even miss her.

Now, she made it to her bedroom without incident and then pushed open the door, stepped inside, and then closed it behind her, exhaling slowly. She had done it.

Alexa locked the door behind her and then she set about finding a hiding place for the map, one that wouldn't be discovered by the maids if they decided to change her sheets or gather up her dirty laundry. It was nice having people to clean up after her, but in a way it was one more invasion of her privacy.

Alexa quickly scanned the bedroom and the closet, finally spotting a jacket that hung near the back with its tags still on, the uncool one with the stupid removable liner the old lady had given her for her birthday. She grabbed it from the rack, carried it out to the bed, and unzipped one side. Carefully, she slid the folded paper between the nylon of the jacket and the fleece of the liner. Then she zipped it shut again.

Perfect.

She hung the jacket back in the closet and left, making her way through the house, out the back door, and across the beautiful lawn to the studio. It was going to be a long evening, she knew, trying to keep her very intuitive art teacher, Nicole, from sensing her excitement, and then killing time until she could get a taste of freedom tonight.

Alexa couldn't wait to escape and make her way back to the Grave Cave.

"Water?"

Jo snapped up to see a policewoman holding out a bottle of water. It was dripping with condensation, and suddenly Jo was thirstier than she'd ever been in her life. She took it and drank a long sip. When she was finished, she tried to find her voice.

"Thank you," she croaked.

"No problem. Do you feel up to answering a few questions?"

Jo shook her head, trying to get her bearings. Where was Bradford? Why had they taken him away?

"Is Bradford okay?" she asked, not wanting to hear the answer.

"The fellow that got hit by the train? He's hurt pretty bad," the cop replied, pulling a notebook from her pocket, "but he's hanging in there. They're taking him to the hospital on Lexington. You can go there once you're finished here."

"Okay," Jo whispered, standing. "Sure."

The woman began her questions starting with the basic facts: names, next of kin, what time she and Bradford got there, where they had been standing. Once they got through that, she asked Jo to describe what happened.

Closing her eyes, Jo tried to walk back through the whole incident as best she could. She described the press of the crowd, the hand on her back, the push that propelled her forward. When Jo opened her eyes, she was surprised to see the cop looking at her skeptically.

"You're trying to tell me that someone intentionally pushed you onto the tracks of an oncoming train?"

"That's exactly what I'm saying. Somebody tried to kill me."

Jo told how she had started to fall when Bradford seemed to sense her movements and did what he could to pull her back to safety.

"This station gets busy at rush hour," the cop replied, closing her notepad and tucking it into a pocket. "A lot of tourists might feel all those folks pressing in on them and think they were pushed. Doesn't mean somebody was trying to kill you."

"But they were. And I'm not a tourist. I grew up in this city."

That wasn't exactly true. Jo had grown up in different places all over the world, dragged along on each new business assignment of her father's. But throughout her childhood her family had maintained an apartment in Manhattan, and she had lived there, on and off, for months at a time. Not counting her grandparents' house in Mulberry Glen, New York City was as much "home" as anywhere else had been.

"Well, if you grew up here, then you know what it's like. We got a lot of people all stuffed together on this one little island. Accidents happen."

Jo studied the woman's face, wondering why she was being so skeptical. Then the woman closed her eyes and pinched the bridge of her nose, and Jo realized she was just an exhausted transit cop, overworked and probably underpaid, who really thought Jo was just paranoid.

Reluctantly, Jo went on to explain how the situation was more complicated than it seemed, that in fact Bradford had been warning her for the past hour that she was in danger.

"There's even more to it than that," Jo added, wishing she hadn't given the printouts of the anonymous e-mails over to her grandmother. "This isn't the first time today I had to talk with the police."

Jo explained about the e-mails and her visit to Kreston, and the cop seemed to grow more convinced, especially when she realized that Jo was *the* Jo Tulip, of Tips from Tulip fame.

"Oh!" the cop cried suddenly. "Get out! You're Tips from Tulip?"

"Yes."

That seemed to change everything. The cop whipped out her notebook and asked Jo to repeat her story. This time through, however, Jo's word was valid and all that she was claiming was absolute truth. As the cop enthusiastically began asking more questions, Jo was relieved. Sometimes a little celebrity came in handy.

The cop took thorough notes and asked good questions, but when she asked Jo if she knew *why* she was in danger, or from whom, Jo was reluctant to answer. If this had to do with her family and the family

company, she knew it would be best to keep her mouth shut for now.
Who knew what can of worms awaited her there, or what problems she
might create for them, all based on the desperate whispers of a man who
might or might not have been telling the full truth? Better to keep the
authorities out of that part of it for the time being, at least until she'd had
a chance to talk to her father.

"Bradford was going to explain once we got on the train," Jo hedged.
"Now I might never know."

The cop nodded, again tucking away her notebook.

"Well, you sit tight for a few," she said. "The detective will need for
you to repeat everything you've told me and then some." She gestured
toward a man who was talking to someone else nearby. "He'll probably
be getting to you next. Don't go anywhere."

"Don't worry," Jo said emphatically. "I won't."

5

Alexa dipped her brush into the light blue paint and then hesitated in front of the easel that awaited her. Slowly, reaching out with the brush, she painted a small circle in the center of the empty white canvas.

Once the circle was done, she thought about it for a moment, rinsed her brush, and then dipped it into the red, using it to paint a ring all the way around the blue. After red, she added a ring of yellow, then green, then black. As she painted, her concerns about hiding her excitement from her art teacher melted away. She was lost in the moment, so focused on capturing the image on the canvas that tonight's escape was the furthest thing from her mind.

"There," Alexa announced, looking up at her art teacher. "I'm done."

Nicole Stebbins walked behind the easel and stood there for a long moment, obviously studying the display. She always wore soft, fluttery clothes, and today's outfit was no exception. Her shirt looked as though it were made of pastel scarves, the sleeves hanging down in elegant points at her wrists. With the bright art room lights shining on her wavy blond hair and through her gauzy sleeves, she looked kind of like an angel. A really colorful angel.

"Interesting," Nicole said finally. "Tell me about it."

"You wanted me to paint an abstract of my mother," Alexa answered, shrugging. "That's her."

Nicole pointed to the center of the multihued ball.

"That's a pretty color," she said. "You began with light blue. Why?"

Alexa hesitated, not knowing how to explain—or if she even wanted to. When she was young, her favorite blanket had been that exact soft shade of blue. She thought maybe mothers were supposed to feel like that color—when they loved you, at least.

"I guess that's the 'mom' stuff. You know, like being nice. Playing dolls. Putting on Band-Aids. I think she used to do that sort of thing when I was a kid. Sometimes."

"But it's been a while?"

"I'm fourteen," Alexa answered, rolling her eyes. "What do you think?"

Nicole looked at her with a strange expression, sadness mixed with pity, her vivid blue eyes piercing through to Alexa's heart.

"I think even fourteen-year-olds need the mom stuff sometimes."

Alexa swallowed hard. Why was Nicole always so insightful? It was creepy, as though she could crawl inside of Alexa's head and read what was in there.

"And the red?" Nicole prodded, pointing toward the canvas.

"Her temper," Alexa answered quickly, glancing away. "It doesn't always show, but it's there."

The next ring, the yellow one, was even bigger than the red. The yellow was her mother's *energy*, which was kind of intense and volatile, because it would come and go and always make trouble whenever it got too yellow. Alexa hated her mother's energy. But she didn't feel like explaining that. She didn't want to talk about this stuff at all.

"Okay," Nicole told her. "How about the yellow?"

"I don't know," Alexa said, trying to describe it and then quickly moving on to the next. "The green is money."

"Money?"

"It's a big part of who she is. Not that we ever had any. But she's always thinking about it, always scheming to get it, always hoping for more of it."

"That must seem odd, in a way, for money to be such a major focus that it becomes a part of who she is."

Alexa didn't respond. It didn't seem odd to her, because that's how it had always been. What did Nicole know about it anyway? She was a rich doctor's wife who lived in Greenhaven and probably hadn't had to worry about money since the day she got married. Life was different in a dumpy little apartment in a dumpy little town across the river in New Jersey: hand-to-mouth, paycheck-to-paycheck. That's just how it was.

"I mean, earning and handling and spending money are necessary parts of life," Nicole added, "but sometimes our priorities get a bit askew."

Understatement of the year. Everything about my mother is askew.

"Okay, well, tell me why you chose to finish in black," Nicole added after a moment.

Alexa was quiet. How could she explain the black? That's what the money was for, mostly, the addiction. The drugs.

"Black swallows all the rest," Alexa said softly, "so that's all anyone can see anymore."

At that, she dipped her brush in more black paint and smeared it across the colorful ball, wiping back and forth in an attempt to obliterate it. She wished it were that easy to wipe out everything—everything that had come before, everything that had changed.

"Does it feel good to do that?" Nicole asked.

"It feels real," Alexa replied, swirling the brush with even more vigor. "That's what she is these days, just one big globby mess."

Finally, she tossed the brush into the water and wiped her hands on the towel.

"I'm tired. I want to quit," Alexa said, feeling inexplicably angry. Sometimes, she wondered why her art lessons with Nicole always seemed to stir up her feelings. She padded across the studio and sat on the floor, pulling on her sneakers and tying them. She was ready to be done for the hour, even though they were just getting started.

"Funny, isn't it," Nicole said, still standing in front of the easel, studying the canvas, "that even with all that black, the light blue still peeks through here and there. As do the other colors."

Alexa finished tying her shoes and looked up at the mess she had made on the canvas. Nicole was right. Even in the midst of the giant glob of black, little streaks and swirls of the other colors were still there. Alexa leaned back against the window seat, resisting the urge to cry, though she couldn't even say why. Just a short while ago, she had been so happy. Now she couldn't imagine feeling any worse.

"Why do you always keep pushing, always get all symbolic on me?" Alexa asked miserably. "You just won't let things rest."

Nicole turned from the canvas and crossed the room to where Alexa still sat on the floor. Nicole sat across from her, cross-legged, elbows on her knees.

"The art doesn't lie," she said matter-of-factly, her curls falling perfectly into place. "That's why it's such a good starting point for conversation."

Nicole was so pretty, not in a glamorous way, but in a slightly plump, mom-ish sort of way—all soft curves and friendly smiles and gentle eyes.

Sometimes late at night, Alex pretended that Nicole was her mom. She would imagine her tucking her in at night, reading her a bedtime story. And cookies. In Alexa's fantasies, they were always baking Nicole's secret family recipe for cookies. But that was dumb, Alexa knew.

Nicole probably didn't even *have* a secret family recipe for cookies.

"Of all my teachers and tutors and medical people," Alexa said, "how come you're the only one who worries about what I'm feeling? Can't we just stick to the art lessons? You'd think this was counseling or something."

Her words came out sounding more bitter than she meant, but when she looked at Nicole to apologize, she didn't understand the expression on the woman's face.

"Alexa, what do you think this is? What do you think we're doing together?"

"Art lessons."

"Art *therapy*," Nicole corrected.

"Yeah, like to go with my physical therapy. Art therapy. Coordination. Physical movement. That kind of stuff."

Nicole shook her head, and she seemed so disconcerted that Alexa frowned in confusion.

"Honey, I'm sorry you didn't understand. Art therapy isn't physical. It's emotional. We're using the art to understand your feelings."

Alexa felt like such a dummy. Of course. Therapy. Counseling. Art therapy. How many of these once-a-week lessons had they had now? Five? Six? And every time, Alexa just thought Nicole was especially nice, especially chatty. Especially insightful.

Figures.

"I'm so stupid," Alexa said softly, covering her face with her hands.

"No, you're not," Nicole said. "Look at me, Alexa. Look at me."

She reached up and gently pulled Alexa's hands from her eyes.

"What?" Alexa asked, blinks sending tears down her cheeks.

"This is my fault and my husband's fault. You are not stupid. You misunderstood because we didn't make it clear. You probably never even heard of art therapy until Dr. Stebbins asked you if you wanted to meet me and give it a try. And since you were already in physical therapy and occupational therapy, you made a logical conclusion."

Alexa nodded, wishing she had just kept her big mouth shut about the whole thing. Dumb, dumb, dumb.

"Why do my feelings even matter?" she asked finally, wiping at her cheeks. "What does that have to do with anything?"

Nicole explained, saying there were two reasons Alexa needed therapy—one, as yet another part of the research, one more area that needed to be cataloged and documented. That wasn't too surprising, since Dr. Stebbins had had Alexa tested and examined in a thousand other ways.

"That's not fair. Isn't counseling supposed to be confidential?"

"It is," Nicole said. "All I do is fill out a checklist once a week, evaluating your emotional state. I never add any notes or include any specifics."

Alexa considered, and then she decided that made it okay.

"What's the second reason?" she asked.

Nicole seemed to study her face for a moment before speaking.

"Because Dr. Stebbins and I care about you, Alexa, and we worry. In less than a year, your entire life has done a complete one eighty. Everything's changed—your body, your mind, your living situation, your schooling. That's hard enough, but add to that practically living under a microscope, and you've got a recipe for major stress. I want to help you learn how to cope."

"Cope?"

"And grow. When the trial phase is over and Dr. Stebbins is finished collecting his data, we want you to be much, much better for all of this, not worse. You're not just our medical subject, Alexa. You're also our friend—not to mention our responsibility."

Responsibility.

Alexa closed her eyes, in her mind suddenly seven years old, hovering in the hall outside of her classroom, listening to the second grade teacher yell at her mother. It wasn't anything her mother had done; it was Alexa's fault. Again.

"This is your responsibility!" the teacher was practically yelling. "It falls on you!"

"Look, we both know Alexa is a handful," her mother said calmly, trying to soothe the old battle-ax. "In fact," she added with a conspiratorial chuckle, "that's what my fiancé and I call Alexa when we're alone, 'The Handful.' But that doesn't mean she needs to be on medication. I won't put a seven-year-old child on drugs just to make your job easier. You give it all the fancy names you want—attention-deficit/hyperactivity disorder,

whatever. *My kid's not a psycho. She just has a lot of energy. And maybe a little trouble staying focused."*

Even at seven, Alexa knew what irony was: It was her mother calling this week's live-in lover her "fiancé"; if so, he was about her tenth fiancé so far that year. It was also her use of the word "drugs," the heroin addict refusing to give her kid the prescription medication she needed for a legitimate condition. *Irony.*

What the teacher and the doctors didn't know was that Alexa's mother filled the amphetamine prescriptions, all right, but rather than give the medicine to her child, who needed it, she sold it on the street for $10 a pill. When you had a kid like Alexa, speed was easy to get, and even easier to sell.

What stung the most, though, was the nickname: *The Handful.* Alexa knew she was a bad girl and that she was always getting in trouble and that adults didn't like her, not even the nice student aide who tried really hard to get along with all of the children.

But for Alexa's own mother to turn against her, to give her such an awful nickname, to giggle over it in bed with a virtual stranger, not to mention with the latest teacher who hated her guts? That hurt more than anything.

That was betrayal, pure and simple.

At seven, Alexa had learned betrayal. Now, at 14, she kept wondering when these people were going to betray her too. She was their responsibility, yes. But was she really their friend? Though Alexa was deeply fond of Dr. Stebbins, her relationship with him was purely professional. Things were a little more relaxed with Dr. Stebbins' wife, Nicole—including the fact that she had invited Alexa to call her by her first name the day they met—but she was still one more adult who had come into Alexa's world after the stroke and the treatment, one more person who would eventually cash in on the medical miracle.

You can't get something for nothing, her mother had always told her. These days, Alexa was still trying to figure out exactly how the "something" and the "nothing" fit into the picture of her coming here. Nicole and Dr. Stebbins and the old lady had all seemed to do so much for her without asking anything in return except the opportunity to study her, to teach her. It was a lot to cope with.

Hardest of all, though, was living with the fear that eventually it would come to an end.

By the time Jo finished answering questions for the police and got to the hospital, Bradford's parents, his brother, and two cousins were all in the waiting room. According to them, Bradford was suffering from a number of broken bones and a punctured lung, and right now he was in surgery.

They asked Jo to explain exactly what had happened, but she left out a lot of the details as she talked, making it sound much simpler than it was—that she and Bradford had been waiting for the train to North Ulton, Jo lost her balance, and Bradford fell trying to save her.

His parents were bitter and angry, and at first Jo didn't blame them. He was in there because of her, after all. But then she kept thinking that Bradford had started it by accepting money to marry her. Anything that came after was simply fallout from that act.

"Why couldn't you just let it go?" Mrs. Quinn pleaded. "It's over, Jo. When my son told you goodbye at the wedding, he meant it."

Jo's mouth flew open in a silent gasp.

"What are you talking about?" she said finally, once she'd found her voice.

"I'm sure you came up here to the city to chase after him and try to get back together again. But it wasn't going to happen, Jo. He's not the same person he was then."

"First of all," Jo replied, fighting to keep her voice steady, "your son has been chasing after me, not the other way around. I only agreed to see him today so that we could get some closure and he would leave me alone. His behavior toward me in the last few weeks has bordered on harassment."

If possible, Mrs. Quinn seemed even angrier than Jo.

"Harassment? Why, you lying—"

"Mom. Mom!"

Both women turned to look at Bradford's younger brother, Ty, the one who had served as best man at their almost-wedding. A laid back "surfer dude," Ty was about as different in personality from Bradford as a brother could be—though equally as handsome. He was just 23, with blond hair that hung messily in his eyes and an easy gait that always reminded Jo of boys at the beach.

"Mom, Jo's right. Bradford's been weirding out on everybody lately. And we all know why."

"Why?" Jo asked.

In response, Mrs. Quinn turned, closed her mouth, and simply walked away. Jo looked again at Ty, who pretended to take a swig from an invisible bottle.

"He's developed a bit of a problem."

Shocked, Jo sank into a chair and sat next to her almost brother-in-law.

"Alcohol? Bradford's been drinking?"

"Whenever he can. I've been trying to get the family to do an intervention, but they'd rather pretend the problem doesn't exist."

Ty spoke loudly, trying to make a point to the relatives nearby. In response, they simply turned their backs and patently ignored him.

"See?" he continued, more softly. "If we don't mention it, it's not there. Par for the course with this crowd."

Jo was surprised. When they were dating, Bradford often enjoyed a glass of wine or two with dinner, but she'd never seen him have more than that, and she'd certainly never seen him get drunk. Then again, maybe that was all a part of who he was pretending to be back then, to court her. Jo didn't drink, so Bradford curtailed his consumption—at least when he was with her.

"How long has he had a problem?" she asked.

"It's only been bad the last couple months," Ty said, considering. "Actually, things have been going downhill for him in a lot of ways. After your failed wedding, he was demoted and transferred to Chicago. But he wasn't happy there and he wanted to come back to New York, so after a few months he came back here, and went to work for one of the company's subsidiaries instead. I guess the drinking got really serious once he realized what a piddly, dead-end job he'd landed himself in. More than anything, he wants to get back into your father's good graces and return to the Bosworth fast track. He had it so good there for a while—until he walked out on you, actually."

"If he has such a drinking problem, how is he holding down a job at all? He hadn't been drinking when he showed up today."

"Oh, he can pull it together when he wants to and seem fine. But right now he's living on my couch, and I can guarantee you that the last time he made it through an entire day sober there was snow on the ground."

Jo thought about that, feeling terribly sad. Bradford may have his character flaws, but he was without question smart and talented when it came to business. Had he not gone down such a deceitful path, he might have seen all of his dreams come true in the end.

"Almost every night," Ty continues, "he sits around the apartment getting on my roommates' nerves, cooking up conspiracy theories, and obsessing about you."

"Me?"

"About winning you back. He keeps your engagement photo in his wallet, and he's always pulling it out and looking at it and talking about how you were the best thing that ever happened to him. Considering how things have turned out, I'm not sure I'd agree. No offense."

"None taken."

Jo sat there for a while, thinking about all that Ty had said. Conspiracy theories? If not for the hand on Jo's back, pushing her toward the train, she'd be tempted to believe that's all today had been about—a theory. But that hand was real. Bradford's injuries were real. And certainly whatever was behind all of it was real too.

"What sort of conspiracy theories?" Jo asked carefully.

Ty shrugged.

"Who pays attention? Secret deals, double crosses, corporate infighting—he's got a real love/hate thing going for Bosworth Industries. I stopped listening a long time ago."

Jo started to reply, but she was interrupted by the sight of the doctor, who was coming out to report on Bradford's condition. As the family gathered around, he told them that Bradford had made it through surgery and was now in recovery. His prognosis was good, though they weren't anticipating an easy road.

"Can we speak to him?" Bradford's mother asked tearfully.

"Not right now," the doctor replied. "We'll be moving him up to intensive care when he gets out of recovery. You might want to relocate up there."

As they prepared to move upstairs, Jo decided to make her exit. She said a quick farewell to Ty, traded cell phone numbers with him, and headed for the door, so thankful that these people had not ended up being her in-laws after all. None of them tried to stop her. She had a feeling they were as happy to see her leave as she was to go.

Outside under the brightly lit awning, Jo inhaled deeply and tried to clear her head. Now that Bradford's family was here to look after him, she could stop thinking about him for a moment and consider her own ongoing safety.

First she had received e-mails from a stranger, telling her she was in danger.

Then Bradford had told her she was in danger.

Finally, a hand, placed firmly on her back, had tried to push her into the path of an oncoming train.

Heart pounding, Jo suddenly felt, again, like a target. Who knew if the person who had pushed her was watching her now? Who knew how soon he or she might to try again to kill her? Shrinking back inside the entranceway, Jo hesitated, weighing her options. Then she turned around and went back into the hospital.

Avoiding the part of the waiting room where Bradford's family was congregated, Jo passed through the emergency department and followed the signs down a long, wide hallway to the main hospital lobby. Once there, she saw that it was well lit and empty except for a security guard near the door and one person sitting behind the front desk, reading a magazine. Ignoring the posted notices about not using cell phones, Jo retreated to a quiet corner behind a water fountain and dialed her grandmother's house. She had to go through two different people to get the woman on the phone, but once she heard her voice, tears sprang into Jo's eyes. She felt a rush of something she couldn't describe—relief, mixed with terror.

"Gran," she said, trying not to sob. "It's Jo. I need your help. Can you send a car to the city to get me?"

6

Alexa tucked the covers around the pillows, poking them here and shifting them there until she was satisfied that the lump in the bed looked like an actual person. Stepping back, she admired her work, trying to remember how long it had been since she was caught making her last escape. Three weeks? Four? Long enough that she was ready to try it again, albeit armed with better knowledge this time.

Ever since she got back to her room after her art therapy session, she had put the conversation with Nicole out of her mind and focused on the map of the estate that she had taken from the study. Nobody ever bothered her once she went to her room for the night, not even the maids, and with her door locked she had felt safe spreading out the map on her bed and taking her time plotting her route.

Just as she had hoped, it looked as though there was another way to get out of here. Along the far north wall of the fence, behind the stables, were several dotted lines indicating what looked like a gate. She had a feeling it was for bringing in horse trailers or hay trucks or something, but since there weren't any horses currently living here—and probably hadn't been for a while—the gate was more than likely overgrown to the point that she hadn't even noticed it.

The walk across the back pasture might be a little creepy, and she wasn't sure what lay on the other side of that gate, but she was a big girl. She could handle it.

Now she was dressed all in black, her hair pulled tightly into a ponytail and tucked under a knit cap. She would bring along her little backpack, inside of which was a hairbrush, a wide belt, and some chunky jewelry to make herself look better once she was free. In the meantime, however, she needed to be silent and sleek, with only a flashlight, a bus route map, some money in her backpack, and a good bit of nerve.

Alexa turned off the light and crept to the window, slowly sliding it open. The night was warm for May, and she could feel the heat swooshing into the room along with the fresh air. Carefully, she slid up the screen as well, and then swung one leg over the sill, shifted her weight, and lowered herself down the other side until her toe touched the stone of the second floor wraparound balcony. The setup of this place was perfect for climbing out at night, as all she had to do was cross under the hall window and slip down the balcony stairs to get to the backyard.

Alexa reached in through the window for her flashlight and backpack then slid the window shut except for the last quarter inch. As long as she returned before sunrise, she'd be able to slip inside and crawl into her bed, no one the wiser. Keeping the flashlight turned off, she slung the pack over her shoulder, crouched down, and started moving.

She had to stop short of the stairs to keep from passing through a beam of light that was coming from one of the empty guest bedrooms. That was odd. Before proceeding with her escape, she carefully crept to the window of the room and tried to peek in, but the curtains were drawn except for the slightest gap where the light was coming through. She held her face close to the glass and peered inside, disappointed that she could see movement in the room but couldn't tell who it was or what they were doing.

Alexa was concerned. Did they have a guest she didn't know about? Maybe someone had switched rooms for the night? It wouldn't really matter except that everyone was supposed to be asleep by now. What if something was going on and someone came to her room to get her, and she wasn't there? She'd be busted.

Alexa crept back to the hall window, which had no curtain, and slowly raised herself to eye level to peek inside. The hall was empty, but the door to that guest room was wide open, the light forming a rectangle on the hall rug. Alexa watched but no one went in or out. She didn't know what to do.

She sat down under the window and thought about it, trying to decide whether or not to abort her mission. Almost desperate to escape by this point, she was just about to bite the bullet and go ahead with it when she heard a noise.

It was the crunch of gravel. A car was coming up the driveway.

Quickly, Alexa ducked all the way down, flattening herself against the cold stone floor, hoping the sweep of headlights would be low enough not to shine on her and give her away.

It was after midnight! Who would be coming here now? Slowly, she crawled toward the front of the balcony and took refuge behind a giant marble column, hidden in the shadows and hoping to catch a glimpse of whoever was coming up the drive.

By the time they reached her grandmother's estate, Jo had been lulled by the rhythm of the road into a quiet numbness, a sort of grim stupor except for the knot of nerves in the pit of her stomach. As they pulled through the gate and down the long, winding driveway, she felt the knot in her stomach loosen just a bit. •

Maybe, for the time being at least, she would be safe.

The limo followed the curve of the driveway, finally pulling to a stop where it looped in front of the house. Even at night, the place was stunning, a stately rambling stone-and-marble structure that simply screamed elegance and old money. Above the front door was a big curved window that revealed a magnificent chandelier. Outside, strategically placed lights beamed up from behind neatly landscaped bushes and plants, illuminating the front of the house and giving the whole area a warm, safe glow. Jo knew there was nothing warm about her grandmother, but Bradford had said she was safe, and that's what was important right now.

Fernando opened the door for Jo, took her things, and then offered her his arm. Jo liked to think of herself as a very independent person, strong and brave, but tonight she had reached her limit. She needed someone to lean on.

Slowly, she took his arm and held on, allowing him to support her as they walked up the steps and through the massive front double doors into her grandmother's foyer.

The car that came up the drive had been the old lady's limo. Alexa couldn't see very well for fear of being spotted herself, but it looked like the person was a woman with blond hair. Fernando had to help her out of the car and up the steps, as though maybe she was sick or hurt or something.

Alexa sat back again behind the column and considered her options. She was so ready to get out of there. But she didn't want to make a costly mistake.

She decided to give it half an hour, keep an eye on the upstairs hallway, and see what happened next. Since she had been living there, a number of guests had used that room, most of them relatives of the old lady, a few of them business associates. It was so late. Maybe this particular guest would go to bed soon, the house would settle down, and Alexa could leave after all.

Quietly, she crept back to her own window, sat against the wall, and waited. Lucky for her it was a warm night, because the coldness of the stone floor was seeping into her bones.

Jo's grandmother was waiting for her in the study, sitting in a high-back armchair in a silk robe, reading. She pulled off her glasses and put the book down as they entered, dismissed the driver with a wave of her hand, and gestured for Jo to sit on the couch. Wearily, Jo sank into the cushions, wishing she could simply sink right through to the inside and never come out again.

"Jo, dear, are you all right? You're as white as a sheet. Let me have Fernando make you a brandy."

Jo shook her head, her eyes still closed.

"No, thank you. I'm okay. I'm still in shock, that's all."

"Well, you were right to come here. I'm glad you called."

When Jo had phoned her grandmother from the hospital, all she had said was that Bradford had been injured in a terrible accident and that she needed somewhere to stay. Her grandmother hadn't asked any questions, other than to find out where to send the car and driver. Now, however, she would be wanting a full explanation, and Jo didn't blame her.

"What on earth has happened?"

Jo exhaled slowly and opened her eyes, fixing her gaze on her grandmother.

She's really the only one who might be able to help, Bradford had said.

Jo was here now and glad she had come. But did Bradford mean that Jo should tell the woman *everything*?

She didn't see that she had much choice. Her grandmother was the matriarch of the family, not to mention the major shareholder of Bosworth Industries. If there was something funny going on in the family or the company, as Bradford had implied, then her grandmother needed to know about it more than anyone.

Swallowing her pride, Jo told her grandmother everything, starting from the moment Bradford arrived at the Marriott and announced that he had been paid to marry her.

Eleanor's face remained impassive throughout the story, which would have seemed odd considering all that Jo was telling her—except that Jo knew that this was her poker face, perfected through a lifetime of sitting on the board during business negotiations and corporate maneuvers. Just by looking at her, you'd never know what she thinking, or even if she was even fully absorbing what was being said.

When Jo was finished talking, however, it was evident that her grandmother had, indeed, taken in every word. She asked a number of questions, zeroing in on the details, trying to get a handle on the situation.

"Jo, I don't know what to tell you," she said finally, her expression guarded. "I think our first step should be to contact your father and get him here as soon as possible. Perhaps he can shed a light on things."

"Let's call him right now."

Eleanor pursed her lips for a moment, thinking.

"Why don't we wait until morning? If we call him over now, he'll know something's up and that might give him a chance to cover his tracks and put a spin on things. You know my motto: Give away nothing and always hold onto the upper hand."

Good grief. Was that her grandmother's philosophy even when dealing with her immediate family? No wonder the woman was so successful—and so cold.

"Yes, I'll call him first thing," Eleanor continued decisively, "and get him over here on some other pretense. Then when he arrives we can confront him together. Let's hear his explanation for all of this face-to-face. Paying a man to marry his daughter, indeed. Even *I* wouldn't stoop that low."

Jo ran a hand through her hair, more tears threatening at the back of her eyes.

"Gran, are you positive you have no idea what Bradford was talking about when he said my life was in danger? He told me that there are people who need me 'out of the way' at Bosworth Industries. How could I possibly be in the way if I have nothing to do with Bosworth?"

Jo looked imploringly at the older woman and was startled to see a flash of something in her eyes. She *did* know something, but she wasn't saying what.

"Darling, you're exhausted," she said, ignoring the question. "Why don't you go on to bed and we can pick this up in the morning? I had Consuela prepare the Rose bedroom for you. It should be ready by now. In the morning we can send for your things. Is there someone you could call at home?"

"Danny—" Jo started and then stopped. Her first thought was Danny, who always stepped in when she needed help. Unfortunately, right now he was on the other side of the world, wrapped up in his own life. "Um, I mean, we don't need to send for them. I'll go home tomorrow and get what I need myself."

"Not without a bodyguard, you won't."

Bradford had also wanted her to get a bodyguard. Right now, that sounded like a good idea.

"Do you know how to get one?"

"Of course. I'll make a call right now. In fact, I think I'd like someone in place tonight, posted outside your door."

"Oh, Gran, I don't think that's necessary. Bradford said I would be safe here."

"Bradford's half dead in a hospital right now, Jo, injured while trying to protect you. I'm afraid he's not the best judge."

Jo shuddered, remembering how nervous he had seemed in the subway. Maybe her grandmother was right.

"Fine. Whatever you think is best."

"Good."

The old lady moved to the desk, made a few calls to arrange for the bodyguard service, and then buzzed Fernando and told him to come to the study. Once there, she gave him his instructions.

"Please show Jo up to the Rose room and then put a chair in the hall outside her door. Wait there until further notice. We're concerned for her safety."

If the request seemed odd, it didn't show on Fernando's face. He simply nodded and once again offered his arm. This time, Jo kindly refused his help. When she reached the door she hesitated, the image of her beloved dog, Chewie, suddenly filling her mind. While in the limo, Jo had called the friend back home who'd had Chewie for the day and asked if the dog could stay the night as well. But this had been an emergency, not a long-term solution. Summoning her nerve, she looked back at her grandmother and spoke.

"Gran, when I come back with my things tomorrow, my dog *will* be with me. I don't expect for him have the run of the house, of course, but I want him here."

Her eyes met and held her grandmother's, as if they were poised for a duel. Jo wasn't usually a stubborn person, but being with Eleanor almost always dug up all sorts of behaviors and feelings she didn't know she possessed. Sometimes she thought the problem might be not that they were too different, but that they were too much alike. Eleanor Bosworth was used to getting her way, but in this Jo was not going to budge.

As if sensing Jo's resolve, her grandmother finally broke their gaze and sighed, clasping her hands together.

"I'll speak to Muck tomorrow," she said stiffly, referring to the gardener. "Perhaps he can put up some sort of temporary fencing."

Stifling a smile, Jo uttered a quick "thank you" and then continued on her way. She may have won this particular battle, but she didn't plan on sticking around long enough for her grandmother to change her mind.

Alexa crouched under the hall window and peeked in, quickly ducking back when she realized that someone had just reached the top of the stairs. Cautiously, she tried again, this time watching as the blond lady she'd spotted out front came walking down the hall and into the Rose bedroom. Alexa couldn't see her all that well, but she could tell the lady was younger than Alexa had originally thought, probably not even 30 years old, and pretty too. Fernando was walking right behind her, carrying a chair, and after he showed her to her room, he did the strangest thing. He put the chair in the hall just outside the room and sat down. Was the lady being held prisoner there or something?

Oh, man.

Whatever was going on, it was weird. Reluctantly, Alexa had to admit defeat. Tonight was not the night to make a getaway. She'd have to wait until tomororrow.

Ah, well. There's always tomorrow.

As quietly as possible, she crept to her own window, slid it open, and climbed inside. After closing and locking the window, she undressed in the dark, putting away the backpack and flashlight and finally donning her T-shirt and pajama pants and slipping under the covers. She *was* kind of tired. She'd get a good night's sleep and in the morning find out what the heck was going on. Then she would try again, making her escape tomorrow night.

Alexa pulled the comforter up to her chin and closed her eyes, feeling not unlike a prisoner herself—though, admittedly, a prisoner with a really comfy bed.

When Jo reached her room, she was surprised to see that the table in the corner had been set with one place setting of fine china. Moments later the head cook and housekeeper, Consuela, entered the room with a tray, which she balanced against the table to unload.

"Your grandma wanted me to make you something to eat," she explained, putting out what looked like a basket of rolls, butter, and a crock of soup. "Just a little snack, nothing heavy. Unless you'd like me to add a sandwich or something."

"No," Jo said softly. "This is fine. Thank you."

She didn't think she was hungry, but when Consuela lifted the lid from the soup and the smell came wafting out, her stomach actually grumbled. Thinking back, she realized that all she had eaten since breakfast was an apple on the train between Kreston and Manhattan. Now she was starving.

"It's good to see you again, by the way," Jo said. "I believe it's been a while. Since last Thanksgiving, maybe."

"Yes, I think so."

Jo didn't know Consuela or her husband, Fernando, all that well, but she knew that her grandmother depended on them. They were the only live-in employees, occupying the apartment out back, over the garage.

"I put a nightgown and robe in the closet for you," Consuela said. "And there's a basket of toiletries next to the sink in the bathroom. Once you get changed, if you'd like, I can wash the clothes you're wearing so you can wear them again tomorrow."

Jo started to decline but then thought about the day she'd just been through. Between all the trains and train stations, downtown Manhattan, the subway, and the hospital, her clothes definitely needed washing. She'd begun the day wearing brown linen slacks and a peach twinset, though she'd had to give the light sweater from the twinset to the police so they could check for fingerprints where the hand had been when it pushed her. She'd spent the rest of the evening in just the sleeveless top, and it had become dirty. Suddenly, she was overwhelmed with the thought of getting clean. From her head to her toes, she felt grimy.

"That'd be great," Jo said, going to the closet for the robe and gown. "Maybe I'll take a quick shower right now."

"In that case, I'll cover the soup to keep it warm until you're ready to eat. Just tell Fernando when you're finished, and he'll clear the table for you. I'll come back for your clothes in a bit."

"Thanks."

Jo felt much better once she had bathed and towel dried and combed out her hair. Luxuriating in the silky feel of the gorgeous nightgown and robe—the tag said Dior—she sat at the little table and placed the linen napkin on her lap. Sometimes wealth made life so much easier, so much less trouble: limo rides, hot meals that magically appeared, fancy nightgowns, laundry that got done without lifting a finger. With wealth, a few phone calls and some well-trained staff could handle almost any problem.

On the other hand, from what Jo had seen in her lifetime, wealth was a double-edged sword. For one thing, it was numbing. Life's rough edges could become so smoothed over that a person could be lulled into the kind of complacency and self-sufficiency that was spiritually dangerous. God? Why do I need God when I've got all this stuff? The sad thing was, the unhappiest people she knew were also some of the richest.

Figuring that out at an early age, Jo had made the conscious decision not to live that way, leaving her trust fund intact and never asking for financial help from anyone on this side of the family since college. Sometimes it felt silly to pinch pennies when her net worth was so substantial, but it was a trade-off she thought worth making. Someday she would be able to take all that money in her trust and do something important with it, not just toss it all away on a lavish lifestyle.

Still, on a night like this, Jo had to admit that she'd rather be sitting here in a Dior gown in a beautiful mansion eating homemade bread and gourmet soup than shivering in rags in some hovel with crackers and ketchup. But before she started eating, Jo bowed her head to say grace. She asked God to keep her from being lulled and seduced by the rich life her grandmother led.

"And please be with Bradford and make him whole," she prayed softly. "Oh, and bless this food to my health. Amen."

She picked up a heavy silver spoon and ate, the soup helping to fill the deep ache inside. She wondered how many days it would be before Bradford could eat solid food. Would he ever heal completely? Would she always have to live with the thought that he was nearly killed trying to save her life?

What was Danny going say when he found out? From the limo, Jo had called his apartment in Paris but had received no answer. Considering the situation, she hadn't left a message except to tell him to call her. She couldn't imagine where her boyfriend might be at this time of night—or morning actually, as the case may be, considering that he was so many time zones ahead of her. She trusted him, but his absence from his apartment at this early hour made her strangely uncomfortable.

More than anything, she wished Danny were there, right now, by her side, holding her hand, stroking her face. Tears began to well up in her eyes, but she blinked them away and forced her mind to other, more mundane thoughts—the gorgeous rose wallpaper, the elegant china, the taste of the soup.

Sometimes Jo hated being so independent.

Because right now, all she really wanted most was to be completely and utterly *dependent*. She wanted to crawl inside Danny's embrace, close her eyes, and make the whole world disappear.

Send   Chat   Attach   Address   Fonts   Colors   Save As Draft

To: JoTulip@tipsfromtulip.com

From: anon6592@mailnet.com

Date: Thursday, May 7, 11:50 PM

Subject: Question for www.tipsfromtulip.com

Dear Tulip,

Isn't your slogan "Be a Smart Chick"? Then why are you running around New York City making a target out of yourself after I told you that your life is in danger? 'Cause that's just dumb. Or maybe you didn't believe me. I guess you believe me now!

I know you tracked down my computer because the library was crawling with plainclothes cops tonight. Thanks a lot. I told you I can't get involved. Too bad they sent out some of the most obvious guys they had. In my life I never seen so many stupid-looking people acting so thoroughly interested in books. It was hard not to laugh, especially 'cause one of them was holding his book upside down.

I got more than one way to get online, though. You can trace this computer too, I'm sure, but that still won't help you figure out who I am. I'll keep moving from now on.

Forget trying to find me and worry about protecting yourself. If it helps, I think the person after you is trying to make it look like an accident. But I guess you figured that out this afternoon at the train station.

Signed,

Trying To Stay Out Of It

P.S.—I've about decided to get the toaster oven with the Teflon, but now I'm afraid it's going to get scratched when I clean it. Is there some trick for how to handle things with a Teflon coating?

7

Danny awoke at the sound of knocking, and it took a moment to remember where he was: in a sleeper car, on a TGV train, on the way to Switzerland. Propping up on his elbows to look toward the source of knock, he saw that Luc was already up, dressed, and opening the door for the steward with their breakfast. Luc took the large tray from the uniformed man, tipped him, closed the door, and then set the tray on the hinged tabletop that swung out from the wall under the window. As Luc removed the lids from the various foods, Danny tried to wake up and clear the sleepiness from his brain. He and Mr. Bashiri had stayed up until 2:00 AM, just talking and sharing stories of the road.

"*Bon matin, mon ami,*" Luc said, looking up at Danny with a smile. "What is wrong?"

"The view," Danny said, trying to sit up further without bumping his head. "I was hoping to see the Alps, but it doesn't look like that's going to happen."

He swung his legs over the side, climbed down, and stepped to the window for a closer look. Visibility was only about 20 feet; beyond that was merely swirling gray mist. Perhaps the fog would burn off once the sun finished coming up. It was tough to be so close to the gorgeous Swiss Alps for the very first time and not even be able to see them.

Assured that Luc had already checked on Mr. Bashiri, Danny sat down to eat. The food was yet another weird European idea of "breakfast," but Luc paid more attention to the coffee than the food, pouring from a heavy silver carafe, carefully stirring in sugar and cream, and sipping slowly as he gazed out of the window at the fog.

"I've never seen anyone who can drag out a pot of coffee longer than you can," Danny teased as his friend poured his third cup.

"*Eh?*" Luc said, looking up with a smile. "What do you know? You are from America, land of the 'go cup,' guzzling your coffee on the run, always while you are doing other things." Luc dropped a sugar cube into the steaming brown brew and stirred, slowly shaking his head. "I like Americans, but when it comes to food and drink, you are all in too much of a hurry."

"I like Europeans," Danny replied, smiling, "but for my taste, in that area I'd say you're all a little slow."

Luc laughed.

"*Touché,*" he told him, raising his coffee cup in a toast. "We both like what we are used to, *n'est pas?*"

They chatted easily over the meal, discussing various cultural differences between the United States and Europe. For some reason, Danny found that the conversation was making him homesick, something he'd worked hard to avoid in the past six weeks. When Luc asked about Jo specifically, Danny felt a surge of loneliness deep inside his chest. He missed her so bad it hurt.

"Tell me what is so special about this lady of yours," Luc said, leaning back in his chair, "that the very thought of her keeps you from even looking at the beautiful women of Paris. If you are so in love, why are you not yet married?"

Danny tried to explain that it was still a little too soon.

"Too soon?" Luc cried. "Did you not tell me that you met her when you were a little boy? That her grandmother and your grandmother were neighbors and that is how you became friends?"

"Yes, but we were just friends. After twenty-something years, we were best friends. Then, last fall, I realized I was in love with my best friend."

"So all of a sudden you did not just love her any more, you *loved* her, eh? *Ooo la la.* Tell me more."

Danny jabbed a sausage with his fork and moved it to his plate.

"It's not an easy decision, you know, moving from best friends to boyfriend and girlfriend. You risk the entire friendship, because if things don't work out in the love relationship, in the end you've got nothing."

"But let me guess—as soon as you admitted that you had fallen in love with her, she said the same thing had happened to her, *non?*"

"No. In fact, she had a hard time with it at first. It was complicated."

"Sounds like it."

Danny remembered the torment of telling Jo that he loved her and not immediately hearing the same sentiment in return. At the time he tried to be patient and put the entire matter in God's hands, but it hadn't been easy. The moment when she finally admitted that she was in love with him too had been the single best moment of his life. She had done a lot of thinking and realized that the only thing holding her back from a love relationship with Danny was the fear of losing him. He promised her he would always be there for her, and he meant it with every fiber of his being.

"Love prevailed in the end," Danny said, remembering.

"And that is when you decided to live happily ever after?"

"No. That's when I decided to come to Paris."

Luc let out a groan, tossing his hands in the air.

"Just when you get the girl of your dreams, you go off and leave her? What kind of a lover are you?"

Danny smiled.

"Jo understood. In fact, she insisted. She knows how important my career is to me. She's very supportive."

Luc set his napkin on the table, shaking his head.

"No job or career would be worth it to me. Love like that, it does not come along every day. If I had a true love who was also my best friend, I would never leave her side."

"It's only for three months," Danny protested. "And this was the career opportunity of a lifetime."

He didn't add that the situation was actually even more complicated than he had described. When he left town, in fact, not only were he and Jo just beginning the transition in their relationship, but her home had burned to the ground *and* she'd been terribly injured in the explosion.

At least he'd managed to postpone the internship for a week so that he could be there when she was released from the hospital. But with nowhere to go and no one to care for her, the best they could come up with was for her to move into the guest room of his parents' house, where his mom could help out. After Danny got Jo settled in there, he had left town. A week or so later, homesick and missing her dog and feeling stronger and more agile with her cast, Jo had bid his parents goodbye, picked up Chewie from his temporary caregiver's, and moved into Danny's house, where she and Chewie were living now.

When Danny thought about it, the big picture kind of gave him a sick feeling in the pit of his stomach. Had he been selfish to accept the internship and fly away to Europe right when Jo probably needed him more than she ever had in her life? He promised he would never leave her, and then he went and did just that.

Jo was simply so capable, so independent, that once she urged him to seize this opportunity, he had taken steps to leave, telling himself that it was only for a few months. And though his mother and three sisters had promised him that they would be there in his stead, helping out with the logistics of Jo's recovery and her housing situation, the truth was that *he* should have been the one to do all that. He should have been there for her.

Had coming to Europe been a mistake?

Danny swallowed down the last of his breakfast, which suddenly felt like a big rock sitting in his stomach.

"I can see all of this talk of Jo has made you miss her, *mon ami*," Luc said, finishing his final cup of coffee. "Cheer up. The fog is lifting, *non?*"

Danny looked out of the window to see that it had indeed grown a little clearer. They were speeding past a mountain lake, and though they still couldn't see the Alps in the distance, glimpses of turquoise-blue water were visible among the misty trees.

Danny tried to shake off his concern and confusion, comforted by the knowledge that at least Jo's recovery was going well. Despite all she'd been through, she sounded fine, both in her e-mails and whenever they talked on the phone. Maybe leaving her at such a tough time hadn't been the best idea, but she was such a trooper that she'd managed to make it work. The worst if it was over now, anyway, so there was no reason to lament decisions already made. It wasn't as though they'd be separated forever.

"Time to pack up," Luc said. "We should arrive in Zurich in about half an hour."

Putting thoughts of Jo out of his mind for now, Danny got up and got moving. Once he was dressed and his own bag was packed, he went next door to make sure that Mr. Bashiri was all set. All three men were ready to go by the time they rumbled to a stop at the station in Zurich. Cool air rushed in when the steward opened the outside door, and Danny realized that it was a good 15 degrees cooler here than it had been in Paris.

"Welcome to the City of Money," Luc said as he stepped from the train.

Danny stepped out behind him, noting that the station was sleek and modern and bustling with people.

"That is why it makes the perfect counterpoint to our photo essay," Mr. Bashiri said solemnly. "The pictures we take here will contrast enormously with the pictures we will take in the Congo."

Because of all the baggage, they rented a Volkswagen minivan. Danny was worried when Luc took the wheel, but fortunately his driving here ended up being much more sedate than it had been in Paris. As they made their way across the busy city streets, Luc tried to teach Danny a few key phrases he might need. The language sounded strange and guttural, a dialect of Swiss German spoken mainly in Zurich.

"Have you ever been to Zurich, Mr. Bashiri?" Danny asked as they turned onto a bridge which carried them over a serene, winding river.

"A few times, Mr. Watkins," the man replied. He was perched in the front passenger seat, camera bag clutched neatly on his lap, eyes taking in the scenery all around. "It is an impressive place, but I much prefer the quieter outlying areas, such as Engelberg and Lucerne."

Luc disagreed, and the two men entered into a good-natured debate about the bucolic-but-boring countryside versus the fascinating-but-congested city. Danny tuned them out and took in the sights instead, impressed with the cleanliness of the city, the striking mix of historic and modern architecture, the river that flowed lazily through the center like a deep turquoise ribbon. In a way, from the car at least, he thought Zurich was so well kept and organized that it looked like something from Epcot or Disneyland, a fake version of a real place. But it was indeed real and quite lovely. Fortunately, the fog that had shrouded the train on the way was nowhere in evidence here.

After several miles they reached their destination: the headquarters of Global Mobile Medical on a street whose name was so long that it looked like three or four German words squeezed together into one. Though parking was supposedly scarce in downtown Zurich, this place had its own private lot, to which they'd been given a special permit. Luc turned in, found a spot down a narrow row, parked, and placed the permit on the dashboard.

Danny had a copy of the itinerary in his pocket, so before they got out of the car he pulled it out and they went over the logistics of the photo shoot. They would spend an hour or two photographing the headquarters, the workers, and the warehouse. From there they would focus specifically on the businesses and the residences of three of the doctors who would be going with the team to the Congo. Georgette wanted photos of those three doctors at work, at home, and at play—an effort that would probably take the next two days and involve a number of locations. Tonight, they were supposed to go to a GMM fund-raising event and photograph there as well.

"I'm supposed to check in with Georgette later this morning," Danny continued, "to talk about getting my travel documents squared away for the next leg of the trip. But that shouldn't take long. In the meantime, Mr. Bashiri, how can Luc and I best help you?"

Mr. Bashiri was thoughtful for a moment before speaking.

"If the two of you will handle the equipment, the driving, and the translating, then I can focus on the photography. Just do not wander off without telling me first because you never know when I might need something."

"Of course," Luc said. *"Allon nous.* Let's go."

Danny thought they might want to go inside without any equipment at first, to meet the people and take a quick stroll through the facility and get a better idea of the pictures they wanted to take. But as they climbed from the car, Mr. Bashiri twisted his neck to look around and announced that the morning sun was at the perfect angle right now for some exterior shots of the building.

"Mr. Watkins, I will need the large format, the digital, and the Leica," he told Danny before setting off to walk around the building and choose his angles.

Danny did as the man asked, pulling equipment out and assembling it so that each camera was on its own tripod, ready to go. Finally, Mr. Bashiri waved him over to where he stood across the street and down the block. Danny obliged, leaving Luc beside the van while he trotted over to Mr. Bashiri with the equipment.

Once the photographer had finished attending to the details of placement, framing, and exposure, he began snapping. Danny stood behind him and watched over his shoulder, wondering why Mr. Bashiri had chosen this particular angle. It made no sense to him, because the sharp morning sun was glinting problematically off of almost every shiny surface between them and the building. He wanted to ask how the man was compensating for that, but Mr. Bashiri was so deeply immersed in what he was doing that Danny didn't dare speak at all.

In fact, he spent most of the morning confused about Mr. Bashiri's methodology. When they were finished photographing the exterior, they went in and met the staff, were given a tour, and took many more pictures, often with strange angles, bad lighting, and odd filter choices.

At least Luc ended up coming in handy, for he wasn't just the translator but also the self-appointed schmoozer. He kept conversations going with the staff, mostly in German, with lots of charm and laughter all around. That left Mr. Bashiri and Danny free to quietly focus on the photography. When they took a break for tea, Danny finally summoned the nerve to ask about Mr. Bashiri's methodology.

"Take a look at the shots I did with the digital, and see if you can figure this out yourself. You tell me what I'm doing."

Danny did as he suggested, pushing the button that would slowly take him through each picture. By the time he was about half finished, he could see some similarities.

"You have a theme here. Glint. Glare. Shiny. Sparkly. You've done it on purpose. The essence of Zurich is all about money and wealth, and you're showing that through the subtleties of reflection and light."

"Correct. Now take it one step further. What do you suppose my plans are for the pictures I will take in the Congo?"

Danny thought for a moment.

"The opposite, I suppose. No flashes of light, no chrome or stainless steel, everything sort of dull and dirty?"

Mr. Bashiri nodded.

"This is a contrast I began to notice on the first part of the photo shoot, when I was at the refugee camp in Myanmar. Nothing shines there. Nothing sparkles. The Congo will be the same."

Mr. Bashiri went on to explain, in photographer's terms, about his use of color and placement and reflection. Danny listened intently, wishing he could take notes, committing the settings and filters and film stock choices to memory as much as possible.

There was so much to learn, and he was grateful that Mr. Bashiri was a willing teacher. Danny just hoped the man wouldn't get tired of his questions—and that everything on the photo shoot would continue to go as smoothly as it had thus far.

Alexa awoke at 6:15, and couldn't get back to sleep. She tossed and turned for a while, finally giving up around 7:00. She thought she might as well get up for the day. She showered and dressed and put on makeup, thinking about her schedule as she used the blow-dryer on her short dark hair.

It was a Thursday, which meant her day was packed: piano at 9:00 with Mrs. Gruber then hours of tutoring with Mr. Preston, then physical therapy with Yasmine, then her weekly exam with Dr. Stebbins. Though sometimes the exam seemed repetitive—how many times was she going to have to point her finger and touch her nose—she liked seeing Dr. Stebbins. In a way, his visits kept her feeling more connected to the whole project, like a part of the team and not just a dog who was training to perform tricks for the crowd.

The old lady had given Dr. Stebbins a room out in the carriage house to use as an office, and sometimes Alexa wished that was his main office so he could be there all the time. Every Thursday he would come in around 4:00 in the afternoon and do paperwork for a while, though sometimes she had a feeling he wasn't so much doing paperwork as he was using the paperwork as an excuse to observe her physical therapy without making her feel uncomfortable. The office was off the main part of the room, with just a glass wall separating it from the therapy area, and his desk was set so that he was facing toward the glass as he worked. Sometimes, she would be on the treadmill or working out with the rubber bands, and she would glance up and see him studying her in that way he had, like a scientist studies a slide in a microscope.

Her exam would follow the therapy, usually at 5:00, but then he'd stick around and do more paperwork for another hour or two. On those nights Alexa usually skipped dinner with the old lady in order to hang out and do the treadmill again just so she could be in the same building with him in case he felt like chatting. He was a nice man, and very smart, and the way he talked to Alexa made her feel smart too.

She turned off the blow-dryer and tossed it in the drawer along with her brush. After heavy spritzing of hair spray and a little more eyeliner, she was done. She studied her own reflection in the mirror for a moment, thinking about that.

"Who would have guessed," she said out loud to herself, wishing she was talking to her friends, not to mention her mom, "that you could use the words 'smart' and 'Alexa' in the same sentence!"

Even though she was a medical miracle, even though she was a freak of nature, even though all of her progress had more to do with Dr. Stebbins' fancy science than with her, sometimes she felt pretty special.

If only she weren't so alone.

8

Jo awoke early and reached for her cell phone, conscious of the fact that there was a probably a man sitting in a chair outside of her door acting as her bodyguard. Trying not to think about it, she dialed Bradford's brother, Ty, who was home from the hospital but had just received an update from his mother. He said Bradford had made it through the night, but he was in such intense pain that his doctors had him on heavy doses of morphine. Jo thanked him for the update and hung up the phone, saying a quick prayer for healing.

Climbing out of bed, Jo wasn't surprised to see that at some point during the night her clothes had been washed, dried, and hung up on the back of her door. She got dressed, strapped on her cast, and tried to fix her hair as best she could, considering that she didn't have any styling tools with her. In her purse was a lipstick, compact, and mascara, which were better than nothing. She was just applying the final touches of lipstick when she heard male voices in the hall. She opened the door to see two big strong men standing there, shaking hands.

"Miss Tulip?" one of them said quickly, in response. "How do you do? We're from Executive Protection Services."

Apparently, she had interrupted them in the middle of a shift change. She walked downstairs with the two men as they explained how her protection would work. Four men would be rotating in approximately six-hour shifts each, and one would never sign off until the next one had signed on. For the most part, she was to ignore them and let them do their job. They had already been apprised of the details of the situation by her grandmother. They asked that she be respectful of and respond immediately to any request they might make of her, as it would be for her protection. Otherwise, she should consider them as part of the background of her life and leave them to their work. Anything she might say or do in their presence was considered confidential unless it endangered others.

It all sounded reasonable to her, and she liked their neat clothes and professional demeanor. They looked like Secret Service agents, which was a relief, as she hadn't known what to expect and in fact had worried they might look more like bar bouncers or mafia goons.

Breakfast was already well underway by the time Jo made it to the dining room. She could hear the clink of dishes and soft conversation from around the corner, and as she hobbled through the doorway after the bodyguard she steeled herself to face her dad. Much to her relief, however, he wasn't there. The bodyguard looked around the room and then took a position near the doorway, against the wall.

"There you are, Jo," her grandmother said from her place at the head of the table. "Come have a seat and get started with breakfast. I've spoken to your father already this morning, and he should be here in about an hour."

Jo hesitated, surprised to see two extra people at the table: Aunt Winnie, who was seated at the far end of the table, and a young woman in her early teens sitting directly to Eleanor's right, sipping black coffee and picking at a plate of mostly uneaten pancakes. The teenager was cute and petite, though kind of urban-looking, with short black hair, multiple ear piercings, and eyeliner so dark and heavy that it almost made her look like an adorable, wide-eyed raccoon. Jo couldn't imagine who she was, what she was doing there, or why she seemed so comfortably at home.

"Jo, honey," her Aunt Winnie said, rising to give her a hug, "long time no see. I was so pleased to hear you were visiting. Who's your friend?"

Winnie looked expectantly at the muscular bodyguard and then back at Jo.

"I, uh..." Jo stammered. Obviously, Eleanor had not made Winnie aware of the situation. "He's not—"

"Just ignore him," Eleanor interrupted. "He's Jo's new personal assistant."

Winnie seemed to struggle with that notion for a moment, and then she leaned in and gave Jo a kiss on the cheek.

"Va va va voom," she whispered as she did so. "Some assistant!"

Her face flushing bright red, Jo took a seat at the table. Obviously, her grandmother didn't want Winnie to know about what was going on. In a way, Jo could understand. Winnie had a nervous condition, and something like this might throw her into a bout of anxiety-driven angst.

"You look great," Jo said to her aunt, meaning it. The woman was dressed sloppily, with no makeup and her blondish-white hair pulled back into a messy ponytail, but her face was radiant and calm. Perhaps she had found a medication that was helping. "Are you staying here?"

Winnie nodded happily.

"It's planting season. I always stay for the month of May, to help Muck outside. We've been preparing the beds and doing the pruning and the fertilizing. Soon we'll start hardening the seedlings, and then we'll plant."

"Sounds fun."

"It is. I love living in Manhattan, but this time of year I've simply got to come out to the country, where I can garden to my heart's content."

Consuela emerged from the kitchen door with a basket of muffins, which she set on the table.

"Good morning, Jo," she said, looking chipper despite the fact that she'd been up late preparing the guest room for Jo and washing her clothes. "Would you like eggs or pancakes or both?"

"Eggs are fine."

"How would you like them cooked?"

"Um, scrambled, please. With whole wheat toast, if you have it. And coffee."

"You got it," Consuela said, returning to the kitchen.

After she was gone, Eleanor proceeded to introduce Jo to the young woman at the table.

"Jo, this is Alexa, a houseguest of mine. Alexa, this is my granddaughter Jo."

"Hi," Alexa said, her voice surprisingly timid and sweet for having such a tough-looking exterior. "Nice to meetcha. Where are you from?"

"Pennsylvania. How about you?"

"Jersey."

"Oh, which part? New Jersey's a lovely state."

The girl rolled her eyes.

"Not the part I'm from," she said, describing an area near Newark, just over the river from New York City. Jo had flown in and out of the Newark airport many times in her life, and she had to agree that the general region was not the best Jersey had to offer, by any means.

"Are you here with Winnie?" Jo asked, glancing at the end of the table to see her aunt taking her last bites of breakfast and then wiping her mouth with her napkin.

"Nope," Alexa replied, "but we've been getting to know each other. She's been teaching me about horticulture. Right, Pixie?"

"Pixie?" Jo and Eleanor asked simultaneously.

Alexa and Winnie both smiled.

"That's my nickname for her," Alexa said, "'cause she's always eating Pixie Stix—you know, those little straws with the flavored sugar powder inside?"

"Oh I haven't had those in years," Jo said, smiling. "Probably not since I was your age, Alexa."

"I keep them in a jar in the guest house, Jo, if you'd like some," Winnie said.

"Should you really have that much sugar, Winnie?" Eleanor asked. "That can't be healthy."

"It's either that or go back to cigarettes, Mother. Take your pick."

Jo winked at Alexa, who looked as though she felt bad for bringing it up.

"Alexa will be helping me with the hardening of the seedlings," Winnie continued, returning to the original subject. "But speaking of seedlings, I've got to get out to the greenhouse. I'll see you folks later."

Winnie dropped her napkin on top of her dirty plate, pulled out her chair, and headed for the kitchen, which had an exit to the outside.

"She really does look good," Jo said softly to her grandmother after she heard the back door close.

"May has always been Winnie's best month," Eleanor replied. "Something about all that gardening seems to keep her quite occupied and content."

"Is there something wrong with her?" Alexa asked. "She seems cool to me."

"Usually she's very…high-strung," Eleanor replied in answer to Alexa's question, "though I know that seems hard to believe right now. She's like a different person this time of year. The more she can keep her hands in the dirt, the happier she is—which is odd, considering that the rest of the year she can't tolerate dirt of any kind."

Jo cleared her throat, hoping to change the subject.

"So tell me more about you," Jo said to Alexa. "If you're not here with Winnie…"

"Alexa is my guest," Eleanor said. "She's been staying here for a few months."

A few *months?* How come Jo didn't know anything about this? And what was she doing here?

"I'm sorry if I seem surprised. I just hadn't heard."

Jo wondered if perhaps the girl was here in some sort of foster care situation—but the thought of that was almost laughable, considering that her grandmother was the last person on earth who might take in some needy child out of love or compassion. Maybe Alexa was one of those "Fresh Air Fund" kids? Again, not really a credible thought, considering Eleanor's personality and temperament. Perhaps Alexa was the daughter or granddaughter of one of the staff.

"How did you two meet?" Jo asked.

Mrs. Bosworth glanced at Alexa and then back at Jo.

"Alexa is a patient of Dr. Stebbins, my neurologist. She's staying here to help with her stroke recovery."

"Stroke recovery? But you're so young!"

"I didn't have the same kind of stroke *old* people have," the girl said, gesturing toward Jo's grandmother. "Mine was a ruptured cerebral aneurysm."

Jo didn't know what that meant, but her grandmother explained, apparently not offended by the "old people" remark.

"There's more than one kind of stroke, Jo. What I had was an ischemic stroke, where a blood clot moved into my brain and caused a blockage. In Alexa's case, a blood vessel burst in her brain, causing internal bleeding. Dr. Stebbins treats both kinds."

"What caused it?" Jo asked Alexa.

The girl shrugged.

"Dr. Stebbins says I was probably born that way, with a little bulge in the artery wall that was bound to rupture sooner or later. I was just lucky they got me to the hospital so fast when it happened. They say every second counts in a situation like that. I was double-lucky that Dr. Stebbins helped treat me. He's a really amazing doctor."

Jo watched as the girl poured herself more coffee. She certainly seemed agile enough now. In fact, she seemed so normal that Jo was having trouble believing what she was hearing.

"So how did this houseguest arrangement happen?" Jo asked, looking from one to the other. "Did the two of you meet in the doctor's office and just hit it off?"

"Don't be ridiculous, Jo," her grandmother said, pushing away her plate just as Consuela appeared from the kitchen with fresh coffee for Jo. She set the insulated pot on the table, cleared the dirty plates, and returned to the kitchen. Once she was gone, Eleanor continued. "Dr. Stebbins told me about his young patient and the particular...needs that she had. We both thought it would be a good idea for her to live here during her convalescence and recovery. I must say, I was a little reluctant at first, her being so young, but I think it has worked out swimmingly. Alexa's a delight and simply no trouble at all."

"How old are you?" Jo asked, studying the girl. She was sure there was more to the story than either of them was saying.

"I'm fourteen," Alexa said shyly, glancing down at her plate. As she did, a few locks of hair fell across her forehead, and Jo could see that in and among the black strands were red and blue highlights.

"Fourteen? Wow, you must really miss your friends and family."

"Yeah, I do," she said. "I miss my friends a whole lot. My mom too. I don't really have any other family."

"Do you get to see your mother much?"

"Alexa knows she's free to visit her mother at any time," Eleanor answered for her. "And she knows Fernando can bring her to see her friends too, if she wants."

Jo could just imagine that—this poor kid having to pull up to her modest little New Jersey school yard in a fancy limo. Yeah, that would go over well.

"What about schooling?"

The girl shrugged.

"I have tutors who come here," she said, a hint of Jersey accent in her voice. "It's not bad."

"They teach her in the studio. At some point, Jo, you'll have to go out and look at the changes we've made."

"Oh?"

"As you know, after my stroke, we converted the carriage house to a workout center for my physical therapy. Since Alexa came, we've added even more equipment along with several small offices for the therapists and the doctor."

"Impressive."

"And the studio is delightful now. It almost looks like a classroom. There are desks and tables and an art area with a sink. We even put in a piano out there."

"A black baby grand," Alexa added wistfully. "It's beautiful."

A black baby grand? Tutors in the studio? This all seemed so strange. Later, when they were alone, Jo was going to ask her grandmother some pointed questions about the whole situation.

The kitchen door opened and Consuela emerged with Jo's breakfast. She set the steaming plate in front of Jo and set down a tiny pitcher of fresh cream for the coffee before returning to the kitchen.

As Jo began eating, Eleanor excused herself from the table, reached for a nearby cane, and stood.

"Just so you know, Jo, Fernando and the limo are at your disposal all day if you want to go back to Pennsylvania to get your things. First, however, we have to talk to your father. Why don't you join me in my office in half an hour?"

"Sure."

"And as for you, Miss Alexa, don't be late for your piano lesson."

Alexa stood up awkwardly, for a moment looking very young and earnest. Despite the tough exterior, there was something endearing and almost innocent about her.

"No, ma'am. I won't. I'll go out there right now."

Jo glanced up at her grandmother, who was looking at Alexa, and for a moment there was a flash of an emotion Jo had never, ever seen on the woman's face before. In fact, if she didn't know any better, Jo could have sworn that what she witnessed was a moment, albeit brief, of *tenderness*.

Go figure.

"I believe that is our hotel over there," Luc said, gesturing toward a five-story building at the end of the block. "Too bad we do not have time to check in now."

The men were squeezing in several quick errands between destinations, the most important of which was to drop Danny's passport off at a travel expeditor service, where they would do the footwork for him to secure a last-minute visa to the Congo. The only other requirement—a yellow fever vaccination and certificate—would be taken care of tomorrow afternoon by one of the doctors at GMM. After that, assuming the expediter had no problems getting the visa, Danny would have everything he'd need to go on to Africa.

The woman in the travel service office did not speak English, which was a bit disconcerting, considering that her job was to handle international issues. Except for taking Danny's picture and showing him where to sign on the dotted line, she dealt exclusively with Luc, who assured Danny once they left that she seemed as though she knew what she was doing and that all should go well with his visa.

"I got her phone number too," he added with a grin. "But I am not sure I will use it. She was pretty, yes, but a bit, how do you say, bucktooth, *non?*"

"I didn't notice," Danny replied as they walked. "I was paying more attention to that cool, retro twin-lens camera. I wonder how old that thing was."

"Ah, Danny," Luc said, throwing an arm over his friend's shoulders. "What am I going to do with you and your tunnel vision? Women are the spice of life!"

"I thought variety was the spice of life."

"Variety in women, *oui!*"

Laughing, they made their way toward a delicatessen-like restaurant, called a *gaststätte*. When planning the shoot, Georgette had said that she wanted many of the Switzerland photos to include food to further show the contrast between the haves and the have-nots. Though several of the doctors were willing to cooperate, it was up to *Scene It* to provide the actual fare. Danny and Luc entered the deli, paid for their order, and carried various platters and containers back to the van.

Their next stop was the home of one of the GMM doctors, an infectious diseases specialist who lived in a fancy condo situated right along the river in Zurich. When they arrived at the condo, the doctor's beautiful young wife used the food they brought with her own fancy serving pieces to set up an elaborate buffet on the balcony.

The spread was sumptuous: colorful fruit, Swiss meats on German breads, and hearty sides of pickles and potato salad. Once the scene was set, Mr. Bashiri began photographing the doctor and his wife pretending to dine al fresco with an incredible view of the city behind them. Danny helped with the lighting and Luc with the screens, and as they worked, it felt to Danny as though they were quickly becoming a creative and efficient team.

Finally, once they were finished, they all made a late lunch out of the food for real. To Danny, it was even more delicious than it looked, and he was glad that Mr. Bashiri had not needed to tamper with the food artificially to make it "pretty" for the camera, something many professional photographers did. This was, after all, a journalistic endeavor, not a hamburger billboard.

As they relaxed and ate, the doctor told them more about the refugee camp where they would be going in the Congo. He had just come back from there six months before, and he was already eager to return. His English was so difficult to understand that he ended up speaking in the local Swiss German dialect instead and getting translated by Luc; but just from the man's voice and body language, Danny could see that despite the difficult conditions there, he seemed to have found an enormous amount of joy and purpose through his work in the sub-Sahara. As the doctor described his work among the refugees, he gestured broadly with his hands and he had a happy, excited gleam in his eye.

At one point, the doctor asked Danny a question, something about "*schutzimpfungen,*" and Danny looked to Luc for translation. Smiling ruefully, Luc told him that the good doctor was asking about vaccinations, suggesting that when Danny got his required yellow fever shot, he should also ask for vaccinations for hepatitis A and hepatitis B as well, which were not required for travel to the Congo but were highly recommended.

"*Ja,*" the doctor said, counting off on his fingers. "*Die shutzimpfung der gelbe fieber, die shutzimpfung der hepatitis A, und die shutzimpfung der hepatitis B.*"

The next doctor they went to photograph added even more shots to the list, telling Danny he would also want to get boosters of all of his childhood inoculations—tetanus, diphtheria, even polio. Danny didn't like shots, but he was willing to do whatever it took to stay healthy on this trip.

This doctor lived in a beautiful villa a half hour outside of the city, toward the distant Alps, and with such a lovely home, Mr. Bashiri had much to work with. Danny unloaded the equipment from the van, and then they got busy shooting photos in several different places around the property. The only problem was Luc, who had to excuse himself several times to take calls on his cell phone. Danny couldn't imagine what was so important that it was worth interrupting the photo shoot for, but apparently something was going on with Luc that simply couldn't wait.

The weird thing was, every time a call came the Frenchman would quickly answer, tell the person to hold on, and then walk far away out of earshot before speaking. Danny supposed Luc was just being polite and trying not to disturb the creative process, but more than once, Danny had glanced up to see Luc looking directly at him as he talked.

Danny hated to seem paranoid, but if he didn't know better, he could almost swear Luc was talking about him.

Once Jo's grandmother and Alexa had both left the room, Jo felt a little strange eating by herself as the bodyguard stood nearby. A bit self-consciously, she tried to make conversation, even offering him breakfast, but his answers were short and monosyllabic. Finally he reminded her that she was supposed to ignore the fact that he was there and go on with her day.

She tried, finishing her meal quickly, thinking about her father and how this encounter was going to go. More than anything, she wanted to talk to Danny. Besides the simple fact that hearing his voice would help to calm and ground her, he needed to know what had happened, to help her figure out how to proceed. If she hurried, she would probably have time to call him before her father arrived.

Upstairs in her room with the bodyguard stationed just outside, Jo used her cell phone to dial Danny's office. Instead of getting Danny, however, she was connected with Danny's boss, who told her that Danny was currently out of the country.

"Out of the country?" Jo asked, for a moment daring to hope that he was on his way home. Maybe he found out about what had happened with Bradford and he was rushing to her side. Maybe he had even left last night and would be here soon.

"Yes," the woman said. "He is on a photo shoot to Switzerland and Africa. One of our staff members had to cancel at the last moment and Dah-nee was able to take his place. Right now, they are in Zurich."

Jo inhaled slowly, feeling more alone and adrift than she'd ever been in her life. Switzerland? Africa?

He might as well be on the moon.

The woman was nice enough, and she obviously knew who Jo was. She gave her the name and number of the hotel where Danny would be staying in Zurich, suggesting that Jo leave a message there. Jo thanked the woman and hung up, sitting there for a moment, feeling hurt that Danny hadn't tried to call and tell her in person about his big trip, even if he had been pressed for time.

Of course, there was always a chance that he hadn't been able to reach her and had simply left a message on her home phone. Jo dialed her house in Pennsylvania and accessed her machine remotely, pleased to find that he had done just that. Much to her surprise, the very sound of his voice made tears spring into her eyes.

"Jo, *hi*," Danny's voice said, "I can't believe I can't reach you in person! I've been racing around like crazy but right now I'm on a train, calling you from my friend Luc's cell phone. I'll try to talk fast. Listen, you won't believe what's going on. Have you ever heard me talk about the photographer Kalunga Bashiri? I actually got to meet him today, in person. Anyway, he was leaving tonight on a photo shoot and our guy who was supposed to go with him had to cancel because his wife went into labor a few weeks early. Jo, they let me take his place! And I'm a nobody! Just an intern!

"The best part is, according to Luc, Mr. Bashiri asked for me specifically. You can't imagine what this means. Luc had to come too, to translate, but then he'll be going back to Paris once we're finished in Switzerland. The whole trip is supposed to take about seven days, three in Zurich, one in transit, and three down in the Congo, in Africa. *Africa*, Jo, *I'm going to take pictures in Africa with Kalunga Bashiri!* That's, like, the biggest dream of my life come true! Okay, I guess my time is up and now I'm sounding stupid, I just wanted to tell you my big news and to let you know where I am in case you needed to reach me."

He rattled off his friend's cell phone number and said for the next few days, at least, she should feel free to reach him that way if she wanted him.

"Anyway," he continued, "I wish you could be here with me right now. It's a dream of a lifetime, and in the whole world you're the only one who would understand that. I love you so much! I'll talk to you soon. Love you. Bye."

Jo pressed the button to save his message and disconnected the call.

Big news...dream of a lifetime...the only one who would understand...

She *did* understand. She was thrilled for him, really she was. In the part of her brain that was concerned with reasoning and commonsense, she knew this was a good thing, that all of his hard work was finally starting to pay off. Yay for him.

In the other part of her brain, the place where her mind intersected with her heart, all she knew was that she needed Danny and he wasn't there. Just the way no one had ever been there for her, ever, in her whole life. Born alone, lived alone, would die alone. Right now, all Jo really wanted to do was bury her face in her hands and have a good cry.

But her father would be here any minute, and the last thing she wanted was to greet him with eyes red and puffy from tears.

Instead, she pulled herself together, resisting the tears by breathing deeply in and out and in and out until the frog was out of her throat and the tremor was gone from her lips.

Finally, the urge to cry under control, Jo put away her phone, retouched her makeup, and headed downstairs. Show no weakness. Keep the upper hand always.

Her grandmother had trained her well.

9

Alexa hit the final chord of the piece and then held her hands still, the notes resonating around the room in a beautiful echo. Though she hadn't really been in the mood for piano lessons, the music had managed to pull her in, as always. She wasn't ready for Carnegie Hall, but everyone agreed that she had made astonishing progress in a very short time—yet more proof to herself that, these days, she was a true freak.

"Excellent," Mrs. Gruber said in a soft German accent. "You have been practicing."

"Like, forty-five minutes a day," Alexa replied proudly. "It's more fun now that we're doing harder stuff."

"What a perfect segue into science class."

Alexa and her piano teacher looked up to see Mr. Preston, Alexa's tutor, standing in the doorway.

"Did you feel the vibrations of the music, Alexa? Do you see it in that glass of water over there? That's *resonance*."

Alexa liked Mr. Preston. He was a dork, but he loved learning so much that she couldn't help but be swept up by his enthusiasm. That was one of the good things about having private classes. If she wanted to get excited about education, there was no one to make fun of her. Around here, it was cool to learn. Where she came from, learning was the last thing anyone wanted to be caught doing.

No wonder she'd been so stupid all her life.

"I'm sorry, I didn't mean to interrupt," he added. He hesitated in the doorway, struggling to hold a big green plastic container. "Go ahead and finish."

"No problem. We are done," Mrs. Gruber said as she began gathering her papers. "By all means, come in and put that heavy thing down."

He did as she suggested, lugging the bin over to the counter.

"Alexa," her piano teacher continued, "let's bring your practice time up to an hour a day. The Haydn and the Chopin sound good, but you have to do *all* the scales on your list, not just the fun ones."

"Yes, ma'am."

"It was a good lesson. You are doing very well."

"Thanks."

As Mrs. Gruber prepared to go, Mr. Preston spoke again.

"Good is right," he said as he unloaded the items from his container. "I was listening from outside the door. Thought it was a record I was hearing, not a live performance."

Alexa glowed under his praise, as did, by extension, her piano teacher. They all knew that Alexa had never even touched a piano until six months ago, so her progress had, indeed, been nothing short of spectacular.

The two adults chatted for a moment as Alexa tucked the beautiful wooden bench up under the piano, scooped up her sheet music, and placed it in a nearby cabinet.

The large, sunny studio had different areas for music and art and regular classwork, but lately they had been having science class over in the art section because they were conducting experiments that tended to get a little messy. Alexa loved experiments. Prior to coming here, the only thing she'd done that even came close to conducting an experiment was watching her mom cut cocaine with her little pocket knife, or sitting by while the guys made speedballs for the crackheads at the Grave Cave.

Once Mrs. Gruber was gone, Alexa and her tutor got right down to business. They were almost to the end of the eighth grade textbook. Alexa was originally so behind in science that they'd had to start with the fourth grade textbook and work their way forward. Between the one-on-one tutoring and putting forth a huge effort after hours on her own, Alexa had managed to learn five years of science in six months. This was one of her last lessons in this book, and then she'd move on to the ninth grade stuff. She couldn't wait, because then for the first time in her life she'd be ahead of where she ought to be and not behind.

It was a thought that grew more and more normal by the day. Sometimes when they were sitting there working, she'd look up at the long windows that faced the garden and picture her own self, the self from before, outside looking in. That kid wouldn't have believed her eyes. She wouldn't have understood any of it, nor would she have cared.

Or maybe she would have. Alexa was never quite sure.

"Do you know what this is?" Mr. Preston asked, pulling out a strange metal object that looked like a long, two-pronged eating utensil.

"A fork for an alligator?"

The tutor chuckled.

"Good guess. It is a fork, of sorts. It's called a tuning fork, and we use it to measure frequency. Today we'll be calculating the wavelengths of sound waves. We studied about this the other day, remember? We were dividing the speed of sound by the frequency and then multiplying that number by one hundred?"

"The speed of sound," Alexa replied, trying to recall. "Three hundred forty-three millimeters per second at twenty degrees centigrade?"

"Correct. Put some water into the cylinder, and then I'll show you a nifty way to measure frequency."

Alexa carried the cylinder to the sink and filled it up, smiling to herself as she did. If the old Alexa were outside looking in, right now she'd be holding her sides, laughing at a man who wore a pocket protector and used words like nifty. That thought took the smile from her lips.

Even though Alexa wasn't quite sure how she felt about herself these days, sometimes she really hated who she had been before.

Kent Tulip strode into Eleanor's home office tall and handsome and crackling with energy. As a teenager, Jo had been the envy of all her friends as the one with the best-looking dad. Age had lined his face a bit, but otherwise Jo thought he was more striking than ever, especially now that there was a hint of gray at his temples. Today he was wearing a black suit with a crisp white shirt and a cerulean tie. Truly, he looked like a million bucks.

"Eleanor, I don't understand why you think we need to go over the minutes of the board meeting again," he said brusquely to his mother-in-law, who was sitting behind her massive antique desk. "What is it that you don't understand?"

"Actually, Kent, you're right. We don't need to. I only said that to get you over here."

Obviously, that gave the man pause. He stood in front of the desk for a moment, hesitating, and then he turned back and closed the door before speaking again, more softly this time.

"What do you mean? Is something wrong?"

"Yes, something is wrong. We have a question for you."

With that, Mrs. Bosworth gestured toward Jo, who had been sitting quietly in the corner, wondering when she was supposed to jump in. Her grandmother had said to hit her father with the big guns the moment he arrived, with no pussyfooting around, just short, sweet, and to the point. Apparently, that moment was now.

"Why, Jo!" her father said, confusion mixed with pleasure on his face. He seemed genuinely glad to see her. "You should've said something. I didn't see you over there. How are you?"

He stepped forward as if to give her a hug, but rather than stand and accept his embrace, she merely held up one hand to stop him, as she summoned her nerve.

"Daddy, why did you pay Bradford to marry me?"

He stopped short, looking for a brief moment as though he'd been hit by a truck.

"Why…what?"

Eleanor surprised Jo by groaning and rolling her eyes.

"Sit down, Kent. Your daughter asked you a direct question. She expects a direct answer."

Jo studied her father's face, a million emotions flashing across it all at once. Obviously, he wasn't merely confused. He was also guilty, embarrassed, and stunned. As he took the chair closest to the door, Jo understood immediately that Bradford had, indeed, told her the truth—at least about this.

"I know all about it," Jo said. "I know about the Jaguar and the condo and the raise and the promotions. I know you and Mother told him how to make me fall in love with him." At that, her voice caught. "I just want to know why."

She swallowed hard, forcing herself to remain calm and cool and not cry. Her father might be sweating, but she wasn't going to show one speck of emotion other than a very controlled anger.

"How did you find out?" he asked finally.

Somehow, just hearing the question gave Jo a great sense of relief. At least he wasn't going to try and deny it.

"We'll get to that in a minute. Tell me why."

Kent ran a hand over his face and looked directly at his mother-in-law.

"*You* know why, Eleanor," he said. "Do you really want to have this discussion in front of her?"

Last night, Jo had felt sure that her grandmother knew more than she was saying. Now, the woman didn't even squirm. She simply reached for a drawer, opened it, and pulled out a file.

"Obviously, you've given me no choice," she said. "And do not for one moment take that self-righteous tone with me, Kent Tulip. In my wildest dreams I couldn't have imagined that you and Helen would pull a stunt like this."

"Eleanor," Jo's father said defensively, "you had a *stroke*. Your doctors were telling us at the time that you'd be lucky to survive through the end of the *year*. We felt that we had no choice. Fortunately for all of us, you rallied."

Before Eleanor could reply, the telephone rang and she answered it.

"Send him in," she said after a pause.

Jo wasn't sure who else was going to join them, but a moment later the door opened and a man entered the room. A distinguished-looking fellow in his sixties, Eleanor introduced him as her lawyer, Sidney Shaw.

"Sid, we have a problem that needs your immediate attention. And I do mean immediate. Have a seat, please."

Sidney shook hands with Jo and Kent and then took the middle chair between them.

"Just to bring you up to speed, Jo," Eleanor said, "I do believe that all of this insane behavior—both what your parents did to you with the wedding and what happened last night—was probably brought about because of certain stipulations in your grandfather's trust."

"His trust?"

The woman sighed heavily, looking every bit of her 86 years.

"As you know, Bosworth Industries is a private company established by your great-great-grandfather. In his lifetime, he was judicious about the company's stock, following a plan for its distribution that would echo down through many generations—and hopefully keep the company always under family ownership and control."

"Okay..." Jo said, this information not unfamiliar to her. All of the family members owned shares of Bosworth Industries in varying degrees. Jo had been given two shares herself when she was born, though she hadn't been allowed to touch the profits from those shares until she came of age, nor could she ever sell them to anyone outside of the family.

"Controlling interest in the company was passed down to your great grandfather and then to your grandfather, my husband. At the time of his death, my husband owned sixty percent of the company's shares. But rather than divide them evenly between our two daughters, he chose to distribute his shares a bit differently."

Jo glanced at her father, who looked as though he might burst a blood vessel any moment. Was he embarrassed? Angry? Whatever it was, the vein on his temple was bulging up the way it always did when he became upset.

"Upon my husband's death," Eleanor continued, reaching for a piece of paper from the file on her desk, "his will decreed that his shares would go into trust, for my benefit, but that upon my death they would be split."

"Split?" Jo asked.

"Yes. Half would be divided among our children and half among our grandchildren. Of course, neither your grandfather nor I realized that we would end up having only two grandchildren. His original intention, of course, was to see the shares divided out among a much larger base of descendants. You were quite young when he died, Jo, so you wouldn't know this, but your grandfather expected Helen and Winnie both to procreate much more prolifically than they did."

Jo forced herself not to roll her eyes. As though it was any of his business to dictate how many children his daughters had.

"Which brings us to the marriage clause," Eleanor said, "the part of this whole thing that has a bearing on the situation we now find ourselves in."

"The marriage clause?" Jo asked, glancing at her father. He was staring straight ahead, his chin set like stone.

"To wit," her grandmother said, looking down at the paper and skimming it. " 'Upon my wife's death'…so on and so forth…here we go, 'shares to be distributed thusly: one-half to be divided equally among my children and one-half to be divided equally among my grandchildren, not including unmarried females.' "

Jo's head jerked up.

"Excuse me?"

" 'One-half to be divided equally among my grandchildren, not including unmarried females,' " Eleanor repeated.

She set down the paper, folded her hands, and looked directly at Jo.

"It was nothing personal, dear. This was written when your grandfather was just a young man back in the forties, and long before women were respected in the workforce. At that time, it was simply a given that unmarried females would have neither the desire nor the capability to be involved with the company. He was acting to protect both Bosworth Industries and his female descendants."

Jo tried not to be hurt or look shocked by the fact that her own grandfather had inadvertently cut her out of his will because she wasn't married. She thought about the implications of such a stupid clause, but she didn't know enough about who in the family already owned how many shares to calculate where such a bizarre division would place the controlling interest. Judging by the look on her father's face, though, it couldn't be good.

"Help me out here," Jo said slowly to her grandmother. "If you dropped dead tomorrow, once the dust settled, exactly who would have controlling interest of Bosworth Industries?"

By all rights, that should be Jo's mother, Helen Tulip, since not only was Helen one of the Bosworths' two daughters, but Helen's husband, Kent, was the chief executive officer of the company.

The second-best option would be an even division of control between Helen and her sister, Winnie. Winnie's husband, Neil, was the chief operating officer which made him second in command to Kent. Neil was also one of the few members of the family that Jo actually liked and respected.

"Unfortunately," Eleanor said, "if I died tomorrow, once the dust settled, controlling interest would end up in the hands of your cousin, Ian."

Ian?

Even Sidney, who had known all of this already, looked mortified at the thought.

The only offspring of Winnie and Neil, Ian was a few years older than Jo. As a child, she had adored him. Riotously funny in a subversive way, Ian had made long family dinners and boring get-togethers feel wild and exciting. As a teen, Jo didn't find his dangerous antics quite so funny, and as an adult her feelings for him vacillated between concern and disgust. Quite simply, Ian had never really grown up, choosing instead to live the lifestyle of a rich, self-indulgent playboy. Now Jo realized that once her grandmother died, Ian would be a millionaire many times over—not to mention the deciding voice for Bosworth Industries.

Given the circumstances, in a way Jo could almost understand why her parents had tried to buy her a husband.

10

Mr. Bashiri was looking tired.

It was only 3:30 in the afternoon, but already he seemed weary and in pain. Danny was concerned because their itinerary called for a full day's shoot with only a two-hour break to grab dinner and check into the hotel, and then they had a night shoot at a benefit gala in Zurich's Old Town district. They would be up quite late, something Danny suddenly realized might not happen if Mr. Bashiri was already fading fast this early in the game.

Danny didn't want to insult or embarrass the man, but after a while he discreetly pulled him aside and asked if he needed to take a break.

"You're holding your back very stiffly, sir," Danny said out of the earshot of the others. "You don't want to push yourself too hard or you might end up completely incapacitated."

Mr. Bashiri thought for a moment and finally agreed.

"I will pull up a chair and rest my feet right over here," he said. "Why don't you switch to the digital and finish this series for me? I'm using the 82B cooling filter. Make sure you turn the fire on under the meat for some of the photos, but keep the flames as low as possible. I'm looking specifically for that low, blue glow of gas, not the higher oranges or yellows of the flames."

"Okay."

Danny got Mr. Bashiri settled on a full-length lawn chair and then went to work, switching out the cameras and filters to photograph the doctor on the patio near the pool, pretending to cook giant hamburgers on his grill. At first, Danny took the shots exactly as Mr. Bashiri had said, but once he was finished with those, he decided to experiment a little. First, he told the doctor to turn up the flames and try flipping a burger. After about ten tries, Danny managed to capture the shot perfectly, with the burger high in the air, the doctor grinning widely, and the spatula glinting in his hand.

Next, Danny had Luc bring out more raw meat and stack it artfully on a tray near the grill. Focusing was tricky, but by playing with the camera settings to increase the depth of field, he was finally able to focus sharply on the bright red meat in the foreground while still depicting the man at his grill in the background. There was something almost obscene about the meat and its gristly, bleeding abundance that would juxtapose well against shots of starving children in Africa.

When Danny was finished, he was surprised to see that Mr. Bashiri had fallen asleep. Watching the man there with his head tilted back against the lawn chair, his mouth slightly agape, Danny felt a surge of sadness for him. This great man could not keep up the pace of his youth. Soon, perhaps, he would have to give up these sorts of photographic assignments completely.

"I guess we can load the car first and then wake him up," Danny said, gesturing toward Mr. Bashiri.

Luc nodded, apparently lost in thought as they disassembled the flash units, light stands, reflectors, and other equipment and carried it all out to the van.

"I think that went well," Danny said to Luc as they reached the vehicle. "Long day, but we got a lot of good stuff."

"*Oui.*"

Luc seemed oddly preoccupied, and as they walked back to awaken Mr. Bashiri, Danny asked his friend if he was okay.

"Sorry. There is much weighing on my mind. Nothing to do with any of this."

"You got a lot of phone calls today. Is everything okay back home?"

"*Oui.* I just have some thinking to do."

They woke up Mr. Bashiri and thanked the doctor for his time and hospitality before getting underway.

"Can I ask you a personal question, Danny?" Luc asked as he pulled onto the main road and sped up. He was obviously starting to feel more chatty.

"Sure."

"This Jo person that you so love and hope to marry, have you met your future in-laws? The extended family?"

"Wow, that's out of left field."

"*Eh,* I only ask because I am thinking of a young woman I know. We might have become serious once, but her family was too difficult for me."

"Well, to tell the truth, Jo's parents would not be my first choice for in-laws. They're very cold and uncaring people. Self-centered. The flip side is at least they won't bother us much. As it is now, Jo only sees them a few times a year. I can deal with that."

"Just remember," Mr. Bashiri said, wagging a gnarled finger, "when you marry a woman, you marry her family as well."

Mr. Bashiri had never mentioned a wife, and Danny wondered if he spoke from experience.

"Actually, Jo will probably have a much harder time with my family because they'll be around a lot and sticking their noses into everything. They're nice and all, but I've got three sisters, and from the way they act, sometimes you'd think I have three extra mothers."

"Three sisters?" Mr. Bashiri laughed. "Growing up with sisters will teach a man much about the female mind. Other women sense this and are drawn to it, like the lion is to the gazelle."

"Don't lions devour gazelles?"

"Yes, I suppose they do. Okay, then like the gazelle is drawn to the watering hole. This is how women are drawn to Danny."

Luc laughed as well.

"You see, Danny?" Luc said. "Women flock to you wherever you go, even if you are oblivious to it. Why not forget about this girl back home and sample the delights of Europe instead? Mr. Bashiri, tell him that he needs to loosen up a bit."

Mr. Bashiri was quiet for a long moment, as the light mood of the moment seemed to dissipate into the air.

"When a man finds his true love," he said slowly, "he should hold on to her with every fiber of his being. No price is too high for the right woman."

After that, all three men were silent on the ride back to the city, each lost in his own thoughts.

Jo felt like a puppet.

As they sat in her grandmother's office and discussed the legalities and stipulations of the trust, all Jo could think about was how easily she had allowed herself to be manipulated. It was bad enough that her parents had paid Bradford to make her fall in love with him. Worse yet was that she had stepped right into their trap, convincing herself that she loved Bradford in return and that the two of them were going to live some sort of fairy-tale life together. Truly, for the first time since the failed wedding, Jo was realizing how utterly foolish she had been. Desperate for normalcy and companionship and romance, she had allowed herself to be swept up into an incredible deception. All through that time, as the wedding date had drawn closer and closer, the only voice of reason in her ear had been Danny's. His influence on her at that time had been merely as a friend, and essentially Jo had cut him out of her life. When she thought of how she'd ignored his advice, resisted his warnings, and finally told him to butt out of her business, she felt a deep flash of shame.

Thank You, God, for Bradford's last-minute exit, as it saved me from a lifetime with the wrong man!

Now that she knew about the terms of the trust, Jo wished she could believe that her parents had done what they had done for her own protection, to ensure her inheritance for her sake. But she knew that wasn't what had motivated them.

They had done what they'd done so that they could protect themselves. With Jo married, Eleanor's death would have meant an even split of stock shares down both sides of the family. Jo had no interest in running the company and would have gladly given her proxy over to her father to do with as he saw best. And that would have given Kent the control and the profits he coveted.

The simple truth, Jo realized now, was that her parents had played with her life like a pair of puppet masters, trading off her future and happiness for the sake of their own money and power. That's what life had always been about for her parents: money and power. It was no wonder she had chosen to turn her back on both, live a simple life, and eschew all of the riches she had always assumed would eventually be dumped in her lap. Now that she knew there was a condition in the trust that could prevent her from inheriting those riches, she was almost relieved.

Of course, she was also a bit indignant about that one condition. A marriage clause, indeed. In this day and age she could hardly believe something like that could be legal and binding. Still, here she sat with her grandmother's lawyer, learning what would be involved if she desired to fight the terms of the trust in court. Sidney's opinion was that although there was a possibility she could win, she'd be more likely to lose, especially because the courts usually favored privately held companies over individuals. Sidney said that the marriage clause might be outdated and sexist, but it wasn't illegal, and her chances of winning would be slim indeed.

"Well, I hate to break it to all of you," Jo said finally, "but as indignant as that clause makes me feel on a personal level, I have no intention of fighting it in court. You guys don't seem to understand. I don't *want* more shares in Bosworth Industries. I don't need the money, and frankly, in a way, it's a relief not to get it. Ian can have it all for all I care."

She didn't add that if her relationship with Danny progressed as she hoped it would, they would get married in a year or so anyway, and the whole point would be moot because her grandmother certainly seemed healthy and would probably still be around a lot longer than that.

"Let Ian have it?" Kent said. "I didn't slave for this company my entire adult life just to be superseded by a spoiled, rich playboy."

Feeling a surge of bravery, Jo responded in kind.

"And I didn't get heartlessly dragged all over the world my entire childhood just to grow up to be manipulated into a fake marriage by people who call themselves my parents but obviously care more about their own interests than they do about me!"

"Now, now," Eleanor said, holding up her hands like a referee at a boxing match. "Let's not get out of line. Jo, you have every right to be angry with your parents—and in the long run you may decide it's simplest just to leave the trust unchallenged. But let's not forget the main reason we're all here now. Someone wants you dead."

"Dead?" Kent asked, jerking his head back as if he'd been struck. Sidney also looked shocked.

"Someone tried to kill Jo last night," Eleanor said simply. "Bradford warned her that her life was in danger and that it had something to do with Bosworth Industries."

"Then, sure enough, someone tried to push me in front of a train, and Bradford nearly died protecting me," Jo added, looking at her father. "He's in the hospital now, in intensive care."

Kent seemed genuinely shocked and upset as Jo told the whole story, from the moment Bradford showed up with roses at the Marriott to the instant he was hit by the train at Grand Central Station.

"He told me that something big is going on at Bosworth and that I'm 'in the way,'" she repeated. "So does someone want to tell me what that big thing is that's going on and how on earth it has anything to do with me?"

The others were silent for a long moment as Jo's question hung in the air.

"There is something big going on," Kent said finally. "Probably the biggest thing to come along in quite a while."

"What is it?"

Kent hesitated before speaking.

"The specifics are unimportant, Jo, but to put it simply, one of our subsidiaries is at a major crossroads. There are two directions we can go with something, and I feel very strongly about which direction that should be. Unfortunately, your Uncle Neil is taking the opposite stand. He's even been trying to rally the board of directors against me. In the last few weeks, I've spent much of my time feeling like a politician, trying to soothe people, sway them back, and defend my agenda. It's not a simple matter. The right choice could have major financial benefits for all of us. Conversely, the wrong decision here could…well, it could cause serious financial ramifications. And I do mean serious. Unfortunately, Neil and I have not been able to see eye to eye. I believe the direction he wants to go in could be a disaster, and he feels the same about mine. We're at a stalemate right now."

"You've got controlling interest, Gran," Jo said. "Where exactly do you stand?"

Eleanor glanced at Kent, who answered for her.

"Your grandmother has chosen to remain neutral in this issue. Frankly, as the CEO, I respect her decision to stay out of it and let me run the company as I see fit. That's how business has always been done at Bosworth."

Jo didn't care. Corporate maneuverings of any kind were about as exciting to her as watching paint dry. Actually, watching paint dry was preferable. She focused on the part of all of this that was relevant to her.

"Again, what does any of that have to do with me? How is it that I'm in the way?"

They all fell silent, lost in thought. The longer no one spoke, the more concerned Jo became. She had expected this to be a no-brainer, that they would be able to tell her exactly what Bradford had been talking about as soon as they heard what had happened. Instead, they all looked completely stumped, as if they had no idea how or why Jo was in danger.

"It could be related to the trust," Sidney ventured, "and how it distributes the shares. I mean, if Jo were killed and then Eleanor died or became incapacitated, Ian would get the bulk of the shares, putting him in the power seat. He would be able to break the stalemate between Kent and Neil by casting the deciding vote."

"Not that Ian gives one whit about the business," Eleanor added, "but I feel certain that he would vote in line with his father's opinion."

"Which would mean it was either Ian or Neil behind the attempt on Jo's life," Sidney concluded.

Jo ran a hand through her hair, refusing to believe that either her cousin or her uncle could be so evil. Her father seemed to agree.

"I'm sorry," Kent said, shaking his head, "but that's ridiculous. Neil may be a thorn in my side much of the time these days, but he's not capable of *murder*. Even Ian, the waste of life that he's turned out to be, couldn't—wouldn't—have done this."

"You bought a husband for your daughter, Kent," Eleanor snapped. "I don't think you're in a position to talk about who is capable of what."

Jo took secret pleasure in seeing her father cut down to size on that one.

"If the distribution of shares is the motive for murder here," Kent said, pretending to ignore Gran's remark despite the fact that his face had flushed bright red, "and we are assuming that somehow the confidential details of this trust have been leaked, then Neil and Ian aren't your only suspects, by any means. The fact is that a number of high-ranking executives at Bosworth Industries would also be greatly impacted by how those shares are divided." He looked at Jo. "I could name ten or fifteen people off the top of my head who are taking Neil's side in this conflict and who would benefit greatly if he were to win. Are we really going to pursue the idea that one of them would want this badly enough to kill Jo for it? I'm not sure you could ever narrow down that many suspects to find the one responsible."

Jo's head was spinning, and she wasn't sure she even understood the complex situation in its entirety.

"There's something I don't get," she said, shaking her head. "Right now, I'm not married. So why is there a target on my back at all? If this theory is correct, shouldn't Gran be the one who's in danger? I mean, I hate to say it, but if she died right now, because I'm not married Ian would get my shares, right? So why try to kill me? Why not just go straight for her? It's not like I'm in a gown, carrying a bouquet. I may not be married for another year, at least."

Sidney reached for the copy of the trust that Jo's grandmother had been reading from earlier. He ran a finger down the text, reading, until he came to a paragraph below the one with the marriage clause.

"This is why," he said simply. Then he began reading right where Eleanor had left off. " 'In the case of unmarried females, shares will revert to the Bosworth Charitable Trust. Dividends on those shares will go to the unmarried female for the period of her lifetime, after which dividends will be paid to the trust.' "

He looked at Jo, but she shook her head. "Can you translate that for me?"

"Of course. What we're talking about are three different scenarios. First would be if you got married and then your grandmother died. In that case, you and Ian would receive equal shares."

"Which is why my parents tried to buy Bradford for me."

"Correct. The second scenario would be if you were still single and your grandmother died. In that situation, Ian would still only get half of the shares. According to the provisions of the trust, the other half would go into a charitable trust which would pay dividends to you for your lifetime. Upon your death, the dividends would then pay into the trust."

Jo thought about that.

"So I would still get the money from the shares. I just wouldn't have any control or ownership of the company?"

"Exactly. Your grandfather wasn't trying to give the short end of the stick to the unmarried females in the family. He was still providing them with an income, just not any control to go along with it."

"Well, that's not so bad," Jo said, feeling somewhat consoled about the unmarried female clause. She'd love knowing her shares went into a charitable trust, especially one that was well-funded enough to do some really good work. "That wouldn't bother me at all."

"But there's a third scenario here," Sidney said. "And this is the one that I think has put your life in danger. If you were to die first and then your grandmother died, Ian would get his shares *plus yours* since he would be the only surviving grandchild. That's what I'm talking about when I say he would end up with controlling interest. You'd have to be dead first in order for that to happen."

Jo thought about that and then looked at her grandmother.

"Then it's a good thing you got me a bodyguard," Jo said grimly. "But if somebody does succeed in killing me, you'd better make sure you get one for yourself next."

Back in Zurich, the three men finally checked into their hotel, which was conveniently located but otherwise quite modest. Danny and Luc were given a simple room with two single beds and a shared bathroom down the hall. At least Mr. Bashiri had a private bathroom, though neither room had a telephone or television.

They agreed to meet in the lobby in exactly two hours, and Danny was glad to learn that Luc had a few errands to run in the meantime. That would give Danny the room to himself for a while, which would be a welcome relief. Mr. Bashiri still looked very tired, and Danny suggested he squeeze in a nap before the evening's festivities.

Upstairs, Danny shut his own door and took a deep breath, relishing the silence. Used to living alone, all the togetherness in the last 24 hours had been a bit tiring for him. The room was stuffy, so he opened the window and pulled back the curtains. Cool air breezed in, fluttering the bottom of the gauzy fabric. Danny leaned on the windowsill and watched the traffic for a moment down below, glad he was a few peaceful stories up and above the fray.

The view from there was nice, though not as good as what they'd had from the doctor's balcony earlier in the day. This room faced away from the river, mostly looking out on other buildings. Down the street, he spotted Luc coming out of a bank, talking on his cell phone. Danny gave him a wave, but Luc's eyes were trained straight ahead and he didn't see Danny. Luc seemed wrapped up in the phone call anyway, his gestures choppy and almost angry. Finally, he stopped walking, hung up the phone, slipped it into his pocket, and turned toward another store.

Danny recognized it as the visa expeditor service where they had gone earlier in the day. As Luc pushed open the door to step inside, Danny wondered if the Frenchman had decided to ask out the bucktoothed girl after all.

Smiling at the thought of his incorrigible friend, Danny stepped away from the window, kicked off his shoes, and stretched out on the bed. He had a lot to do, but he was so tired that he thought maybe he'd grab a ten-minute nap and then he would get up and get rolling again.

Just ten-minutes' rest was all he needed.

11

The meeting in Jo's grandmother's office was adjourned without reaching a real resolution. At least they decided that the security at the estate would be tightened, and Eleanor said that she would make arrangements to stay posted on Bradford's condition at the hospital, in case he regained consciousness and could supply them with more information about what he knew and had been planning to tell Jo. She also said she would sit down with Winnie and let her know the full story about what was going on.

"The details of the trust were supposed to remain confidential until after my death," Eleanor said. "But now that all of this is happening, I suppose the cat's out of the bag."

Sidney said his goodbyes and left, and though Jo's father tried to make a quick exit as well, Jo came hobbling outside after him, asking him to wait, her bodyguard close behind.

"Daddy, I think you and I need to speak privately about the whole Bradford wedding issue, which is far from being resolved."

"We'll have to deal with it later," Kent replied, continuing on to his car, which was parked in the front circle. "Right now, I've got to get to work. I have an important meeting."

He got in and drove off without waiting for a reply or even looking his daughter in the eye. Jo stood on the bottom step and watched him go until his car was out of sight.

She was hurt, yes, but she just wasn't surprised enough to cry.

"You okay, miss?" the bodyguard asked.

Jo glanced at him, mortified that someone else had been a witness to her father's cruel brush off. Then again, what did it matter? She'd been treated that way by Kent Tulip her whole life, like a lesser being, like someone who was worth dealing with only after all other matters of importance had taken priority.

"Can I get you anything?" the bodyguard tried again, gesturing toward the house.

"Yes," she replied, standing up straight and squaring her shoulders. "Tell Fernando to bring the car around. We're going to Pennsylvania."

Danny's ten minutes of relaxation turned into a deep sleep—so deep, in fact, that the next thing he knew, it was an hour and a half later and Luc was shaking him awake. After that, Danny had to rush to be ready to go in time. As he returned from a quick shower wearing slacks and a button-down shirt, he was dismayed to see Luc sporting a tuxedo.

"Oh, no," Danny said, tucking his toiletries into the zippered pocket of his suitcase. "Is this a formal event?"

"I think so."

Polishing his dress shoes near the window, Luc seemed distant and preoccupied. Danny continued to get ready, pulling a slightly wrinkled tie from his duffel bag, looping it around his neck, and wishing he'd thought to throw in his tuxedo for good measure. He wondered what Mr. Bashiri might wear.

They ran into the photographer in the hallway to see that he was dressed all in black in a high-collared crisp linen outfit that was neither suit nor tuxedo but seemed perfect for the occasion just the same. The fund-raiser was at a deluxe hotel within walking distance, so the three of them set off, Danny carrying most of the equipment and Luc making light conversation with Mr. Bashiri as they went. Along the darkened street they went right past the visa expeditor's office, though now the lights were all off and a closed sign was in the window.

"Hey, I saw you going back in here this afternoon," Danny said to Luc as they walked past. "Did you make a date with the woman after all?"

Luc looked sharply at Danny and then away.

"How did you see me?"

"Our hotel room faces this street," Danny explained. "I waved at you but you weren't looking."

"Yes, well," Luc replied, forcing a smile, "*Eh,* I let her down easy. Told her I wouldn't be in town long enough to get together after all. I did not think I could get past that crooked smile."

"Whatever happened with the young woman you met on the train?" Mr. Bashiri asked.

"The Dutch one, from the compartment at the end of the hall?" Luc replied, this time his grin genuine. "If all goes as planned, we will be meeting on the Paradeplatz tonight after we finish at the gala. She is going to show me the Zurich nightlife."

"Sounds like fun," Danny said, so glad that his dating days with anyone except Jo were over. He'd spent years going out with different women, only to find that the one he really wanted had been under his nose the whole time.

Once the three men reached the gala, they got right to work, again trying for photos that would emphasize the opulence of life here in Zurich. Danny took care of the lighting, while Mr. Bashiri chose the different angles and cameras and took the pictures. Luc handled the reflector screens and the crowd, mostly trying to get them to ignore the fact that they were being photographed. After a while, Danny had to stifle a smile at the sight of all the elegant women and well-dressed men who pretended not to care that they were being photographed for *Scene It*—all the while doing everything they could to place themselves within range of the camera. One man nearly danced his wife into the buffet—and ended up having his picture snapped as he used a linen napkin to wipe cocktail sauce from her backside.

At one point an older woman decked out in emeralds spoke warmly with Mr. Bashiri, like an old friend. Later, the same woman cornered Danny out of earshot and asked about the photographer.

"You're his assistant, aren't you? How is he? Really?"

"Excuse me?"

"Kalunga. He looks so old, so sad. I wonder how much longer he'll continue to punish himself."

Punish himself? For what?

She started to walk away, and then she turned back and placed a wrinkled but heavily bejeweled hand on Danny's arm.

"Take good care of him, would you?" she asked. "He's not just a sweet man, he's also one of the most gifted artists I've ever had the pleasure of knowing."

"I agree. I have great respect for Mr. Bashiri."

Absently, she reached up to adjust a huge diamond-and-emerald tiara that was nestled in her elaborate hairdo.

"So many people blamed him for what happened with his family, but I've always felt that it wasn't his fault. Sometimes life is so unpredictable. Don't you think?"

Danny wasn't sure what he was agreeing to, but it didn't seem prudent to stand there and discuss Mr. Bashiri's personal life with a stranger. He nodded and tried to think of an innocuous reply.

"It sure is," he said finally. "Life is funny."

Then he excused himself and went back to work, wondering if he'd ever know what she'd meant.

The back of the limousine felt huge and empty. Jo sat beside the window and rested her head against the beige leather seat, watching absently as they crossed into Pennsylvania. Her bodyguard had taken the front passenger seat, and through the soundproof glass that separated her from the front of the vehicle, she could see him chatting with Fernando.

Though nothing of value had been accomplished in the meeting in her grandmother's office, at least the whole situation was more clear than it had been before. Jo reviewed that meeting in her mind, counting off the things she now knew.

Jo knew why her parents had wanted Bradford to marry her.

She knew also how her marital status would impact the distribution of shares of Bosworth Industries upon her grandmother's death.

Jo knew that the "something big" at the company to which Bradford had referred involved a decision that had divided upper management into diametrically opposing positions, locking them in a stalemate that needed to be broken one way or another.

Finally, she knew that killing her and then killing her grandmother would be one way to break that stalemate—something that would have a favorable impact not just for her uncle and cousin, but for an entire list of Bosworth executives.

In other words, if that's why she was in danger of being killed, there were so many suspects involved that she had no recourse at all but to stay safe until the entire matter had passed or until the killer was rooted out some other way. It wasn't as though she could go out investigating on her own. In the past year, Jo had become a pretty good sleuth on behalf of others. How ironic that she was helpless to do anything about it now that she was in danger herself.

Jo needed to feel constructive, to be in control of something, so she pulled a pen and some paper from her purse and began to make a list of all that she would retrieve from the house once they arrived there. She listed clothing, toiletries, and all the items in her office she would want to have in order to set up a temporary workspace at her grandmother's house.

At least that part wouldn't be too hard. Since the explosion, Jo had significantly simplified her work schedule because of her health. She had taken a leave of absence from her part-time job teaching home economics at the high school and from her weekly radio show where she answered caller's questions about household hints. She had even put on hold her agent's efforts in securing a book deal, syndication for her column, and a reality TV series about home care. All she was left with now was the daily "Tips from Tulip" column in the newspaper and her online household hints blog, both of which were easy to keep up with.

Her life had also been simplified through the efforts of her friends, who had all been a huge help to her since she got out of the hospital. Most of Jo's clothes had been destroyed in the fire, so Marie had done the footwork of gathering a new wardrobe for her. Putting the word out for castoffs and donations among their more well-dressed size-five and six friends and fellow church members, Marie had managed to collect tons of stuff, much of it nicer than the clothes Jo had lost.

Jo's friend Anna, who was a lawyer, had stepped in and handled several legal and financial matters for her, most notably being a bulldog with Jo's insurance company to make sure that they paid out her homeowner's policy quickly and completely. Once the big check was in hand, however, and Anna had tried to talk to Jo about her plans for rebuilding the house, Jo had put her off. She wasn't ready to deal with that yet.

For the time being, she had simply been holing up in Danny's house, trying to regain her strength and get completely well with as few outside distractions as possible. She never could have imagined what it would be like to have her health blown out from under her, much less how it would feel to lose her home and most of her possessions to a fire. Even now, six weeks later, Jo would think of something else that had been lost to the flames, and she would be overwhelmed with sadness. From what she'd read, that wasn't at all unusual and in fact might even continue for a while. Material goods didn't matter in the grand scheme of things, Jo knew, but it was still hard to let go of all the family photographs and mementos and little treasures she had lost.

At least the fire had spared her office, which was in a separate building out behind her house. All of her notes and writings and archives were still there, intact, thank goodness. Jo thought of the column as the legacy she'd been given by her paternal grandmother, and it would have broken her heart to lose that.

Thinking of her Nana now, Jo smiled, her heart filled with a rush of warmth.

I'm not worried about leaving you, Jo Jo, her Nana had said on one of her last days before dying of cancer. *You've got a good head on your shoulders, a good heart, and a rock-solid faith in God. In this life, if you've got all that, you'll do okay.*

Jo blinked away a single tear now, missing the woman with an ache from somewhere deep inside. In the last six weeks, Jo had had to part with her home, her health, her boyfriend, and almost her life.

"I hope you were right, Nana," she whispered out loud. "Because these days, my head, heart, and faith in God are about all I have left."

"Let's measure with the goniometer," Yasmine said, "then you can give me fifteen minutes on the bike."

"Okay."

Alexa stood on the exercise mat and raised her left arm straight up in the air so that the physical therapist could measure her range of motion. As always, the left side was a perfectly normal 180 degrees. The right side, though, still had a little way to go. Alexa raised that arm as high as she could and held it there shakily while Yasmine adjusted the device under her arm.

"Excellent, Alexa. You're at one sixty-five," Yasmine said as she sat at the desk, flipping her long, black braid out of the way and making notations on the chart.

Alexa climbed onto the exercise bicycle and started pedaling. She would never admit it to anyone, of course, because it was way too babyish, but sometimes when no one was paying attention, Alexa would turn on the box fan, point it toward herself, and pedal as fast as she could, imagining that the wind in her hair was the real wind blowing past as she sped down the road. She had never ridden on a real bike, so she used this one to pretend. She was studying about Europe with Mr. Preston, and sometimes if she closed her eyes she could picture herself in London or Paris or Rome, maybe pedaling down to the Sistine Chapel and taking a look at its famous ceiling, or swinging around the Louvre and giving a hand to the Venus de Milo.

"Up your tension there, honey, and slow it down," Yasmine said as she finished her notations and closed the file. "Focus on the program. You seem a million miles away."

Alexa adjusted the controls so that it was a bit harder to pedal. It wasn't as much fun that way, and she could feel the pull in her right leg.

"I was just thinking about real bike riding. It must be fun, if you can keep your balance."

"You've never ridden a real bicycle before?"

"Where I'm from? Duh. Where am I going to ride it? On the Turnpike? Maybe the railroad tracks?"

Alexa's voice sounded a bit sharp, but at least she got her point across.

"Maybe I could ask Dr. Stebbins about getting a bicycle for you here," Yasmine said. "There's certainly room to ride around on the estate. It's not hard to learn."

"Sounds great," Alexa replied, but she knew better than to get her hopes up. "Dr. Stebbins never lets me do anything dangerous. He already said no to skateboarding."

"Bicycling's a lot safer than that. Dr. Stebbins would probably approve as long as you always wear a helmet. Some of the others have real bikes, and it seems to be helping with coordination and balance, not to mention their gross motor skills."

Yasmine put away the goniometer and then the rubber bands, not looking at Alexa, obviously not realizing what she had just said. *Some of the others.*

There were others?

Others like her?

Heart pounding, Alexa spoke, trying to sound nonchalant.

"Yeah, so how many others are there? Dr. Stebbins never said."

Yasmine instantly stiffened, and Alexa knew that she had asked the wrong question.

"I, uh, I just meant other people who've had cerebral hemorrhage," Yasmine said lightly after a pause, closing the cabinet.

Alexa slowed the pedaling until she stopped. She stared at her physical therapist.

"No, you didn't. That's not what you meant at all. You meant others in my same situation, others who got treated with Fibrin-X, like me."

Yasmine turned to her, her expression grim.

"No, you misunderstood."

Yasmine busied herself with straightening the room, nervously adjusting the papers in Alexa's file and sliding the chair up under the desk. Alexa watched her for a minute, and then she climbed off the bike and simply stood there.

"If you knew what it felt like to be me," she said slowly, "you'd tell me the truth. I have to know, Yasmine. Are there others? I'm not the only one?"

Finally Yasmine stopped puttering and focused on Alexa.

"If there were—and I'm only saying *if*—I couldn't tell you that anyway. That would have to come straight from Dr. Stebbins."

"He says I'm one of a kind. A medical marvel. I thought he meant it literally."

"You are a medical marvel."

"But I'm not one of a kind, am I? There are more. Tell me. You've met them. You work with them! Are there kids? My age? Kids who know what I'm going through?"

"Alexa, please, I can't—"

"Tell me!" Alexa cried, hating the desperation in her own voice. Until that moment, she hadn't realized how miserable she was to think she was the only person in the world who had ever been through what she'd been through. "Where are they? Are they close? Do they live around here?"

"Alexa, you've got to bring this up with Dr. Stebbins."

"But he doesn't want me to know! He doesn't care how this feels. He just wants to do his stupid evaluations. It doesn't matter to him that I'm a freak."

"You are not a freak."

"That's how it feels! And he doesn't care! Neither do you!"

Alexa stomped off to a far corner of the room and sat down on the low, wide window ledge. Tucking her legs against her body, she wrapped her arms around her knees and began rocking back and forth.

"Dr. Stebbins and I both care very deeply about you," Yasmine said, stepping closer. She went on to give Alexa some spiel about ethics and procedures and confidentiality laws. "I'm afraid our hands are tied."

Alexa knew enough to realize that was probably true. Still, there had to be a way to find out.

"What if he didn't have to tell me?" she asked, her mind racing. "What if I found out on my own?"

"What do you mean?"

"What if I looked at his files or read the data or something? Then I could find out without him having to say a word."

"That's against the law, honey. Besides, all of the data is probably under lock and key down at the pharmaceutical company. That sort of information isn't just lying around. Patient rosters are highly confidential, especially in new drug development."

Alexa thought about the small side room where the doctor kept a desk and a file cabinet. He did a lot of paperwork in there. Even if the main notes weren't kept on site, there might be something in there that she could find—some kind of list or printout.

"Look, honey, the doctor's running late today, but you can talk to him about this when he finally gets here. Tell him how you feel. Maybe...I don't know...maybe he can try to put together a support group or an Internet loop or something for kids in stroke recovery. No one involved here wants you to feel like a freak. I think you just need some interaction with kids your own age for a change."

Alexa nodded, her plan already set. She was going to break into the office tonight and find the information that she sought. Dr. Stebbins might get angry if he found out, but that was nothing compared to the thrill of finding someone else—anyone else—who was just like her.

12

Three hours and forty-five minutes after leaving her grandmother's estate in Westchester County, Jo finally spotted the exit sign on the highway that said "Mulberry Glen." She had already given Fernando directions to her neighborhood, and she watched now as he took the exit and drove them there, steering through the lazy, tree-lined streets, past modest homes and rolling parks. Mulberry Glen.

Home.

Why did it feel as though she'd been gone forever? She had only left early yesterday morning, but it seemed like ages ago. She was glad now that she had asked Danny's dad to drive her to the train station yesterday morning, intending to take a taxi or call Marie for a ride home, so that at least she didn't have to retrieve her car from there now.

The driver put on his blinker at Jo's driveway, turned in, and pulled up beside the pile of charred rubble that had been her house, a roughly-repaired fence, and her lone little home office sitting in the backyard looking like a lost puppy.

Jo went into the office after the bodyguard checked it out, and then Fernando showed up at the door a moment later with two huge Louis Vuitton suitcases on wheels, loaners from Jo's grandmother. As the bodyguard stood near the doorway, Fernando opened each bag in turn so Jo could fill them with her necessary papers and equipment.

"Is there more luggage in the car?" she asked, wondering whether she needed to leave room for her clothes as well.

"Two more this big," Fernando replied, "plus three smaller ones."

Okay. Obviously her grandmother expected her to stick around a while.

In that event, Jo filled the second suitcase also, mostly with her chemicals and testing supplies. She'd miss the ease and convenience of having a built-in test kitchen right at her fingertips, but maybe her grandmother would let her set up something temporary that would suffice.

Finally, when both bags were full, Fernando brought them back to the car and loaded them into the trunk.

"You see that house there?" she asked him, pointing across the back lawn to Danny's. "We'll walk over and meet you. Just go around the block that way and come back up."

Fernando did as she said, though as he started up the limo and shifted into reverse, Jo noticed her across-the-street neighbor standing near her mailbox, eyeing the luxurious vehicle.

"Jo?" the woman called out. "Everything okay?"

Mrs. White had lived in the same house Jo's whole life and was probably her favorite of all the neighbors. When Jo was young, whenever she came to stay with her grandparents, inevitably she would end up at some point over at the Whites with the other neighborhood kids, just hanging out or playing a game of Uncle Wiggly or learning how to knit. Trained as an RN, the woman was a nurturing sort who simply drew children like a magnet. When Jo grew up and finished college, Mrs. White insisted that she call her by her first name, Jean.

"Hi, Jean," Jo said now, walking toward the tiny octogenarian with the salt-and-pepper hair and sparkling blue-gray eyes. "Don't worry. I'm fine."

"I saw the limo, and I wasn't sure if someone died or if you were getting married again."

Jo cringed, wishing she could tell her the whole truth.

"Neither. I…uh…I'm taking a vacation with my grandmother. She likes to travel in style."

"I can see that. And how do you do?"

Jean introduced herself to the bodyguard and shook his hand, probably assuming he was Jo's date. Not wanting to start any rumors in this small town, Jo quickly interjected that he worked for her grandmother.

"I needed somebody strong to help with the luggage."

Not wanting to linger, Jo bid her sweet neighbor goodbye and hobbled back across the street, through her yard, and past the gate into Danny's yard. The path between the two homes was well worn from years of use, a sight that almost always made Jo smile.

Loving thoughts of Danny were on Jo's mind as she waited inside the back door, the bodyguard doing a quick sweep through the house before giving her the all clear. Thinking of the man who was her best friend and also her true love, Jo found herself practically humming as she went about the business of packing up her clothes and personal items that were in his house. While Jo was living there, she had slowly been cleaning and organizing the place, not so much so that it would seem intrusive to him once he returned—as though she had rearranged his life or invaded his privacy—but just so that it was livable for her in the meantime.

More than once she had resisted the urge to put up a fresh coat of paint in the living room or totally reorganize the way he had set up his kitchen cabinets. He probably wouldn't have cared on either account, but she did. This was his home, and she wanted to respect all of the boundaries that ought to come with that.

At Jo's request, Fernando tossed out all of her perishables from the refrigerator and carried out the trash as she packed her things. Once she was finished, she told the two men she'd just be a few more minutes, and then she walked down the hall and opened the door to Danny's tiny darkroom, stepped inside, and pulled the door shut behind her.

The room hadn't been used for weeks, not since Danny left, but there was something about being in there that made her feel close to him. She thought it was probably the smell—the odor of photochemicals and special papers and developer fluid—mixed with the worn spot on the floor where he stood as he worked, and the places on the counter where he had rested his hands so often that there were permanent smudges there.

Placing her hands in the same spot, she simply closed her eyes and inhaled, wishing desperately that he would come home to her, knowing that she would never ask him to. In fact, she wouldn't even tell him what was going on so that she would never be the one to have come between him and the dream come true he was currently living. Just a few more months, and then they'd be together again anyway.

If she wasn't killed in the meantime, that is.

Alexa didn't think Yasmine would ever leave. By the time the physical therapist said her goodbyes, got in her minivan, and drove away, Alexa had only a 15-minute unsupervised gap in which to break into the doctor's office and search his files.

At least she knew how to do it. She'd never done any breaking and entering, as some of her friends had, but she knew the techniques for getting past certain locks. She'd taught herself how a long time ago, when her mother would pass out on the couch inside their apartment and Alexa's only choices were either to climb through a window or jimmy the door.

All she needed was a little screwdriver or a slim piece of metal. Quickly, she rooted through the drawers of the workstation, but all she could come up were two paper clips. If the lock was simple enough, they might work.

Running to the door she wanted to open, she knelt in front of it, bent the paperclips a 45 degree angle, and placed them horizontally above the knob. Then she jiggled the clips with one hand while she twisted the knob with the other. Fortunately, this was no deadbolt, just a household key lock. Within 30 seconds (though it felt like 30 minutes) the knob twisted all the way and she was in.

Holding her breath, Alexa got up, stepped inside and pulled the door quietly shut behind her. With the big glass window that separated the office from the rest of the room, she couldn't exactly hide. On the other hand, at least there was enough light spilling through the glass that she didn't need to turn any lights on. She simply sat at the desk and went to work, flipping through drawers, looking at files, and trying to find some clue about the others, the medical marvels like her.

Jo's last stop before leaving town was to get Chewie, who had spent the night at the home of Chief Cooper's father, Harvey Sr. During Jo's hospitalization and the week following that she'd spent at Danny's parents' house, Chewie had remained happily ensconced with his new best friend, the man everyone called Harv. Harv had lovingly cared for Jo's dog until she was well enough to take him back herself, though he refused any sort of remuneration for his trouble other than a gift certificate from his favorite restaurant, the local pizza parlor.

Jo stopped off now to buy another one and then called Harv to tell him they were coming. When they pulled up in front of his house, he was sitting on the front stoop, petting Chewie and holding tightly to his collar. He let it go as soon as the limo came to a stop and Jo climbed out. She simply got down on her knees right there on the grass, awkward though it was with the cast on, and held open her arms as the dog ran to her.

Jo closed her eyes and embraced her big baby, knowing how foolishly dramatic their reunion must look, considering they'd only been apart for one day and night. She didn't care. Jo was as happy to see Chewie as he was to see her, and she cooed and rubbed and cuddled him as he yapped and nudged her and furiously wagged his tail. They were together again.

Jo thanked Harv and slipped him the pizza certificate, which he accepted with a laugh and tucked into his shirt pocket, thanking her.

"Chewie here has a thing for spiders. Did you know that?"

"You mean how he likes to torment them?"

"Apparently, he likes to eat 'em too. Sort of." He went on to explain how he had swatted a spider down from the ceiling with the broom, and the insect ended up sailing right into Chewie's open mouth. The man laughed just thinking of it. "That dog got the weirdest expression on his face, kind of crossed his eyes like he was trying to look down his own throat, swallowed a couple of times, and walked away. Funniest thing I ever saw."

"Chewie will keep you entertained, that's for sure."

Back in the car with Chewie this time, they set off toward the highway, Jo saying a prayer of thanks that the Lord had put so many kind people in her life.

Chewie sniffed furiously at her cast, stepped on every inch of seat and floor while exploring the entire back of the limo, and finally settled down next to her, so close that she could feel his chest expand and contract against her leg with every happy, excited breath he took.

Jo scratched him behind the ears and thought about Harv and Chief Cooper and Jean White and her friends Marie and Anna and Danny's family and everybody at church and all the ladies in her Bible study group and the teenagers at the high school and on and on until she felt a huge swell of gratefulness for all that God had blessed her with in Mulberry Glen.

Somehow, He had given back to her, as an adult, the connections she'd never been able to make as a child. Being moved from place to place for many years had left Jo feeling rootless, essentially friendless, and empty.

But as she had put down roots in this little town and slowly allowed them to deepen, something had changed in her heart. She realized now that despite her recent problems, those roots had finally begun to allow her to blossom and grow in a way she never could have imagined before.

Jo realized, with startling clarity, that she felt complete now, as if that gnawing need for connection that had eaten away at her for most of her life had finally been filled. Just seven and a half months ago, when Jo had been ready to marry Bradford, that need had been at its greatest, its most frenzied. That must have been what had made her so ready to jump into such a shallow and speedy relationship—because at least then she might be able to fill the void and silence the pain of her isolation.

It wasn't until the wedding fell apart and she was left to face the hurt and loneliness by herself that she had finally begun to deal with the void for real. Wanting to honor God and fix what was broken inside of her, Jo spent the next six months immersing herself in introspection, Bible reading, prayer, and sharing, even joining a Bible study group for single women, led by Danny's sister, that often felt more like a group therapy session than a mere lesson. Jo had known that true healing could only come through her relationship with God, but what she hadn't expected was the different ways God would heal and grow her, not just through His Word, but also through the loving ministrations of His people. Jo had literally been led into wholeness not just by her King but by His kingdom here on earth. Those six months had been a time of serious personal growth on many levels. In the end, the most important step for Jo had been to let go of the notion that a mere man—any man other than Jesus—could make her whole. Once she did that, everything else seemed to fall into place.

After that, when her best friend Danny told Jo that he loved her, she had done even more soul-searching, finally coming to understand that real love—true, gut-level, forever-kind-of-love between a man and a woman—was about trust and vulnerability and real sharing and bonding, not just the pale imitation that she had found with Bradford. With God's help, Jo understood that she could now give her heart fully because it was already whole on its own. Finally telling Danny that she loved him too had been the easiest, most natural words she'd ever had the opportunity to say, even if she had been flat on her back in the hospital at the time.

Nowadays, she was simply waiting for him to come back to her so that they could move on toward the next phase of their lives, together. It was hard to wait, but just as God had used the pain of the failed wedding to help her grow, Jo had no doubt that He was also making use of this time apart from Danny as well. Her biggest prayer was to understand what lessons God was still trying to teach her. In her best moments, Jo had to admit that she wanted to keep learning, to continue to become the person He truly wanted her to be. When she wasn't feeling quite so pious, she was more likely to stomp her feet and demand to know why God was keeping them apart.

Either way, she missed her true love more than she'd ever thought possible. Perhaps, she realized now, what God most wanted her to get from this situation was empathy. For the first time in her life, Jo finally understood how Danny must have felt all those years when she was traveling around the world with her parents and he remained back in Mulberry Glenn, just waiting for her to return. The waiting was pure torture. More than anything, she wanted Danny to come home, so they could go on with their lives and get married and live happily ever after.

Correction, she thought. *I'd like to live happily ever after...if only I could figure out who's trying to kill me.*

Alexa's search seemed fruitless. As the clock ticked on the wall across the room, her efforts grew more and more frantic. There were some files and notes in here, and a lot of computer printouts, but it was all just numbers and codes and scientific-type stuff. She couldn't make sense of any of it, and there wasn't a name or address to be had in the whole bunch.

She was about to give up completely when she found one thing that was promising, a single sheet of pink Phone Message paper that had been shoved up in the corner of a drawer and forgotten, hand written from some secretary for Dr. Stebbins. There was a name and a callback number, and the message filled up almost the entire bottom of the tiny page: "Mrs. Finch called about the scan on Emma. Call her at above number to discuss. Ethan doing great, wants to know how much longer before he can go horseback riding." The message was dated from last summer, which made the timing about right.

Alexa wasn't sure, but she thought this might be exactly what she needed. It was worth a try anyway. She slipped the note into her pocket and tucked away everything else. Then she reached for the door and quietly swung it open. As she took a step out, she heard the surprised voice, deep and distinct, of Dr. Stebbins, only a few feet away.

"Alexa?" he demanded. "What were you doing in my office?"

On the way back to New York, Jo had Fernando make a detour through Gilbertsville, so that she could go to her favorite pet store and pick up some supplies for Chewie. Once there, Jo wished that she had time to stroll the aisles and shop for a while. But with a very ostentatious limo sitting in the parking lot under the "Zimmers' Pets" sign, a hovering bodyguard who was making her nervous, and an agitated Chewie at her side desperate to play with all of the puppies that were for sale, Jo needed to hurry.

Moving quickly through the family-owned-and-operated store, she was able to find everything she needed except the smoked bones, a treat that helped prevent the buildup of tartar on Chewie's teeth. She asked a polite young man, one of the Zimmers' sons, where they were keeping the bones now. As he led her there, she noticed the familiar bright, neon green socks peeking out at his ankles. She had spotted the socks on other employees and family members on previous visits to the store, and now she wondered if Alexa might like a pair. It seemed like something a teen-ager might wear.

"Hey, Kevin," Jo said to the owner as she approached the cash register and put down her items. "I have a question for you."

"Shoot."

"As usual, everyone in here seems to be wearing neon green socks. Is that part of the store uniform, or just a teen fad?"

The man grinned and held up his own leg, tugging up his pants to reveal yet another flash of neon green at the ankle.

"Not a fad or a uniform," he said, "and not just for the kids. It's the Zimmers' family trademark."

He rang up her items as Jo dug out a credit card from her purse.

"Why neon green?"

"Well, to give the short story of the long story," he said as he took her card and slid it through the machine, "it all started on a nighttime scouting hike." He went on to explain how one of the other leaders just happened to be wearing a pair of neon green ski socks, which had made the man's legs and ankles completely visible even after dark. "For our next night hike, I brought the same kind of socks for everybody to keep track of all the boys. Really worked like a charm."

He tore off the charge slip and slid it across the counter to Jo with a pen.

"It sort of evolved from there," he continued. "I bought a whole bunch and started wearing 'em every day. Told my kids to wear them too. They love 'em, and even my wife is happy, because she never has to match or fold socks any more."

He gestured toward a woman who was perched on top of a ladder, looking through boxes on a high shelf.

"I wasn't crazy about it at first," Mrs. Zimmer said with a smile as she looked down on them, "but when the whole family wears only one color and one kind of sock, they *all* match. Saves a lot of time. Believe it or not, Kevin even wears his to formal events."

Jo signed on the dotted line, smiling at this interesting man and his unique take on personal style. Even though she doubted she would ever recommend neon green socks with formal wear, there was something to be said for buying only one style and color of sock. She thought she might put that tip in her blog for people who hated the whole time-consuming socks-in-the-laundry problem. If everything matched, then these people were right. No sorting would be required.

"Where could I get a pair?" she asked, thinking again of Alexa.

"I have ours specially made by a sock lady," Kevin replied. "We don't sell 'em, but I'd be happy to give you some."

Before Jo could object to his kindness, he called to a cute young girl in a "Cheerleaders Rule" T-shirt who was busy cleaning a fish tank nearby.

"Gracie, hon, see if you can find Jake and get him to bring out a new pair of socks from the pack that just came in."

"Oh, that's not necessary," Jo objected.

"It's our pleasure," he insisted. As they all waited for Gracie to find Jake and retrieve the socks, the bodyguard grew visibly agitated at Jo's side. Fortunately, the young man who had led Jo to the smoked bones showed back up and took an interest in Chewie.

"What's your name, boy?" he asked, kneeling down and holding out a hand so the dog could sniff him. Chewie took to him almost immediately.

"This is Chewie," Jo told him.

"Hi, Chewie. I'm Sam," he said warmly, scratching the dog's chest and then giving the dog's upraised paw a shake.

"How many pairs of socks you want, Dad?" a male voice called from in back.

"Just one is fine," Jo answered for Kevin, calling back. At this point the bodyguard looked as though he might blow a gasket from the delay. Jo figured he was probably a New Yorker, used to the rush, rush, rush of the city and intolerant to the slower, friendlier pace of rural Pennsylvania.

Finally, Gracie returned with her older brother, who looked to be about 17 and was handsome enough to be an actor.

"Here you go. Sorry for the delay," the young man said, flashing her a smile and handing the plastic-wrapped socks directly to Jo.

"Are you sure I can't pay you for them?" she asked Kevin.

"Nope," he replied, picking up her bag of items and handing it to her. "Just be sure to come back next time Chewie needs something."

Jo thanked him again and followed her bodyguard out of the door, not surprised to find another Zimmer kid hovering near the limo. He was tossing a baseball up and down in his glove—and wearing neon green socks. From what she could recall of her last visit, his name was Tom and his big dream was to play for the Phillies.

"Sweet wheels," he said now, with a grin. "Forget pro ball. I want to know what *you* do for a living!"

Jo just laughed as the bodyguard opened her door.

"It's called 'old money,' sweetie. You don't earn it. It's just sort of there."

"Impressive."

Jo started to climb in, and then she hesitated, remembering that when she was Tom's age, she would have traded all the fancy vehicles in the world to be a part of a normal family who simply put down roots, worked together, and cared about each other.

"You know what, Tom? This limo may seem impressive, but trust me. It's not worth a fraction of what you and your family have right here."

13

Alexa was busted. She didn't know what to say and couldn't have found her voice at that moment even if she could have thought of something.

"I asked you a question," Dr. Stebbins said, stepping closer. "What were you doing in there? That door was locked. That's a private office."

"Nothing," she said finally, shame burning her face.

"Alexa," he repeated, his voice a heartbreaking mix of suspicion and disappointment. Except for the time she got caught sneaking in after a night out, this was the first time he'd ever been really upset with her. "Tell me the truth."

He reached past her to push the door open and stepped inside, flipping on the bright overhead light. He looked around for any obvious tampering, fooled with the doorknob for a minute, and then sat in the chair at the desk. She stood in the doorway, hardly able to meet his eyes.

"You fooled with the lock. I can see there where you scratched it. What were you looking for?"

She used to be such a good liar, such a great storyteller, always talking her way out of trouble, especially at school. But since her stroke, she hadn't gotten in much trouble at all, and now she was out of practice. Summoning her wits, she tried to pretend that Dr. Stebbins was the principal at her old school and she'd been caught putting cherry bombs in the toilets or spraying graffiti in the gym.

"Nothing," she said, jutting out her chin in a gesture that used to seem cocky but now only felt silly. "I was hungry, and I thought you had some microwave popcorn packs in here."

He remained silent for a long moment, and she finally forced herself to look him in the eye—though that was too hard, so she ended up staring at his forehead instead.

In his early forties and already half bald, Dr. Stebbins wasn't exactly superhandsome, but there was something appealing about him. He wore wire-rimmed glasses over deep blue eyes, his face free of wrinkles except for a single line that creased on each side of his mouth. Always dressed neatly in slacks, shirt, and a white doctor's jacket, he was just a little bit plump, like his wife, Nicole, but in a pleasing way. The few times she had seen them together, they got along really well, the way she always imagined married couples did, except that they didn't call each other "Pookey" or give Eskimo kisses.

"I'd like to give you the benefit of the doubt, Alexa, but I know very well you're lying."

"It's not that big of a deal. I just wanted popcorn." That was her story, and she was sticking to it.

"Maybe what you were really looking for was drugs. I don't keep anything in here, but I am a doctor, so maybe you thought I had a secret stash or something—"

Alexa took a step back, feeling like she'd been slapped in the face.

Drugs? He really thought she'd been in there looking for drugs?

"How can you say that?" she cried, bursting into tears. "I'm *not* my mother! I don't take drugs!"

"Then what did you want?"

"Names!" she yelled. Then she put a hand to her mouth, holding back more sobs. "I wanted names," she repeated, collapsing onto the mat on the floor. "I can't do this anymore, Dr. Stebbins. I've got to know if there are other kids like me. I don't want to be the only one. I wanted to find a list or a file or something that would tell me how to find the rest."

Alexa put her face in her hands and cried. After a while, she could feel a warmth nearby, and she peeked out between her fingers to see that he was sitting in front of her, on the mat.

"I'm sorry," he told her softly. "Drugs were the only thing I could think of. I should've known better than that. I believe you."

She pulled her hands away, only to see that they were all smeared black from eyeliner. Without even being asked or having to get up, he handed her the box of tissues he was holding in his lap. Then he just quietly sat there while she tried to clean herself up.

"I'm sorry I broke into your office," she told him after wiping her face and hands and blowing her nose. "But nobody seems to understand what it's like for me. I mean, I appreciate everything you've done, and everything the old lady's done, but sometimes it's not enough. It's hard being a kid without any other kids around—especially for a medical freakazoid like me."

The doctor surprised Alexa by smiling.

"Is that how you think of yourself?"

"Of course. What else would you call it?"

He shook his head.

"Just a kid who had a problem that got fixed. Two problems, really, both fixed at the same time by the same solution."

She shook her head.

"I was a medical experiment that just happened to work in freaky ways."

"No, that's not true. You were what's known in the drug development world as a serendipitous discovery. It's not that uncommon, you know. There are a lot of drugs that were intended for one thing and now doctors use them to treat other, unrelated conditions. That's what's called off-label use, Alexa. That's the study you're involved in now, an off-label-use study."

"But until I came along, nobody knew what Fibrin-X could even do to people."

"As a stroke treatment we certainly did. It was already into phase three drug trials at that time. We knew that it would dissolve the fibrin that the hemorrhaging had created in your brain without releasing more hemoglobin or kicking off the clotting cascade."

Alexa didn't exactly understand what he was saying, but she wanted him to keep talking just the same. Something about the way he spoke was always so reassuring.

"We just didn't realize," he continued, adjusting his glasses, "that Fibrin-X would also promote reconnection of the proximal and distal segments of the CNS nerve fibers, or that that would somehow have a significant affect on attention-deficit/hyperactivity disorder—you know, your ADHD. Certainly, reconnection had already been achieved with other drugs in peripheral nerves, but never before in the central nervous system. At first we didn't understand the mechanism that was making it work, but our animal studies are showing that as the drug dissolves the fibrin, it's also causing nerve growth all around the circle of Willis and in other areas that relate to ADHD. It's really quite exciting, and you're a part of it."

Alexa sniffled, thinking it *was* kind of exciting when he put it that way. She had seen a plastic model of the brain once, and the circle of

Willis, where her aneurysm had been, was just a big ring of arteries in a circle at the base of her brain. For a long time she had rolled that name around on her tongue, circle of Willis, thinking it sounded cool. If she ever formed a club with the others, maybe they could call themselves that, the Circle of Willis, like a play on words.

"I'm a part of it, yeah, but am I the only human part? Are there any others out there like me?"

"Statistically speaking," he hedged, counting off on his fingers, "it wouldn't be all that common to find a person, a, who has ADHD, b, who ruptures a cerebral aneurysm and, c, then gets treated with Fibrin-X. That's a very rare set of circumstances that would all have to come together."

"Rare, but not impossible. You gotta tell me, Doc. Am I the only person this ever happened to?"

He hesitated a long time before answering.

"No," he told her finally. "You're not the only one."

"Are the others adults, kids, or teens like me?"

"All of the above."

She closed her eyes, exhaling slowly.

"I knew it," she whispered, more tears threatening to spill down her cheeks. "Did the same thing happen to them that happened to me? Did they all get better too and then get really smart?"

Again, he hesitated.

"They have all shown significant improvement with their stroke and their ADHD, yes. Eventually, we had enough data from those of you that it happened to by accident that we were able take the serendipitous discovery back to animal trials to study it further, on purpose. Eventually, of course, we will use Fibrin-X on ADHD patients even if they haven't had an aneurysm."

"But I thought you told me that nobody even knows what causes ADHD."

"Until now," he replied, his eyes sparkling. "Thanks to patients like you, Alexa, my colleagues and I have managed to crack the code, so to speak. As it turns out, the condition is both chemical and anatomical in nature, similar to depression or obsessive-compulsive disorder. The brain is a marvelous and complicated organ. There's still much about it that no one knows—but our discoveries are going to advance the field of neurology by eons. What we've done is groundbreaking."

"So now you can help other kids like me? Well, like I used to be, at least?"

He nodded.

"Soon, very soon, you'll see that what happened to you was the beginning of what is going to become the cure for ADHD around the world. No longer will it be a condition where the best we can do is manage the symptoms. Now we'll be able to *eradicate* it. Do you understand how important that is?"

"I might, if I knew what 'eradicate' meant."

Dr. Stebbins burst out laughing and surprised Alexa by giving her a hug.

"Sometimes you're so intelligent I forget that you're only fourteen," he said, letting her go, though the warmth of his affection stayed with her, making her feel safe and appreciated. "Eradicated means eliminated. Soon, thanks in part to what's happened to you, we will be able to get rid of ADHD altogether. No one will have to suffer for years the way you did, or spend their life taking drugs with dangerous side effects, just to manage the symptoms. We'll simply diagnose the problem, inject the Fibrin-X or a finely-tuned derivative, the brain will heal, and the ADHD will go away."

"You make it sound simple. Like a dream come true."

"It's only simple at the end, once science has done its part. Once people like you have done your part too."

She thought about that for a moment, feeling somehow brave and important. *Significant.*

"So when can I meet the others?" she asked, her face glowing. "The other teens, like me, who had a stroke and got treated with Fibrin-X and were accidentally cured of their ADHD too?"

Dr. Stebbins smile faded.

"I'm sorry, Alexa, but not anytime soon. We're going to announce our preliminary findings at a symposium next month. It's going to be huge news, really groundbreaking. After that, maybe I can a arrange a get-together. But until then, things must remain very quiet and completely anonymous. There are others out there, but for right now I can't tell you who they are."

The night air was downright chilly as Danny, Luc, and Mr. Bashiri stepped from the doorway of the hotel. Danny was tired but pleased with the work they had done. Better yet, Mr. Bashiri seemed pleased as well.

They walked along the clean and quiet street, parting ways with Luc after a block. He was off to meet the lady from the train for a date.

"Are you certain you can handle all of this equipment by yourself?" Luc asked, carefully taking a strap from his shoulder and placing it on Danny's. His concern was laughable, since Danny was usually stuck carrying most of the stuff anyway.

"I'll manage somehow. Have a good time. Don't do anything I wouldn't do."

Luc stuck his hands in his pockets and started walking.

"Thanks," he said, turning around and taking a few steps backward. "But if I didn't do anything you wouldn't do, I would end up not doing anything at all!"

With a laugh he turned and sprinted off down the street, whistling as he went.

Danny and Mr. Bashiri continued toward the hotel, a comfortable silence between them. Danny wanted to talk, to find some way to ask about the woman at the gala who had referred to Mr. Bashiri's family and his ongoing need to "punish" himself. He was trying to think how to broach the topic when Mr. Bashiri spoke instead.

"I want to talk to you about the photographs you took today, Mr. Watkins," he said. "At the hotel earlier, when we had our break, I went through the digital photos one by one."

"Oh?" Danny asked, trying to keep his voice even. "What did you think?"

"Obviously, you have great technical skills. You also have a good eye, and a knack for composition."

His words sounded like a compliment, but Danny could hear the reservation in his voice.

"Thank you, sir. Were there any problems?"

"Yes, though none you could have anticipated. I should have explained more fully, at the beginning, my intentions with this shoot. I realize now that you wasted a good amount of time taking perfectly decent photographs that will be of no use to us for this article."

Danny could feel his pulse pounding in his neck. What had he done wrong?

"I shall try to explain," Mr. Bashiri continued, his expression thoughtful. "You remember this morning in the break room at GMM, we discussed my technique of reflection and light? I should've gone on to say that I am also using the contrast of cold against warmth."

"I don't quite understand," Danny said, trying not to sound defensive. "I thought you wanted to make Zurich appear wealthy, clean, and abundant. Didn't I do that? The big bleeding globs of meat in the foreground? The doctor with his glinting spatula and five-thousand-dollar gas grill and custom-designed pool behind him? I caught him flipping the burger for the sake of action, but what I didn't anticipate was the absolute glee that would appear on his face at that moment. When we finally got it right, it was a great shot. Maybe you overlooked the best one. We could go through them together. I could show you."

They paused at a light, waiting for the cross signal.

"No, I saw the best one," Mr. Bashiri said. "Again, it was an excellent photo. Just not in keeping with my theme."

He went on to explain that his intention was not simply to contrast the wealth, cleanliness, and state-of-the-art equipment and procedures of Switzerland against the poverty, filth, and behind-the-times tools and methods in the Congo. He said that the Congo offered something that Switzerland did not, and that his intention was to show that as well.

"The difference between the two countries seems tragic, yes, but I also hope to demonstrate how the Congo is so much more real, and much *warmer,* than what we are seeing here."

"Warmer?" Danny asked, wondering what could possibly be "warm" about the suffering of the refugees.

"Spiritually speaking. I always intentionally infuse most of my work with spiritual undertones and even lessons—though such things are not necessarily understood by everyone, at least not on a conscious level. This series is no exception."

Danny braced himself for what Mr. Bashiri had to say, wondering what, exactly, he meant by "spiritual." Was he talking New Age, transcendental stuff, Zen?

"To put it simply," Mr. Bashiri continued, "I am using blue undertones here, as opposed to oranges and browns down there. Cool colors here, warm colors there. The reason I told you to keep the fire on the grill at the level of blue gas was because I am reserving the reds and oranges and yellows for later. The blue pool in the background today was fine. It was the bright red meat in the front, the orange flames flickering at the beef, that created the problem."

"I think I understand," Danny said. "The Zurich shots will be aesthetically pleasing, but it sounds like you intend for the pictures in the Congo to be more emotionally pleasing. Is that correct?"

Mr. Bashiri nodded vehemently.

"You see," the man explained, "there is something very lovely but also very *cold* about the sparkle of this rich city. The refugees in the Congo may be miserable, but there is a realness to their experience that the people here lack. The refugees have more physical problems, yes, but there is also much less there to weigh down their souls."

Danny was silent for a moment, trying to understand how anything about a refugee camp could be preferable to this stunningly beautiful European city.

"Perhaps you would have to be a man of faith to grasp fully the spiritual symbolism," Mr. Bashiri added, reaching into his pocket and pulling out his pipe. "Even the doctors we spoke with today, did you not get the feeling that they are more at peace and happier with themselves down there than they are here? That what they do down there matters more to them than their high-paying jobs and fancy possessions here? It's not just about being fulfilled through altruism or good deeds. I am convinced that when they are among the people of the Congo, even though the work is difficult and the conditions are miserable, the doctors have left behind most of what stands between them and their Maker and are drawn closer to the true heart of God."

Mr. Bashiri paused at a tall, cylindrical trash can and began rapping the pipe sharply on the edge, knocking the ashes and burnt leaves into the receptacle.

"Now that you mention it, I did sense a real fervor in the doctors we spoke with."

"That is their spiritual hunger, my young friend, eager to be filled at the well."

Danny nodded, starting to understand.

"So now do you see? Through the warmth of the photos I will take in the Congo, I am trying to show, primarily, a biblical principle, that 'blessed are the poor in spirit, for they shall inherit the earth.' This is how I give God's messages to the world: through my photographs."

Mr. Bashiri smiled self-consciously, looking almost sorry that he had brought it up.

"Please do not tell your magazine I said that, though, because their agenda is not a spiritual one. Probably, I should not even have told you, but with all of your hard work, I felt you deserved to know. Also, I thought perhaps you would understand what I am saying."

Mr. Bashiri finished tapping out the pipe and they began walking again. From his other pocket, he produced a small, resealable pouch of tobacco, and slowly he used it to fill the pipe.

"Are you a Christian, Mr. Bashiri?"

"Yes, I am," the man replied quietly, after long pause. "And you?"

"*Yes,*" Danny said emphatically. "My faith is the most important thing in my life."

Mr. Bashiri turned to look Danny in the eyes, considering for a long moment. Finally, he nodded solemnly and then spoke.

"I am not surprised," he said. "In fact, now that you tell me this, I recognize that the light of God shines through you, in all that you do."

"And in you as well, sir."

"Just be careful, Mr. Watkins, that you do not confuse personal ambition with God's plan for your life. That was a lesson it took me many years to learn, and by the time I did, it was too late."

Halfway back to Westchester County, Jo decided to check her e-mail, hoping that Danny had been able to get to a computer and write, giving her more details about his trip.

She pulled out her handheld digital assistant and accessed her account, holding her breath as the list of incoming e-mails appeared on the screen line by line. Checking e-mail was usually the most fun part of the day for Jo, that time when she felt connected to Danny despite the distance between them. He couldn't go online off and on all day the way she did and send little notes, but he made up for it by sending her a single, much longer e-mail almost every night. Danny's replies were always a delight, filled with the kinds of visual descriptions that only a photographer could provide. Through his letters Jo could picture his apartment, his office, and much of Paris. He was loving the work but hating the separation from her, enjoying the city but missing his home country, loving the culture but merely enduring much of the food, especially the breakfast.

Now, sadly, there didn't seem to be anything from him, which came as no big surprise, considering that he was busy traipsing around Europe and Africa.

There also wasn't anything from the detective in charge of her case, despite the fact that she had just that morning forwarded him the most recent e-mail from the person she was starting to think of as "Toaster Man." At least her grandmother had the connections to stay on top of things, but Jo missed the communication she was used to with Chief Cooper back home. He always returned her calls right away and did everything he could to help her in times of trouble.

Jo smiled gratefully at the thought. She would gladly trade all of NYC's high tech resources and experienced manpower for just one small-town cop who actually cared.

As they reached the hotel, Danny felt disappointed and elated at the same time. The news that Mr. Bashiri wasn't even going to consider including his photos for *Scene It* was devastating, of course, but once he understood why, at least he was consoled. And the man had been very complimentary of the pictures themselves. Next time, Danny would ask more questions and get more information about the overall thinking and planning of a shoot before setting out to prove himself as an *artiste*.

More importantly, he understood now why he felt such a growing connection between himself and the famous photographer. It wasn't just about professional compatibility, it was about the Holy Spirit, who filled their hearts and their lives.

They were brothers in Christ.

Stepping into the hotel lobby, Danny wanted to find a quiet corner and sit and continue their conversation where it had left off, maybe urging Mr. Bashiri to explain what he meant when he said he learned his lesson "too late." But the photographer was looking very tired, and he said goodnight, suggesting they meet in the café across the street for breakfast at eight in the morning.

"Okay, see you then," Danny replied as the elevator doors opened and Mr. Bashiri stepped inside. "I've got to check something before I go up."

"Very good. See you in the morning."

The elevator doors closed, leaving Danny alone in the empty lobby. He strode to the front desk and asked if there were any messages for their room.

"*Nei*," the man replied after checking, and then he said it again in English. "No."

"Is there a pay phone somewhere nearby?"

The man directed him down the hall and gave him a printed sheet of instructions in several languages, including English, on how to use the phone with a calling card. Danny followed the directions step-by-step, taking a chance on dialing Jo's cell phone number first. Quickly calculating, he realized that it was about 5:00 PM back home. She was probably out in her office, just wrapping things up for the day.

"Hello?" she asked, and suddenly Danny broke into the biggest grin he'd had in a long time.

"You have no idea how sweet it is to hear your beautiful voice."

"Danny!" she gasped, and he could hear her excitement as well. Though they e-mailed every day, they hadn't spoken on the phone in more than a week. Until that moment, he hadn't realized how much he missed being connected in this way.

"Hi, babe," he said. "Am I catching you at a good time?"

"Are you kidding?" she replied. "Anytime is a good time for you to call. I got your message. Where are you now?"

"Still in Zurich," he said. "It's going really well, but it's a lot of work. We'll be here again tomorrow, and then the next morning we leave for Africa."

"Africa," she said breathlessly, sounding very happy for him. "Tell me everything, Danny. I want to hear all about what you've done and what you'll be doing."

"Okay, but first, are you doing okay? I didn't catch you in the middle of making dinner or anything, did I?"

"No, sweetie. I'm in the car."

"Going somewhere fun?"

"Well, actually, I'm on my way back to New York. I'm going to stay at my grandmother's estate for...for a little while."

"Your grandmother's? Why? What did the doctor say? What did the Bronx police say?"

"Oh, I'll e-mail you with all of that. Gran just wanted me to come for a visit. Right now I want to hear about your trip. Tell me all about it. Start at the beginning."

Leaning as far as the wire would stretch, Danny hooked one foot under the side of a nearby green velvet wingback chair. Sliding it toward him, he finally grasped it with his hands, spun it around, and got comfortable.

"Let's see," he said, reviewing the past 24 hours in his mind. "This whole thing started just yesterday, when my friend Luc invited me to dinner…"

Jo listened to Danny's adventures, relieved that it had been easy to deflect the conversation back to him. Really, it just felt so wonderful to hear his voice and share in his excitement and forget all about her own problems for a while that it was almost a relief to pretend that nothing was wrong on her end.

As Danny talked, Jo could tell that this trip really was the chance of a lifetime for him. It sounded as though the photographer, this Kalunga Bashiri fellow, was turning into a mentor and friend, and that the whole trip would end up greatly enhancing Danny's photography and his career.

The more he told her, the more Jo knew that she wouldn't destroy this opportunity of his for anything. At some point down the line, of course, when he finally learned about what had been going on back home at this time, he would be angry with her that she had kept him out of the loop. But as he talked now about all he was experiencing, she decided that her silence now and his resulting anger later would be worth it in the long run. If he knew what was going on here, and that her life was in danger, he would hop on the next plane home—and she couldn't let him do that. The price was too high.

Besides, if he really could have been of significant help to her in some way, then she might consider telling him what was going on. But the truth was, she already had the considerable resources of her grandmother and her parents, a staff at her fingertips, and round-the-clock bodyguard protection. What could Danny give her that she didn't already possess? There was nothing he could bring to the situation except comfort and love, and the need for them wasn't worth the sacrifice he would have to make to give them.

Jo leaned back against the leather seat and looked out of the window, loving the familiar cadence of his voice, growing misty-eyed just picturing him in his excitement, gesturing in all of those cute ways he had and even drumming absentmindedly with his feet against the floor.

He had worked so hard to get where he was. He deserved this.

"Wait, you have to get *how* many shots?" she asked now, laughing. Danny always had turned into a big baby at the doctor's office.

"The number keeps growing!" he exclaimed. "Tonight at the gala, somebody else told me to throw in cholera and typhoid. By the time I get on that airplane, I'm going to feel like a pincushion!"

Smiling, Jo closed her eyes and listened to his voice and tried to imagine that she was there with him now. The thought warmed her heart and made all of her current problems seem very far away indeed—at least until he had to hang up.

"This is the only pay phone around," he told her regretfully, "and there are two other people sort of hovering off to the side, waiting to use it."

"I understand."

"I probably need to get on to bed, anyway. It's late here." He went on to tell her that he loved her, and that he'd call again in a few days.

"If you can't reach me on my cell, try my grandmother's house," she replied, waiting as he grabbed a pen to write the number down. "I'm not sure how long I'll be staying there."

As they said their final goodbyes and hung up the phone, Jo felt a warm rush of love spread from her head to her toes. She leaned her head back and watched the world go by, allowing that warmth to hold the realities of her own situation at bay for the rest of the drive.

14

Danny was sound asleep, dreaming of Jo, when a loud "thunk" woke him up. Confused, he reached for the bedside light and flicked it on, surprised to see a half-dressed Luc sprawled across the hotel room floor.

"Whoa!" Danny cried, swinging his legs over the bed and sitting up. "You okay, man?"

"Dah-neeee!" Luc replied, rolling over onto his back, completely drunk. "Why is ze room spinning around in ze circles?"

Taking a deep breath, Danny ran a hand across his face and then reached down to help his friend. Apparently, too much alcohol made the Frenchman sound just like Pepé Le Pew.

"You're drunk, buddy. Can you sit up if I help you?"

Together, they managed to get Luc from the floor to the bed. There, he laid across the top of the covers in only his tuxedo pants and cummerbund.

"Where's your shirt and jacket and tie?" Danny asked, surprised that he didn't see them anywhere in the room.

"In the bathroom, I think. I hung them on a hook on the back of the door."

Grunting, Danny pulled slacks on over his shorts and padded down the hall to the shared bathroom. Sure enough, there he found Luc's clothes, hanging messily from the shower head. He carried them back to the room and closed and locked their door.

"Is there anything else you lost along the way?" Danny asked, patting the inside jacket pocket of the tuxedo, relieved to find Luc's wallet and cell phone tucked safely in there. Thank goodness his clothes hadn't hung in the bathroom all night, where anyone could have rifled through them.

"*Non*," his friend said, raising a hands in front of his face and studying them as though they were foreign objects. "I have lost nothing but my pride."

Wearily, Danny helped Luc off with his shoes, and then he moved the trash can next to his bed.

"If you need to puke, the trash can's right here, okay?"

Danny then climbed back into his own bed and turned off the light, desperate to slip back into sleep, but Luc wasn't having any of it.

"Do you sink I am a bad person, Dah-nee?" he asked, his accent heavy and slurred.

"No, of course not."

"Some people must think I am," he continued. "They keep throwing money at me and asking me to do things. Terrible things."

Danny opened one eye, looking over at his friend in the dark.

"What happened?" he asked. "Did you have problems with the Dutch girl?"

"*Non*. She was *mignonne comme tout*. It was all the phone calls, the interruptions. She finally left me at the bar and told me to call her when I was ready to give her my full attention."

Danny smiled, understanding how she must have felt, remembering all of the calls Luc had taken today during the photo shoot.

"Who keeps calling you? What do they want?"

Luc didn't answer Danny's questions, though he did keep talking.

"You cannot trust a person in this world, you know? Even the people you think you should be able to. Even the ones who are closest to you."

Danny didn't reply, torn between wanting to get back to sleep and wanting to know what had made his friend so upset.

"Watch your back, my friend, is all I can say. Watch…your…back."

Danny exhaled slowly, wishing Luc would either come out with it or be quiet so he could go to sleep.

"Why should I watch my back, Luc?"

There was no reply for a long moment, and then the snoring began, loud and long. Danny put the pillow over his ears, counting the minutes until Luc went back to France and he could get some sleep.

Alexa was just slipping the black cap over her hair when she heard rustling out in the hallway. *Oh, great.* There were soft voices and lots of footsteps, and she had a feeling that the old lady's granddaughter was back from wherever she had gone for the day. Alexa had asked why Jo wasn't at dinner, but all the old lady said was that Jo was out and she'd be back later.

That time must have come. Now Alexa would have to wait even longer to get out of there. She moved more quietly, tucking every loose strand of hair under her cap, wondering when the coast would be clear for her escape. It was early still, not even 8:00 yet. But this time she really couldn't wait until everyone was asleep to make her getaway.

The rustling seemed to die down after a while, but then, suddenly, there was a soft knock at Alexa's door. She froze, her heart pounding.

"Yeah?" she called, trying to make herself sound sleepy, as she frantically ripped off her "escape" clothing and pulled on her T-shirt and pajama bottoms instead.

"Oh, I'm sorry, were you asleep?" a female voice called through the door. "It's Jo. Mrs. Bosworth's granddaughter. Never mind. We can talk in the morning. Sorry I bothered you."

Quickly, Alexa shoved her backpack, tools, and clothes under the bed. Then she opened the door. She didn't want anyone getting suspicious of what she was planning to do tonight for any reason. Better that she go ahead and show her face and act as though nothing was wrong.

"That's okay. What's up?" Alexa asked, seeing that Jo had already gone halfway down the hall, where she was talking softly with Fernando and some big guy. In Jo's hand was a leash, which led to a dog.

Alexa gasped. A dog? In this fancy house? A *dog!*

Jo turned back, saw Alexa's gape, and smiled. The two men left, and then Jo and the dog walked toward Alexa, who took one step backward, into her room.

"Hi, Alexa. I just wanted to let you know about Chewie here. He'll be staying in my room, so if you hear any growling or barking or anything, I didn't want you to be scared."

Alexa's eyes were wide.

The dog looked harmless, like a pet. But where she came from, most folks couldn't afford pets. The only people she knew with dogs were the dealers who had dobermans or pit bulls.

"Does it bite?"

Jo laughed softly.

"Are you kidding?" she said, kneeling down next to the big brown creature and putting an arm around him. "He's a big sweetheart. He wouldn't hurt a fly. Though he might eat a spider or two."

Alexa wasn't so sure. He had a cute face and all, but he was breathing heavily, his mouth open, and those teeth looked really sharp.

"Are you afraid of dogs, honey? I'm sorry, I didn't think about that. You don't have to worry. He's not going to be loose."

"He's not?"

"No, during the day he'll be outside, mostly, out behind the carriage house. Muck put up a temporary fence for him. At night, when he comes inside, he'll be in my room."

That didn't sound so bad. At least he wouldn't be out there at night, when he might hear Alexa sneaking past and start barking.

"You can pet him if you want."

Alexa thought about it and shook her head.

"Maybe later."

Jo stood, brushing off her knees.

"That's fine," she said. "Oh, and I brought you something. Just a sec."

Taking the dog with her, she disappeared into the Rose room and came back out a moment later with a little plastic package. Alexa took it from her and unwrapped it to find a pair of neon green socks.

"What's this?"

Jo shrugged.

"I just thought they were cool, like something a teenager would wear. Not that I know a whole lot of teenagers."

They were kind of cool, but Alexa sure wasn't going to put them on right now, as she had a feeling they would glow in the dark.

"Thanks," she said, feeling awkward. The people in this house were always giving her gifts, one of those rich-people habits like talking about investments or eating with cloth napkins. Alexa liked it, of course, but she still hadn't grown used to it.

"Anyway," Jo said, "I'm sorry I woke you up. I think I'll hit the sack too. I just didn't want you to wonder what was going on if Chewie decided to bark or something."

"Yeah. Thanks. Goodnight."

"Goodnight."

Alexa closed the door, tossing the socks onto the dresser and listening for the thud and click of Jo's closing door. Once she heard it, Alexa went to the bed, pulled out everything she had shoved underneath, and slowly changed back into her getaway clothes, wondering how long she would have to wait tonight before it would be safe to make her move.

Jo felt terrible. Here she was with a labrador retriever and the poor girl across the hall was scared of dogs! Jo knew she'd have to take things slowly, showing Alexa how sweet Chewie was, and how fun. Maybe tomorrow they could play catch in the yard with his big new bone. He was sure to win over the girl's heart eventually. And at least Alexa seemed to like the socks.

Jo began to unpack, sliding her clothes onto hangers or slipping them into drawers. She put the suitcases with the stuff from her office near the door and left them alone for now, deciding that she would talk to her grandmother in the morning to see if she could have a little corner in either the newly enhanced carriage house or the studio to do her work. That was one good thing about living on an estate—there was always room for whatever you wanted to do.

Jo put down food and water for Chewie, and soon after, Consuela appeared at the door with a tray of food for Jo, which she set up on the table in the corner, as she had the night before.

"We've got to stop meeting like this."

"It is not a problem," Consuela replied. "We knew you would be late, so I kept your dinner warm in the oven."

Unfortunately, Jo didn't have much of an appetite. When she had eaten all she could, she put the tray in the hall, said goodnight to her bodyguard, came back into the room, and opened up her laptop. Glad to see that the house had wireless Internet, she went online and typed out a careful reply to the e-mail she had received that morning from Toaster Man. Although the police might disagree, Jo decided the best way to handle him was to sound as though she was making friends with him. The more she could get him to say, after all, the more clues she might have for discovering his identity.

It was more than the police had done so far. According to Jo's grandmother, who had just been turning in for the night when Jo arrived, she had managed to get an update on the case but it wasn't looking good, with no new leads or breaks. Even Jo's sweater had no clear fingerprints

on it at all, which the lab blamed primarily on the type of fabric. Bradford was doing a little better in the hospital. Though he had been questioned by the police, he was so out of it that his answers had made little
sense and had not shed any new light on things.

Exhausted, Jo got ready for bed and slipped under the covers, Chewie
settling down at her feet. She closed her eyes, glad that he seemed to be
adapting well to his temporary new home. She prayed she would remain
adaptable too.

Jo was almost asleep when she heard Chewie growl, but she had a
feeling that he was just bothered by the sound of the bodyguards' shift
change in the hallway outside of her door. Jo put a hand on his back and
spoke in soothing tones until he quieted down. Then, not hearing any
more sounds, she closed her eyes again and finally drifted off to sleep.

To: anon6592@mailnet.com

From: JoTulip@tipsfromtulip.com

Date: Thursday, May 1, 7:43 PM

Subject: Question for www.tipsfromtulip.com

Dear Trying,

Thank you for the warnings about my life being in danger. It was just hard to believe until I saw it for myself. Trust me, I won't make that same mistake again. But I do appreciate your concern.

I have been thinking about your toaster oven questions, and I've decided to run some cleaning tests so I can give you some really good advice on this before you buy. (Or, if you've already bought by now, I can teach you how to do a better job of keeping this one clean for longer.) I keep thinking that the reason toaster ovens are so much harder to keep clean than regular toasters is because of the various things we cook in them, such as melting cheese, buttered toast, greasy meats, etc. The machines may be small, but since they never seem to come with a self-cleaning feature, they're also harder to clean than full-size ovens. It's a real conundrum.

Have you been shopping online and just looking at pictures or actually going into the stores to try them out? Because I would encourage you to get a good look at what you think you want, in person, before you buy. Sometimes a picture doesn't tell the whole story. If you're in the Kreston area, there are several stores I could recommend. Just let me know. And I'll keep you posted on my cleaning tests.

With regards,

Jo Tulip

15

If she hadn't dropped her flashlight as she was closing the window, Alexa would have made it out of there without a sound. As it was, at least the thing landed on her foot first with just a soft thud, but then it rolled across the stone floor of the veranda, making a bit of a clatter.

Alexa crouched down under the window, pressed herself against the wall, and waited in case anyone had heard and tried to take a look. At least the dog didn't bark.

After counting to one hundred, she crawled several feet to retrieve the light, slipped it carefully into her pocket, and then took the chance to peek in through the hall window. There was a man sitting in a chair outside of Jo's room, only it wasn't Fernando this time but some big, muscle guy. At first Alexa thought maybe they were keeping Jo prisoner in the Rose room at night, but then she realized that it must be the opposite, that the man was there to keep other people out, almost like a bodyguard. Alexa wasn't sure why that might be necessary, but she didn't have time to worry about it now.

Silently, she crept to the back stairs and went down, pausing at the bottom to listen for the sounds of the night. Having spent her entire life in the city, she didn't like the quiet out here when it got dark. Where were the distant sirens, the honking horns, the families yelling at each other a couple of houses down? Here, instead, there were just crickets and rustling trees, and sometimes far in the distance other animal sounds she didn't quite recognize.

Now, however, she heard something else, and it sounded like voices. Men's voices, from around the front of the house. She could smell cigarette smoke too.

Crouching, Alexa pressed herself against the bottom of the banister and listened as hard as she could. Finally, she heard one of them say "back to work," and then feet crunching on gravel. Suddenly, the beam of a strong flashlight clicked on, illuminating the curve of the driveway out front. Alexa held her breath, remaining perfectly still and watching as the person holding the flashlight appeared in view, walking along the driveway toward the garage, playing the beam of light out in front of him. She couldn't quite tell in the dark, but it looked as though the man had on a uniform of some kind.

Was he a cop?

Torn about what to do, she decided to go back up the stairs and look over the front balcony to see if she could spot the man he'd been talking to. Sure enough, once she crept up to the front of the house and peered over the side, she was directly above a guy who was just standing there, hands on his hips, surveying the driveway in front of him. There was a walkie-talkie crackling softly from his hip, and then suddenly another voice came out of the static, saying, "All clear around the garage. I'm going to sweep the perimeter."

This man took the walkie-talkie from his belt, pressed a button, and said, simply, "Ten four." Then he put it back and just kept standing there.

Alexa studied his uniform and finally decided that he was a security guard. They were both security guards.

Great. Just what she needed. Added security. Alexa couldn't imagine why that might be necessary, but around rich people, she had learned, you just never knew. The old lady had probably bought some expensive new diamond necklace or something and they needed to guard it.

Whatever it was, Alexa felt certain it had nothing to do with her—though it sure was going to make it harder to get out of here.

She hesitated for a moment and then made her decision. Creeping back down the stairs, she stayed next to the banister until she spotted the man's flashlight far in the distance out back. If he was the one who was sweeping the perimeter, then she needed to go now, behind him, so she could make her escape before he came around again.

Alexa clenched her teeth and took off, running through the shadows to a big tree near the garage, then running from tree to tree all the way to the fence along the pasture. She climbed over, devastated when she ripped a hole in her leggings at the knee. From there, she could see the flashlight beam a lot better, and from what she could tell, the guy really was just walking around the edge of the property along the stone wall.

He was far enough away for her to take off running, which she did as best she could, terrified about crossing the wide, open expanse of the pasture, knowing her weak right foot might give out on her at any time. The foot held, though, and except for nearly tripping once or twice, she made it past the old well and all the way to the stable.

The building was creepy and dark, but she hugged it tightly as she made her way along the side, looking for signs of the road that was supposed to be here, the one on the map she'd found yesterday. Behind the stables, things were kind of overgrown and weedy, but once she spotted two rusted old handles, she realized that they were connected to two huge double doors. Guessing that the driveway led right to those doors, she walked directly from there to the stone wall, thrilled beyond belief when she finally spotted a big gate that was almost completely overgrown with ivy.

Making her way through the undergrowth and praying there weren't snakes in the grass, she ran her hands all along the gate, moving the ivy out of the way until she found a rusted old padlock hanging from the center. It was locked up tight, but now that she'd made it this far, she wasn't about to let that stop her. Her biggest reservation was simply that she hated to mess up her clothes. She had worn one of her favorite outfits tonight, not any of that classy, expensive stuff the old lady had bought but something Alexa had brought back with her the last time she snuck out: black leggings, a supershort jean skirt, a tight, black tank top, and a jean jacket.

Careful not to stretch the hole she'd already torn at the knee, she stepped up on the lowest wrought iron rail of the gate and tried to figure out how she might climb over. She never would have been able to make it over the top of the stone wall, but the gate might be a different story. It had three horizontal bars reinforcing the vertical ones, and she used them like a ladder, mustering every bit of strength she had to pull herself up.

Maneuvering herself over the top of the gate wasn't quite so easy, especially because her right hand was starting to feel very shaky and weak. Concentrating, she simply focused on not falling, and eventually she was able to swing herself over the top and come back down the other side. When her feet touched the dirt, she took a deep breath and said a prayer of thanks that she had made it.

Then she stood up straight, brushed the grass and leaves from her clothes, and tried to figure out where she was. Sure enough, there was a road on this side of the gate, but it was old and dusty and obviously hadn't been used for a while, at least not right there. Looking up the road, she could see that it was lined on each side by split rail fences and then pastures. She had a feeling that the road ran between two different estates because she could see two different barns in the distance, one on each side of the road.

Taking her chances, Alexa simply started walking up the dirt road, hoping it would lead to the main road where she expected it to. If it did, there was a bus stop just a little way down, used primarily by all of the hired help who came into this rich area each morning and left each evening. According to the schedule she had pulled off of the Internet, a bus would be along there in about 20 minutes. She started walking, dirty and sweaty, proud of what she'd pulled off, and not even all that scared anymore.

She reached the bus stop without incident, and though it took her a while to get where she was going, after two transfers and countless stops, Alexa was almost there. She finally had fixed herself up the best she could along the way, brushing the dirt and grass off of her clothes, adding a wide metal belt and some chunky plastic jewelry, teasing up her hair and putting on more eyeliner. Now that she was close, she was really nervous. Getting there had taken so long that she was afraid they might all be in bed by now.

The bus pulled to a stop, but as Alexa walked up the aisle to get off, the driver said, "You sure this is your stop, kid?"

His voice sounded nice, but when she looked at him to reply, she could see disdain in his eyes. Was it really that much of a stretch to think she could live in a rich neighborhood like this one?

Maybe it was.

"I'm here to visit my aunt."

He just sat there, still looking suspicious, until she added, "She's the maid at the Peterson's, fourth house on the right."

That seemed to placate him. He swung open the door and she climbed off, wishing a spring would pop in his seat and give him a good spanking. What a jerk.

The street was quiet once the bus rattled away. Alexa pulled the printout from her backpack, studied it for a minute, and then put it back and started walking. By her calculations, she only had to go two blocks up and one block over and she would be there.

From what Alexa could tell in the dark, the neighborhood was really nice, with huge lawns and pretty houses. The people around here weren't as loaded as the old lady, of course, but they weren't hurting, either. Alexa didn't know why, but she had expected the Finches to be poor, like her.

She just hoped she had the right place. After dinner she had gone online, pretending to do her homework but really trying to find out more about the information on the pink Phone Message paper she had taken from Dr. Stebbins' office. She knew there was a website where she could enter a phone number and it would respond with a name and an address. Sure enough, the number she typed in gave her the last name of Finch and an address in a town just over the state line in Connecticut.

With that information in hand, Alexa had looked up the bus schedules between there and here, a challenge made more complicated by the fact that not as many buses ran at night as they did during the day. Eventually, she figured out some connections that would work.

Now that she had made it this far, there wasn't much more to go. As she walked, she tried to focus on how good it felt just to be *free*. Nobody on the whole planet knew where she was right now, which was a strange and exhilarating feeling. Before she went to live with the old lady, she was often out on her own, with nobody knowing or caring. But things were different now. She mattered now. In a way, she realized, maybe it was worth the trade-off.

Alexa finally reached the Finches' house, disappointed to see that there were almost no lights on at all. She started up the front walk, wishing she could peek in the windows but knowing that in a nice area like this, if someone spotted her sneaking around, they would call the cops first and ask questions later.

Fortunately, as she neared the door, she spotted a flickering glow coming from a room off to the side, and she realized it must be a television. Taking her chances, she stepped off the walkway and crept over to the window, relieved that her actions didn't turn on a motion-sensitive light or kick off some kind of security system. All was dark and quiet except for the television inside. The bottoms of several of the windows were open by a few inches, and the sounds of the show floated through.

Through the window, she could see two couches in an "L" facing a giant, flat screen TV. Looking at the backs of people's heads, she counted three people lounging along the couches, one of them eating popcorn.

She just watched them for a few minutes until the one with the popcorn stood up and started to leave the room. It was a guy, about 16.

"Are you going in the kitchen?" a girl's voice asked. "Get me a soda, would you?"

"Get your own soda, moron," he replied, throwing a handful of popcorn at the girl's hair.

She sat up, angry, shaking the kernels out of her long blond locks.

"Ethan!" she yelled. "You jerk!"

Ethan. This was the right house. Alexa knew it in her very bones.

Summoning all of her nerve, she went to the front door and knocked, so lightly at first that she was sure no one had heard it. She knocked again, louder this time, until the girl yelled, "Ethan, get the door, would you? You're right there."

Alexa heard the click of several locks twisting, and then the heavy door swung open to reveal the boy. Through the window, he had looked kind of cute, but now, up close, she realized that there was something wrong with his face. Studying his features, she decided that one whole side sort of hung slack, not a lot, but enough to make his eye look droopy and his mouth a little crooked.

Just like a person who'd had a stroke.

"Yeah?" he said, not seeming at all surprised that there was a teenage stranger standing on his front step.

"Ethan Finch?"

"Uh-huh."

"My name is Alexa. I think we need to talk."

He opened the door further, but as she started to step inside, the girl came running, blocking her way.

"Don't be stupid, Ethan. You don't just let anybody in. Especially when Mom and Dad aren't home."

The girl stood there next to the boy, and Alexa realized that they were about the same age. They were also the same size and height, and they looked a lot alike, though the girl didn't have the droopy face like the boy did. She wondered if they were twins.

"What do you want?" the girl asked, scowling.

"Are you Emma?"

"Yeah?"

"I came to talk to you guys. I'm a patient of Dr. Stebbins."

She thought that might get a reaction out of them or something, but they didn't even seem surprised. The girl just shook her head and said that they weren't allowed to let anybody in when their parents weren't home.

"When do you think they'll be back?" Alexa asked, wishing they could have this entire conversation without any adults present.

"I don't know," the girl replied, shrugging. "A couple more hours, I guess. They went to a party."

Suddenly, another girl appeared in the doorway as well, obviously a younger sister. Ethan shooed her away, telling her to go back and watch the movie.

"Maybe we could talk outside," Alexa offered after the kid was gone. "Do your parents have a rule about that?"

The two of them looked at each other and then back at her.

"I guess not," the girl said, shrugging.

Together, they both came out and hovered on the front stoop. Feeling awkward, Alexa stepped back down to the walkway, facing them.

"It's kind of hard to explain why I'm here," she said, wondering why she hadn't thought about what she would say once she found herself in this hard-earned position. How could she put it? *I'm looking for people like me, people who are also medical freaksters?* She didn't want to scare them off. "Just to make sure I'm at the right place, did you guys by any chance have a medical problem, in your brain?"

"I did," the guy answered. "Last year. I fell off my horse and busted an aneurysm."

"Was it in the circle of Willis?"

"No, it was near the barn."

"In your brain, I mean," Alexa said. "The circle of Willis."

Both kids just stared at her blankly.

"Okay. You had a stroke, right?"

He nodded.

"Then, did you get an IV drip of a new drug, one that worked really well?"

"Yeah. Fiber-something. It had side effects."

"Like what?"

"It made me nauseous and kind of jittery."

"Don't be stupid, Ethan," Emma said, elbowing him in the ribs. "She's talking about your ADHD."

"Oh, yeah, it cured my ADHD."

Alexa's face lit up.

"Mine too!" she cried. "How about you, Emma?"

"I don't have ADHD. Never did." Alexa thought about the message that she had found, *Mrs. Finch called about the scan on Emma.* "But they thought I might have an aneurysm too," the girl added, "just one that hadn't busted yet. They made me get a brain scan. Our little sister too. Turns out, we were both fine. No problems at all."

"How's your recovery been, Ethan?" Alexa asked. "Do you get physical therapy?"

"Yeah, twice a week. Sometimes when my leg gets really tired I have to wear a brace on it or use a crutch. That helps."

"Do you go horseback riding?"

He shook his head.

"Dr. Stebbins said not for another month, not until after the big symphony thing."

"Symphony?" Alexa asked, her pulse surging. "What instrument do you play? Did it make you gifted too?"

"Gifted?"

"You know, music, art, all of that. The Fibrin-X made you really good at it now, right, even though you didn't do any of that before?"

"If he's good at art or music, I'm a rocket scientist," Emma said.

"But what about the symphony? You said you had a symphony thing."

"Not me," he replied, rolling his eyes. "Dr. Stebbins."

Dr. Stebbins? Alexa considered for a moment and then spoke.

"You mean the *symposium?*"

"Yeah, that's it. Symphony, symposium, one of those."

Alexa nodded, a black sort of despair creeping heavily across her chest. This wasn't what she had expected at all.

Why didn't the drug make them smart, like it did me? Why didn't it make them talented?

Alexa realized suddenly that she was done here.

"Hey, listen," she said, "would you guys mind not telling anybody that I came here tonight? I kind of snuck out."

"Sure," the boy said.

"Why?" asked the girl. "I mean, why'd you come?"

How could she even reply? *Because I needed to know that I'm not the only medical miracle on the planet? Because I wanted to find like minds? Because I wanted to form the Circle of Willis?*

"I guess 'cause I thought I was the only person, ever, who was cured of ADHD," she said finally. "Then I found out today that there were others too. I just wanted…I just wanted to meet you. Sometimes I feel kind of isolated. Like a weirdo."

"Yeah, well, Ethan was already a weirdo, so there's nothing new there!" the girl cackled, poking her brother again in the ribs. "At least he's not hyper anymore, but he's still dumb."

"Hey, I'm not the one who made straight D's in eighth grade, moron," he said to his sister.

"Yeah, just 'cause the teachers felt sorry for you so they threw in a few C's, moron."

They told Alexa goodbye and then continued to bicker all the way back into the house. She waited until they had shut the door. Then she turned and started running.

She ran all the way to the bus stop.

By the time the next bus came, it was almost midnight, and for some reason she couldn't stop shaking, even though it wasn't really all that cold outside. When she made the transfer at the big station, there was a bus leaving for Newark, and impulsively she got on that one instead. Maybe she would feel better if she went home for a while—to her real home.

It took another hour to get across the river, through Newark, and into her town. Despite how late it was, though, things were hopping. Almost as soon as she started walking down the main drag, she spotted a couple of the guys from the Grave Cave.

"Well, if it isn't the magical disappearing act," one of them called. "What happened to you, Trip?"

"What do you mean?" she asked, flashing her old smile. Alexa couldn't remember the guy's name, but she always had thought he was cute.

"I mean, where you been? It's like you went into the hospital and you never came back."

Alexa shrugged, trying to act cool about it.

"I'm livin' with a guardian now, but I been back, once or twice."

"Yeah, but not to stay."

She took a few steps toward him, one hand on her hip.

"Why are you asking? You miss me?"

The other guys burst out laughing, poking him and whistling.

"We can use another runner, is all," he said, his face flushing bright red. "Then again, we need a runner, not a tripper, Trip."

His lip curled in a sneer, and Alexa realized he was making fun of her. Running was what she'd been doing the night she tripped on the railroad tracks, hit the ground, and ruptured the aneurysm.

Before she could think of a reply, someone else called her name from down the street. She turned to see three of her girls heading her way. They wouldn't make fun of her. They were her friends.

After a lot of squealing and hugging, the four girls linked arms and set off. They walked toward the end of the street to an old, abandoned factory that had once upon a time manufactured caskets and coffins—hence the nickname, the "Grave Cave." The building was huge and cavernous, and even though there were "Condemned" signs all over it, kids were in there almost every night. Most went to deal or make or buy drugs or get high, but some of them, like Alexa, just went to hang out, shoot the breeze, and sometimes pick up a little extra cash as a runner. Before her accident, the going rate was fifty bucks to make deliveries to the corner and a hundred and fifty to go the four blocks over to Creston Street.

Situated right along the old railroad yard, Creston Street was sort of the dividing line between the good part of town and the bad. That was as far as some of the rich people were willing to go to buy their drugs, since they didn't want to risk taking their Corvettes and BMWs into the poorer areas. The night of her last delivery, Alexa had been told to look for an indigo blue Jaguar parked just across the tracks, near the rusted old caboose.

She had spotted it and was almost to the car when she tripped on an uneven metal rail and fell. Next thing she knew, she was in a hospital with the world's worst headache and an IV stuck in her arm, her right side completely useless and numb. Of course, nothing in her life had been the same since. All they kept telling her over the next few days as she began to recover was how lucky she was: lucky to have gotten to the hospital so fast, lucky to be given a newly-approved medication, lucky that the neurologist treating her was working with an expert in the field of stroke recovery, the man most responsible for the new medication, the great Dr. Stebbins himself.

Yeah, they all thought she was lucky.

"Yo, you seen your mom lately? She's messed up, girlfriend."

"She's always messed up," Alexa replied nonchalantly, despite the shudder of fear that ran through her. "What'd she do now?"

"I heard she ran out of veins so she started injecting into her eye. Like right in her eyeballs."

"Ewww," the other girls squealed.

That set them off, talking about all the gross places a person could use to get drugs directly into their system. Alexa was quiet, glad when they reached the Grave Cave and had to stop talking as they went inside.

Even before she stepped into the building, Alexa could smell the familiar, acrid burning of pot, mixed with the stench of body odor and urine. They squeezed in through the busted doorway and made their way past the sleaziest part of the building, the area where there were always dark shapes on the floor. Some were kids who had passed out from drink or drugs, but most of them were just homeless people who were sleeping. No matter how many times Alexa walked through there, she always expected one of the lifeless forms to wake up, reach out a hand, and grab her by the ankles.

Finally, the four girls reached the stairs without incident and went up to the second level, where the guys mostly worked the phones. If she held her nose, closed her eyes, and just listened, Alexa thought the place could be mistaken for any office, any business. They spoke of shipments and deliveries and profit margins. The only difference was, if the lookouts up on the roof pressed the buzzer, these guys could close up shop and be out of the building without a trace in less than a minute.

"You girls wanna do some running?" one of the guys called out to them as they went past.

"Not tonight, hon. We're just going up top."

They took the stairs two more flights—past the guys with their test tubes and chemicals and hot plates—climbed out a huge, open window, and used the outside fire escape to reach the roof. The roof was where Alexa liked to be. Up here, nobody was allowed to get high because they had to keep their eyes peeled for the cops. Instead, they mostly sat around and watched the streets down below and passed the time together by talking. Alexa had a spot she liked to sit, leaning against an old exhaust chimney. But instead of watching for cops, she would tilt her head back to gaze up at the stars. She loved the stars.

Of course, in the old days, she could never sit still for long. Usually, she'd get bored with the sky pretty soon and start throwing spit bombs at the other buildings or braiding somebody's hair or making up jokes and songs about the teachers at school or doing whatever else passed the time.

Now, after greeting more of her old friends, she claimed the familiar spot by the chimney, sat down, and looked up at the sky. She realized she couldn't see nearly as many stars from here as she could at the old lady's place. Here, there was so much light coming up from the city that it blotted out all but the brightest planets. She wondered why she never realized that before—and why she used to be willing to settle for so much less than what was really out there.

Alexa sat for a long time, an hour or so, just listening to the conversations that swirled around her, contributing to the talk once in a while herself. Somehow, it all seemed so inane, so wasteful. Was this really how she used to spend most of her time? Sitting on the roof of a giant drug factory and hanging out with a bunch of losers?

Slowly, she realized something, and with that knowledge came a strange lightness in the pit of her stomach. She really *was* lucky.

Tripping on that train track and blowing the aneurysm in her brain was the single best thing that ever could have happened to her.

Danny was up and dressed and ready for the day before Luc was even out of bed. Despite Danny's proddings, however, the Frenchman refused to move at all, until finally Danny told him that if he hadn't made it downstairs by the time they were finished with breakfast, they would be taking the car without him and Luc would just have get to GMM on his own.

Mr. Bashiri was just stepping off the elevator into the lobby as Danny came down the stairs. He greeted the photographer, who was looking crisp and fresh in cotton khaki shirt and pants. As Danny locked the equipment into the car and they walked to the café together, Danny told him that Luc was running late and would be joining them later.

Breakfast was a quick and tasty array of fresh fruit and pastries, eaten at an outdoor table in the early morning sunshine. Luc still hadn't shown up by the time they were finished eating, so Danny took the wheel of the van himself, relieved to find that it wasn't difficult to get the hang of driving in Zurich. Fortunately, he had paid enough attention on their previous maneuverings that he was able to find GMM's headquarters without even needing to consult the directions. He parked in their private lot and they went inside to find that the place was already buzzing with activity and excitement.

He realized that it must be this way every time GMM sent off a fresh batch of doctors to a foreign location. Tomorrow's contingent was actually going to be big, with not just the doctors but also a number of nurses and aides and even a couple of dentists—not to mention a certain pair of photographers. On top of that, this afternoon the GMM staffers would be packing the plane with tons of equipment—medical instruments and medicines and other supplies. Danny was looking forward to photographing that, or at least observing Mr. Bashiri as he photographed it. Now that Danny fully understood the man's artistic intentions, he thought he could learn a lot by seeing how they were carried out.

Danny carried their equipment into the warehouse area, where a number of people were busily moving among the supplies, checking off lists, and taking an inventory. With Danny's help, Mr. Bashiri quietly went to work, assembling the cameras and then capturing the scene on film.

"I had a thought," Danny said to the photographer after a time, hoping it wouldn't be too forward of him to make a suggestion.

"Yes?"

"How about a bird's eye view from the top of that ladder, with a supertight ap and an extended shutter speed?"

Mr. Bashiri considered his suggestion for a moment and then nodded, understanding that what Danny was suggesting would create an interesting perspective where all of the boxes would remain sharply in focus but the people would appear on the film as a bunch of blurs moving among them. It also helped that the boxes were gray and the people all wore blue GMM shorts—two colors that were in keeping with the theme of "coldness."

"Yes," Mr. Bashiri said finally, adding some thoughts about the settings. "I like that idea very much."

Stifling a grin, Danny set up an unused ladder that had been propped against the wall, climbed up with the camera, a cable release, and a tabletop tripod, and went to work. He didn't know if the pictures would come out quite like he expected, but he did know that he'd never had so much fun in his life—and that he was thankful to his very core for the opportunity to get a second chance.

Alexa told her friends that she had to leave, and then she headed back down alone, this time using the fire escape all the way. It creaked and moaned as she went, but at least she didn't have to walk through the first floor again. And except for a few broken steps, it was safe enough.

Once on the ground, she dusted herself off, rearranged her backpack, and started walking toward her mom's apartment. Probably she wouldn't even say hello, but it was hard to be this close and not even peek inside. She'd be seeing her mom on Friday anyway, since a visitation weekend was coming up.

Alexa had just reached the corner of her street when she spotted her Uncle Rick. He wasn't really her uncle, just one of her mother's ex-boyfriends. But of all the guys who'd been in and out of her life that way, Uncle Rick was the only one who ever seemed to care about Alexa. Tall and skinny with spiked-up hair and both arms covered in tattoos, he wasn't handsome, exactly, but he had a nice smile. Even after he and her mom had broken up, probably two years ago, he tried to stay in touch with Alexa as much as he could. She had heard he'd moved away, across the river, so she couldn't imagine what he was doing back here, sitting on the stoop in front of a bar by himself, smoking a cigarette.

"Uncle Rick?"

He looked up and broke into a wide grin.

"Alexabear!" he cried, standing up to give her a hug. "What's happening, kid?"

She wrapped her arms around him and held on tight, thinking he was the closest thing to a dad she'd ever had.

"How come you're not any taller, squirt?" he teased, patting her on the top of the head.

"How come you're not any fatter, slim?" she replied, poking him in the stomach.

Laughing, they sat side by side on the concrete step, and for the first time all night Alexa didn't even feel cold anymore. They talked for a while, but from the things he said, Alexa realized that something about him had changed.

It wasn't until he started to apologize to her for some long-forgotten hurt—okay, he passed out and fell on her seventh-grade science fair project and crushed it the night before it was due, and she'd never really forgiven or forgotten—that she realized what was up.

"You doing a twelve-step program, Uncle Rick?"

"Yeah," he said, smiling sheepishly. "It works if you work it."

"So why you hanging out in front of a bar?"

"Just waiting here for your mom," he said, and in his eyes Alexa could see a lot of pain. Her mom did that to people, gave them pain. "She wasn't ready to leave, but I didn't think I should wait inside. Too tempting."

"I'm proud of you."

Though he seemed touched by her words, he shook his head, lighting his next cigarette off the one he'd been smoking.

"Don't be proud. I've done a lot more things wrong than I've done right."

He flicked the smoldering cigarette butt into the gutter.

"But isn't that what the twelve steps are all about? Starting fresh? Getting another chance?"

He inhaled deeply on the new smoke, peering at her through squinted eyes.

"How'd you get so wise at fourteen?" he asked as he exhaled.

She held her breath until the smoke dissipated.

"I know all about second chances," she said. "I'm a living example of a second chance."

16

Danny was beginning to feel embarrassed. They were nearly finished with the warehouse photos and Luc still hadn't shown up. Mr. Bashiri brushed off Danny's apologies, focusing instead on a discussion about which equipment they would be taking with them on the next leg of the trip, and which pieces they would be shipping back to Paris. It would have been nice to bring everything to the Congo, but that simply wasn't prudent. Since they were flying down on the GMM jet, the less equipment they brought along, the more medical supplies could be carried in their stead.

They were making a list of the items that were absolutely necessary when Danny heard a woman calling his name.

"Danny Watkins?" she asked again, crossing the room to where they were working.

"Yes?"

"You are getting shots today, *ja? Die shutzimpfungen?*"

"Vaccinations, yes," he replied, butterflies rising up and flitting around in his stomach.

"*Bitte,* the doctor would like to do that now, if you do not mind."

Swallowing hard, Danny handed the list over to Mr. Bashiri and excused himself.

"If you are a good boy," the photographer teased with a wink, "perhaps they will give you a lollipop."

Steeling his nerve, Danny followed the woman from the warehouse into the main building and up the hallway to a small room, the inside of which looked very much like an American doctor's office, complete with examining table, blood pressure cuff, and a scale.

Danny introduced himself to the doctor, a transplanted Australian wearing jeans and a faded T-shirt. The man apologized for his attire but

176

said that he'd come today prepared only to load boxes, not to practice medicine.

"Not that I mind doing it, of course. A couple of last-minute volunteers also need to be inoculated."

The doctor told Danny to sit on the table and then he pulled up a stool and sat. He took a brief medical history and then one by one, he named all of the vaccinations and boosters he felt Danny ought to get. The list was long and disturbing.

"I guess you can do 'em all," Danny said bravely, "but will we really run into every one of those diseases down there?"

"Sure, mate, and lots of others too, I bet, including some that've got no vaccinations at all—nor even any cure."

Before giving the shots, he gave Danny a rudimentary exam, taking his blood pressure and temperature, and then checking his ears and nose and throat. As he worked he talked about what he called "orphan diseases," which were conditions rare enough that even though they were probably curable, the pharmaceutical companies weren't willing to fund the research to find those cures.

"Developing new drugs costs an arm and a leg," the doctor said as he pressed Danny's wrist to find a pulse and then consulted his watch. "As a result, lots of needed drugs are never developed. It's real sad. Take Buruli Ulcers, for example. We'll see a lot of those down there, and they're not pretty. They stink too."

"Stink? Like bad breath?"

"No," the Aussie smiled, releasing Danny's wrist and reaching for a rubber mallet to check his reflexes. "These ulcers aren't in the stomach, they're on the skin—arms, legs, whatever. Like rotting flesh. They're disgusting."

He tapped Danny's left knee with the mallet, seemed pleased with the reflex, and then checked the right.

"We treat 'em with skin grafts, tuberculosis drugs, even amputations. There's no cure. In fact, we're not even sure how the infection is contracted. Airborne bacteria? Stagnant water? We don't know. But once someone gets a Buruli ulcer, not only are they in tremendous physical pain, they are also socially ostracized as well."

"That's horrible."

Satisfied with Danny's exam, the doctor went to the cabinet and the refrigerator, pulling out different bottles of colored liquid. In varying combinations, he pulled the liquids into the syringes, holding them up to the light to flick out the air bubbles.

"I've got to warn you," Danny said, watching him work, "I don't do well with shots. If I can get through this without passing out, I'll be doing good."

"Just be thankful these shots exist, mate," the doctor said with a laugh, placing the final syringe on the tray. "I mean, what's a little moment of pain compared with the value of protecting yourself from dreaded diseases? Trust me, once you see yellow fever or cholera in action, you'll be thanking your lucky stars that all you had to do was get a shot."

"If you put it that way..."

The doctor carried the tray of colorful syringes over to the exam table and set it down. He was just wiping Danny's arm with an alcohol swab when there was a knock at the exam room door. It was flung open, and there stood a bleary-eyed Luc, with the very flustered receptionist right behind him.

"I am sorry, Doctor. He insisted."

"Did you get the shots yet?" Luc demanded, his voice tight.

"We were just about to—" Danny began, but Luc interrupted him.

"Stop!" he said. "You don't need them. I'm sorry, Danny, but you won't be going to Africa."

Uncle Rick wanted to know all about Alexa's life now, so they sat there on the steps and she told him about the estate and the old lady and her teachers and the Stebbins and everybody else. Alexa wasn't supposed to mention the Fibrin-X or the ways she had changed, so she just stuck to the story they told her to tell people, that she was living with a guardian until her stroke recovery was complete. When Alexa mentioned the latest guest at the house, Jo Tulip, Uncle Rick seemed really surprised and interested, saying that Jo was a famous newspaper columnist.

"Get out," Alexa replied, laughing.

"No, really. Haven't you ever heard of 'Tips from Tulip'?"

"No, but maybe that explains why she always has big muscle guys around. She must need bodyguards to protect her from the paparazzi."

"She does?" he asked, tilting his head and blowing out smoke. "Bodyguards?"

"All the time. They even sit in the hall outside her bedroom at night."

"Imagine that."

Suddenly, the door to the bar swung open behind them, and Alexa's mother stepped out, her arm around the big, burly man who owned the place. The smell of beer and the blare of rock music spilled from the open doorway.

"You wanna take her home now?" he said to Rick in a voice filled with irritation. "She won't take no for an answer."

"Just one little drink," she slurred, her eyes a swollen pair of slits in her face. "I don't know why I can't have just one more little drink."

She pointed at Alexa and gestured toward the door.

"Why don't you run in and buy one for me, hon?" she said. "You look like the kind of person to help a girl out."

Rick put his arm around Alexa's mom, shouldering her drunken weight.

"Gosh, Misty, don't you even recognize your own daughter?"

The bartender waved them all off and went back inside as Misty struggled to open her eyes.

"Alexa? My baby!" she cried, throwing her arms around Alexa and nearly knocking her down—not that she was much more than skin and bones. She began to cry and coo and tell Alexa how much she loved her and missed her. Then she passed out, and Alexa and Rick had to carry her the rest of the way home.

Moving through old familiar motions, Alexa put her mom to bed in the dinky little room in the crummy little apartment where she was slowly drinking and drugging herself to death.

"We've got to get her into rehab before she kills herself," Alexa said to Rick as she tucked the woman in.

"She's been sober the last few weeks. I was hoping to move back in, thinking we could give it another go. But she got loaded Wednesday night and hasn't stopped partying since."

"What if we just took her to a dry out place right now and dropped her off?"

He shook his head, wearily taking a seat in the chair beside the bed.

"Doesn't work that way, honey. Until she wants to change, she'll never get any better."

Alexa left them both there in the bedroom and went into the front of the apartment. She needed to get out of there, but she was reluctant to leave things like this. She decided to tidy up for ten minutes first, and then she would say her goodbyes and go. Her mom would be coming up to the old lady's for visitation on Friday anyway—if she was sober by then.

Alexa walked around with an empty trash bag, filling it with boxes and bottles and cans. She tied it off and set it beside the door, and then she gathered up all the dirty dishes and carried them into the kitchen. The sink was already full of dirty dishes and she wasn't about to wash them all, so she simply stacked everything as best she could. Reaching under the sink for a rag, Alexa wet it and wiped down the table and the counters and then straightened the chairs. When she was finished, the room looked a little better, but not by much. She couldn't help but compare it with the sparkly kitchen at the old lady's house. About the only thing that sparkled here was what looked like a shiny new toaster oven, next to the stove. Otherwise, the place was a dump, and it always had been.

Alexa returned to the bedroom to tell Rick goodbye, but he had fallen asleep in the chair. It was just as well. Chances are, if he was awake, he might not let her head out into the streets by herself at this hour of the morning anyway.

At least she could get home from here by train rather than by bus. Slinging her pack over her shoulder, Alexa walked out the front door, pulling it quietly shut behind her, and headed for the train station.

The doctor moved the full tray of syringes back to the counter and said he would be in the warehouse when Danny was ready for him, if Danny was ready for him.

"You let me know either way, 'kay mate?" he said, and then he exited the room, pulling the door shut behind him, leaving Danny and Luc free to speak in private.

"What do you mean, I'm not going to Africa? Is there a problem with my visa?"

"Yes, there is a problem with your visa. Yesterday afternoon, when you saw me going into the travel service, I was canceling your application and putting in one for myself instead. Here is your passport."

Danny took it from him, truly shocked. Was Luc really that ambitious, that he would sabotage Danny's visa so he could take the trip in his place?

"I don't know how to say this to you," Luc told him, moving to the doctor's stool and taking a seat. "For the past few days, I have been wrestling with a tremendous dilemma. It started with Chester Parks, who wanted me to convince you to take the job with *Haute Couture.*"

"Chester Parks? What on earth does he have to do with this?"

"First of all, I lied to you about how he and I met. It was at the gallery party, *oui,* but our encounter did not go exactly as I described. He actually came there that night specifically to meet you. When you did not show, and then he learned that we worked together, he paid me to arrange the dinner instead."

"Paid you?" Danny asked, still not understanding what this had to do with Africa.

"*Oui.* A hundred dollars, just to make sure you showed up at the restaurant. At the time, I did not think much of it. I knew he was going to offer you a job. I thought I was doing you a favor."

"Okay."

"When you turned down his ridiculously lucrative offer and left the restaurant, he told me that if I could convince you to take the job in the next twenty-four hours, I would be given a thousand dollars as a finder's fee."

"Good grief."

"Then this opportunity to travel with Mr. Bashiri came up, and I knew I would not be able to talk you into it even if he paid me a million dollars. After you and I parted ways the other night at the *Métro,* I called and told him what had happened, and he simply upped the offer."

Luc stood and began pacing, misery clearly on his face.

"He told me that he would arrange through the magazine for me to take this trip as well, so that I could continue to work on you until you changed your mind. If I convinced you to take the job within the week, I would get a five-thousand-dollar finder's fee. Of course, I took him up on it."

Danny nodded. Five thousand dollars was nothing to sneeze at.

"We started out on the trip just fine, and I was still trying to figure out how I was going to convince you to take the job when he called me back late the next day and said the agenda had been changed. He said that my primary purpose at this point was simply to get you fired from *Scene It.*"

"Fired?"

"Yes. Sabotage your work, make you look bad, whatever it took to get you kicked out of the trip and off the magazine. If I succeeded, he said that he would pay me twenty thousand dollars."

Danny could feel the blood rushing from his face.

"But why?"

"I did not know, though he implied that it had something to do with your girlfriend, Jo, or her family."

Jo? Her family?

"I was not sure what he meant or if I could do what he asked of me," Luc continued, "but for that much money, I still had to think about it. I have to confess, my friend, I almost did some things I would not have been proud of. I considered opening some of the cameras to expose the film, breaking some of the expensive lenses and blaming you, or telling Mr. Bashiri some sort of lies about you…I don't know, I tossed around a lot of ideas in my head. Chester Parks continued to call, and every time he did I told him that you were my friend and I simply could not bring myself to do it, he offered me more money. Yesterday afternoon, while you were busy taking photographs at the barbecue grill, he called and said that if I could get you fired by the end of today, I would be paid a hundred thousand dollars. That was his final offer."

Danny didn't know what to think. Or say. Or even feel.

He didn't understand.

"With that dollar amount floating around in my head, you must see how it was becoming harder and harder to postpone or turn down. I told him if he wired me a twenty-thousand-dollar down payment, I would begin by canceling your visa application so that your travel plans would have to fall through. He put the money into a Swiss bank account for me, and then I had no choice but to do it."

"But why? Why did he want me fired? Why was it worth that kind of money?"

Luc sat again on the stool, shaking his head.

"These are the questions I asked him. Last night, when he called yet again, I said I would not do anything else to cause problems for you unless I knew the reason behind it."

"And did he tell you?"

"He said he would think about it and call me back. A half hour later, just as I was about to kiss my beautiful date, I got a call from someone else instead, the person Chester Parks had been working for all along."

"Who?"

"She said her name was Helen Tulip—and that she was Jo's mother."

The train station was just a few blocks away, and though waiting there for the train was scary, at least nobody else ever showed up and nothing bad happened. Alexa got onboard and chose a seat on the nearly empty train car. She had to change trains twice to get all the way to Westchester County. By the time she finally got off at her stop, she was practically dragging her bad leg behind her. She knew for a fact that even if she could walk all the way back to the estate, she would never make it over the gate.

Taking a chance on a different approach, she waved at a lone cab that was sitting under the street light in the train station parking lot, got inside, and gave him the address of the old lady's house. After seeing those two new security guards at the house earlier in the evening, her hope was that the men manning the gate and the front door were also new and wouldn't recognize her.

"You're awfully young to be out and about by yourself at this hour," the cabbie said as he clicked the meter on and started driving.

She pulled out her hand mirror and a tissue, and started wiping off every speck of makeup, including the eyeliner. According to the clock on the dash, it was 4:55 AM. By her estimation, that should still give her enough time to get to her room before the sunrise started lightening the sky.

"Sometimes you've got to get an early start," she told him, "when you're working in a greenhouse."

When she finished removing the makeup, she brushed her hair, took off her belt and jewelry, and then put everything away in her bag. Her hope was that the security guards would let her right on through once she told them she was there to do some early yard work. Coming in the front gate in a taxicab took a lot of nerve, but in a way it was the sneakiest entrance of all because it was so overt.

Sure enough, when the cab pulled up at the gate, all she had to do was roll down the window and repeat her lie to the security guard. He spoke on the walkie-talkie and let her through, telling the cabbie not to leave until she had been cleared by the guard at the house. Once they made it up the long curved driveway and came to a stop, she paid the cabbie with the money she kept in her backpack and then smiled at the next security guard as he opened the door for her.

"It's pretty early to be coming to work," he said, looking vaguely suspicious. "You're not on my list."

"I'm supposed to help Winnie in the greenhouse. We're hardening the seedlings today. Gotta get an early start."

He pulled out a piece of paper and looked at it.

"Can't let you stay if your name's not on here."

She bit her lip and thought for a moment.

"It doesn't have an Alexa?"

He scanned it again and then nodded.

"Yep, there you are. Somebody goofed and put you down under family."

"I wish," she said, smiling.

"I hear you. You have a good day now."

"You too."

Then she walked around the house toward the garage and made a wobbly beeline along the back of the house once she was out of sight.

Somebody goofed and put you down under family.

Just the thought of being listed as "family" warmed her to the very core.

At the stairs, Alexa began climbing up, one step at a time, though her leg was so weak she practically had to crawl. Almost to the top, she had to pause and catch her breath, afraid her leg was going to give out completely any minute now. There wasn't much more to go—surely, she could pull it together long enough to get up four more stairs, across the veranda, and into her window.

She was about to make that last push when she spotted movement in the backyard. Someone was coming her way. Alexa crouched down and sat perfectly still, praying that she was well hidden in the shadows. As the person drew closer, she saw that it was Winnie, walking over from her apartment in the guest house. Oh no! The security guard must have woken Winnie up to make sure Alexa was really supposed to be here, and Winnie was coming to check it out.

But then she did the strangest thing instead.

When Winnie reached the main house, she didn't head for the back door or even the back stairs. She looked all around, as though to make sure that nobody was watching, and then she slid open a window and crawled inside. Being kind of chunky, it wasn't easy for her to squeeze through, but she finally made it, her little white Keds dangling out the window for a minute before disappearing inside.

What was up with that?

After a moment, a faint, moving light could be seen inside the room where Winnie had gone. Despite her exhaustion, Alexa couldn't help but crawl back down the stairs and over to the window to take a peek inside and see what she was doing.

From what Alexa could tell, Winnie was in the front part of the old lady's bathroom. She was there holding a flashlight in her mouth and going through the medicine cabinet, grabbing bottles of pills, reading the labels, and putting them back, one by one. Was Winnie a druggie? Looking for a fix? If so, Alexa doubted she'd find anything more interesting in an old lady's medicine cabinet than arthritis medicine or a bottle of laxative.

Finally, Winnie seemed to find the one bottle that she wanted, but what she did next was totally weird: She took out the capsules, opened each one, dumped its contents into the sink, and then refilled it with something else. Alexa would have thought she was putting in poison or something, but from what she could tell, Winnie was filling the capsules with the sugar powder from some Pixie Stix.

Pixie Stix?

Alexa could not begin to imagine what that was about. But with the sun due to come up soon, she couldn't stick around long enough to find out. Reluctantly, she pulled herself away from the window and returned to the stairs. She made it all the way up this time without stopping, crept across the veranda to her window, slid it open, and climbed inside.

Her leg made a bit of a thump as she hit the floor, but she didn't even pause. She just slid the window shut, stripped off her clothes, and pulled on her pajama pants and T-shirt. Then she pushed the lump of pillows out of the way and got into the bed, wondering what kind of a game Winnie was running in there and thinking she'd never been so tired in her life.

17

For some reason, Jo awoke early and couldn't get back to sleep. She tossed and turned for a while but finally had to admit defeat. If she couldn't sleep, she might as well get up.

Quietly, she left the snoring Chewie at the foot of the bed and padded over to the window. Looking out, she saw that the sun was just peeking through the trees. Though she didn't catch the sunrise often, it was still her favorite part of the day. She pulled the easy chair closer to the window, sat, and simply gazed out at the morning, listening to the chirping birds and thinking about God. She tried to remember a verse from the book of Psalms, something about protection and fear. Retrieving her Bible from the nightstand, she looked for it now, flipping the pages until she found it: *The Lord is my light and my salvation—whom shall I fear? The Lord is the stronghold of my life—of whom shall I be afraid?*

That was it. Jo read it again, several times, until she committed the verse to memory. Really, that was all she had to hold onto right now when she was under attack, just as King David had been under attack when he wrote it.

Grateful for the Lord's continued love and protection, Jo closed her Bible and began to pray. She spent a while with her head bowed, bringing to God every question she wasn't able to answer and every problem currently seeming so insurmountable. By the time she was finished, she felt as though she had covered it all—and she felt much more at peace.

Jo finally opened her eyes to see that the sun had come all the way up and Chewie was awake and wagging his tail. Jo gave him a big hug and then dressed as quickly as she could, eager to check out Chewie's new fenced-in area out back and then get them both some breakfast.

Danny listened, his mouth agape, as Luc related the conversation he'd had with Jo's mother, Helen. According to him, her intention was to get Danny home quickly, no matter what it took, for Jo's safety. It was complicated, but apparently it had something to do with the family's wealth and a will and a certain clause that was preventing Jo from inheriting her rightful share of the family fortune.

"Helen said that she had connections at *Haute Couture*," Luc continued, "so when she arranged for a job offer and you turned it down, she simply directed Chester Parks to keep upping the offer until you had no choice but to say yes."

"You're telling me that Chester's going to call me back and offer me even more money for that job?"

"*Non*. Something has happened to change their plan—to make it much more urgent for you to come home than before."

"Something happened? What?"

"She wouldn't tell me, just that it was imperative that you come home *immediately*. I asked her why she didn't call you up herself and explain the whole situation, but she said that if you felt you were being manipulated, you wouldn't cooperate. She said it would be best for her purposes, not to mention my bank account, if you were simply fired and sent on your way."

"But this is crazy. If I knew Jo needed me, I would be there in flash. Without question."

"I know. I do not doubt that. But there is something very fishy going on here, my friend. I simply had to tell you the truth—though last night, with all of that money being thrown at me, I must confess that I accepted her offer. I agreed to sabotage your position. She still thinks that is what is going to happen."

For a hundred thousand dollars, Danny almost understood why Luc had made such a decision.

"What went on between last night and right now to change your mind?" Danny asked, knowing that the inner conflict must have been what had sent Luc to the bottom of a whiskey bottle.

"I am not sure," Luc replied, "except that this morning, when I got up and looked at myself in the mirror, I decided that I did not want it to be the last time I could look at myself in the mirror. Could I really sell my soul and betray a friend—especially one with such talent and passion for his work? I do not think so. Not for any price."

Before Danny could respond, they were interrupted by a knock at the door. It opened, and Mr. Bashiri looked inside.

"Is everything all right?" he asked. "We still have much work to do, but the doctor said that the two of you are in here arguing. May we postpone your conversation until lunchtime, perhaps?"

Mr. Bashiri seemed irritated, and Danny didn't blame him. The problem was, suddenly there were more important things going on here—including the fact that for some reason Helen needed him home in a hurry, and it had to do with the family fortune. Danny did not like Jo's parents, and he certainly didn't trust them, but if Helen was willing to throw a hundred thousand dollars at Luc just to get Danny to come home, then something very big must be going on there.

Suddenly, an image of Jo popped into Danny's mind. She might be independent and self-reliant, but she was also sweet and trusting and vulnerable, and he knew she could easily become an unwitting pawn in somebody's financial game if she wasn't careful or if she didn't understand what was really going on. If Helen Tulip was pulling out the big guns, then it must be time for out-and-out war.

Danny just wished he knew what they were fighting for.

"Well?" Mr. Bashiri said, glancing at his watch. "We do not have much time to waste."

"Come in, please," Danny told him, feeling terrible for what he was about to say. But even Mr. Bashiri himself had told Danny to make sure his priorities were in order, and that professional success was not always worth the cost.

Danny only wished he had realized that truth six weeks ago, when he first abandoned Jo to take this job.

"I'm afraid there's a problem with my visa," Danny said now. "I think we need to make a change of plans."

Breakfast was a decidedly unpleasant affair, beginning with Eleanor's announcement that Bradford was doing so much better that he was being moved out of intensive care and into a regular room—but that he was being uncooperative with the police and refusing to answer any of their questions.

"He'll talk to *me*," Jo cried, but Eleanor said that Bradford and his parents had specifically requested no visitors, especially not Jo Tulip.

Jo couldn't understand why he had done that, but it sounded for some reason as though he was trying to weasel out of the situation entirely. She could only wonder what he might do next—perhaps deny ever saying any of those things to her in the first place?

Jo had been in a good mood when she first sat down, but the wind quickly sputtered from her sails after that. The looming presence of her bodyguard only served to remind her of the gravity of it all.

Down at the end of the table, Winnie was sullen and morose. Apparently, Eleanor had talked to her yesterday while Jo was in Pennsylvania and told her everything that was going on. Now, the woman who had been so bubbly about her gardening the day before had not said two words since sitting down.

Eleanor looked as though she was worn out. With a listless appetite and dark circles under her eyes, Jo knew that the situation was taking a serious toll on the woman. Jo could only pray that it would be resolved soon. At 86, her grandmother didn't have the stamina to get through something like this unscathed.

Alexa hadn't made it to breakfast at all. According to Eleanor, she had come down earlier and complained of a sore throat and a headache, so they had canceled her tutor for the day and she had gone back to bed to sleep.

Only Consuela seemed to be in a good mood, singing to herself as she carried in a platter of homemade waffles and set it down next to the heated syrup.

"For goodness' sake, Consuela, this is breakfast, not Carnegie Hall. Please be quiet."

Jo looked up at her grandmother, surprised at the outburst.

"I think Consuela's just in a good mood," Jo said, trying to smooth things over.

"Yes. It's watching your dog out the window that's making me happy," Consuela concurred. "So sweet and funny. He reminds me of my little Koko, best pet I ever had."

She babbled on a bit about her childhood dog, obviously not realizing that no one except Jo was interested. Once she left the room, Eleanor let out a sigh and then went back to picking at her food.

Jo thought it might be as good a time as any to mention her need for a little office space to do her work and ask if any of the outbuildings could accommodate her. Her grandmother said that she should feel free to use either an empty office in the carriage house or a table in the studio.

"There's a sink in the studio, isn't there?" Jo asked. "I'll work in there. I'm going to concentrate on some household hint questions today."

She didn't add that the questions would all revolve around toaster ovens to give her more fodder for drawing out Toaster Man and encouraging him to write back. Perhaps if Jo was able to sneak enough details out of him, she could track down the case that way. Given the confines of her situation, she figured that was better than nothing.

"Oh, please," Winnie interrupted suddenly, her voice harsh. "Household hints? There are more important things going on here than that. I think you both should know that my son, Ian, called me in the middle of the night. He said that he had a visit from the police, asking him questions about what happened."

Jo turned to her grandmother, one eyebrow raised, wondering how the cops knew to question Ian.

"Don't look at me like that," Eleanor snapped. "Yes, I'm the one who gave his name to the police. They have received my full cooperation. I will not tolerate this sort of behavior in my home, my family, or my company. Lying, double-dealing, contract killing—whatever. I won't have it."

"Mother, do you honestly think my son—your own grandson—could be a murderer?" Winnie demanded.

"Actually, no, I don't. But he is the most likely suspect, and we had to start somewhere. For what it's worth, the police will probably question you and Neil too."

"Perfect," Winnie snapped. "Turned in by my own mother. Will you look the other way as they beat me with a rubber hose?"

"Uh, the cops don't really do that," Jo said, fighting the urge to smile.

"Do you want me to move out of here and back to Manhattan, Mother? Go as far away from Jo as possible, just in case I might be trying to kill her myself?"

"It's an investigation, Winnie," Eleanor explained tiredly. "The police have to go through a systematic process of eliminating suspects. You and your husband and son would each benefit quite handsomely from Jo's death. They simply need to rule you out so they can move on to the real murderer."

Jo put down her fork and wiped her mouth with her napkin, wishing this entire mess could simply go away. She knew she could be wrong, of course, but she'd almost be willing to stake her life on the fact that the killer was not Winnie or Neil or Ian.

"Winnie," Jo said, "according to my father, there are plenty of people in the company who would stand to gain by my death. The police will be talking to all of them eventually, I'm sure. Don't take it personally."

"Don't take it personally?"

Winnie threw her napkin onto the table, slammed her hands down, and stood up so quickly that the bodyguard sprang into action, poised to take her down if necessary.

"My nerves can't take this," Winnie said, near tears, her hands shaking. Jo was sad to realize that the carefree, happy Winnie she'd glimpsed yesterday was now completely gone. "It's not fair!"

"It may not seem fair right now, but—"

"I wait all year for planting season," Winnie interrupted. "*All year.* And you people are just *ruining* it for me."

With that, she ran from the room in tears. They could hear the back door slam and then Chewie barking and then another door slam in the distance. Jo looked at her grandmother, her eyes wide.

"Well," Eleanor said precisely, dabbing at her mouth with her napkin, "what were we thinking? How very thoughtless of us to have placed a greater value on human life than we have on planting season."

Danny decided that he was going to catch the next possible flight home. Above all else, he needed to be with Jo. He didn't intend to quit his job with *Scene It* or close out his Paris apartment or anything like that. He simply had to find out what was going on and make sure she was okay. He'd deal with whatever ramifications came from his actions later.

Though Mr. Bashiri seemed disappointed that Luc would be the one going with him to the Congo rather than Danny, he was gracious about it. All Danny told him was that he had a personal matter back in the States that needed attending to, and that since it didn't look like his visa for the Congo was going to come through in time anyway, he was going to bow out from this trip now and fly home as soon as possible.

"There will be other photo shoots, other trips," Mr. Bashiri said to Danny, nodding his head. "I feel certain that this is not the last time you and I will work together. And Luc, with his language skills, will be an asset of a different kind, of course."

"Thank you, sir. I appreciate your understanding."

Danny got the number of a local travel agent from the receptionist and then made the call from a telephone in the warehouse. She told him that his only choice for today was a flight leaving from the Zurich airport at 1:45 PM, with one seat left in business class, if Danny wanted it. According to the travel agent, he would have to change planes in Amsterdam and then fly straight to the JFK Airport in New York, arriving at 8:32 tonight, local time. The next available flight wasn't until Saturday afternoon.

"I'll take the one forty-five today," he said, not even wanting to hear the price. He was willing to pay whatever he had to. He'd just have to figure out some way to cover the cost on his credit card later. "And rent a car for me in New York too, would you? The cheapest thing you can find."

Giving her his credit card number over the phone, Danny looked across the room at Luc, who was trying to pack up all of the extra equipment. The Frenchman was already looking overwhelmed with having to assist Mr. Bashiri by himself, not to mention rather green around the gills after all of those shots on top of a nasty hangover. Finally, the reservation complete, Danny called for a taxi, and then he crossed the busy room to say his goodbyes.

"Listen, before you go," Luc said under his breath, "would you please tell me why this is the tripod Mr. Bashiri keeps insisting we need to bring to Africa rather than any of the others? The others have so many more features, and they're all so much lighter than this one."

Danny thought for a moment and then reached out for the tripod in question, flipped it upside down, and showed Luc the bottoms of its feet.

"My guess is because this one has solid legs," Danny said. "All of the others are hollow."

"So? That is what makes them so light!"

"Yeah," Danny replied, putting it back down. "But in the conditions you'll encounter in the Congo, that's also what makes them fill up with dirt or mud every time you use them."

Luc slapped a flat hand against his forehead, as though he couldn't believe he hadn't figured that out on his own. Danny knew his friend had a lot to learn about the practicalities of in-the-field photography, but he had a feeling that spending this time with Mr. Bashiri, the consummate professional, would have a great influence on him.

Suddenly, Danny felt a pang of reluctance over what he was about to do. He had paid way more than he could afford to hop on a plane and fly to America without so much as a single conversation with anyone there, all based on secondhand information, leaving behind the best job he'd ever had and the professional opportunity of a lifetime.

It made no sense.

But what did make sense was the feeling that had been growing in his gut ever since Luc said the name of Helen Tulip. Maybe it was the Holy Spirit's leading, but somehow Danny simply *knew* that he needed to be home with Jo, even if he didn't understand why.

Danny's final words with his traveling companions were bittersweet. He thanked Luc for coming to him and telling him the truth.

"Listen, man, about the money..." Danny said, a sly smile on his lips.

"The hundred thousand that I have to give back?"

"Yeah. Helen was paying you to get me fired, so that I would go home to America, right?"

"Right."

"Well, the way I see it, I'm on my way home. The finer details aside, it sounds to me like that's money you earned. I'd plan on keeping it, if I were you."

Luc seemed to think about it for a moment as his own smile grew.

"*Oui!*" he said finally, giving Danny a strong hug. "I do believe you have a good point, *mon ami*. She achieved her end goal, which was to get you home. Ultimately, that's what she was paying for."

Luc seemed very happy as he returned to his work. Danny stepped toward Mr. Bashiri. This goodbye would be much more difficult, as Danny didn't expect to see him again any time soon. He was so grateful for the man's patience and instruction and gentle nature. If he could, Danny would like to be just like Mr. Bashiri throughout every level of his career.

He was flattered when the photographer offered to walk him out front to wait for the taxi. As they went, Danny tried to think of a way that, again, he could apologize for simply taking off like this. But when he tried to put it into words, it just came out sounding stupid. He babbled something about his girlfriend needing him, but that she was much more than just a girlfriend, she was also his best friend and more than likely soon-to-be fiancée.

"Let me tell you a little story," Mr. Bashiri said, interrupting him. "One I do not share often."

Danny nodded, listening, glad to see as they stepped outside that the taxi had not yet arrived.

"Many years ago, when my four children were small, I spent much time away from them, working hard to succeed in my field. My wife was a very capable woman, so I knew they were in good hands. Through my work, at least I was able to provide for them well. Eventually, I even bought for us a beautiful home on a beautiful hill, but I was gone so much it was almost like I did not live there at all."

"You were working hard," Danny said. "Earning a living."

Mr. Bashiri shook his head.

"In my country, a man does not just provide for his family, he also defends his family. This I did not do. I was not there to do that."

At the corner, Danny could see a taxicab waiting at a red light, heading in their direction, and he willed the light to stay red just a little longer.

Mr. Bashiri continued, his eyes very sad and faraway.

"Rebel forces came through our village one day, with the goal of eliminating anyone with ties to the government or with obvious signs of prosperity. Because of our beautiful home on a beautiful hill, my entire family was murdered."

Danny looked away, a sudden heat threatening at the back of his eyes.

"I was deep in the jungle at the time, on an extended shoot. No one could reach me for two weeks. By the time I came home, my family had already been buried. I was not there to spend time with them, I was not there to protect them, and I was not there to bury them. I was only there to mourn them."

After what that woman had said last night, Danny had assumed there had been some sort of accident or minor tragedy in Mr. Bashiri's family, but nothing on a scale of this magnitude. He took in an uneven breath and tried to think of how to respond.

"Your wife and four children," he said quietly. "How did you manage to go on after that?"

"I did not manage, not for a long time. But eventually, the preacher in our village led me to Jesus Christ. He said that while I was gone, before the massacre, my whole family—except for me, of course—had come to faith and had been baptized in the river. Me, I had always scoffed at Christians, but after talking to the preacher I came to understand that the only way I might see my beloveds again was to join them in heaven. And I know that I will, when that time comes. Truly, God pulled me from the pit of my sorrow and gave me the strength to carry on."

Danny was stunned.

"Thank you for sharing that with me," he said finally as the light on the corner turned green and the cab made its way over to the curb.

Mr. Bashiri seemed to snap out of his daze, shaking his head and lightening his posture. Danny thanked him again, shook his hand, and reached for the handle of the cab. He opened the door but paused before getting in, to hear Mr. Bashiri's final words.

"I say this only as a cautionary tale, Mr. Watkins: Threats come in many forms. There may not be rebel forces in Pennsylvania, USA, but there is still good reason to stand at the side of the one you love in times of trouble. If you do not, the cost may simply be too high to bear."

18

In the wake of Winnie's outburst at the breakfast table, Jo and her grandmother finished their meal in relative peace and quiet. After Jo took her last bite, she wiped her mouth with her napkin, set the napkin beside her plate, and looked over at the empty spot where Alexa had been sitting the morning before.

"May I ask you a question, Gran?"

"Certainly."

"I don't mean to be nosy, but I've been wondering about Alexa. What's really going on with her living here? You have to admit, the situation is a little odd."

Rather than answer Jo's question directly, Eleanor pushed away her plate, placed her napkin on the table, and suggested that Jo come to her office in an hour or so, where they could speak about it privately. Then she simply reached for her cane, got up, and left the room.

Obviously, the subject was closed for the time being.

Now feeling even more curious than before, Jo decided to use the hour until their meeting to set up her work area. She asked Fernando to retrieve the two heavy suitcases from her room, and then she went out to the studio with the bodyguard. Fernando showed up with the bags soon after, just as the bodyguard was giving Jo the all clear.

She stepped inside the empty building, impressed with the renovation. The studio had always been her favorite of the estate's several outbuildings anyway, a charming remnant of days past. Now, she saw that the room had been expanded and enhanced with a gorgeous piano, plenty of workspaces, and a beautiful old wooden easel set up near the floor-to-ceiling windows.

Eager to unpack, get organized, and get down to work, Jo chose a table that was out of the main area but not too far from the sink. She didn't want to get in the way of where Alexa usually had her lessons, but there seemed to be plenty of room, and she would gladly work around the girl's schedule.

Jo unloaded her supplies, one by one, until she was set up and organized. Glancing at her watch, she decided she still had time to go on a toaster hunt. If she was going to test some cleaning techniques, she needed a few guinea pigs.

With the bodyguard tagging along behind and Chewie giving a few friendly barks every time they came past his pen, Jo collected toasters from all over the estate. Consuela gave her two from the main kitchen and one from her apartment over the garage. As Jo lined up the toasters along her worktable, she realized that she was just happy to be doing something, anything, that might propel this case forward and give her at least some sense of control. It might not be safe for her to pound the pavement and question subjects or examine evidence, but at least she could try to establish a relationship with the one person who might be willing to come forward, Toaster Man, if only she could only get him to keep writing back.

Danny's eyes were glued to the window as the airplane landed in Amsterdam. He wished circumstances were different and that this was just an ordinary trip and that he could take the time to explore what looked like yet another beautiful and unique European city. More and more, he had been thinking lately about backpacking through the Continent once his internship with *Scene It* was finished. Living in Paris—not to mention having visited Zurich—had whetted his appetite to see more of the countries he'd always wanted to visit. He wondered if Jo might ever consider making a trip like that with him after they were married.

After they were married. How funny that he thought of it that way almost all the time these days. Never "if," always "when." He hoped she was starting to think the same way too.

Once Danny was off the plane, he headed toward his next gate, relieved to find a bank of payphones on the way. He had several calls to make, so he decided to start with the most difficult: his boss, Georgette, who was not going to be happy when she learned that he had abandoned his charge in Switzerland and was now on his way to America. It took a while to figure out how the use the phone, but once he finally got it he was connected with *Scene It* and then with Georgette.

His pulse surging, Danny decided to launch right into it the moment he heard her voice.

"Georgette? This is Danny. I know this may sound crazy, but I'm calling you from Amsterdam."

By the time Jo's appointment with her grandmother had rolled around, her curiosity was definitely piqued. She showed up promptly on time and then took the seat her grandmother indicated.

Sighing wearily, Eleanor told Jo that the whole story of Alexa was quite confidential, but that she was willing to share it now as it had some bearing on Jo's situation as well.

"You've probably already guessed that Alexa comes from a rather unstable background," Eleanor said. "Absentee father, mother on and off drugs and alcohol, poverty-level existence."

"I gathered it was something like that just from the things she said."

"What she didn't tell you is that for the first thirteen years of her life, Alexa also suffered from a severe case of attention-deficit/hyperactivity disorder, or ADHD. I'm sure you've heard of it."

"Of course. I had a few of those in my home ec classes at the high school, both the ones who couldn't sit still and the ones who spent most of their time just staring out the window, off in another world."

"According to school records and other information, Alexa was just about the worse case of ADHD they had ever seen—extremely hyperactive, unable to concentrate, sometimes unable even to complete a full thought in conversation before her mind had already flitted off to something else. Needless to say, she barely passed any of her classes. According to her mother, they pushed her through the system anyway, but by the ninth grade she could still barely read and was doing math at about third grade level."

"I don't understand," Jo said. "The child you're describing is nothing like the girl I met yesterday morning at breakfast. Did they finally find a good ADHD medication for her? I know there are supposed to be some out there that work pretty well."

"Just wait. I'm getting to that."

Jo sat back and listened, unable to fathom where this might be leading.

"A little over a year ago, late one night, Bradford was passing through Newark on his way to a meeting, and he happened to see something very disturbing on the side of the road: a young teenage girl, lying on the ground."

Bradford? A little over a year ago? That was just about when he and Jo first started dating.

"Of course, he stopped to check on her. She was conscious but groggy and disoriented. Her speech was slurred, and when he tried to help her up, he realized that she had no control over the right side of her body. There was no one else around, and he didn't think he should waste the time waiting for an ambulance, so he put her in his car and drove her to the nearest hospital."

Jo ran a hand through her hair, feeling like Alice in Wonderland gazing down the rabbit hole. *Shouldn't this have come up in conversation at some point during six months of dating and engagement? Why had he never mentioned it?*

"By then Bradford was rather invested in the situation, as you can imagine. He waited as the doctors did some tests and determined that the girl had had an aneurysm in her brain that had ruptured. Alexa was able to tell them her name and address, and Bradford himself rushed to the girl's home to retrieve her mother. They only had about a four-hour window of opportunity, you see, to get her started on the right medication. Bradford had a feeling that she was a perfect candidate for something called Fibrin-X, a new stroke drug being developed by one of our subsidiaries that had just moved into the final testing phase. Fortunately, the neurologist at the hospital concurred."

Jo nodded, knowing that one of Bradford's responsibilities at Bosworth Industries had been to monitor a group of subsidiaries that included a large pharmaceutical company.

"I won't bore you with the details, but suffice it to say that Alexa's mother gave permission for the medication, they got the IV started in time, and her symptoms showed rapid improvement. Within several days, Alexa was speaking normally and had regained some control of her right arm and leg."

"That's wonderful."

"Amazingly, she also no longer exhibited any symptoms whatsoever of ADHD."

Jo blinked, looking at her grandmother.

"What do you mean?"

"I mean she was cured. More than that, she was not the first person in the country with a similar scenario. Doctors involved in the phase three trials of Fibrin-X were watching for off-label-use situations, and it was rapidly becoming apparent that the drug might eventually be prescribed not just as a stroke medication but perhaps primarily as a cure for ADHD."

"Currently, there is no cure for the disorder?"

"No, none, so you can imagine the impact something like this might have. The company decided to bring Fibrin-X back to animal studies, in order to determine the mechanism that was making it work. Until this happened, doctors weren't even sure what caused ADHD, so of course they hadn't been able to cure it. But by working backward and starting with the cure, they have been able to trace out the cause. Next month, Dr. Stebbins is expected to announce his preliminary findings at a medical symposium. I hate to speak prematurely, but according to our experts, his work thus far is extremely important, perhaps even of Nobel Prize caliber. Not only will his announcement have a tremendous impact on the treatment of ADHD, but on the whole field of neurology and eventually a host of other brain disorders as well."

Jo was impressed with the story, impressed with the doctor—even impressed with Bradford for his role in the story.

"So how is it that Alexa ended up living here with you?"

Her grandmother shook her head, saying that it all happened rather quickly.

"Dr. Stebbins had been monitoring the ongoing progress of all of the Fibrin-X/ADHD patients, but he was particularly intrigued with Alexa's case. In reviewing some of her old records, he realized that she had had some IQ testing as a child and had scored at a near-genius level, but that her ADHD had been so severe that she had barely functioned in school. He came to me, to ask if I might considering sponsoring her—paying for a boarding school education, all of the best and brightest opportunities, whatever it might take to see if this child could reach her full potential in the wake of her treatment with Fibrin-X. We both agreed that she would make an amazing case study for his presentation."

Jo could understand why. Her story was compelling.

"Frankly, I didn't think boarding school would present the best opportunity for her as she simply had so much catching up to do. I thought it over and decided to make an alternate proposal: Private tutors, private lessons, and one-on-one instruction with some of the best teachers that money could buy. Before I knew it, we had managed to work out the details for her to come and live here. Her mother signed over temporary guardianship, grateful that her daughter might have the chance at a better life than she was able to provide."

"I can imagine."

"In the beginning, I really didn't expect to have Alexa here for very long, perhaps a month at the most and then we would make more long-term arrangements. But she was very little trouble and really quite pleasant to have around. One month turned into two, which turned into three and, well, you know the rest. Given her age, living in a mansion with an old lady probably isn't the best situation for her, but it's certainly better than what she had at home."

Much to Danny's surprise, Georgette wasn't as upset as he thought she'd be about the change of plans. Apparently, Luc had been her first choice for making the trip anyway because of his language skills.

"Let us be honest, Dah-nee. You may be a hard worker and a very likeable person besides, but you have been living in France for more than a month and your French still sounds like something you learned from a book. Yesterday."

While she didn't mind that the Africa trip had turned out as it did, she was not as happy about the fact that Danny might not be at his desk first thing Monday morning.

"I do not care which one of you comes back here to Paris and which one goes down to the Congo, but if I am not getting Luc back on Monday, then I need Dah-nee instead. It is that simple."

"I'll try, Georgette," he said, knowing that it would be difficult, if not impossible, especially considering the time difference. That would give him only about 24 hours in the States before he'd have to turn around and get on an airplane to return. Considering that he wasn't sure why he was going home or what he might find when he got there, he wasn't going to make any promises. "Again, this is a family emergency. I don't know what's going to happen."

"Well, I tell you what is going to happen here. Wednesday, at the latest. You have until Wednesday. If you are not back by then, you do not need to come back."

"That seems a little harsh."

"It is a harsh business. I am not trying to be mean. I get dozens of internship applications every month. If you will not take advantage of this opportunity, then there are plenty of other people waiting in line who gladly will. An internship is not like a regular nine to five job, Dahnee, where you can take personal time if you need it. By design, it is an intensive, three-month commitment that must be an absolute priority."

Danny closed his eyes and pinched the bridge of his nose, a headache just starting behind his eyes.

"I understand," he said, feeling that same helpless urgency he'd felt when they offered him the internship in the first place—and then gave him only one week to wrap up his affairs, move to Paris, and begin. If the job hadn't come with an apartment, measley as it was, he never could have made it work. "I'll keep you posted."

"Please do," she said, and then she said goodbye.

Sighing heavily, Danny hung up and tried to focus on his next call.

It was time to speak with Jo.

As he dialed her cell phone number, he decided that, unlike in last night's conversation, she would have to be honest with him this time and tell him if anything strange was going on. The more he thought about it, the more suspicious he became about that whole interchange. Pumped about his trip and excited to hear her voice, he had done almost all of the talking. But now that he thought back on it, he realized that when he had asked her how she was or what she was doing, she would turn the conversation back to him. Even her brief mention that she was on her way to stay at her grandmother's house seemed very odd in retrospect. Jo's grandmother made her crazy. When had she ever willingly gone just to stay with her?

Was Jo hiding something from him? Just trying not to burden him? Or was he jumping to conclusions?

All he knew was that he had 30 minutes before they would begin boarding his next flight. Using the calling card, he dialed Jo's cell and listened to it ring.

Jo could feel her cell phone vibrating from her pocket, but she decided to ignore it and call whoever it was back later. At least the volume was turned off, so that there was no ring tone to interrupt what her grandmother was saying. Eleanor was just getting to the part where she was explaining how Alexa's situation had some bearing on Jo's situation. Other than the Bradford connection, Jo still didn't see how it related at all.

"Do you remember in the meeting here yesterday," Eleanor said, "when Kent told you that one of our subsidiaries is at a major crossroads, and he and Neil have taken opposing views on the matter?"

"Yes."

"The subsidiary in question is the pharmaceutical company. The argument between your father and your uncle has to do with the release of the information about Fibrin-X and its ADHD connection at next month's symposium."

Jo sat back and exhaled slowly as the phone finally stopped vibrating. That certainly wasn't where she thought her grandmother was going with this.

"For very good reasons, Neil is eager to support Dr. Stebbins' efforts, and he is doing everything he can to facilitate the development of drug and prepare to get the word out about the findings. Your father, on the other hand, for equally good reasons, is opposing the release of data at this time. He thinks it's extremely premature and wants to push the matter back by several years at least."

"Several *years?*"

Jo's phone began vibrating again, so this time she reached her hand into her pocket and simply turned it off.

"That's not unusual," Eleanor said. "The average drug takes twelve years to go from conception to completion. As it is, for every five thousand new substances developed, only five will make it to human trials, and of those only one will ever end up on the market. Drug development is a phenomenally costly endeavor."

"Gran, while I appreciate having a little background here, I don't really understand the implications. Your theory—and my father's—is that someone is trying to kill me to gain control of my shares so that they can take this particular decision in one direction or the other. Correct?"

"Yes."

"Why on earth is this worth *killing* over? It sounds like any one of a dozen similar business decisions that these folks have to make every month. I just don't see why it's that big of a deal."

"I'll tell you why," her grandmother said, folding her hands and putting them in her lap. "Because the average cost of bringing one new drug to market is one *billion* dollars. It's an astonishing amount of money, but the return profits on successful drugs, if the process is handled correctly, are well worth it."

"Meaning..."

"Meaning the right decision here, on this particular drug, could mean a multibillion-dollar windfall for everyone involved. The wrong decision could bankrupt the pharmaceutical company."

"Wow."

"There is no room for error. Someone, it seems, wants to make certain this decision goes their way, even if it means they have to kill for it."

Alexa woke up and glanced at the clock, trying to figure out how many hours she had slept. Not the full eight, but it would have to do.

She sat up on the edge of the bed and thought about how nice it was to have a day off, with no tutors or teachers or therapy or anything. She had a feeling she should play sick more often.

But now she needed a shower and then she thought she would go down and look for something to eat. She had to play this just right, because if she acted too sick the old lady might call in a doctor, but if she acted too well she might get mad that Alexa had asked them to cancel her lessons. Maybe later she would do some homework anyway, just to keep up. She needed to practice her piano too.

Most important on the agenda, though, was trying to figure out what Winnie had been doing last night in the old lady's bathroom. When Alexa thought about what she had seen—Winnie crossing the lawn in the darkness, climbing into the house through the window, and messing with the old lady's medicine cabinet—she couldn't make any sense of it at all. But if she told the old lady or anybody else about it, she'd have to admit that she had snuck out herself, and that she couldn't do.

As her tutor was fond of saying, it was a real catch-22.

Jo stepped outside, chilled to the bone despite the bright morning sunshine. Walking slowly toward the guest house, her mind was spinning with what her grandmother had told her, trying to make sense of it all. At least now she understood why someone was after her. When billions of dollars were involved, life suddenly grew a bit cheaper. Like the Bible said, the love of money was a root of all kinds of evil. And how.

Trying to put the conversation with her grandmother out of her mind for now, Jo continued toward the guest house, bodyguard in tow, eager to collect one last toaster so that she could get down to work. That would take her mind off of things, at least for a while.

Of course, Jo thought as she walked up the stone path toward the small but elegant building, *getting this last toaster means facing the wrath of Winnie. I hope she's calmed down by now.*

Jo reached the door and knocked but got no answer. She decided to try the greenhouse instead. As she went, she thought about Alexa, her heart going out to the girl. She seemed incredibly well adjusted, considering how much her life had changed in the past year. "The resilience of youth" was the phrase that came to mind.

Some kids could withstand so much and still come out shining in the end.

Danny paced near the telephones, trying to figure out what to do. The plane would begin boarding in ten minutes, and he still hadn't been able to reach Jo. Finally, he decided to try the number she had given him last night, for her grandmother's house. He pulled out the crumpled paper and called it now.

A woman answered on the second ring. Danny identified himself and asked for Jo Tulip, but instead, after a few clicks, Jo's grandmother came on the line instead.

"Danny, this is Eleanor Bosworth. How are you?"

"I'm fine, ma'am. I'm calling from Europe, looking for Jo. Is she around?"

He hated to rush her, but people were already starting to get out of their chairs and line up at the gate.

"I'm sorry, but she's out in the studio right now. I'll have to have her call you back. Can I give her a message for you?"

He hesitated. What should he say? That he was on his way? That he'd see her tonight? Suddenly, he felt like the biggest idiot on the planet.

Should he skip this plane and not get on at all?

"I'm sorry, Mrs. Bosworth," he said, thinking he might have lost his mind. "This might sound crazy, but I'm standing in the airport trying to decide whether or not to get on a plane to New York to come see Jo. It's hard to explain why, but can you tell me if she's okay? Is everything all right?"

"Well, the police are doing what they can, but they don't really have any solid leads. Jo's safe for the time being, now that she has twenty-four hour bodyguards. And Bradford's still in the hospital, though he's out of intensive care. Does that tell you what you need to know?"

Danny stood there like a stone for a long moment, simply staring at the receiver. Did that tell him what he needed to know?

"My flight gets in at eight forty-five tonight," he finally replied. "I'd like to come straight to your house, if I may. Could you give me directions? I haven't been there in years."

She offered to send a car and driver to the airport to pick him up, but he declined, telling her that his travel agent had already reserved a car. Danny preferred to have his own set of wheels.

"That's fine," she replied, rattling off a simple route that would take him from JFK to her estate in Westchester County. "Of course, you'll stay here. There's plenty of room. Frankly, I'm relieved that you're coming. In a way, the key to Jo's safety lies in your hands."

"Ma'am?"

"If you were to marry her, then this whole problem would be solved."

As Danny watched the people at the gate filing onto the plane, he was unable to form a coherent reply.

"You told me last fall," she added, breaking his silence, "of your intentions toward my granddaughter. I assume they still hold true?"

"Absolutely," he said, finding his voice. "I love Jo more than life itself."

"Then do the right thing and get here so the two of you can tie the knot. You can still have a big church wedding and all of that down the line. The important thing now is to get those shares vested, which would happen the moment she says 'I do.'"

"Mrs. Bosworth, I don't know how to say this, but I have no clue as to what you're talking about. Jo has told me nothing. We spoke just yesterday, and she acted as though she didn't have a care in the world. Unfortunately, if I don't hang up this phone in about two minutes, I'm going to miss my flight."

Mrs. Bosworth was quiet for a moment.

"She hasn't told you anything?"

"No, ma'am. The only reason I was flying home was—" he hesitated, not wanting to mention the Helen Tulip connection just yet. "Well, it's complicated. But from what you've been saying, it sounds like things are even more complicated there."

"Complicated and confusing and frightening. Strangest of all is why Jo hasn't shared any of this with you."

Danny had to agree. He wasn't sure whether to feel hurt or suspicious or simply scared.

"Mrs. Bosworth, would you do me a favor? Would you not tell Jo that we talked or that I'm coming? She doesn't seem to want me there and, knowing her as I do, I'm sure she has her reasons. But that's not going to stop me. It sounds like she needs me, whether she's willing to admit it to herself or not."

"Hear, hear! You go ahead and get on that airplane, young man. In the meantime, my lips are sealed."

19

Jo hobbled to the greenhouse, her bodyguard a few steps behind. Through the foggy glass she could see Winnie at the potting table, deeply immersed in her work. Jo stepped inside, inhaling the wet, loamy smell of green, growing things. Muck, the gardener, was sitting on a cement bench nearby, sorting through a big box of sprinkler heads.

Jo greeted him and then walked toward the back of the structure, calling out a hello to her aunt. Winnie glanced up, did not reply, and simply returned to what she'd been doing.

"I'm sorry to bother you," Jo continued, "but I wanted to see how you're doing. Plus, I need to ask you a favor. First, though, are you okay?"

"What do you think?"

Jo could see that Winnie's hands were shaking and that she was handling the seedling much too roughly as she moved it to a bigger pot. Not wanting to set her off into a rampage, Jo quickly tried to change the subject, admiring the plants and commenting on some early blooming hothouse roses. Winnie seemed to be growing more and more agitated, though, picking up the spritzer and vigorously pumping out squirts of mist at the newly potted plant.

Suddenly, Jo could feel the bodyguard's hand on her elbow, gently leading her backward a bit so that he could insert himself between the two women. As he did, Jo felt a brief flash of fear—and she wondered for the first time if it was possible that one of her closest relatives really *could* be a killer. Winnie had always been a little "off," as the family would say, but Jo had never, ever seen anything in her that was evil.

Eager to distance herself even more, Jo walked back toward Muck, who seemed to be dealing with some frustration of his own, though not in a frenzied way like Winnie. Clearly, there was a problem with the sprinklers. Jo asked if he needed help, and all he said was "Clogs." Muck had always been a man of few words.

Jo picked up one of the sprinkler heads to examine it more closely and found that many of the tiny holes where the water was supposed to come out were indeed clogged. This problem she could handle. She advised him to use a three-step approach: scrub the heads with a toothbrush, use the hose to force water backward through the holes, and finally clear any remaining clogs with a wire. Considering how many sprinklers he was dealing with, though, that was going to be a tedious and time-consuming process.

Jo glanced back at Winnie, who seemed to be calming down. Now she was spritzing a nearby tray of seedlings, much more gently than before, her expression vague and distant.

"Thanks," Muck mumbled.

"Those clogs are caused by sediment in your water," Jo added, turning her attention back to him. "Are you drawing from the old well?"

He nodded. Back in the pasture was a picturesque stone well, now slightly crumbling, but still, apparently, functional.

"House is tied into municipal now," he said, "but I still use the well for the grounds."

In that case, she suggested that he install an inline filter, which he could probably find at any hardware store.

"That might save you from going through this mess every spring," she added. "By removing the sediment, you'll eliminate the clogging problem."

"Hmm," he mumbled, nodding. "Good to know."

Jo was just about to go when Winnie called out to her.

"Jo! You said you came in here to ask me a favor."

Jo hesitated, not wanting to set off her unstable aunt again.

"It's not important. I just wondered if there was a toaster or toaster oven in the guest house and, if so, could I borrow it? I'm trying out some different cleaning techniques."

Winnie was quiet for a long moment, her disdain and anger communicated through her silence.

"I'll have to take a look later," she finally replied. "I take all my meals in the main house, so I've never had need to notice."

"If there is one, just let me know. I'll be working in the studio."

Jo forced her tone to sound matter-of-fact and light, but as she stepped out the door and into the sunshine, she couldn't help but breath a big sigh of relief just to be out of there.

Alexa finally emerged from her bedroom at noon, feeling almost human again after a long, hot shower and some quiet time slowly getting ready for the day. For some reason, she decided to forego the usual makeup and hairspray and try a more natural look instead, with just a little lip gloss and a dab of mousse in her hair. She kind of liked the way it looked, different than before, just the way she was different than before.

Downstairs, the kitchen was empty, so she made herself a peanut butter and jelly sandwich and ate it standing at the window, watching the dog jump around in the grass outside. It looked like Muck had run some temporary fencing in a big loop out from behind the carriage house, creating a nice shady area for the animal to run around in. Though it was fun to watch him play, she just hoped the fence would hold and that the dog wouldn't break out and try to bite her.

"Good morning, sleepyhead," Consuela said, coming into the room, walking directly over to Alexa, and placing the back of her hand against Alexa's forehead. "How are you doing? You don't feel like you have a fever."

Alexa waited until she pulled her hand away and then took another bite of her sandwich.

"Actually," she replied, "I'm feeling a whole lot better. Still got a little headache, but my throat doesn't hurt any more."

Consuela seemed genuinely relieved, which Alexa found kind of touching.

"I'm glad I slept in, though," she added. "Otherwise, I might've gotten really sick."

"Maybe so."

Consuela took a package of frozen meat out of the freezer and stabbed at the plastic cover with a knife.

"Your mother phoned here this morning," she said, and instantly Alexa was on alert. Had her mom said anything about last night? Was she busted?

"Oh?" Alexa asked, taking another bite and trying to sound nonchalant.

"It's a visitation weekend, you know, but she was calling to say that we didn't need to pick her up from the train station because she has a ride. She's driving up with a friend instead."

Alexa just nodded, relieved that it didn't sound as though her mom had blown it for her. Consuela slid the frozen meat into the microwave and, with a few beeps, started it defrosting.

"I told her you were a little under the weather," she added, "but to be honest she didn't sound too healthy herself."

Coming off a 24-hour bender, Alexa wasn't surprised. She hoped this meant that Uncle Rick was coming too. Maybe together, the two of them could talk to her mom in a sober moment and convince her to check herself into rehab. Alexa was worried about her.

Truly, if something drastic didn't happen soon, Alexa was afraid her mother was going to end up dead.

In the studio, Jo lined up the three appliances she had acquired, which so far amounted to one regular toaster and two toaster ovens. Though they weren't completely spotless, they were cleaner than she would have liked for a starting point. With a smile, she thought of all the dirty toaster ovens she could have probably collected from friends in Mulberry Glenn. Most of the people she knew usually kept the outside neat with a sponge or washrag, but never bothered to clean the inside unless they had a melted cheese spill. Danny was so bad that sometimes he didn't even bother with that. He'd just keep using it until it stopped smoking. Oh, how she missed him. She wished he were there right now.

Next to the appliances she lined up the supplies she thought she might need: washcloth, toothbrush, nylon scrubber, vinegar, ammonia, stainless steel polish, paper towels, and a dishpan. She also needed dishwashing liquid, which she had forgotten to bring, so she left everything where it was and headed for kitchen to get some. Alexa was in there with Consuela and Fernando, who were discussing the cleaning of the big chandelier in the foyer.

"Hi, Jo," Consuela said, interrupting herself as Fernando left the room. "Listen, I just remembered that there's another toaster in the garage, but it's pretty old and dirty. Would you like that one too?"

"Absolutely. For my purposes, the dirtier the better."

"I'll get it right now. Should I just put it out in the studio?"

"That would be great. Thank you."

Consuela headed out to the garage, leaving Jo and Alexa in the kitchen alone. Jo realized that she had to concentrate on not showing anything in her facial expressions that would give away what she had learned about Alexa just a while earlier. Jo had no trouble believing the girl was a genius, but she found it almost impossible to picture her as she'd been before—a kid who could hardly get a passing grade in school.

"You look like you're feeling better. Any fever? Nausea?"

"Nope. I think I was just tired, mostly."

"That's good. Sometimes we all need a break."

Jo found the dishwashing soap under the sink and was squirting some into a paper cup when she noticed Alexa standing at the back door, watching Chewie through the glass.

"He's really a sweet dog," Jo said. "You can go out there and play with him if you want."

"Okay. Maybe later."

Jo was describing how to play double fetch with two tennis balls when Consuela returned, mission accomplished. She then grabbed her rag and spray cleaner and went toward the foyer, where Fernando was apparently waiting to hold the ladder as she cleaned the chandelier.

"Go ahead, Alexa," Jo urged. "Try to make friends with him."

Smiling nervously, the girl went outside, and Jo knew that she was in very good hands with Chewie.

Jo walked to the foyer to thank Consuela for the extra toaster. Unfortunately, when Jo walked in it was to see Consuela perched up on top of the ladder, spraying cleaner directly at the fixture. Jo gasped, unable to hide her dismay. Trying not to sound obnoxious, she explained that Consuela should spray the cleaner on her cloth and not directly at the crystals, because otherwise it might leech into the frame through tiny nicks and cuts and eventually corrode the finish.

"For that outer row of crystals," Jo added, "you should take them down and hand wash them. Just use warm water with a capful of vinegar and only a drop of dishwashing liquid."

Consuela thanked her for the advice.

"No problem," Jo said, returning to the kitchen. "Sorry to be a pain."

"You're not a pain. Never. I'm one of your biggest fans. I never miss 'Tips from Tulip.'"

Jo was surprised that Consuela was even aware of the connection. On the Bosworth side of the family, they were so embarrassed of Jo's occupation that they rarely talked about it at all. Sometimes, in fact, she practically felt like a black sheep.

Glancing toward her grandmother's office, Jo came back into the room and climbed halfway up the stairs so that she was closer to Consuela on the ladder and could speak softly.

"Just don't let my grandmother catch you reading my column. You might lose your job."

Laughing, Consuela asked why.

Jo shrugged. She never was sure what they had against it, but she suspected it was simply too pedestrian for them, as if writing about cleaning was just one tiny step up from being a chambermaid or a window washer.

"Let's just say I think my grandmother would prefer I had a different occupation. Something a little more, um, corporate. Either that or be some sort of society matron."

"Are you kidding?" Consuela said, spraying her cloth and then wiping a crystal. "Your grandmother's so proud of you she could bust. Not that she'd ever let you know it, of course."

Gran, proud of me? Never.

"She's always talking about how smart you are," Consuela continued. "She reads the column too, every day when she eats her lunch. She likes it when people write in something dumb and you tell them to 'Be a Smart Chick!' She thinks that's funny."

Jo was truly surprised and deeply pleased.

"Thanks for telling me. I had no idea," she said, going back down the stairs and returning to the kitchen. As she went, she wondered why the people in this family had so much trouble simply affirming each other.

Would it have been so hard for her grandmother simply to say, just once in her life, "I'm proud of you, Jo"?

Of course it would have been too hard.

Eleanor was a Bosworth, and the Bosworths never gave an inch.

High over the open water, Danny was being spoiled by business class, wondering how he would ever fly coach again. He hadn't realized when booking the trip that not only would his seat be roomier and more comfortable, but that he would get much better service and all sorts of little amenities. From the cotton slippers for his feet to the hot towel he'd been given prior to the meal, he was starting to feel like a prince.

Of course, all of that pampering was the only thing that was keeping him from climbing the walls. Over and over, he kept reviewing his brief conversation with Jo's grandmother, trying to figure out what on earth was going on there.

The police are doing what they can, but they don't really have any solid leads. Jo's safe for the time being, now that she has twenty-four-hour bodyguards. And Bradford's still in the hospital, though he's out of intensive care. Does that tell you what you need to know?

Based solely on those words, Danny had created a dozen different scenarios in his mind—though none of them gelled with her further statement that if Danny were to marry Jo, then this whole problem would be solved. What whole problem? Why? How?

He knew he'd make himself crazy if he tried to puzzle it all out without the facts. Better that he not obsess on it for now and just wait until he was there to get the full story. In the meantime, he thought he might try to get as much sleep as possible on the flight over.

Goodness knows, he probably wasn't going to get much sleep once he got there.

Walking back out to the studio, Jo smiled at the sight of Alexa happily playing fetch with Chewie. From the girl's relaxed body language, it was obvious that she had overcome her fear of the dog. Good ol' Chewie. No one could resist his charms for long.

Jo's bodyguard was just reaching for the door to the studio when it swung open and Winnie stepped out. Startled, Winnie jumped back and gave a little yelp.

"Jo, darling," she said, patting her chest, "I'm glad you have a body-guard, but could you please tell him not to sneak up on people like that? He almost gave me a heart attack!"

"Did you need something?" Jo asked, offended for her bodyguard's sake, at the way Winnie had spoken about him as if he wasn't even there or couldn't understand, like a pet or a small child.

"I was taking a break and thought I'd check the guest house for a toaster," Winnie explained. "Sure enough, there was one there. I didn't know if you wanted the flowered cloth cover too, so I brought it just in case. I put mine next to the other appliances."

"Thanks. I appreciate it."

Jo and the bodyguard continued into the studio, but Winnie paused before heading for the main house.

"Jo, I'm sorry for my behavior earlier at the breakfast table and in the greenhouse. I'm just having trouble with all of this…drama."

Jo wondered if Winnie realized the irony of her statement, that she herself was the root of much of the day's drama.

"I understand," Jo replied, trying to be kind. "The whole situation has been incredibly unnerving for all of us."

Satisfied, Winnie continued on her way.

"Oh, and Jo," she said, turning back one more time, "I heard from Neil. He and Ian are on the way from New York. They want to talk to you."

20

Chewie wasn't so bad, not bad at all. He did have those big teeth, of course, but after playing with him for a while, Alexa had to admit that he was as gentle as a teddy bear—a big, slobbery teddy bear with bad breath, that is.

Once Alexa was finished playing with him, she went to the studio. She sat down at the piano, intending to practice, but she was really more interested in what Jo was doing.

Jo had lined up toasters and toaster ovens in a row on the far table and now she was looking closely at each one and making notes on a pad of paper. Alexa asked Jo what she was doing, and she said she was going to clean them. She was especially excited about the dirtiest one that Consuela had brought. It didn't make much sense to Alexa, how somebody could get excited about cleaning, but then Alexa remembered what her Uncle Rick had said about Jo being a famous newspaper columnist. Maybe her column was about cleaning.

"You can go ahead and play," Jo said, glancing up to catch Alexa staring at her. "You won't bother me. I just hope I don't bother you."

"Okay."

Embarrassed, Alexa began her scales. Once she was warmed up, she propped open the sheet music in front of her and began. It felt a little weird with someone listening, but soon she forgot all about that.

Something about playing the piano always sort of took Alexa away, as though she could climb inside of it and go for a long, beautiful ride away from everything except that strange connection between the marks on the page, her brain, her fingers, and her ears. It was like a big loop that she didn't understand. If she put her hands in position and looked at the page, it was almost as though the music just happened, independent of her. Somehow, her eyes told her brain what she needed to do, and her brain sent that information down to her fingers. It was magical, and the more she practiced, the easier it all became.

When the first song ended, she held the pedal for a long moment and then released. The room was silent except for Jo, who let out a loud sigh. Alexa turned to look at her.

"That was amazing. I think you have a real gift, Alexa."

"Thanks," she replied shyly, turning back to her music.

She was about to try it again, with the metronome this time, when Consuela appeared at the doorway, followed by Alexa's mom and her Uncle Rick.

"Excuse me, but we have some visitors," Consuela said, stepping into the room. "Everybody's showing up at once."

Jo looked up to see a woman, painfully thin, who resembled Alexa, albeit a much older, battle-weary version, wearing dark shades and sporting an inch of black roots in her bleached blond hair.

This must be mom.

Behind her was a tall, lanky fellow in a muscle shirt, with tattoos down his slim arms and a silver loop in his eyebrow. A heavy silver chain hung around his neck with an even heavier one around his hips, in place of a belt. A boyfriend, maybe? As they stepped into the room, the bodyguard suddenly stood up straight, on full alert.

Before Jo could even take off her rubber gloves and introduce herself, Consuela told her she was needed in the house.

"Jo, your uncle and cousin are here to see you," she added before exiting.

Jo's stomach churned at the thought. She hated confrontation, especially with family, but she had a feeling this one was going to be a doozy. Quickly, she put down her cleaning supplies, took off her gloves, and washed her hands at the sink, all while Alexa awkwardly hugged her mother and the fellow who was with her.

"Sorry about that. I'm in middle of cleaning some toasters," Jo said to them after drying her hands on a towel, folding it, and setting it on the counter. She walked over to the woman and reached out for a handshake. "I'm Jo Tulip, Mrs. Bosworth's granddaughter. You must be Alexa's mom."

The woman offered a limp handshake in return without taking off her sunglasses.

"A pleasure," she said in a throaty voice.

Jo shook hands with the man also, who reeked of cigarette smoke.

"I'm Rick," he said, his gaze intense. "Misty's friend."

"Nice to meet you both. Sorry I have to run."

Jo introduced her bodyguard simply by name, and then the two of them left the studio and walked to the house. As she hobbled through the dining room, she could hear her Uncle Neil talking with Fernando about hiring him for a side job, something to do with moving his boat out of its dry dock winter storage and putting it in a wet slip for the summer. She reached the doorway to the foyer, where they were talking, Fernando standing there holding the folded-up ladder. As Jo stood and waited for them to finish their conversation, she glanced up at the chandelier to see that it was all aglow and sparkling beautifully. Consuela had done a great job.

"Uncle Neil?" Jo said softly.

Both men turned to see her. Fernando excused himself, taking the ladder as he went. Jo stepped forward into the room, wondering what to say. *I'm sorry you got questioned by the police, but by the way, did you try to kill me?*

"Josie," he said warmly, using the pet name he had for her. "Come here."

Once she heard that, she knew it was going to be okay. They embraced for a long moment, and for some weird reason she could feel tears threatening at the back of her eyes. All she needed to know was that her favorite person in the Bosworth family wasn't mad at her—or had wanted her dead.

When they pulled apart, he stepped back and held her out at arm's length.

"I haven't seen you in so long. I'd say you've grown even more beautiful, if that were possible."

"I've missed you," she told him, trying to remember the last time they'd been together. Neil was the same dapper figure as always, silver hair set off nicely by a tanned face and navy suit. "Thanks for coming out. Where's Ian? They said he was here too."

"He went to find Muck. The radiator's overheating."

"Some things never change, huh?"

Ian collected vintage sports cars, and he was forever dealing with the details of leaking oil, busted hoses, and thirsty radiators. Sometimes, Jo wondered if Ian might have had a happier and more productive life if he'd simply chucked all of his wealth early on and become an auto mechanic.

"He can join us when he comes in," Neil said. "Obviously, we need to talk."

"Yes."

"But first things first. After I heard what happened, I just needed to see that you were okay. I'm so sorry you're having to go through this."

Before Jo could reply, she heard a swooshing sound and then suddenly the bodyguard was tackling her from behind, throwing his muscular arms around her and pushing her forward. As they went, somehow he managed to flip around so that they both landed on the ground, with her fall cushioned by his body. At the same moment, a loud crash reverberated around the room.

By the time Jo extracted herself from his grip and sat up, others had come running and were standing in doorways, faces pale with shock. Jo looked up at Consuela, Fernando, and her uncle. Then she looked at the ground where she had been standing, shards of crystal from the chandelier shattered against the marble floor.

"What are you doing here so early?" Alexa said to her mom and Uncle Rick, though she wasn't disappointed. "You usually don't come 'til around four or five."

"Wanted to beat rush hour," Rick replied. "I thought the car might overheat in heavy traffic."

"You guys didn't say anything to anyone here about last night, did you? I'll get in big trouble if they find out I snuck out."

They both shook their heads.

"When I woke up this morning, I thought I had just dreamed you were there," her mom said. "Then Rick told me it really happened. You can't do that anymore, Alexa. Don't make them mad. It's not worth the risk. What if they catch you and say that's it, you're outta here?"

"They wouldn't do that."

"Even if they wouldn't," Rick said, "it isn't safe to be running around at night by yourself."

"You didn't fuss at me last night."

"Last night, I thought you were there with permission. I thought maybe they dropped you off in the neighborhood or something."

"So I took the train by myself, big deal." She didn't add that the evening started with sneaking past security, climbing over a gate, and taking a bus to Connecticut.

"Anyway, you shouldn't have left," Rick said. "I was very worried about you when I woke up an hour later and you were gone."

"The train was leaving soon," Alexa said, shrugging. "I was okay. I know how to take care of myself."

"Alexa, don't do that again, you hear?" her mom said, looking awkward, as she always did when she tried to be parental. It was kind of a joke, really, considering that most of the time Alexa felt more like the mother than the daughter.

Hoping to smooth things over, she decided to change the subject. She pointed to the nearby table and told them if they wanted to sit they could see her latest schoolwork. Relieved, they did as she suggested. From her cubby, Alexa pulled out some folders and removed her best papers and tests. Proudly, she set everything down on the table and watched over her mother's shoulder as she went through each one and then handed them off to Rick.

In a way, Alexa knew her mom didn't care all that much. But this was always how they started out a visitation weekend, sort of as a way to catch up. Her mom would ooh and aah over the A's and A+'s, and Alexa would feel something deep inside of her begin to heal, just a little bit. She'd spent a lifetime being a scholastic disappointment and the subject of dozens of emergency parent-teacher conferences, with the news getting worse every year.

You have to do something about your daughter.

She's obviously a bright girl.

She's not living up to her potential.

She can barely follow a linear thought pattern.

She's hyper and impulsive.

She's impossible to control.

She's a danger to herself and others.

She's failing almost every class.

It was a nice change to be the opposite of all of that now, a pleasure rather than a pain. A success rather than a failure.

"Gosh, Alexa," Rick said proudly. "Look at this math. It's like something they'd be doing in college. Impressive."

Alexa smiled, glad that Uncle Rick had come. It would be the first visitation when it hadn't been just her and her mom, but she didn't mind him tagging along. Alexa looked forward to visitation weekends, mainly because it gave her something different to do. And they had their own little routine. Usually, Fernando and Alexa would pick up her mom at the train station on Friday afternoons and then he would drive them both to Mariner's Village, which was a cute little tourist town about 15 minutes away, right on the Long Island Sound. There was a motel there that wasn't half bad, and he would take them there, drop them off, and leave.

With something like 45 regular television channels plus a few premium ones, Alexa's mom mostly liked hanging out in the room and watching TV. Sometimes, though, Alexa could get her to go out and do stuff. Since the whole town was within walking distance, they would eat in the restaurants, stroll the shops, maybe catch a movie in the dinky theater or play games in the arcade next door.

Alexa liked it most because it gave them a chance to spend time together in a way they never had before. Her mom liked it because the old lady always paid for the hotel and gave them plenty of spending cash besides.

Of course, the best weekends were the ones when her mom would actually stay sober the whole time and not leave Alexa in the room late at night so she could "take a walk" or "get some air." Alexa always knew what that really meant. Her mom wouldn't be back for hours, and when she returned she would reek of smoke and beer and collapse on the bed in a stupor. At least she never tried to bring any guys back with her, something she was always doing at home.

Suddenly, the thought of the upcoming weekend gave Alexa an idea. Maybe together, she and Uncle Rick could talk her mom into going to rehab. Maybe they could even drop her off at a place before the weekend was over.

Finally, Mom can get some help.

Alexa needed to talk to Rick about it privately, but the conversation needed to take place *now*, before they left the estate. As her mom read through an essay, Alexa tapped Rick on the shoulder.

"While she's looking at my schoolwork, could you help me move something heavy over in the carriage house? It'll just take a minute."

"Sure thing," he said, getting up and following her from the room. At the doorway, she paused and told her mom they'd be right back.

"Okay," she said, deeply engrossed in what she was reading.

Once they were outside, Alexa led Rick down the walkway and around the corner to the next building, but she didn't talk until she opened the door and they had stepped inside.

"I don't really need you to help me with something heavy, Uncle Rick," Alexa said as she walked past the first row of exercise equipment and over toward the window where they could sit on the wide sill. "I just wanted to talk to you. We need a plan before we even get in the car. We've got to talk Mom into going into rehab."

She sat but he remained standing, running a hand through his short, spiky hair. She could see the fingers of his other hand twitching toward his chest pocket, and she knew he was wishing he could smoke.

"You want to do an intervention, Alexa?"

"Don't you?"

"I want her sober, yeah. Are we prepared to do a real intervention? Not really. Usually, you should wait until there's a third party there, a person who knows what they're doing—not to mention, you probably ought to have details about where and when the person could go into rehab, just in case they say yes. It's an opportunity you don't want to miss."

"I could call Dr. Stebbins. He might have ideas about where we could take her."

"Okay. For what it's worth, I already checked for AA meetings in Mariner's Village, and I'm hoping she'll go with me while we're there. That'll help."

Feeling excited, Alexa crossed the room to use the telephone on the wall, glad that she had memorized Dr. Stebbins' private cell phone number. She was only supposed to use it for medical emergencies, but she figured this was one. Sort of.

Dr. Stebbins was actually quite nice about it when Alexa explained what she wanted. Though he didn't have any answers for her right away, he said he'd be glad to have his secretary look into it.

"We don't have any money, so it's got to be a place covered by Medicaid. And it's gotta be local too, because if we have to take my mom far away, she might chicken out."

"Got it."

Alexa told him that she was headed out for the weekend so she would have to call back from the road. He gave her his secretary's direct line and said to wait an hour or two before calling.

When she hung up, Alexa beamed at Rick.

"They're going to help us," she said. "Let's plan to do it at dinner tonight, okay?"

"Okay. It's a deal."

Walking carefully around the glass, Fernando helped Jo up first and then her bodyguard, the man who had pulled her to safety. The bodyguard's face was flushed and his expression was concerned, but at least he seemed unhurt. Jo thanked him, knowing mere words were not enough. He brushed off his clothes and replied that he was only doing his job.

The foyer floor was covered with the shattered glass, but when Jo looked at it, she realized that only one piece had actually fallen—the loud crash had only made it seem like more.

Jo looked up at the huge fixture, spotting the empty place along the outer rim where the crystal had hung. Each piece on that rim was in the shape of an upside-down teardrop, pointed at the bottom, about four inches wide and ten inches long. Truly, if it had hit her, even just the one piece could have done some major damage.

Consuela looked up as well and burst into tears.

"This is my fault!" she cried, sobbing.

Her husband, Fernando, took her in his arms and tried to comfort her. Eleanor, on the other hand, looked furious, and she began to berate Consuela for her carelessness in front of everyone.

"Gran, wait," Jo said, stopping her. "Listen, this was actually *my* fault. I'm the one who told Consuela how to clean the chandelier. I said that the crystals in the outer rim needed to come down so they could be hand washed."

Jo climbed halfway up the stairs so that she could get a closer look.

"I see what happened," she said, pointing toward the frame. "They're not clicked all the way into place. Everybody watch out, because if we don't fix these, another one might fall too."

Though the incident had been disturbing, Jo had no doubt it was an accident. There was no way someone could have purposely planned that. After all, it could have fallen at anytime on anyone. It was just bad timing that it had nearly fallen on her.

Or so she hoped.

Alexa realized that she still needed to pack. Her mom and Rick had finished going through the school papers and now were checking out her artwork—not the art therapy stuff she did with Nicole, but from her regular lesson during the week. Alexa didn't think her paintings were all that good, but it was fun to hear their reactions. They seemed genuinely impressed.

"Okay, while you guys look at that stuff, I guess I'll run over to the house and pack my suitcase. It's getting so warm outside, I might even throw in my bathing suit. Maybe they've opened the pool at the hotel!"

Alexa went outside, but before she was halfway up the walk, she heard her mother calling her name. Alexa turned around to see her mom coming toward her, shielding her eyes from the sun despite the fact that she was wearing sunglasses. She kept glancing nervously toward Chewie, who was across the lawn, standing at the fence and eagerly wagging his tale. She didn't like dogs.

"Listen, honey," her mom said, "I wanted to talk to you. We're going to have a good time and all, but…"

Alexa stared at her own reflection in her mother's sunglasses as her voice trailed off.

"But what?"

"But you probably don't need to bring a suitcase."

It took Alexa a minute, and then she understood.

"I don't want to hurt your feelings or anything," her mother added quickly, "but it's just a small hotel room and there's already two of us. We can all go have some fun, show Rick the town, eat dinner. But maybe we'll bring you back here tonight and then pick you up again tomorrow."

Alexa was *not* going to cry, no way, no how.

Her mom wasn't concerned about Alexa or her privacy. She just wanted to have some time alone in a nice hotel with her boyfriend.

Considering that they could have all the alone time they wanted the other three weekends out of the month, it just wasn't fair.

Alexa crossed her arms and fixed her mother with a cold stare, her face showing disdain but her heart feeling something much more painful.

"Whatever," Alexa said finally. "It doesn't matter to me."

Everyone scattered: Fernando retrieved the ladder and climbed up to fix the chandelier, Consuela and Eleanor moved into the kitchen so Eleanor could berate her some more, and Jo and Neil moved into the study, where they could sit and talk. Jo hobbled to the couch, propping up her bad ankle on an ottoman. She realized her uncle had sat on a chair across from her and was using the ottoman to put his leg up too. He rolled back a stained and torn pants leg until it revealed a bleeding gash in his shin.

Jo gasped.

"Looks like one of the shards got me," he said, sucking in air between clenched teeth. "I thought so."

The bodyguard alerted Eleanor, who called her private physician for a housecall. From what Jo could see, it looked as though her uncle would be needing stitches.

"Well, I came out here today to check on you," he said, "and ended up almost killing you instead. I'm so sorry."

"How was that your fault?"

"I was standing right under the thing when you came in the house. If we had moved in here right away, you wouldn't have been in danger."

"And you wouldn't be bleeding all over those nice slacks, either. Don't worry about it. It was an accident. I'm certain."

Feeling not quite as sure as she sounded, Jo looked up at the bodyguard, who nodded.

"I don't know how anyone could've done that on purpose," he agreed, "with the placement and timing and everything. I'd say accident, and I'm trained to know the difference."

Jo nodded, reassured, as the muscular man took a less conspicuous position near the wall.

Jo decided to seize the moment of relative quiet to ask Neil if he had any idea what was going on or who he thought might want her dead. They discussed the situation for a while with apparently no need for holding back any information or theories since it sounded as though Jo's dad had already told Neil everything.

"If Bradford said you were a target because of 'something big' going on at the company, then I'd have to agree that it has to do with the pharmaceutical branch. That's by far the biggest thing we've got going on right now in both the main company or in any of the subsidiaries."

They tossed around the names of some of the executives who would profit most from the upcoming announcement about Fibrin-X, but every time a new name came up, Neil would have some good reason why that person simply wasn't capable of doing something so diabolical.

"Your father's convinced the motivation has to do with financial gain, but I'm not so sure. Somewhere, there is someone who will gain more than just financially from this. Otherwise, why construct such an insane and far-removed plot? You realize, if this person, whoever it is, ends up killing you, then they'll have to kill your grandmother next or your death will have been in vain."

Jo's grandmother entered the room at just that moment.

"What's this? Who's killing me off?"

Neil repeated his statement to his mother-in-law.

"Kent's theory requires a huge sequence of events," Neil explained, "each of which has to take place in a certain order: Jo would die, then you would die, then we would all inherit, then Ian would combine his stocks with mine, and we would force the majority decision of proceeding with the Fibrin-X announcement as planned. Sounds like a lot of a-b-c-d-type stuff, any step of which could get messed up along the way."

"But if he's right, I do see some solutions," Jo told them. "For one thing, why don't you have the announcement made sooner, like today or tomorrow? Then the cat's out of the bag."

"I talked to Dr. Stebbins about that this morning," Neil said. "Even if Kent would okay it, which he wouldn't, Stebbins isn't ready. The data simply isn't finalized."

"Okay, then why doesn't my father simply change his position to vote with you, so that I don't have to die in order for either side to win?"

"Kent and I talked about that," Eleanor said, taking a seat in her chair, looked even more tired and pale than usual. "He refuses."

Jo looked at her grandmother, her eyes wide.

"He refuses? My own father refuses to do the one thing that might save my life?"

Eleanor shrugged, saying that in a matter such as this, where the lives and livelihood of so very, very many people would be affected, he simply had to consider the greater good and make the noble decision.

"Like a soldier, going to war," Neil added sarcastically. "Go ahead, Jo. Die on that battlefield so that the rest of us may be saved."

21

What about you, Grandmother?" Jo asked, ignoring her uncle's sarcasm for the moment. "You're the one who holds the majority. Why don't throw your weight Neil's way, and then neither you nor I will be in danger?"

Gran was quiet for a long moment. When she spoke her eyes were distant and sad.

"In the history of this company," she said, "I have never intervened, never interfered with the choices of the CEO. I have cast my vote in stockholders' meetings, but otherwise I have kept myself far removed from the decision-making process. I cannot change that policy now."

"Why not?"

"It's too hard to explain, Jo," she said, focusing in on her granddaughter. "But I simply have to stand firm on this. In any event, I believe I have found another solution, one which will become clear tonight."

"Hey, Granny!" a loud voice said suddenly from the doorway. "Somebody forgot to take out the trash!"

Jo's cousin, Ian, stepped into the room with a laugh, making a flamboyant entrance, as usual. Dressed in black slacks, magenta sportscoat, and a wildly patterned shirt, he looked like an object lesson in which of this season's designer fashions *not* to wear.

"Don't call me Granny. You know I hate that."

"But you love *me!*" he cackled, walking over to his grandmother and throwing his arms around her in an exaggerated hug. "You gorgeous babe, you."

Eleanor clucked her tongue at him but smiled indulgently and gave into his hug. Somehow, Ian could always get away with things no one else ever could.

Ian stood up straight and fixed his eyes on Jo.

"Hey, cuz! Somebody call Sherlock Holmes and give him a magnifying glass. We've got ourselves a bona fide mystery on our hands! How are you, train bait?"

He came and kissed Jo wetly on the cheek before plopping down next to her, squeezing tightly between her and the arm of the couch.

"I've been better," she replied, feeling the energy radiating from him like a pulse.

"Hey, what happened to you, Pop?" he asked, suddenly growing serious as he gestured toward Neil's bleeding shin.

"We had an incident with the chandelier," Eleanor answered for him. "Neil, my doctor is going to swing by on his way to the tennis courts in just a bit."

"That must hurt," Ian said.

"And, Ian, no one forgot 'to take out the trash,' as you put it," Eleanor continued tiredly. "Consuela simply has to sweep up the broken glass."

"No, not that trash," he said. Then he pointed to the window, which looked out of the front of the house. Alexa's mother and the mother's boyfriend were standing there, obviously waiting for Alexa. "*That* trash!"

Ian laughed at his own joke, not even noticing that everyone else in the room was silent. Jo was angry on Alexa's behalf, embarrassed for her family, and ashamed that Ian was a blood relative. She wasn't sure where Alexa had gone or why they were waiting, but she could only hope that the girl hadn't heard him.

"Hey, where's Mom?" Ian asked, oblivious to the chill that had settled in the room. "I miss seeing the old bag rattling around the penthouse in Manhattan."

"Your mother is probably out in the greenhouse," Eleanor said coldly. "You are more than welcome to go and find her."

"In a minute," he replied. "First I want to know what we're talking about here. Personally, I think it's time to hire a private investigator to get to the bottom of this. Obviously, the cops involved are a bunch of goons who don't know a crime scene from a Krispy Kreme."

"Are we to assume that your own interview with the police went poorly?"

"Heck, no. The guy was a Vette-head. Asked me a couple questions about where was I on Wednesday at six PM and what was I doing. When I said I was in Hackensack buying a sixty-three split window, he went nuts. We talked cars the rest of the time."

"A Vette-head?" his grandmother asked.

"Yeah, a Corvette aficionado. I spent all week trying to decide between the split window and a sixty-seven big block, but I went with the sixty-three in the end. It's a beauty."

"I'm glad to know you had a successful car-buying venture while I was busy nearly getting myself killed," Jo said, knowing she sounded cranky and tired. Ian usually had that effect on her.

Suddenly, he stood and began pacing as he spoke.

"Right, right. Okay, so let's think about that. What is it the cops are always looking for on TV? Motive, means, and opportunity? Well, a lot of us have motive, if your dad is to be believed, and I suppose we've got means, considering that all it took was the push of a hand. That leaves opportunity. I was in Hackensack. Dad was at a business dinner. Now, if we can just eliminate ten or twenty other people in the company, we'll be doing great."

"Don't be sarcastic, Ian," Eleanor said. "It doesn't become you."

"Was I being sarcastic?" he stopped and asked no one in particular, putting one finger to his chin. "Is that how it sounded? I was going more for *irony*. I'll have to try harder next time."

As he had so many times before, Jo could tell that Ian was getting himself worked up. In a way, he was just like his mother. Both of them reacted to stress by becoming agitated and antagonistic.

"You always do this, Ian," Jo said to him, her own frustration suddenly nearing the breaking point. "Just stop it."

He paused again, but before he could reply, the chimes rang at the front door. They all turned to look, and a moment later, two more people walked into the room: Helen and Kent Tulip.

"Hail, hail, the gang's all here," Ian said.

Just one big happy family.

Alexa felt bad leaving before she had a chance to do anything about Winnie and what she'd seen last night. But her mom and Rick were ready to go, so Alexa guessed that she'd have to wait until she returned, later tonight, to pursue it.

What she'd really like to do was just forget it and not say anything to anybody. But what had happened was just too weird. As nice as Winnie seemed, she had obviously been up to no good, crawling in a window and fooling around with a medicine cabinet. The old lady needed to know.

For a while today, Alexa thought she had figured it out. She nonchalantly asked the old lady if she had diabetes, wondering if the Pixie Stix powder had been put into the pills as some kind of cruel trick to kick up her blood sugar. But the answer had been no. She did have several health issues, but that diabetes wasn't one of them.

Alexa reached her bedroom and grabbed her purse, checking her reflection in the mirror. She knew if she told the truth, she'd be busted. And she couldn't have that. What if, like her mom had said, they told her "that's it, you're outta here"?

Running a brush through her short hair, Alexa realized that maybe there was another way to do this. Maybe somehow she could keep an eye on the guest house tonight, and if she saw Winnie sneaking out again, this time she could take action. She could tell Jo's bodyguard that someone was sneaking around in the backyard and then he would call security to check it out.

That sounded good. Alexa was actually glad now that her mom was bringing her back here to sleep tonight. Happily, she put down her hairbrush, went down the stairs, out the door, and the long way around to the front, where her mom and Uncle Rick were waiting for her.

At least now she had a plan.

"Excuse us, everyone, but we need to have a private conversation," Jo announced suddenly at the sight of her parents.

Not only had her father refused to talk further to her the day before, but she hadn't even spoken to her mother since she learned about their deal with Bradford to marry her. Right now, Jo didn't care what kind of maneuvers they pulled, she wasn't going to listen to anything but the truth, anything but an apology. She had never stood up to her mother before, but today, right now, that was going to change.

"Outside," Jo said, standing and marching from the room, despite her awkward cast. She didn't wait for a reply, but simply walked through the house avoiding the foyer completely, out the back door, and across the lawn to the French garden. The thought of being indoors for one more minute was utterly claustrophobic.

The French garden was one of Jo's favorite places on the whole estate. Set far back from the house, it featured a winding pathway that meandered among fountains and flowers, with stone benches set at various points alongside the path. Not much was blooming this early in the year, but that didn't matter. What Jo was looking for now was privacy.

Pushing open the gate, Jo took a glance behind her to see that both parents had, indeed, followed her from the house, as had her bodyguard. Once inside the garden, she walked more slowly until the others caught up. Then, in single file, she led them toward the butterfly area, where two twisted willow benches sat across from each other. Silently, Jo sat on one and waited as her parents sat on the other. The bodyguard remained standing at a discreet distance.

Jo was determined not to make this any easier for them than it ought to be. Beyond all the talk of attempted murder and corporate maneuvers and share distributions remained the simple fact that Kent and Helen Tulip had tried to buy a husband for their daughter while employing all manner of deception in order to do so. Jo didn't know how their relationship was ever going to heal from that—not that it had been all that great in the first place.

"Where do I even begin?" Jo asked finally.

"I know you're upset with us," her mother said. "And rightfully so. A lot has happened, a lot has been…learned."

"Like the fact that the two of you paid Bradford to marry me?"

Helen looked away, obviously at a loss for words—not a common occurrence by any means.

"Does it help to know that your mother and I were both deeply fond of Bradford?" Kent said. "We had ulterior motives, yes, but it's not like we just picked some stranger off the street. We chose him very carefully, Jo. We would have cared for him like a son."

Jo tore a leaf from a nearby geranium and pressed her thumbnail against it, forming little half moons all along the edges.

"Daddy, there is nothing either one of you could say to me that would justify what the two of you did. Nothing. Don't even try."

They sat there together silently, the only sound that of the rustling leaves in the trees and one lone bobwhite in the distance. There was so much Jo wanted to say, but she couldn't seem to form the words.

"I don't know how you two sleep at night," she said finally. "Or look at yourselves in the mirror in the morning."

"We did what we felt like we had to do at the time," Helen said. "But we are sorry, if that helps."

"Sorry because of what you did, or sorry because you got caught?"

"Don't be disrespectful, Jo," Helen said sharply. "We are still your parents."

"Yeah, well, I'm not sure I still want to be your daughter."

Even as she said it, Jo feel a brief, hot flash of shame. Maybe she was on the verge of pushing it too far. She took a deep breath and tried to calm down.

"I know you think our motives were pure greed, Jo," her father said, "but there was much more to it than that."

"Oh?"

"You're not really a part of the business world, so I don't expect you to understand. But when a company gets to be the size of Bosworth Industries, it practically takes on a life of its own. Do you even comprehend the scope of what we're talking about?"

He scooted forward and counted on his fingers as he talked.

"We've got upwards of forty thousand employees, with nineteen separate corporate divisions, each with its own independent management. At any point in time, we have more than two thousand projects or business ventures going on worldwide."

Jo listened to his statistics, genuinely surprised. She knew the company was big, but she didn't know it was *that* big.

"We've bought and sold many subsidiaries," he continued, "grown and expanded and adapted with the times, survived and thrived and pushed the envelope in many ways. We have grown tremendously while still remaining a good, solid company, thanks in large part to *my* leadership. But if Eleanor had died with you still single, forcing your shares to be diverted to some stupid charitable trust, then who knows what might've happened?"

"So basically it was worth destroying my future to save your lousy job?"

Kent shook his head vehemently.

"It's not just my job or our own personal fortune that would be at risk, Jo. It's everyone who owns shares of Bosworth, who works for Bosworth, who deals with Bosworth. By trying to arrange your marriage, we were acting in the best interests of everyone involved."

He sure sounded convincing.

Then again, a person didn't get to be the top dog in a company that size without learning how to make themselves come out smelling like a rose.

"You were acting in the best interests of everyone involved," Jo repeated softly. "Everyone except me."

To think that her parents could actually justify their behavior this way simply boggled her mind. Had they really convinced themselves that buying Bradford, manipulating their daughter, and forcing a wedding was somehow justified in light of the greater good?

"Oh, good grief, Jo," Helen snapped, "it's not like we tried to marry you off to a robber baron or a criminal or some kind of beast. Bradford is a handsome, capable, intelligent man, and he would have made a good husband. From what I understand, he even grew quite fond of you."

"We didn't see you doing any better on your own," Kent added. "It's not like you had any other prospects, and living there in that small town, who knew if you'd ever find anyone? By hooking you up with Bradford, we were doing you a favor."

Tears filled Jo's eyes, blurring her vision.

"Why didn't you just come to me?" she asked, her voice cracking. "Instead of perpetuating this incredible hoax, why didn't you just tell me the truth? We all thought Gran was going to die after the stroke. I would've understood your concerns about the company if I had known about the trust."

Her parents looked at each other, all sorts of silent communications passing between them.

"And what would you have done, Jo?" Kent asked. "We know you. You're very stubborn, and when it comes down to it, you really don't care all that much about Bosworth Industries. Be honest. If we had asked you to get married for the sake of the company, you would have laughed us out of town. Your mother and I did what we had to do in the way that we had to do it. We had no choice."

"Oh, you had a choice," she replied. Jo looked at her parents, really looked at them, and wondered if she'd ever be able to forgive them.

"Look, we're sorry for the way things worked out," Helen said, "and even sorrier that Bradford ended up reneging on our arrangement. But we've got a bigger problem now. I think you need to get over all of this so we can concentrate on what's more important. Saving your life."

"Does that mean you're going to side with Uncle Neil so that whoever's trying to kill me no longer has a motive? That might save my life."

Kent didn't reply, but the expression on his face told her all she needed to know. He wasn't going to budge.

Jo stood, suddenly done with them and this entire conversation.

"Fine. I can take care of myself."

She turned and walked away, but as she went, her mother called after her.

"Just don't marry Danny Watkins, whatever you do."

Jo froze and then slowly turned around. It had grown fully dark now, though the garden was well illuminated with spot lighting.

"What?"

"I'm begging you, Jo," Helen said, standing and coming to her. "Don't marry Danny. You told me a few weeks ago that the two of you had fallen in love but that he went off to Europe without you. Let him stay gone, let him pursue his dreams by himself. He's not the man for you. He never was and he never will be. I wouldn't even be surprised if he ended up getting fired and coming home with his tail between his legs. He's simply not good enough for you. We both know you can do better."

Jo was enraged. Incensed. Closer than she'd ever been in her entire life to punching someone. Danny wasn't *good enough?* Danny was one of the best people she had ever known!

"This conversation is over," Jo said, unwilling even to dignify her mother's words with a response.

Then she spun on her heel and walked away, knowing that if it were humanly possible, right now steam would be shooting out of her ears.

Alexa was devastated.

According to Dr. Stebbins' secretary, the only rehab places with an available bed were either not covered by Medicaid or too far away. There was a place in Delaware, which was only a few hours' drive, but they didn't expect to have any openings for a couple of days.

"They're going to let me know as soon as something opens up," the woman said. "It could be tomorrow, but more likely Monday or Tuesday."

"Okay. Let me know when you hear from them," Alexa said, giving the woman Rick's cell phone number so she could call tomorrow if they got that lucky.

She thanked the woman and hung up. All she wanted was to get her mom some help, but right now everything seemed to be going wrong.

Alexa walked back into the main part of the restaurant, catching Uncle Rick's eye as she approached their table. With a slight shake of her head, she told him all she could say right now, that it hadn't worked out yet. In response, he looked genuinely disappointed and, most of all, sad. Just the way she felt.

Sliding into the booth across from them, Alexa hoped that the soup she'd ordered might wake up her appetite. She was feeling terrible, especially because her mother seemed to be going to pieces as the day wore on—becoming jittery and irritable and withdrawn, not to mention chainsmoking constantly. Alexa had seen her mom rooting frantically through her own suitcase and her purse more than once, sliding her fingers along the bottom of each pocket, and Alexa had a feeling that she was just hoping to run across some forgotten pill.

At least Uncle Rick, who was usually a real pushover, had finally reached his limit. The last time Alexa's mom snapped at him for no reason, he told her there was an AA meeting in the basement of a local church at 9:00 PM, and they were going there even if it killed her.

Alexa knew her mom needed more than just Alcoholics Anonymous. She needed Everything-That's-Addictive Anonymous.

More than anything, the woman needed a dry out clinic, a place that would basically keep her prisoner until she got through the worst of it, and then help her to heal.

The food arrived, and as the waitress slapped their dishes on the table, Alexa looked up at Rick and spoke.

"Monday or Tuesday," she said, hoping her mom could hold on that long. "At the soonest."

He nodded, understanding.

"Monday or Tuesday what?" her mom asked.

"That's when Consuela will be giving me cooking lessons," Alexa lied easily, picking up her spoon. "I'm going to learn how to make soup just like this."

Jo had managed to calm down somewhat by the time she neared the carriage house. She was done with her parents, finished talking, finished listening to excuses. Finished being a part of this family, if that were possible.

Oh, how she wished she had two good legs! She would strap on her skates and take off down the street and keep rolling all the way to the bay, if possible.

Just thinking of a physical release, she went into the carriage house and tried to find some piece of equipment that would allow her to work out without using her legs. Rejecting the treadmill, the bicycle, and the rowing machine, she turned to the universal and started lifting weights. After she had exhausted the options for arm lifts, she got down on the mat, laid on her back, raised her injured legs into the air, and started doing crunches.

Though she wasn't dressed for it, she didn't care. It was the burn she was after, the focus and the pull and the pain, good pain. After 75 crunches, she was breathing heavily. At 150, she was hurting. Finally, at 200, she collapsed onto the floor and just lay there, catching her breath.

She closed her eyes, wondering among other things if the body-guard thought she was nuts. When she opened her eyes, however, he was standing over her, holding out a towel and smiling.

"Sorry to interrupt, but if I were you, that's exactly what I would've done. Too bad you can't go running or something."

She took the towel from him, sat up, and dabbed at her neck and chest. Strangely, she did feel a lot better. Exercise always helped.

"Did you ever wonder how you could possibly be related to your own parents?" Jo asked, tossing the towel across the mat and into the hamper.

"Every time my father picks his teeth in public."

Jo burst into a laugh. It felt good to laugh.

He helped her up and from there she decided she was going back to the studio to work on her toasters. On the way, she detoured over to Chewie's pen, feeling guilty that she'd left him out there in the dark for so long. She released him, and he gladly ran alongside her as she went to the studio, his new bone clenched tightly in his teeth.

The piano was playing as she neared the building, a boogie-woogie sort of tune, and Jo smiled as she opened the door, expecting to see Alexa. Instead, Jo's smiled faded as she realized that the person at the piano was Ian.

"Hey, cuz!" he said, ending the song with a flourish. "Gran said you'd end up out here eventually. Nice pooch."

"Where is everyone?"

"The doctor showed up to look at Dad's leg, so I made a quick exit. I don't do well with blood or pain."

Jo wasn't surprised. She released Chewie's collar and he ran straight to Ian, gave him a few sniffs, and began wagging his tail. True to form, Chewie was eager to make a new friend. As Ian reached out to pet him, Jo hobbled over to the toasters and started back in where she had left off. Soon, Ian joined her, across the table.

"Your parents were out here looking for you when I showed up," Ian told her, "but they only hung around for a few minutes and then they left."

"Good," she said. "I'm glad they're gone."

Jo wasn't thrilled that Ian was there, either, but if her uncle needed stitches, as she suspected he would, then they would have to leave soon anyway to get to a clinic or ER.

"You used to like me, Jo," Ian said. "When we were kids. What happened?"

She put down the rag and looked at him.

"I still like you, Ian. I just have to take you in smaller doses. You're a little…much for me."

"Yeah, I'm a little much for everybody. Even myself sometimes."

Jo glanced at the row of toasters, wondering if she could simply work on them all night. She missed her own home, where she could use cleaning as the perfect antidote to stress. Around here, they had people to do those things. If Jo got down on her hands and knees and started scrubbing a floor, everyone would think she'd gone mad.

"Well, I won't hang out and interrupt your work," Ian said. "I just had one thing to tell you before I go. Something I thought you'd like to know."

"What's that, Ian?"

"The real reason that your father is opposing the announcement about Fibrin-X. The motivation that is making him stand firm even at the risk of his own daughter's life."

At least he had her attention now. Jo met her cousin's eyes, seeing the family resemblance in the vivid green there. Ian pointed a thumb at the bodyguard.

"Does he have to be here for this?"

"Never leaves my side," Jo replied. "But whatever he overhears remains strictly confidential."

"Yeah, right," Ian said, rolling his eyes. "Whatever. Here it is. You want it?"

"Yes. Actually, I'd love to hear what you have to say."

"Your father doesn't just hope to postpone the announcement about Fibrin-X. He hopes eventually to squash the research completely. He doesn't want that drug ever reaching the market."

"Why not?"

Ian leaned back again, propping his feet on the table.

"Ever heard of Lambremil? The drug?"

"Sounds familiar."

"It's made by our pharmaceutical company, the same folks who are behind the Fibrin-X. Lambremil is the number one ADHD drug in the world. It helps manage the symptoms."

"Okay."

"Do you know the statistics, Jo? Depending on who's counting, right now there are eight million adults and maybe as many as four and a half million kids with ADHD. More of them take Lambremil than any other drug. They take it every day. Every single day, many of them for their entire lives. Do you understand what I'm saying?"

It took a minute, but finally Jo began to get it. She looked at him, eyes wide.

"He doesn't want there to be a cure."

"Bingo."

Ian sat forward, tapping a finger against the table.

"Even if we charged a hundred bucks a pop for the Fibrin-X, even five hundred, a one-time-use drug is pretty limiting in its earning potential. Just think of all the cash flow problems when the Lambremil well trickles dry. As your father likes to say, the financial consequences of that would be astronomical."

Ian was telling her the truth. Jo knew it, in her heart, knew that her father would place his bottom line against the health of millions of suffering people, as well as the safety of his own daughter.

Jo felt sick to her stomach.

"Well, I'd better get moving," Ian said, standing. "I can see my work here is done."

He started to leave, but as he walked away, Jo realized there was still one thing that didn't add up.

"Ian."

"Yeah?"

"No offense, but you love money more than anyone in the whole family, and you're not exactly a well of compassion for the hurting people of the world."

"Gee thanks for that insult. Nice seeing you too."

"Wait," she said, stepping toward him. "I'm just saying, knowing you as I do...why are you against my father in this? Loyalty to your own dad is one thing, but it makes no sense why you, of all people, would support the less economical choice in this matter."

He stood there for a long moment. Then he smiled, but it wasn't his usual fake happy smile. It was real and kind of sad.

"Can't you guess?"

She shook her head.

"Like all ADHD drugs, Lambremil has side effects. All drugs have side effects. I was never able to tolerate any of them."

Jo suddenly realized that Ian had ADHD. In a flash, she realized he always had.

"I'm sorry, Ian. I didn't know."

"Yeah, well, I wasn't even diagnosed until a few years ago. People thought I was just incorrigible. Wild. Way out in left field. I suppose I am, but I suspect that's mostly thanks to my disorder."

"You want the cure for yourself."

"Yes, I do. The moment the Fibrin drug trials go into the next phase, my name is at the top of the list."

22

Danny couldn't believe that he was actually standing on American soil. The last hour of the flight had been torture, watching out the window for the sight of New York City. Landing at JFK and getting off the plane and going through customs had been positively surreal.

Now he was standing beside his rental car, a little white Chevy, wondering how quickly he could get to Jo. Depending on the traffic, Danny figured he might be able to make it to the estate in about an hour.

That meant that in about an hour, he would say hello to Jo and probably give her the shock of her life. He would look deeply into the eyes of the woman that he loved and tell her that he was there for her, for however she needed him.

His biggest question was why she hadn't told him that she *did* need him or what was really going on.

After Ian left, Jo decided to go online and check her e-mail, to see if Toaster Man had responded yet to the note she'd sent him last night. He had not, but there were plenty of other e-mails waiting for her, mostly business matters and reader letters.

She worked on them for a while, taking a break when a contrite and red-eyed Consuela showed up with a warmed-over dinner plate, asking if she was hungry. She had also brought out some dog food for Chewie, which he devoured in a matter of seconds. Jo's dinner was wonderful, and as she ate, she tried to calm any concerns Consuela might have about the chandelier incident.

"The biggest person to blame is myself," Jo said. "I should've told you that the crystals can be tricky to put back in place."

Consuela seemed to feel better by the time she left.

Alexa returned soon after that from her outing and asked if she could join Jo in the studio. The girl spread some books out at the next table for studying, but as she worked, she seemed upset and listless, and Jo wondered if she always got that way after time with her mother. It couldn't be easy to live such a strange life, standing with one leg in each world and not really feeling a part of either.

Jo tried drawing the girl into conversation, and it didn't take much to get her talking. In fact, she seemed relieved to be able to unburden on someone. Alexa talked about her mother's drug addiction, about the need to find a rehab and then accomplish the more difficult task of talking her mother into actually going into it. Alexa seemed so hopeless that Jo thought she might talk to her grandmother later and find out if they could help financially in some way.

Mostly, Jo just let Alexa go on about all of her mother's faults and weaknesses, expressing feelings that had probably been building up for a while. The picture she painted as she talked was of a highly unstable woman, severely addicted to drugs and men, who did not seem capable of parenting a teenager or holding down a job or even making it through one day without a fix of some kind or another. Jo could only imagine how relieved the woman must have been when her daughter underwent a medical miracle and was taken off of her hands by some rich lady across the river.

"The sad thing is," Alexa said, "all afternoon I kept looking at her and thinking that's how I would have ended up. That's what I would have become, if Dr. Stebbins hadn't fixed me and pulled me out of there."

"Somehow I doubt it. You're made of stronger stuff."

Jo thought of her own situation, of the petty, materialistic people her parents were. She might have become like them too, she supposed, if not for the love of her Tulip grandparents, who showed her a better way to live, not to mention the One to live for.

"You know, my mother's not such a piece of cake either," Jo added. "When I was way younger than you, I made the decision that I was *not* going to grow up to be like her. And you know what? If we didn't have the same last name, you wouldn't even know we were related, that's how different we are."

"Really?"

"Really."

"Is she a drug addict?"

Jo smiled.

"No. But she's not a very good person. Lately, I've started to realize that in a lot of ways she's a very bad person."

"But she loves you, right?"

"In her own way, I guess. I think she loves herself too much to really love anybody else."

"That's sad."

Jo shrugged.

"God made sure that I had a lot of other people to love me instead—grandparents and friends. And, of course, God loves me most of all. Having Him in my life fills up all of those other empty spots inside."

"Sometimes I talk to God, but I'm never sure if He's really listening. I went to a youth group at a church once, and they said He hears everything everybody says, but I'm not so sure if that's true."

Jo looked at the young woman in front of her, praying for wisdom and all the right words.

"God hears you, sweetheart. He's listening—and He loves you more than you could ever imagine."

Somehow, that news seemed to reach some hurting place deep in Alexa's heart. Her eyes slowly filled with tears.

"You know that for sure?" she whispered.

"I've never been more sure of anything in my life."

Jo didn't want to overwhelm Alexa with information about God and faith, but as they talked it became clear that the girl already understood plenty—and that, in a way, she had started down that road toward her Creator a long time ago, all on her own. They talked for a while, Jo answering Alexa's questions, and then they even prayed together. Afterward, both of them seemed much more settled and at peace.

Danny put on his blinker, hoping this was the right place. For the last ten minutes, he had passed estate after estate, most of them hidden by iron fences or high, ivy-covered walls. This one had a little guard hut at the entrance, with a man in a uniform sitting inside. Rolling down the window as he pulled to a stop, Danny asked if this was the Bosworth home.

"Name?" the man said, not bothering to answer Danny's question.

"Danny Watkins."

The gate swung open, allowing him to drive through. When he reached the massive house, another guard was standing there, and he also verified Danny's name against a list. Danny wasn't sure, but somehow he doubted that all of this security was the norm around here.

What was going on?

Finally he stood at the front door and knocked.

Back at her own table, Jo closed out her e-mail, glad that almost all of the reader questions had been simple ones, as she had managed to polish off several days' worth of blog entries, along with a week's worth of columns. This time of year, the same sorts of things popped up again and again: bugs, gardening, stain removal for mud and grass. Easy stuff for which no testing was required.

She decided to work on the toasters some more, so she made up a solution at the sink of warm water and vinegar for her first pass.

"Can I help?" Alexa asked, looking up from her books.

"Sure. Do you want to do the scrubbing or the note taking?"

"I'll take notes."

Jo gave her the notepad and showed her where to write as she dictated. Switching to the dirtiest toaster, Jo dipped a toothbrush in the water and was about to start on the inside of the toaster door when Alexa spoke.

"Shouldn't you unplug it first?" she asked.

Alexa pointed, and Jo followed the cord with her eyes from the back of the toaster down to a floor outlet.

She hadn't plugged it in.

A chill starting at the base of her neck, Jo walked around to the back of the table, to see if any of the others were plugged in also. They weren't.

Was it a simple mistake? Had someone misunderstood and thought she wanted it plugged in?

Jo stood there, trying to give someone the benefit of the doubt, trying to figure it out. She looked at the toaster again and gasped, realizing that the cord in question had been scraped bare near the top, and the exposed wires laid flush against the metal frame. Little black flecks littered the table under the cord. If Alexa hadn't stopped her from touching the appliance with the wet toothbrush, Jo might be toast herself by now.

Someone had tried to electrocute her.

Danny was shown into the study by a maid and left there alone for a few minutes to wait for Mrs. Bosworth. In that time, he thought about simply tearing through the house and calling Jo's name until he found her. Standing here like an idiot waiting for her grandmother was ridiculous.

Finally, he saw the older woman coming toward him. She was walking slowly, with a cane, looking pale and exhausted. He ran forward to help her, and as they walked together to the nearest chair, she leaned on him heavily.

"You made it," she said softly.

Her eyes were shiny, though Danny wasn't sure if that was because she had tears in them or because she was old. He looked at her, trying to figure out why she seemed different from the last time he'd seen her last fall, and finally he decided it was her face. It looked strange now, almost puffy and swollen.

"Where's Jo?" he asked, sitting across from her.

"She's in one of the outbuildings," Mrs. Bosworth replied. "We'll send for her in a moment."

She closed her eyes, swaying slightly, and Danny asked her if she was okay.

"No, I'm not," she replied. "In just the last few hours I have decided that either I'm getting sick or someone's trying to poison me."

That certainly wasn't what Danny expected to hear. Had the woman gone a little nuts, or was he coming in on the tail end of something a lot more complicated? More than likely, it was the latter, considering all that he had learned so far, both from Luc and today from Eleanor on the phone.

"Have you seen a doctor?" he asked.

"Yes, and he wanted me to go to the hospital for some blood work, just in case."

"Why aren't you there now?"

"I wanted to be here when you got here," she said, as if that were the most natural reply in the world. "So I arranged for a private nurse to come out instead. She just left with four vials of my best stuff."

Danny simply shook his head, knowing that the very rich had their own ways of doing things, as bizarre as they may seem to someone like him.

"Could you please just tell me what's going on here?" he asked. "I've come a long way to see Jo, and so far all I am is confused."

"I'll explain the best I can and as quickly as I can," she said. "Then you can go to her. She's out in the studio."

Mrs. Bosworth proceeded to tell him a convoluted tale about how Jo met with Bradford on Wednesday after her doctor's appointment, but that Bradford started telling her that her life was in danger. Sure enough, someone tried to kill her, but Bradford saved her and ended up getting hurt badly himself.

As she took a deep breath to launch into the next part of the tale, Danny tried not to think about the idea of Jo and Bradford together. Danny wasn't necessarily a jealous person, but Bradford was a sore spot with him, a real Achilles heel.

He listened as the tale grew more complicated. The fact that Jo was on somebody's hit list more than likely had something to do with Eleanor's late husband's trust and the strange distribution of company shares, depending on the order of who died when. By the time she finished explaining it, what he understood most was that both Jo and her grandmother were in grave danger, but that the possible list of people who would have something to gain from their deaths had dozens of names on it, far too many to ferret out the killer before he or she was able to try again.

"The only way I know to protect my granddaughter," Eleanor said tiredly, "is to make sure that's she's married before I should die or become incapacitated. Her parents pulled a fast one in trying to get her to marry Bradford last fall—but Jo will have to tell you the details of all that herself. All I know is that the last time I saw you, you told me that you loved my granddaughter very much and that you wanted to marry her. I believe your words were something like, 'I want to take care of her for the rest of her life.' Is that still true? Because if it is, the best way you can start taking care of her is by marrying her as quickly as possible. She'll be vested in her stock shares—and safe—the moment the two of you are declared husband and wife."

Though her hands were shaking, for the sake of Alexa, Jo did not make a big deal of the toaster wire being scraped bare, put against the metal, and plugged in. She had a feeling this little setup probably wouldn't have done more than give her a mild shock, if that, but that was beside the point. Someone without much knowledge of appliances had more than likely set this up hoping it would kill her, and that's what mattered. Now, Jo suggested that they head into the house because she needed to talk to her grandmother.

"But what about cleaning the toasters?"

"We'll work on them tomorrow. Do you mind? It looks like that one might have a short in it, anyway."

Jo wasn't sure what to do. She didn't want to mess with any of the evidence, but she didn't want to leave this as it was in case someone else came along and was accidentally shocked instead. Finally, she realized that for the time being, they could simply throw the breaker. The body-guard did that for her, plunging half of the room in darkness.

They all walked to the house together, Jo glancing around at the dark grounds as they went, sensing eyes in every shadow. Once Alexa was back in her room, Jo would talk to her grandmother and together they would call the police. Jo didn't look forward to once again having to talk a cop into believing her when she said someone was trying to kill her, but maybe if the local cops interfaced with the Manhattan transit authority police, they would get the full story and pay a bit more attention.

Inside, the kitchen and dining room were dark, the only sound was that of Chewie's toenails clicking on the tile floor as they walked through. In the foyer, as her bodyguard kept them safely away from underneath the chandelier, Jo asked Alexa if she would mind taking Chewie with her up to her bedroom for a while.

"I would put him in my room," Jo said, "but even with that bone to keep him busy, he'll still go nuts in there by himself, trying to get out. I'm afraid he'll scrape the doors or eat a pillow or something."

Alexa agreed to keep him for a while, as long as Jo would come and get him when she was ready for bed.

Once Alexa and Chewie were gone, Jo went looking for her grandmother. She finally found her in the study, talking to some man. Jo wasn't sure who it was, but a quick glance at the back of his dark head told her it wasn't her father, cousin, or uncle, who all had light-colored hair, and that's all she cared about.

She stood in the doorway and tapped on the frame.

"Gran? If you have a moment, I need to see you in the other room. It's kind of urgent."

Both Gran and her gentleman caller turned to see Jo, and the funniest thing was, to Jo, the man looked just like Danny. Funnier still was when he stood up and took a step closer and Jo realized that it actually was Danny.

Danny?

Jo opened her mouth to speak, but her voice got lost—disappearing somewhere between the moment she took a breath and the moment she passed out from surprise.

Danny watched as Jo's eyes fluttered and she began to collapse, but before he had moved even a foot, the big guy who was with her jumped forward and caught her under the arms. As Danny ran over to them, and Eleanor assured the bodyguard that he wasn't a threat, the man gently lowered Jo down to the floor. Danny crouched down in front of her, slipping an arm behind her shoulders to hold her up. Her eyes fluttered back open, and as they did she gasped and then reached up with both arms and wrapped them around his neck.

Pulling her to him, they simply embraced, rocking back and forth there on the floor. Danny knew that nothing would keep him apart from her ever again.

He didn't care what it would take. He would not budge from her side.

Alexa didn't mind having the dog in her room. In fact it was kind of fun, but it put a big delay on her surveillance plan for the guest house. She wasn't sure how much longer it would be before Jo came and got him, but she decided she'd use the time to scope out all of the upstairs windows, to see which one would have the best view if Winnie tried to pull her sneak-in stunt again.

Leaving Chewie happily settled on her bed, Alexa crept up and down the hall, peeking out the different windows, and finally settling on the bathroom at the top of the stairs. Not only did it provide a good view of the backyard, but it also had Jacuzzi jets in the tub. That way, if the bodyguard wanted to know what she had been doing in that bathroom down the hall for half the night, she could tell him she'd been enjoying the Jacuzzi and had fallen asleep by mistake.

Back in her room, she gathered up her robe and slippers and a towel and carried them down to the bathroom. Then she returned to her room and to Chewie, flipping on the television to pass the time until Jo came and got him.

Jo couldn't let go of Danny, couldn't stop holding on. Eventually, when she lifted her head to look around the room, she realized that her grandmother and bodyguard had both left, closing the door behind them. Thankfully, Eleanor recognized the need for the two of them to be alone.

There was so much to say and yet nothing at all to say, so much to catch up on and yet nothing more important than simply sitting there on the floor together, Danny's hands in Jo's hair, his lips against her forehead. Jo lifted her face to kiss him, this man she had missed so desperately and loved so much. It was a kiss of reconnection, of claiming. Almost desperately, he kissed her back, gripping her head with his hands and pressing his mouth hungrily to hers. After the kiss, they simply sat there together, her hands on his shoulders, making sure he was real, his hands on her arms and back, making sure she wasn't going to go away. She leaned against his chest and he kissed the top of her head and slowly she was able to believe that he really was here.

Finally, he spoke, his voice warm and tender and so familiar.

"I'm not sure we've been introduced. My name is Danny. You must be Jo."

"It's nice to meet you," she replied. "Though I apologize for only giving you my standard greeting. Next time, I'll try for something a little more personal."

She sat up then, facing him, drinking in the sight of his handsome face, his deep blue eyes. How had she ever gone six weeks without him?

"Danny, what are you doing here? How did you know to come?"

"I was in the neighborhood and thought I'd stop by."

His sweet teasing brought tears to her eyes.

"Hey," he said softly. "Hey. I'm sorry. Don't cry."

Jo blinked, twin tears forming a line down each cheek.

"I'm sorry," she squeaked. "I just missed you so much and I'm so glad you're here. I don't know why I thought I could ever be apart from you for so long."

He gathered her in his arms again and began rocking, cooing softly, saying, "Never again, Jo, never again."

"Do you mean that?"

"Whatever it takes," he replied. "We're together from now on."

As glad as she was to see him, she was confused. She didn't understand how he got here or what happened between the last time she talked to him and now, or why he had been sitting in here with her grandmother like two friends having tea.

"We have a lot to talk about," he said finally, releasing her. "First thing we ought to do, I suppose, is to get up off the floor."

Jo allowed him to help her up and lead her by the hand to the couch. There they sat, side by side, fingers entwining.

They talked.

She told him everything, every detail of what had been happening.

He told her everything that had occurred on his end.

He apologized for ever going to France in the first place, considering how it had come so soon after her accident.

She apologized for keeping him in the dark about what had been happening with her, no matter that her intentions were honorable.

"I know you're a very independent person, Jo, but I'm not taking my cues from you anymore. There's nothing wrong with asking for help. I need to be here every bit as much as you need me to. In fact, if being apart these past weeks has taught me anything, it's that I need you too, more than I ever could have imagined."

Jo agreed, saying that she wanted to learn to cleave to him, to be interdependent with him, that she wanted for them to be together forever.

"Speaking of forever," Danny said, suddenly moving from the couch to the floor again. This time, however, he got down on one knee and held both of her hands in his. "I'm sorry I don't have a ring to give you yet, but I can't wait another moment to ask. I have to know you'll always be mine. Jo Tulip, will you marry me?"

She put her fingertips to her lips, knowing this was the moment she had waited for all of her life.

Would she marry him?

"Yes, Danny Watkins," she whispered, smiling through her tears. "Just try and stop me."

Danny closed his eyes, so thankful to God for this woman. He knew that they had the basis for the kind of marriage he had always dreamed about: They were best friends and had been for years. Truly, between their solid friendship and their faith in God, nothing could give them a stronger foundation than that.

But he knew Jo didn't really understand what he was asking. Gently, he explained he wasn't talking about six months from now, a year from now, at a big church wedding with a long walk down the aisle.

He was talking about tonight.

They could have a church wedding later too, of course. But as her grandmother had said, the moment the judge pronounced them husband and wife, Jo's shares would be vested and there would be no more reason for someone to want her dead.

"But I don't understand," Jo protested. "How could that be legal? We haven't gotten blood tests. We haven't filed for a marriage license."

Danny gave her a rueful look.

"Apparently, the moment your grandmother knew I was coming, she made arrangements. With her pull she was able to work it out. Tonight she has a neighbor, a judge, waiting for a call if we should need him."

"Of course she does," Jo said, a darkness passing in front of her face. "It all makes perfect sense."

"So, will you, Jo? It's only be a matter of time, anyway. Why don't we just speed things along and make it legal now so that no more harm will come to you?"

"Danny," Jo said, shaking her head sadly, "don't you see how we're being manipulated? We're like a pair of puppets and my grandmother is holding the strings."

"I know," he replied. "That's why I think we should talk to a lawyer first, and get a couple of matters out of the way."

"Such as?"

"Such as, not only do I not want the puppet master in there to win, I also don't ever want anyone to think I married you for your money. I think we should draw up a document that clearly lays out what happens to your future inheritance."

"And what would that be?" Jo asked, truly intrigued.

"I've been thinking about this, and, knowing you, I believe I've come up with the right solution. What would you say if I suggested that your shares could go into the charitable trust *anyway*, with you named as trustee so that you can call the shots on how the money is distributed?"

"Would that protect me from harm now?"

"No, but it would give you the last word with your parents and your grandmother, basically snipping away the puppet masters' strings. You could shock them all and become a philanthropist, Jo."

Jo studied him, a new gleam in her eye.

"I love it," she said. "But we are talking about a lot of wealth, Danny. To me, the money has always felt like a burden, but you might not think of it that way. I don't know if that's really fair to you, for me to give it all away. You could be a wealthy man, you know."

He took both of her hands in his and kissed them.

"Yeah, the money would be nice," he said, embarrassed that now tears were forming in his own eyes as well, "but having you as my wife would already make me the wealthiest man who ever lived."

23

The next hour passed in a whirlwind. Sidney, the lawyer, came and handled the legal details, even snickering when Jo and Danny told him their intentions for her inheritance.

"You realize your parents are going to flip, don't you?"

"Absolutely," Jo replied, grinning, knowing the victory was even sweeter because she was marrying the one man her mother had told her *not* to marry.

Once the papers had been drawn up and signed, they got ready to have a wedding. Jo knew that they needed to call the police and report the incident with the toaster, but it seemed safer to get married first and act on that afterwards. The more she thought about it, she decided that in a way it was good that the whole toaster thing had happened, as it allowed the list of suspects to be narrowed down significantly. The people who had been in the studio today, alone, could be counted on one hand: Winnie, Consuela, Jo's parents, and Ian. Considering that several of those suspects were on the property even now, she told her grandmother to leave everyone else out of the ceremony except the lawyer, the judge, and the two who were getting married.

"What about witnesses?" Eleanor asked.

"How many do we need? We've got you and Sidney and the bodyguard."

Jo suggested that Sidney also serve as the best man, even though he had never met Danny before tonight.

"And Alexa can be my maid of honor," Jo added, "though she doesn't need to know what's really going on here."

"I'm sure that would please her," Eleanor said.

Upstairs, Jo flipped through the clothes in her closet, trying to find something to be married in. She hadn't exactly made plans for this when she was packing up at home. She had, however, made plans to go to her grandmother's church, which was kind of formal, so she had brought along three dresses, any of which would suffice now. She picked the lightest-colored one, a soft beige tea-length summer dress with tiny pink roses along the neckline.

Before changing clothes, she went across the hall and tapped on Alexa's door, eliciting excited barks from Chewie. As Jo stood there in the doorway, petting her dog, she told Alexa that she wasn't going to believe this, but that her fiancé had just returned from Europe and they had decided to get married—downstairs, right now.

"Would you consider being my maid of honor?" Jo asked.

Alexa nodded, eyes wide.

"I didn't even know you had a fiancé. You don't have an engagement ring."

"We just never had time to get one," Jo replied truthfully.

Alexa said that it would only take her a few minutes to put on something nicer than a T-shirt and flannel pajama pants, so Jo told her to come down to the study as soon as she was ready. In the meantime, she left Chewie there and returned to her own room to get dressed.

Jo wished she had time for a shower and full makeup and hair and everything. But then she thought of her almost wedding last fall, to Bradford, and she decided that what she looked like as she walked down the aisle wasn't important at all.

What *was* important was the man who would be waiting for her when she got there.

"Oh, my, you do look handsome."

Danny returned to the study to see Jo's grandmother beaming at him from her chair. He had freshened up and was now dressed in his slightly-wrinkled sports jacket and slacks, once again wishing he had his tuxedo instead.

"There's a stereo in the cabinet," she said. "Perhaps you'd like to look through the music. I doubt that we have the bridal march, but check the

Mendelsson, just in case. If not, there should be something else suitable."

He did as she suggested, finally selecting a CD with "Jesu, Joy of Man's Desiring" followed by Pachelbel's Canon. He loaded it into the stereo and adjusted the volume as it played.

"Oh, and you don't need to call me 'Mrs. Bosworth' anymore," she added. "Please, make it Eleanor."

"Okay, Eleanor. How are you doing? Are you feeling okay?"

She didn't look very good.

"I'm much better now, knowing that my granddaughter will be safe."

There was a knock on the front door, and Eleanor suggested that he answer it.

"That would be the judge," she pronounced. "It's showtime."

Alexa couldn't believe this!

It was so exciting and so romantic, and she was going to be a part of it. She chose her frilliest, girliest dress, some pink designer thing that the old lady had picked but that Alexa had never worn. There had never been an occasion dressy enough for it until now.

Standing at the mirror, admiring herself once she was ready, she caught sight of the canopy over her fancy bed and got an idea. It was trimmed with a garland of silk flowers, so she kicked off her nice shoes, climbed up on the bed, and reached as high as she could to pull the flowers down. They were a little dusty but very pretty, so she blew on them with the blow-dryer until they were clean and then used scissors to cut the garland into four pieces.

One piece she wrapped into a circle, to wear on her head like a crown of flowers. She made a second one for Jo, in case she wanted it, then the third she fashioned around Chewie's neck, like a collar. Finally, with the small clump that was left, she formed a bridal bouquet for Jo to carry. Alexa didn't know much about weddings, but she knew that the maid of honor should be helpful in as many ways as she could.

Alexa led Chewie out of the room and knocked on Jo's door, and when Jo answered, it was obvious right away that the flowers had been the perfect touch. Jo looked really, really pleased, especially when she saw the flowers on Chewie too. That made Alexa's heart soar. She liked Jo so much, and she really wanted to make her happy.

Instead of wearing the whole ring of flowers on her head, Jo decided to pull out just one and pin it in her hair. Then she put the rest in her bouquet.

"So what do you think?" Jo asked, stepping back from the mirror and twirling around.

"I think you look like a bride," Alexa said, grinning widely.

They didn't waste much time down in the study. With the door safely closed and only Jo and Danny, Alexa, Eleanor, Sidney, and the bodyguard in attendance, the judge started right in with the ceremony.

Though Jo was thrilled to be standing at Danny's side, about to become his wife, she also couldn't help but feel sad. For a day she had dreamed of her entire life, this wasn't exactly how she had envisioned it. She hated that none of their friends were there, or Danny's family, or that their minister was not even the person conducting the ceremony. Instead, it was some judge Jo didn't even know, reading the words for the ceremony out of a black book that wasn't even the Bible. It was just some handbook for civil servants.

"Ladies and gentlemen," he began, "we are gathered here to join this man and this woman in matrimony…"

Not *holy* matrimony? Just matrimony? Jo hated that, hated that they were racing through the biggest moment of their lives, totally pressured, just so some aspiring murderer might be thwarted in his or her schemes. Jo thought of the people who had had access to that toaster, and it struck her that even her own parents might somehow be involved in the attempts on her life.

Jo pictured her mother as she had been today, in the garden, and her words of warning against marrying Danny. When Jo tried to reconcile that with Danny's own story about how her mother had attempted to woo him back to America with a big job offer and then suddenly changed course and took steps to get him fired instead, it didn't make any sense.

He's not good enough for you, she had said. Good enough? Jo thought now. He was far more than she deserved or ever dreamed of.

"Danny Watkins," the judge was saying, instructing them to face each other and join their right hands, "do you take this woman to be your lawfully wedded wife, to have and to hold, from this day forward…"

Jo's mind was spinning.

Just don't marry Danny Watkins, whatever you do, her mother had said.

But why had she said it? A few weeks ago, when Jo finally told her mother about the change in her relationship with Danny—that they had gone from friends to much-more-than-friends—the woman had been thrilled. So why the change of heart today, in the garden? Why the strange tactics with Danny in Europe?

"I do," Danny said now, his voice strong and sure.

Jo looked at him and she felt terrible, terrible that such a dear and loving man was being manipulated, just as she had been manipulated.

Just don't marry Danny Watkins, whatever you do.

"Josephine Tulip, do you take this man…"

As the judge asked her one of the most important questions of her life, Jo gasped, realizing with sudden clarity that her mother had been using reverse psychology on her! Helen Tulip knew that Jo was just stubborn enough and just angry enough that the one way to get Jo to do what Helen wanted was to tell her specifically not to do it. She told Jo "don't marry Danny" so that Jo *would* marry Danny.

"…till death do you part?"

Till death did they part. Slowly, Jo shook her head, her heart pounding.

"I'm sorry," she said suddenly, looking from Danny to the judge to her grandmother. "But I don't. Not right now. Not like this."

Alexa didn't understand what was going on. First Jo stopped the wedding just when it was getting good, then Danny wasn't mad or anything, he just looked concerned, Then the old lady started feeling all weak and dizzy and had to lie down. Alexa would have thought it was all just a bunch of crazy drama until she heard Danny say something to Jo about Eleanor maybe having been poisoned.

Poisoned?

Jo quickly shushed him, glancing at Alexa, but Alexa wasn't stupid. There was something going on that they didn't want her to know about.

The problem was, she knew something they didn't know about too.

"What about poison?" Alexa asked, tugging at Jo's sleeve.

"Nothing, honey. Would you please take Chewie upstairs to your bedroom and wait there? I'll come up and talk to you in a bit."

Unfortunately, Alexa couldn't do as she was asked.

Eleanor was a tough old bird, but Alexa really liked her and always had. She would feel just terrible if something bad happened to her—something Alexa could have prevented if she hadn't been afraid to speak up.

She had to tell them what she'd seen.

Steeling her nerve, she brought Chewie upstairs and locked him away so he wouldn't be in all the confusion. Then she came back down and stood in the study doorway, listening as Jo talked to the police on the phone about poison and toasters and electrocutions. Danny was kneeling on the floor beside the couch, holding the old lady's hand and telling her that everything would be okay.

"Alexa," Danny said, noticing her. "I thought Jo asked you to wait upstairs."

Alexa took a step forward as Jo finished her call and hung up the phone.

"I saw something," Alexa said. "Last night. I saw something outside."

That got all of their attention. Even the old lady twisted her head around from where she was lying on the couch.

"Alexa, what are you saying?" Eleanor demanded. It wasn't until then that Alexa realized the old lady wasn't looking like herself at all. Her face was swollen and puffy, as were her arms and legs.

"About five o'clock this morning," Alexa said. "I'm sorry I didn't tell you sooner, but I didn't want to get in trouble. I was outside, and I saw someone climb in through your bathroom window and mess with your medicine cabinet. "

That earned gasps from all of them.

"Can you describe this person?" Jo demanded.

"I don't have to describe them. I know who it was."

"Who?" they all asked at once.

"It was Winnie."

For the time being, Jo wasn't even going to ask Alexa why she had been outside at five o'clock in the morning. All she cared about was figuring out what substance Winnie had used as a poison, so that they could help Eleanor in time. At least the police were already on their way.

Could it really have been Winnie who pushed Jo at the train, who tried to kill her with the toaster, who had been trying to poison her own mother? Truly, Jo was shocked. She hadn't thought Winnie had it in her.

Once the police were there, it didn't take much explanation to convince them that the woman staying out in the guest house should be detained for suspicious behavior, though they stopped short at calling it "attempted murder" until they had more of the facts. Of course, it helped that both uniformed men who responded to the call were well aware of who Mrs. Bosworth was and her influence in the community. Surely, they knew that they would do well to heed her request to take her daughter into custody.

Jo was relieved to see that they were able to do the apprehending without any trouble. Winnie was watching a gardening show on television, jotting down ideas for a new planter layout, when the cops simply knocked on her door and told her she needed to come with them. Before going, she insisted on talking to Sidney, who coldly told her to phone her own lawyer, who advised her not to say one word about anything until she was at the police station and he could be there with her for questioning. Unfortunately, that meant she was giving no denials or confessions for the time being.

She also wasn't giving any clues about what she had done to the capsules in her mother's medicine cabinet.

Thus, under the careful supervision of a detective who did not want any of the evidence compromised, Jo donned a pair of gloves and went through her grandmother's medicines, trying to figure out which one had been altered.

First she narrowed it down to the three bottles that had capsules rather than pills. She thought she might have to pour out some of each, but as soon as she opened the lid of the first bottle, she was hit instantly with a strong scent of orange flavoring. She read off the label as Danny wrote down the information, and then they called Eleanor's doctor to see what he would have to say. According to him, the medication was for Eleanor's thyroid condition. Once they explained what was going on, he said that his best guess was that Winnie had indeed simply replaced the medicine inside the capsules with the sugar powder from Pixie Sticks, hoping her mother wouldn't notice the difference.

"If that's the case," he said, "then I don't think there was any poison involved. When someone with a thyroid condition as serious as your grandmother's is deprived of her medication, the symptoms would fall exactly in line with what she's experiencing now: dizziness, confusion, swollen face and arms and limbs. The blood work we had drawn this afternoon included tests for TSH and T3 and T4, so as soon as the results come back, we'll be able to confirm if her thyroid levels are indeed off. I'd be willing to bet that's exactly what it is."

He was going to do some checking and call back. After they hung up, Jo realized that she had forgotten to ask him if denying someone their thyroid medication could be fatal or just disorienting. Either way, Jo wasn't sure if Winnie's motivation was greed for the money or the desire to ensure the development of Fibrin-X for her son's sake or just an attempt to stop others from messing with her planting season. As Winnie's lawyer had told her not to talk, she had been driven away from the estate in the backseat of a police car with her lips sealed.

Fernando and Consuela, who had been roused from their garage apartment by all of the police activity, were beside themselves with worry about Eleanor, insisting that she allow them to bring her to the hospital right away. The doctor called back and confirmed that her thyroid levels were indeed a mess. He said that a bed was ready and waiting for her at the hospital in White Plains, and he would meet her at the ER.

"We'll do more tests, of course, but if that's all it is, we should be able to get her stabilized within the next twenty-four hours," he told Jo in a reassuring tone. "Don't worry."

The men helped Eleanor into the back of the limo and Consuela climbed in beside her. Before they drove away, however, Eleanor insisted on speaking to Alexa.

The girl approached the vehicle and stood there self-consciously until Eleanor opened her arms and Alexa fell into them for a big hug.

"You probably saved my life, young lady. Thank you."

"You're welcome," Alexa replied in a small voice.

"But when I get out of the hospital, we're going to talk about this little matter of you being outside at five o'clock in the morning. I do believe I shall have to take that iPod away from you for a while as a punishment for trying to sneak out."

"Yes, ma'am," Alexa replied, her face red. "You get better, okay?"

Together, they watched the limo drive away, Jo's hand on Alexa's shoulder. Jo was amazed to realize that the girl had cracked the toughest nut of all, Eleanor Bosworth. Jo realized now that she and her grandmother had been getting along better in these past few days than they ever had before, and she had a feeling that Alexa's influence was to thank for that.

The old dog had finally been taught some new tricks.

Danny couldn't believe how tired he was, but this long night was not over yet. Though it was late, the police still needed to finish taking statements. Alexa had already given hers earlier, when Eleanor and the lawyer were still there. Now it was Jo's turn, so while the cops questioned her in the study, Danny and Alexa kept each other company in the kitchen.

Alexa was a neat kid, and Danny soon found himself entertaining her with funny Chewie stories.

"But once Chewie ate the remote control," Alexa said, fascinated, "how did you change the channel?"

"We'd just squeeze his tummy to go up and tug his tail to go down. Oh, and we pulled his ears to adjust the volume."

"Now you're teasing me," she said, eyes sparkling, but she didn't seem to mind.

Danny was hungry, so he decided to whip up a midnight snack. Raiding the refrigerator, he was able to find everything he needed to make a massive club sandwich, which he split with Alexa.

Talk turned more serious as they sat at the table to eat. Jo had already given Danny the whole story of Alexa and how she had come to be living there, but he wanted to hear it from her point of view. He asked about the original incident, when she had the stroke. Something had been bothering him since he heard it the first time, from Jo.

"Wait a minute," Danny said, interrupting Alexa's tale almost as soon as it started. "You were out taking a walk, all by yourself, in the middle of the night, near Newark? Is that the kind of place where a kid just goes for a walk in the middle of the night?"

Alexa hesitated, her face flushing bright red. Danny felt bad, because whatever Alexa had been doing when she had the stroke was clearly none of his business—but what Bradford had been doing was.

"Yeah, it's not the best place to be late at night," she finally allowed.

Danny put down his sandwich and looked Alexa right in the eyes.

"You probably just think I'm being nosy," he said, trying to give her a reassuring smile, "but this is important for Jo's sake. Alexa, do you know a man named Bradford Quinn?"

"Of course. He's the one who saved my life."

She went on to describe how Bradford had driven her to the hospital and retrieved her mother and coordinated her treatment and introduced her to Dr. Stebbins.

"And he did all of that," Danny said, "for a total stranger he found on the side of the road, out of the goodness of his heart?"

Alexa nervously tore the crust from what remained of her sandwich.

"He was on his way to a meeting and he saw the strangest thing on the side of the road, and when he pulled over to check it out, he realized that it was a young teenage girl, just lying there. It was me, and my whole right side—"

"Alexa. You're giving me a speech. A nice, convincing, rehearsed speech."

She took a big bite of her sandwich.

"Why don't you tell me what really happened that night?" Danny prodded. "Why was Bradford there, and what were you doing?"

She chewed that bite a record number of times, but eventually she had to swallow. Then she looked at him, her eyes wary.

"I'm not supposed to tell," she said. "He made me promise."

"Some promises shouldn't be kept, Alexa. Not if they put other people in danger."

"The old lady and Dr. Stebbins, they'd be so ashamed of me."

"Why?"

She exhaled slowly.

"Because I was making a delivery. A drug delivery. A hundred and fifty bucks to make a drop at the indigo blue Jaguar by the old caboose. I had done it plenty of times before to the same guy. This time, I was almost at his car when I tripped and fell. I didn't bump my head all that hard, really, but it was enough to rupture the aneurysm. I don't remember much after that, except Bradford making me promise not to tell anybody why he was there. He said if I promised not to tell, he'd make sure I was taken care of. Well taken care of. He kept his promise, but now I've broken mine."

Danny shook his head.

"He was wrong to force you into that deal in the first place. You don't need to feel bad."

She shrugged, obviously not convinced.

"What kind of drugs he was buying?"

"Same as he always gets. Speed. Everybody knows that's how Bradford hides the drinking he does at night, by popping speed during the day."

"Who is 'everybody'?"

Alexa shrugged.

"My mom mostly, I guess."

"How does your mom know that?"

"Probably 'cause she talks to him a lot."

Danny tried not to react too strongly to that statement. What on earth was Bradford doing hanging out with Alexa's mother?

"Oh, yeah? Why is that? Are they dating?"

Alexa laughed, shaking her head.

"Eww! My mom with a hunk like Bradford? Yeah, right."

"What, then?"

"Well, I don't know a whole lot," Alexa hedged, looking as though she was sorry she'd said anything, "and I learned a long time ago not to ask too many questions around my house..."

"Yeah?"

"But I think they're in some kind of business together. I've heard them on the phone, talking about profits and sales and things."

Danny blinked, looking at Alexa.

"Business together? What are they selling?"

Alexa shrugged and looked at Danny, her expression earnest.

"I don't know, Danny. I try not to listen, because I don't want to know."

It was nearly three o'clock in the morning before the final policeman left, along with the extra security personnel. Though Jo would have loved to send the bodyguard packing as well, she suggested he finish out his shift until morning and then they could wrap things up for good.

Jo walked Alexa to her bedroom in order to retrieve Chewie, hanging around just long enough to tuck the girl into bed.

"You're a real hero, sweetie," Jo told her, pulling the covers up and tucking them in along the side. "I'm so proud of you for telling the truth tonight and saving my grandmother."

Alexa just smiled and closed her eyes, looking peaceful but exhausted.

Out in the hall, Jo asked the bodyguard if he would mind taking Chewie outside for a quick potty stop before bed. While man and dog were gone, Jo and Danny took advantage of the privacy to say goodnight.

Jo didn't want to part with him at all, and she was tempted to suggest that they simply cuddle together on the couch downstairs until morning. But she knew they both needed sleep—not to mention that on this almost wedding night, after having been apart for so long, they wouldn't exactly be bubbling over with self-control if they did.

Instead, they kissed goodnight in the hall and then simply hugged, holding onto each other for a long moment before parting.

"You do forgive me for stopping the wedding?" Jo whispered.

"As long as you don't stop the engagement," he replied, giving her one more kiss. "I completely understand."

It wasn't until Jo was in bed, under the covers, that she realized there was still one matter left unresolved.

If Winnie was the one who had been trying to kill her, then who was it who had been trying to warn her? Who was Toaster Man?

Hoping to prod him into action, Jo got up, went to her computer, and wrote another e-mail to him. As she shut down the computer, put it away, and got back in bed, Jo knew one thing for sure. There were still more questions to be answered.

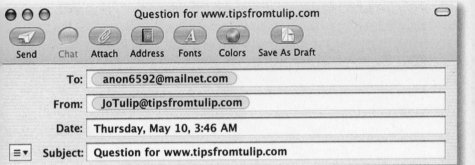

To: anon6592@mailnet.com

From: JoTulip@tipsfromtulip.com

Date: Thursday, May 10, 3:46 AM

Subject: Question for www.tipsfromtulip.com

Dear Trying,

Did you get my last e-mail? A lot has happened since then.

The person you've been warning me about was arrested tonight, just a few hours ago. She's at the police station, giving her confession even as I'm writing this.

My suggestion for you is that you come forward, very quickly, and turn yourself in before she has a chance to do it for you. The police will look much more kindly on you if you do. Maybe when this is all over, I can tell you what I've managed to learn about cleaning toaster ovens.

Sincerely,

Jo Tulip

24

Danny awoke, for a moment unsure about where he was. Paris? Zurich?

Neither, he realized. He was in America, at the home of Eleanor Bosworth.

Sitting up, he glanced at the clock, shocked to see that he had slept until nearly noon. Between jet lag, the mixed-up body clock, and the late hour that they had gone to bed, it made sense. He ran a hand over his face, feeling more rested than he had in days.

In the course of a week, Danny had slept in a grungy flat, a rattling train car, a cheap hotel, an airplane—and now the lap of luxury. He wasn't one for material possessions, but this sure beat the rest. Vaguely, he wondered what the thread count was on the sheets. Eight hundred? A thousand? Whatever it was, they probably cost more than his last month's car payment.

But as he looked around the elegant guest room with its deep leather headboard and ornate carved furniture, as beautiful as it was, he knew he'd rather live in a cardboard box with Jo than a palace without her.

Good thing, too, he thought as he sat up and swung his legs over the side of the bed, because last night they'd essentially signed away her future fortune with the lawyer. Upon Jo's inheritance, they would still get the interest from the shares, whatever that came to, but the actual shares themselves would belong to the Bosworth Charitable Trust. Considering how heavily that money weighed on Jo, Danny thought it was a pretty good solution. Not that he would have minded marrying rich, but some things were worth a lot more than dollars, and Jo's peace of mind was one of them.

If only Danny could find peace of mind of his own and shake the cloud of uncertainty that had been enveloping him since the cops drove away with Jo's Aunt Winnie last night.

So many things simply didn't add up.

Danny was no crime expert, but he did know that matricide was extremely rare, especially without strange and horrifying extenuating circumstances. Eleanor Bosworth would never have won Mother of the Year, but she wasn't a monster, either. The thought of her own daughter attempting to murder her was astonishing indeed.

Beyond that, Danny still wasn't very happy with the whole Bradford element, especially after talking to Alexa last night. He had learned just enough to get some ideas about what might be going on, but not so much that he could be sure if his ideas were correct. With Bradford in the hospital and refusing to speak to anyone except family—refusing particularly Jo—the situation was difficult indeed. What was Bradford trying to hide? And what had made him go from his tell-all intentions at the train station to the closed-mouth stance he was taking now? At least after speaking with Alexa, Danny had some leverage with which to get information.

He just had to figure out a way to get to Bradford in order to use that leverage.

Putting it out of his mind for now, Danny walked to the window and pulled open the curtains, thrilled that it was such a gorgeous spring day. There was something about being home in the States after spending time in Europe that felt so relaxing, so normal. His stomach growling, Danny realized that the one thing he wanted most, right now, was a real American breakfast, even though he'd slept so late that it was nearly lunchtime. He thought he could smell bacon cooking somewhere in the house, so he decided to get ready for the day as quickly as possible and head out to the kitchen.

Danny's hope was that he and Jo could talk about their engagement over bacon and eggs. Now that they had almost tied the knot the night before, he was impatient to see that through.

He wanted Jo Tulip as his wife, soon, and nothing was going to stop him until he made that happen.

Jo was scooping eggs onto a plate when Danny appeared in the doorway. He looked adorable, freshly shaven and no longer road weary, with the sparkling blue eyes that made her fall in love with him, all over again, every time she saw him. He came straight over to her, wrapped his arms around her from behind, and whispered in her ear.

"Good morning, Almost-Mrs.-Watkins."

"Good afternoon, Very-Much-Engaged-Mr.-Watkins."

Somehow, now that they had almost married, Jo could think of little else. She wanted it to happen for real. She wanted to be Danny's wife.

"Is that amazing plate of food by any chance for me?" Danny asked, pulling away to look at it hungrily.

"In your e-mails," Jo replied, grinning, "all you've talked about for five weeks is how much you missed a normal American breakfast. So I made you one. Eggs, hash browns, bacon, fruit, toast, freshly squeezed orange juice, and coffee. May your cholesterol recover somehow."

"How did you know I was awake?"

"I didn't. It was getting so late, I decided to cook it and then wake you up and serve you breakfast in bed."

She turned to face him, and he put his arms around her again. He was still looking hungry, but now his hunger seemed to be more for her than for the food. As he moved in for a kiss, she put a hand to his lips and said that maybe it was better that she hadn't delivered that breakfast in bed after all.

Smiling, he just groaned and pulled her into a tight hug. Grinning to herself, Jo hugged him back and then moved away and said that his meal was getting cold.

They sat together at the kitchen table. As Danny dug in, Jo brought him up to speed on all that had been happening while he was catching up on his sleep.

Consuela and Fernando were still at the hospital with Eleanor, where they would probably remain for the rest of the day. Jo's grandmother was a little better, hooked up to an IV and ordering around the hospital staff as though they were her own personal minions. Consuela was afraid that if they left Eleanor's side she might actually start hiring and firing hospital personnel.

"Yep," Danny said after swallowing a sip of juice. "That sounds like your grandmother all right."

Jo said that the bodyguard service had been terminated this morning and that Alexa was outside playing with Chewie, waiting for her mother and the mother's boyfriend to pick her up for their visitation day.

"She's been dressed and ready to go since ten. I guess they're running late."

"Poor kid."

Jo said that once Alexa was gone, things around there should be quiet, at least until the police returned. Since taking Winnie into custody, the cops had managed to get a partial confession from her. Winnie was claiming that she hadn't been trying to kill her mother by tampering with her thyroid medication, but merely make her seem confused. According to the stipulations of the trust, Eleanor's shares would be distributed upon her death or incapacitation, and Winnie was insisting that that was all she had been going for—trying to get her mother declared incapacitated so the shares could be distributed.

Winnie denied having anything to do with any attempted murder on Jo. Doubtful of her claims, however, the police had obtained a warrant and were coming back out to do a more thorough search of the guest house where she'd been living, to try and find some sort of evidence to the contrary. Winnie had no alibi for Wednesday around the time Jo was pushed. She said she'd simply gone out driving around for a few hours to look at some of the local gardens, and had never interacted with anyone who could corroborate.

As for the tampered-with toaster, though Winnie denied doing that as well, the cops weren't taking it very seriously anyway. Just as Jo had suspected, they said the setup wouldn't have done much harm, and it certainly wouldn't have been deadly.

"Still, what does that have to do with it?" Jo asked Danny as she made herself some tea. "Attempted murder is still attempted murder, even if the person doesn't know what they're doing."

"I agree."

"I'll just be glad when this whole thing is over. All I've been thinking about all day is Toaster Man."

"Toaster Man?"

"That's my nickname for the person who's been sending me the anonymous e-mails—though of course in the end it might turn out to be Toaster Girl. I just don't know."

"If Winnie's the attempted killer," Danny said, "then who do you think your anonymous e-mailer is?"

Jo shook her head, frustrated that she had no good answer for that.

"I would have to say Neil or Ian, or maybe even Muck."

"Muck?"

"The gardener. Winnie comes and helps him out every year with the spring planting. Maybe they're close."

"Maybe, though I can see why he'd want to warn you if he knew something."

"The problem is," Jo said, "whether it's Ian or Neil or Muck or someone else, if they knew Winnie was a threat, why did they allow her to stay here in such close proximity both to me and Gran? A few anonymous e-mails would not have been enough to protect us. I say if it's any of them, they're culpable in the poisoning of my grandmother, not to mention the attempt on my life with the toaster."

Danny took a bite of bacon and chewed thoughtfully.

"I thought you said the e-mail person had had trouble with the law."

Jo nodded.

"That might point to Ian, then," she said. "I know he was stopped for drunk driving a few times during college."

Their conversation was interrupted by Alexa, who swung open the door to announce that her mom was finally there and she was leaving.

"Chewie's inside the fence," Alexa said, looking adorable in jean shorts and her new neon green socks, "and I gave him some fresh water."

"Thanks, honey."

"Hi, Danny."

"Good morning, sunshine."

"Jo, before I go, can I see you outside?"

"Uh, sure."

Curious, Jo went to the door and stepped out, pulling it shut behind her. In the distance, waiting at the curve of the driveway for her daughter, Misty gave a halfhearted wave. Jo waved back.

"Are you ever going to marry Danny?" Alexa whispered. "You *really* should. He's such a hottie. "

Jo laughed out loud.

"Yes, he is a hottie. He's also a good, good man. And what's on the inside of a person is way more important than what's on the outside, you know."

"More important than those gorgeous blue eyes?"

"Yes."

"More important than that sexy smile?"

"Why, Alexa," Jo teased, "I do believe you have a crush on my fiancé."

The girl blushed, and Jo realized that it was true. How cute.

"Yes, I am going to marry Danny," Jo said as she patted Alexa on the shoulder. "So you'll have to find your own hottie, okay? This one's taken, for sure."

Danny was grinning at Jo as she came back inside.

"What?" she asked, crossing back to the table and taking her seat.

"What what?"

"Why are you looking at me like that?"

He wiped his mouth with his napkin and then reached out to put a warm hand on top of hers.

"Because I was just thinking what a wonderful mother you're going to make. Have we talked about how many kids we want?"

The conversation took a more personal turn after that, as Jo and Danny sat at the table and discussed the future and for the first time made a number of concrete plans. Of course, having been best friends for so many years, they had similar life goals and values, so ironing out the details of how they envisioned their life together wasn't very difficult. They both wanted to live forever in Mulberry Glenn, Danny working as a nature photographer and Jo continuing with her household hints. When Danny admitted that he'd been thinking a lot about Jo's burned-down house and had come up with an idea, Jo was all ears.

"What if," he said dramatically, "we used your insurance money to expand my house rather than rebuild your house? We could get rid of the rubble, move your home office closer to the front, and fence in both yards as one. How great would that be? With such a big yard, we'd have room for plenty of little Watkinses to run around in, not to mention the world's coolest swing set, which their father would personally help build."

Jo realized as soon as he said it that the idea was perfect. She had a feeling that the reason she'd postponed doing anything about rebuilding was because she knew subconsciously that there was a better way to go—and that turning the two properties into one was it.

Beyond that, of course, was the thrill in her heart when he talked about "little Watkinses." Her dream had always been to have a big family, and the thought of Danny as the father of her children thrilled her to the very core.

As they continued to talk, Jo was not surprised to find that they agreed on so much—particularly on their intention to marry sooner rather than later. About the only area they disagreed on was travel. Having spent a lifetime being whisked around the world by her parents, Jo wasn't keen on the notion of an extended European tour. She hated to disappoint Danny, but she'd rather stay home, where she was cozy and warm and safe.

The police arrived as Danny and Jo were washing up the dishes. She went to greet them and then stayed outside to keep Chewie calm while they worked out in the guest house, looking for incriminating evidence.

Danny thought it might be the perfect time to run a couple of errands. He returned to his room for his wallet and keys, and then he went outside to tell Jo he'd be back in a few hours if she thought she'd be okay without him.

"Sure, but where are you going?" she asked, surprised.

He merely winked and smiled and said she'd have to wait to find out once he got back.

Driving out of the estate, he reached for his cell phone and dialed the home of his sister Denise, back in Mulberry Glenn. He wasn't sure how to tell his family why he was here rather than in Europe, so he simply said that he'd taken a few days off of work to come home and get officially engaged to Jo.

Of course, that set Denise to yelling and cheering, and she actually wanted him to hold on while she used her cell phone to spread the word along the family grapevine. Laughing, he told her that he had to go, but that before he hung up, he wondered if she could tell him the name of her husband's cousin's jewelry store in New York City where they always got such good deals.

Squealing again, she dug out the name and address of the place and made Danny promise that he would call her back to describe the rings he was considering as soon as he got there.

Danny hung up, glad that the store was in the jewelry district and wouldn't be hard to find. His only concern was that whatever he could afford would never be as nice as the boulder that Bradford had given Jo when they were engaged.

Thinking of Bradford, Danny's mood darkened. He had one other errand to complete. After he had the engagement ring in his pocket, his next stop was the hospital.

Alexa was determined to have a fun day with her mom and Uncle Rick, even if they both seemed quiet and tense. Since they had wheels, something that wasn't usually the case during visitations, she talked them into going to an amusement park that they always passed on the way to Mariner's Village. Fortunately, the old lady had given Alexa enough cash so that she could afford the tickets for all three of them and buy them lunch and treats besides.

Strangely, Alexa didn't want to talk about all of the excitement at the estate the night before with Winnie's arrest. Alexa was terrified that if her mother knew, she might think the place wasn't safe and try to take her out of there. Rick was such a worrier too, and Alexa knew that even if her mother didn't have a problem with it, he would.

So she kept her mouth shut, except for telling the story of how Jo's fiancé showed up from Europe last night and they almost got married but then they changed their minds.

"I was the maid of honor and in charge of the flowers," Alexa bragged, "and I even decorated Chewie."

"Jo almost got married, but then she changed her mind?" Rick asked.

"Yeah," Alexa replied, "she said it was just too soon, too fast. I think they'll probably have a regular wedding next year."

They covered the whole park, standing in every line that wasn't a mile long, getting soaked on the log ride, and eating so much ice cream and cotton candy that Alexa felt sick. The roller coasters seemed to be a big hit with her mom especially, and as the cart was click-click-clicking up yet another steep incline, Alexa glanced at her, to see a wild, expectant excitement on her face.

Alexa knew that was the same look her mom got whenever she went out at night on one of her binges. Just the sight of it made Alexa's stomach plunge—even before the roller coaster crested over the top of the hill and headed back down again.

Choosing a ring took a long time, much longer than Danny expected, mostly due to the three-sister conference call during which he had to listen to a lengthy lesson on how to pick a diamond and then describe each of his top choices as he narrowed them down. At least the sweet old diamond dealer was very patient, and in the end he gave Danny a "family discount," despite the fact that they were only tenuously related through in-laws. Danny was no jewelry expert, but knowing Jo as well as he did, his final choice of a ring seemed perfect, and he felt certain she would love it.

He left the jewelry store with the rock in a box in his pocket and a smile on his face, surprised to see that the day was getting away from him. After sleeping late, lingering over breakfast with Jo, driving into the city, and then haggling with his sisters over the phone, it was almost 5:00 pm. Now he was ready to do this one other errand, and then he could head back.

Danny walked the ten blocks to Lexington. When he was almost to the hospital, he ducked into a florist shop, picked out the biggest bouquet of flowers they had, and burdened his already aching credit card with yet another purchase.

As he waited for the woman to ring him up, he noticed a roll of stickers nearby with the words "Heavenly Days Florist" printed in an elegant script of gold and pink. Discreetly, he pulled off a sticker for himself, and when he got outside with the bouquet he took a moment to slap the sticker on his front shirt pocket.

Inside the hospital, he played the role of delivery person to the hilt, suggesting that since the bouquet was so very huge and heavy he'd be happy to deliver it all the way to the patient's room rather than saddle the elderly volunteer with it. The woman gladly sent him up to the fifth floor. There, he asked for the room for Bradford Quinn and was directed toward the end of the hall.

Danny held the bouquet in such a way that it would block his face, then he lightly knocked, pushed the door open, and stepped inside.

"Floral delivery," he said.

"Whoa!" he heard Bradford reply. "Who's that from?"

Danny walked further into room, hiding his face, and made his way around to the other side of the bed. Then he set down the flowers on a rolling table, thrust out a hand, and quickly knocked the call button out of Bradford's reach. Attached to the rail by a cord, it hung in midair, swinging back and forth under the bed.

On the bed, Bradford sat half propped up, his eyes wide, his face pale. The guy was totally banged up and bandaged, but at least he seemed mentally clear and alert.

"Hello, Bradford," Danny said. "Remember me? Jo's friend Danny? I just thought I'd drop by so we could have a little chat."

25

Jo didn't know where Danny had gone, but she had an idea it had something to do with making their engagement official. Last night, there had seemed to be no need for a ring, but now, in the light of day, she was secretly pleased beyond belief. What would that feel like, to be able to look down at the ring finger of her left hand and see a piece of jewelry that represented their commitment?

Jo didn't want to seem shallow, but she simply couldn't wait.

In the meantime, she busied herself by cleaning up last night's mess, since Consuela was tied up down at the hospital and none of the part-timers worked on the weekends. As Jo vacuumed the areas where the police had stomped around, tracking dirt, she thought about what it would take to put together a small but elegant wedding.

The only problem she could foresee in their plans was an immediate one: the seven weeks that still remained of Danny's internship in Paris. He had already said that he was willing to give that up, but now that this current crisis was being resolved, there was really no good reason for him to have to make that sacrifice—no good reason except that she couldn't bear for them to be apart that long! When they were tossing around potential wedding dates earlier, they had settled on a Saturday afternoon in late August, which would be tough to pull off in such a short time but not impossible. Still, Jo wondered, how could they coordinate a wedding so soon if Danny was thousands of miles away during most of their engagement?

"You've looked better," Danny said to Bradford, taking in the various bandages and bruises. "Must feel pretty rotten too."

"Get out of here, Danny, or I'll yell."

"I'll get out of here as soon as you tell me what I want to know. Trust me, Bradford. Yelling is not in your best interest."

"Why should I talk to you?" Bradford asked, trying to reach for the call button but barely able to move his arm.

"Maybe because I've figured out a few things," Danny said. He pulled up a chair and then sat, making himself comfortable. "You see, I heard your little story about the night you played the big hero in Newark, with Alexa. But unlike everyone else, I was having trouble believing that you *just happened* to be driving through that part of town and *just happened* to see a teenage girl slumped on the side of the road. You were such a big man and all, saving her like that. Funny, but I'm not buying it."

"I have no idea what you mean. Alexa had a stroke. She needed my help."

"Sure she did, but let's get real. You didn't *just happen* to see her at all. You were waiting for her when you saw her fall. Waiting for your little delivery of amphetamines."

"What makes you think that?"

Danny hesitated, not wanting to reveal that his source was Alexa herself.

"I've done some looking around," Danny said nonchalantly. "And now that I know about all of your nasty little habits, particularly your, uh, business venture with Alexa's mother, I just can't help but think that there are others who ought to know about all of that as well. The cops, Jo's dad, your immediate supervisor at the pharmaceutical company..."

"No," Bradford whimpered.

"Feels pretty scary to be so helpless, doesn't it?" Danny asked, hating being cruel but not knowing what else to do. "Kind of like how Jo feels not knowing all the facts."

Bradford shook his head back and forth.

"I told Jo everything I know."

"Oh, I don't think you did."

Danny lifted the receiver from the telephone and began dialing.

"I wonder if Jo's dad has his cell phone on. I think I'll start with him. Too bad you'll have no chance of ever working for Bosworth Industries again."

"Okay, okay! What do you want to know?"

Danny hung up the phone.

"We can make this quick, Bradford. Let's start with your conversation in New York with Jo. The way she describes it, getting any real information out of you was like pulling teeth. Makes me think you probably had something to hide—and you were trying to tell her just enough to keep her safe while not having to incriminate yourself in any way. Am I warm?"

Bradford just looked at him, sweat starting to bead up along his brow. Finally, he gave a slight nod.

"So, let's see. What could be your big secret?" Danny continued. "Maybe that you were involved in the threat on Jo somehow? Maybe that you were double-dealing and triple-dealing behind the scenes and somehow started the ball rolling that put Jo in danger in the first place?"

"Why do you think that?" Bradford asked, averting his eyes.

"Because the terms of her grandfather's trust were completely confidential, Bradford. However, you knew what Jo stood to inherit if you married her because her parents told you. My theory is that when all was said and done, you blabbed that information to the wrong person."

The room was quiet for a long moment, and when Danny looked at Bradford, he was surprised to see that the man had tears in his eyes.

"I love Jo," Bradford said. "I don't want her to die."

Seizing the opportunity, Danny leaned forward, elbows on his knees.

"If you love her," he said, much more kindly, "then tell me what I need to know to keep her safe. Someone tried to kill her again yesterday. Nearly electrocuted her with a toaster."

That seemed to be what Bradford needed to hear to finally make him talk.

"It was my big mouth," he admitted, closing his eyes. "I blabbed. I told the wrong people that the gravy train might be coming to an end."

"The gravy train?"

"Yeah. If Kent Tulip gets his way, the Fibrin-X studies will eventually be squelched completely. There goes all of the funding for poor Alexa's fancy new lifestyle. To make matters worse, if Neil is correct in saying that such a move would spell financial disaster for the pharmaceutical company, then not only would they go out of business, but I'd lose my job, and I'd no longer have access to the Trephedine. Goodbye gravy train for everybody."

Trephedine? The only "Trephedine" Danny had ever heard of was a nasal decongestant that was sold over the counter at drugstores. Not wanting to communicate his ignorance and call his own bluff, however, Danny focused on the first part of what Bradford had said instead.

"Who are the 'wrong people' that you told?"

"My business partner and her boyfriend."

"Business partner? Alexa's mom, you mean?"

"Yeah. Misty. And her on-again-off-again loser of a boyfriend, Rick."

"What did you say to them?"

"I don't know. I wasn't thinking. I was a little drunk. I told them all about the disagreement in the company about the Fibrin-X and the way the trust is laid out. I said that if I could get Jo Tulip to marry me, the money might keep flowing, but without my influence in the matter, then unless Jo were dead, the well was going to dry up. Like an idiot, I actually said that. Unless Jo were dead. I was speaking theoretically, but I'm afraid Rick decided to handle things literally."

"Why do you think that?"

"Because word on the street a week later was that he'd been asking around about Jo Tulip. The guys at the lab told me that Rick had even wondered aloud how you could kill someone and make it look like an accident."

Jo put down her book, surprised at how dark it was getting outside. Where was Danny? He'd said he'd be gone a few hours, but this was pushing it. Since he left, she had bid the police hello and goodbye, given Chewie a bath, done her nails, and read four chapters of a novel.

With a strange, uncomfortable feeling, Jo realized that after several days of extra security and round-the-clock bodyguards, she had now swung to the other extreme and was here in this giant house all alone. The thought was unnerving. At least Chewie was with her.

But were the doors even locked downstairs? Jo thought she and Chewie ought to check and make sure. Halfway down the stairs, she realized that at least there was still one person around, the guard in the little hut at the end of the driveway. Her hands shaking, when Jo reached the kitchen she looked up the phone number for the hut on a list on the counter and dialed. She was comforted to hear him answer the phone and assure her that he'd be there all night if she needed him.

"In fact," he said, "you've got a car coming up the drive right now."

Jo thanked him, hung up, and went to the window, hoping to see Danny's rental car. Instead, it was the old junker driven by Alexa's mother's boyfriend. Feeling relieved to have someone here with her, Jo opened the door as the car came to a stop in front of the house.

Danny dialed Eleanor's house but got a busy signal. Hanging up, he tried Jo's cell phone, but there was no answer. He decided to finish his information-gathering from Bradford before trying again.

"Did you confront Rick?" Danny asked Bradford. "Did you tell him about the rumors you heard?"

Bradford shook his head miserably.

"I tried. But he sort of comes and goes. When I went to talk to him, he had disappeared. That's when I started getting nervous. Misty said he went back to his apartment across the river for a few days to pack up some of his stuff in preparation for moving in with her. But I thought maybe he had gone to Pennsylvania, looking for Jo. I couldn't take that chance. I knew I had to tell her the truth."

"Why didn't you just call the police?"

Bradford looked at him and took a labored breath.

"Why do you think?" he asked. "Because of the Trephedine."

"Yeah, what do you think the cops would do if they knew about all that?" Danny asked, hoping his question was vague enough to lead somewhere.

"Well, let's see. For starters, I'd go straight to prison for a variety of offenses."

"Like what?"

"Oh, gee, I don't know, forged documents, establishing a front company, using circuitous routing for the delivery of pharmaceuticals—the list goes on and on. Misty and Rick would go down for possession and distribution of precursor chemicals. They'd probably both squeal, which would expose the truth behind the entire meth lab at the Grave Cave. It's like dominoes, my friend. Everything would topple against everything else. And all because of a few thousand units of cold medicine."

Lapping at the edges of Danny's memory was an article he had read once about the production of methamphetamines in clandestine meth labs. From what he could recall, the first step in creating the drug was often accomplished by taking an over-the-counter product that contained ephedrine or psuedoephedrine—which must be what Bradford was calling "precursor chemicals"—and boiling it down into a concentrate. That was why, the article had said, that many states were starting to limit the amount of such products that any one customer could purchase.

"I thought it was illegal to buy more than two or three packs of drugs like Trephedine at a time."

"Yeah, duh," Bradford said, "but I work the for the company that *makes* it. It was all Misty's idea. She and Rick hooked in with a bogus Internet pharmacy, and all I had to do was set up an account to which I sell Trephedine in bulk. Individual customers may be limited to three packs at a time, but the retailers aren't. So far, it's proven to be a very lucrative side business. The guys at the lab pay us well, Misty and Rick serve as the middlemen, and I get a commission on the sales."

"Sounds like you've got it all figured out," Danny said, shaking his head, wondering how Bradford managed to sleep at night.

"It's a real sweetheart deal, all right. Unfortunately, to Rick at least, the profits are worth killing for."

Alexa, Misty, and Rick came into the house, their mood light. Apparently they had been to an amusement park, and from the way things sounded, they'd eaten everything from churros to snow cones.

"Before you go, you have to come up and see what I did with the flowers for Jo and Danny's almost wedding," Alexa told her mother. "We'll be right back, Uncle Rick."

"Take your time," he replied.

Alexa and her mother went up to Alexa's bedroom, leaving Jo in the foyer with a man she had met only briefly before. Feeling awkward, she wondered if she should suggest that they take a seat in the living room, and then it dawned on her to bring him to the kitchen instead.

"Would you like a snack or something to drink?" she asked.

He put one hand on his stomach.

"I couldn't eat another thing, but I'd love a glass of water."

"Sure," Jo replied, "right this way."

They both went into the kitchen, Jo making light conversation, talking about how fond she was becoming of Alexa. Using the dispenser in the door of the fridge, Jo filled glasses with water for them both as she talked.

"This is a fancy kitchen," he said, running a hand across the granite countertop. "Funny that it's got a blender and a coffeemaker, but I don't see a...toaster oven."

Jo tried not to react to his comment. Instead, she simply handed him the water and met his eyes. There was something there, something very unsettling.

Then the telephone rang.

Danny was so relieved to hear Jo's voice. He was calling from the road, using a cell phone he'd borrowed from Bradford. By the time Danny left the hospital room, Bradford had been in great pain and exhausted by the effort of their conversation. He was ready for some medication and eager for Danny to go. When Danny asked if he had a phone he could take, the guy had merely pointed to the drawer in the rolling table and told him to feel free to help himself—and to please send a nurse in on the way out.

"It's me," Danny said now, "I'm glad I caught you. I have to tell you something urgent. Listen, Winnie might not be the one who pushed you at the train or messed with the toaster. I won't take the time to explain it all now, but I think that was done by Alexa's mother's boyfriend. His name is Rick."

Jo was quiet for a long moment, and then she spoke in a strained yet singsongy manner.

"Yes, she just got home a few minutes ago. Would you like to speak with her? I can go get her. She's right upstairs."

"Jo? Did you hear what I said?"

"Yes, hold on just a sec," Jo said, and then there was a clunk as she set down the phone. "Can you excuse me a minute, Rick? I've got to tell Alexa about this phone call."

"Sure," a man's voice replied.

Heart pounding, Danny didn't know what to do. Jo was in the same room as the man who wanted her dead.

Jo didn't know how she managed to get out of the kitchen, up the stairs, and down the hall without running. As she forced herself to act natural, Chewie trotting along happily at her side, she could only pray that Danny had understood what was going on here—and that he had heard her address Rick by name. Surely, Danny would summon the police right away and come immediately himself as well.

When Jo reached Alexa's room, she didn't even bother to knock on the door. She simply swung it open and stepped inside, surprising Alexa and her mother, who were sitting on the bed and looking at the silk flowers from last night. Once she and Chewie were inside, Jo shut the door behind her, locked it, and then announced that they were all in danger.

"I don't know how to say this," Jo told them frantically, racing over to the dresser and trying to push it toward the door, "and I know you won't believe me, but Rick tried to kill me on Wednesday and again yesterday. We're not safe, at least not until the police get here."

Danny's mind was racing. He was still far away, just over the bridge out of New York City. Traffic was light in the direction he was going, but even as he pressed the accelerator to the floor, he knew it would take a good half hour to get there.

He was so torn, needing to call the police but not wanting to hang up on the only connection he had to Jo. After listening to dead silence for a full minute, however, Danny finally made his decision. Gritting his teeth, he disconnected the call and dialed 911.

It took a few transfers to get his call to the right police department, but he finally got there. Knowing that what he had to say sounded crazy, Danny explained the situation as quickly as possible.

"We'll send a car right over," the cop said in response. "What's the address?"

Danny rattled the street name off from memory, but he wasn't sure about the house number. He gave the Bosworth name and said for them to look it up—but to do it fast.

"A couple of your men were just out at the house this afternoon," he added. "I'm sure they'll remember it."

"Do you want to hold on until someone is there?"

"No. I'm going to keep calling back until she answers the phone again."

"Help me," Jo said, trying to slide the large dresser against the door all by herself.

Alexa just stood there, loudly and angrily refuting everything Jo had said about Rick. But Misty seemed to believe her. She complied, and together the two women were able to move the dresser into place just as Chewie started barking and there was a loud pounding on the door.

"Jo, are you in there?" Rick's voice demanded. "Come out! You don't know what you're doing!"

Jo looked at Alexa, who burst into tears.

"Tell me it isn't true, Uncle Rick!" she yelled, and almost instantly, her mother was at her side, clamping a hand over her mouth.

"Be quiet, Alexa," she hissed, "or you'll get us all killed. Quick, show me how you sneak out at night. Get us out of here!"

"No, don't leave this room," Jo said, "we're safer in here. Where's the phone?"

"There is no phone," Alexa sobbed. "I don't have one."

No phone in here, and Jo's cell was in her own bedroom across the hall. Rick's pounding grew louder, as did Chewie's barking.

"You can do what you want," Misty hissed at Jo, "but my daughter and I are out of here. Rick keeps a gun in the car. Any minute now he might start shooting through the door."

Clearly terrified now, Alexa did as her mother said, quietly sliding open the far window and climbing out onto the veranda.

Silently, Misty went through the window next, and then, reluctantly, Jo lifted the very heavy Chewie to push him out as well. He fought her, though, for some reason afraid to go through the opening out into the dark. Quickly, Jo handed out his big bone to Misty and told her to wave it at him so he would come. Sure enough, that did the trick. Focused on getting to his treat, he scrambled through the window as Jo helped, lifting his heavy rear end off of the floor. Once he was out, the bone clenched happily in his mouth, Jo followed.

Crouching, the three women and the dog all ran across the veranda and down the back stairs, and then across the lawn toward the pasture. Jo did the best she could in her removeable cast, though she was slower than the others.

"Alexa!" Jo whispered, trying to catch up with them. "Why are you going this way? We've got to escape, not just hide. We should be going toward the front. There's a guard in the hut."

"There's too much light out front," Alexa whispered. "If he's got a gun, we'd be easy targets. Besides, this *is* an escape. There's an old gate behind the stable."

Jo remembered the old gate. Though it probably hadn't been used in a while, that was how they used to bring in the horses when she was a child.

"Don't fall in the well!" Jo warned as they veered close to the stone structure in the dark. By then they were nearly to the gate.

Once there, Alexa announced that they'd have to climb over the top. Jo instantly realized that she'd never make it. With her sore ankle, she was barely even standing at this point.

Besides, even if she could make it over, she had one problem: Chewie. There was no way they could get him over that gate without breaking his neck.

Jo told Alexa to go first, and then Misty.

"Now you, Jo," Alexa whispered as her feet touched the ground on the other side.

"I can't leave Chewie here alone," Jo said. "I just can't. I'll hide back here in the shadows and wait for the two of you to get help. If I know Danny, the police will be here soon too."

Jo looked up at Misty, who had paused at the very top of the gate.

"You're not coming with us?" she said.

"I can't make it over," Jo replied. "Even if I could, I can't leave my dog."

Misty hesitated, looking at her daughter.

"You know where to go from here, to get help?"

"Yeah," Alexa said. "There's a couple houses along the road."

Strangely, Misty swung her leg back over and started down the inside.

"I can't leave Jo here alone," Misty said. "You go ahead and go, Alexa. Jo and I will both hide and wait until you return with help."

26

Danny couldn't stand it any longer.

Calling the Bosworth house merely resulted in a busy signal. Calling Jo's cell simply rang and rang and then went to voice mail.

What's happening there?

As the needle on the speedometer entered the red zone at the very top of the dial, Danny tried again to reach the police. Once he was connected to them, they told him to be patient, that the policemen had reached the property but had not yet entered the house.

"There's always a chance that we have ourselves a hostage situation here," the dispatcher said. "They have to enter with caution."

Someone was coming toward them.

Jo and Misty crouched in tall weeds near the gate, half hidden behind a massive tree trunk. Chewie was growling low in his throat, the bone still clenched in his mouth, but Jo had her arms around him, and she was whispering calming sounds in his ear. Much to her shock, Misty slowly withdrew from her pocket a small knife, which she opened up and held poised and ready, just in case.

The way they were positioned, the knife was close to Jo's face, and even in the dark she could see that it was dirty, flecked with little black spots. Absurdly, Jo wondered if there was a household hint for that, for cleaning a filthy pocket knife.

As the man drew closer, Jo squinted to see who it might be. With the glint of the moon shining off his metal belt and the orange glow of a cigarette tip, she realized that it was Rick. Holding her breath, she prayed Chewie would remain quiet until he had passed.

At least he didn't come very close. He just poked around the empty stable for a moment and then continued making a broad sweep along the perimeter, around back. As he went, he kept saying things like, "Come on, Misty, it's okay. I'll help you. It'll be all right."

Finally, when he was well past them, Jo decided they ought to make a move toward the front of the property. Maybe Danny had misunderstood and hadn't called the police. If they could make it all the way to the guard hut, they could get some help themselves. As quietly as possible, Jo whispered her intentions to Misty. Chewie set his bone on the ground right in front of him, resting his chin nearby. To him, this was all just an interesting nighttime adventure.

"We'll have to go a little at a time," Misty whispered back, pointing toward the well. "Let's run to there first."

Without waiting for Jo to reply, Misty grabbed Chewie's bone, darted out from hiding, and ran across open lawn to the old well. Once there, she crouched down behind it and waved frantically for Jo to join her, holding out the bone so Chewie would come as well.

Jo wouldn't have chosen that particular way to go, but it was too late now.

"Come on, boy," Jo whispered to Chewie, and then they took off toward Misty.

Alexa was almost to the main road when she looked down and realized that her socks were glowing in the dark. Thank goodness Uncle Rick hadn't spotted her running across the lawn!

After so much walking at the amusement park today, her bad leg was really weak, and she tripped a few times as she went. Once she reached the dark and deserted road, she stood and looked both directions, trying to figure out which house was closest. Since it was the more familiar route, she turned right and headed toward the bus stop, knowing she would pass two places on the way.

Unfortunately, at the first big house, not a light was on and no one responded to her doorbell ringing or her pounding. Summoning even more energy, she continued down the road to the next place. But it was protected by a tall iron gate, and when she pressed the buzzer at the entrance, no one responded. She stood there and rattled the gate and yelled, but no one ever came.

What could she do?

By this time she had almost looped around to the front of the old lady's place. Suddenly she remembered the guard in the little hut at the front of the driveway. He could help her.

Clenching her teeth and dragging her right leg, Alexa kept going, making her way there as quickly as she could. As she went, she could hear sirens in the distance, and her prayer was that the cops were coming to rescue them all.

By the time Danny reached the estate and screeched to a stop in the driveway, there were four police cars there, lots of activity, and one very agitated Rick, whom they had just apprehended around the side of the house. Danny didn't see Jo anywhere, and when he asked a cop what was going on, he said that the house was empty and they were now checking the other structures and the perimeter for the three women, who seemed to have escaped from the house and disappeared into the expansive grounds of the estate.

"According to this guy," the cop said, gesturing toward Rick, "he's not the one we should be worried about. It's the woman he calls Misty. He says he can prove *she's* the killer."

"Let me talk to him," Danny said, suddenly infuriated.

The cops didn't even try to stop him. They just stood and listened to the exchange between the two men, one of whom was in handcuffs, his arm gripped tightly by a cop.

Rick defended himself against Bradford's charges, saying that the reason he had been asking around about Jo Tulip—and ruminating about murders that looked like accidents—was because he knew what Misty was planning, and he was trying to gather enough information to circumvent her efforts.

"If you knew about this," Danny challenged him, "then why didn't you do something about it sooner?"

"Because I wasn't sure at first," Rick replied. "After Bradford opened his big mouth and told us all that stuff about Jo Tulip, Misty talked about wanting her dead. But I thought that's all it was, just talk. We've been planning for a while to get back together, but it wasn't until I was moving some of my stuff into her place that I found a piece of paper with information on it about Jo Tulip—her home address, the type of car she drove, her basic schedule. Seeing that paper, I realized that Misty might've been serious."

"Why didn't you tell the police?" Danny demanded, but he knew the answer to that question: because the police would learn about the Trephedine supply and the meth lab—and that would send both him and Misty to prison.

"Look," Rick said defensively, "I've been working this thing from the only angle I could think of: I e-mailed Jo and warned her."

"Where did you send the warning e-mails from?" Danny asked, as a test.

"First one from the library in Kreston. Once the police caught on, though, I've skipped around. An Internet café. A different library, in Jersey. After I heard about what happened on Wednesday at the train station, and I knew for sure the threat was real, I haven't left Misty's side so I could make sure she didn't try anything else. Alexa and I have been trying to get her into a rehab. It's just the drugs making her do this, you know? She's not really a killer."

And that was the bottom line for Rick. Not only had he been reluctant to involve the police for his own personal reasons, he had continued to hold on to the hope that he could get the woman he loved some help without ever having to do anything official about the attempted murders.

Hobbling as quickly as possible toward the old well, all Jo could think about was Alexa's safety out there in the dark, alone on the road. Jo hated to be judgmental, but she couldn't help but think what an awful mother Misty was. Who on earth would let their 14-year-old daughter go out into dark streets alone with a killer on the loose? Misty should have left Jo with the dog and continued over that fence with Alexa.

Of course, Jo realized as she reached the well, according to Alexa this woman had been making bad decisions her whole life. Though living here in this big cold house wasn't the best situation for such a young teen, it had to be better than what she'd been living at home, with a mother to whom drugs and dollars were more important even than her own child.

Jo reached the well and crouched down, careful not to press against the old stone in case it might crumble and give their position away. Glancing at Misty, she realized that she still had the knife in one hand, but in the other she was still holding onto Chewie's bone, despite his eager whimperings.

"Let him have it or he might bark," Jo whispered.

Distracted again by the black flecks on the knife, Jo realized they looked just like the black flecks that had been on the table behind the toaster, where the cord had been scraped down to the wire.

The toaster.

Jo thought again of Rick's words in the kitchen just now, and the expression on his face. If he was the killer, was Misty "Toaster Girl"?

If so, why were there flecks on *her* knife?

Suddenly, before Jo could draw the next logical conclusion, Misty raised up the bone, tossed it as far away as she could, and said to Chewie, "Go get it, boy!"

Before Jo could get a good grip on his collar and stop him, he took off running. In the distance, Jo thought she could see extra lights coming from the front of the house. Were the police here now?

She sure hoped so, because she was standing beside a killer.

Jo looked back at Misty, eyes wide, and at the knife she now wielded toward her.

"It was *you*," Jo said, knowing it with certainty, knowing it deep in her bones. "You pushed me into the train. You rigged the toaster."

Misty was very small, very thin, but there was something almost animalistic in her gaze, and Jo was frightened.

"It's nothing personal," Misty replied, bringing the knife even closer. "I just need you out of the way. Bradford said unless you're dead the whole thing's going to come to an end. And I can't have that. As long as your death looks like an accident, I'm free and clear."

Jo tried to turn and run, but the cast slowed her efforts. In an instant, Misty reached out and gripped Jo's clothes, pushing her toward the hole in the well. Heart pounding, Jo fought back, trying to knock the knife from her hand, surprised at the strength in the small woman. As they grappled there in the dark, Jo tried to scream and yell for help, but Misty managed to work her way around to Jo's side, clamp a cold hand against her mouth, and hold the knife to her throat.

Chewie returned and began barking, and then he went for Misty. Jo managed to break free as Misty screamed, the dog doing what he could to subdue her. Terrified that Chewie might get stabbed by the flailing knife, Jo knew she had to do something. Glancing around, she spotted the bone that Chewie had retrieved. Picking it up, she gripped it in her hands like a baseball bat. Then, praying she'd make her mark and not hit Chewie by mistake, Jo swung as hard as she could.

Finished talking to Rick for now, Danny was desperate to search the grounds for Jo. Fanning out with several cops, he headed toward the garage and past it into the yard, praying that God would guide him to Jo. Far in the back, he heard a sudden sound, a deep, thunking crunch, followed by a cry for help.

It had come from way out in the back pasture. Danny and the cops took off running in that direction. As they got closer, Danny could see someone standing in the distance, but he couldn't tell which of the women it was. As they drew closer, he called out, realizing that it was Jo, just standing there next to an old well.

She spotted Danny, waited until he reached her, and then threw herself into his arms. Chewie was bouncing against him nearby, almost frantic with energy.

"Where are the others?" Danny cried.

"Alexa made it over the gate and ran for help," Jo said. "Misty's in there."

The cops bent over the opening of the well to look down inside, shining a bright flashlight.

Danny was afraid the woman might be dead, but when he looked in he saw that the fall wasn't far enough to have killed her. There was a wide brick shelf about seven feet down, and she was lying there on it, looking dazed but very much alive.

"Jo!" a voice yelled, and Danny and Jo turned to see someone running toward them from the house.

The voice sounded like Alexa's, but all Danny could see, moving up and down in the dark coming toward them, was a pair of neon green socks.

Behind her, more flashlights suddenly appeared, and Danny knew that even more cops had arrived, and that everyone was going to be okay. He pulled Jo in more tightly than before, and closed his eyes, thanking God that the woman he loved was so brave and smart and resourceful.

Jo had survived.

27

Alexa sat in the study, wrapped in a blanket, her eyes so swollen from earlier crying that she could barely see. Her throat also burned from the screaming she had done when she first realized what her mother had done. Now she just felt numb, like a piece of her had died inside.

"Here you go, honey," Jo said, coming into the room with a wet washcloth.

Jo sat at the end of the couch and Alexa laid down, resting her head on Jo's leg. Jo gently folded the washcloth and placed it over Alexa's closed eyes. Then she stroked her hair, the repetitive motion quite soothing. Out front, they could hear Danny still talking with the last of the cops, who were just wrapping things up.

Alexa couldn't believe all that had happened, that her mother had tried to kill Jo and apparently had nearly killed Bradford a few days before. In the end, she had been put into handcuffs and driven away in a police car.

The worst part was that the whole time the cops were working to get her out of the well, she kept crying and saying, "I did it for you, Alexa! I did it for you!"

Alexa knew that wasn't entirely true. Her mom had also done it for herself. According to Rick, it was all about drugs and money, as everything in Misty's life had always been about drugs and money.

At least Dr. Stebbins and his wife, Nicole, had agreed to come out to the house as soon as Jo called them. They lived in Bergen County, New Jersey, about an hour away, but they'd made it in 35 minutes. Once there, they had been a huge help. Besides getting her to calm down, they talked to her about what might happen next.

Alexa had been shocked to learn that they wanted her to come and live with them. Much to Alexa's surprise, they said they had already been discussing the details of eventual custody and guardianship, both with the old lady and with Alexa's mom.

"Alexa, we've always hoped that you would eventually live with us," Dr. Stebbins said, "as long as it was something you wanted too. This whole incident will merely speed that process along." According to him, though the full legal details would have to be ironed out later, they already had the necessary permissions they needed to take her with them tonight, if she wanted.

Did she?

Did they even have to ask?

"But what about the old lady?" Alexa had said, feeling bad for abandoning the woman who had provided so kindly for her in the last year.

"Mrs. Bosworth knows that a girl your age shouldn't be rattling around this big place by yourself," Nicole had said. "You may be fourteen, Alexa, but you still need parenting. You also need some friends your own age, not to mention a more normal, more realistic life. We've got a great youth group at our church, and there's a school for the gifted in our area where we think you would fit right in."

"But I'm not really gifted," Alexa said. "It's just the Fibrin-X that made me smart."

The doctor and his wife had looked at each other and back at her.

"Is that what you think?" he asked.

"It's true, isn't it?"

"No, not at all. The drug merely took away your problem, freeing you to realize your own potential. Fibrin-X doesn't make people smart. It just gets rid of the ADHD that stands in the way."

Alexa was stunned, but what he said made perfect sense. That's why Ethan Finch was so stupid, even though he'd received the drug too. He'd been dumb before, with ADHD. Now he was just as dumb without it.

"I was smart before?" she ventured.

"Early tests indicated a genius-level IQ," Dr. Stebbins said. "That's why we wanted to give you all of these opportunities, to see how much you could accomplish once the ADHD was gone."

"Why didn't anybody tell me?" she asked, feeling something whole, something complete, click into place inside of her.

"An oversight, I suppose. I'm sorry, Alexa. I thought you knew."

No wonder they wouldn't mind if she came to live with them. She wasn't a freakazoid at all. She was just a kid who'd been cured of a disorder.

"If I live with you," Alexa had said, "do I still have to call you Dr. Stebbins?"

He and Nicole both laughed.

"Just until the symposium," he replied. "After that, you can call me anything you want."

Now, the Stebbinses were upstairs, packing up some of Alexa's things so they could go. The thought of going with them was scary and sad and happy and thrilling all at the same time. At least they promised her that she could have all sorts of visitation privileges: out here with the old lady, at prison with her mom, even with Rick, wherever he ended up. Jo had added that once she and Danny were married, Alexa was welcome to come and visit with them anytime she'd like.

"Chewie would be thrilled," Jo added, "as would we."

Now even Chewie had begun to calm down. He was settled nearby, licking from his paws the remains of his favorite treat, a pack of cream cheese. The police had taken away his bone as evidence from the crime scene, so Jo had rewarded him with the white gooey stuff instead.

The biggest concern Alexa had was for her mom. She knew she would go to prison; she just wasn't sure for how long. Jo said that the silver lining in all of this was that at least Misty would be forced to stay sober while in custody. Jo had prayed with Alexa, asking God to turn this whole mess into a blessing in the long run, the first step toward Misty changing her life for the better.

Just as Alexa's life had changed in the last year in so many ways, for the better. Hearing the Stebbinses come down the stairs, Alexa pulled off the washcloth and sat up.

"You okay?" Jo asked.

"I'm okay."

She was thinking about the old Alexa, the one from before, that she used to picture looking in at her through the window. Maybe she was supposed to embrace that girl inside of herself and love her…and forgive her.

"Just remember that everything you've ever been through has worked together to make you who you are now," Jo said, almost as if she could read Alexa's mind. "And who you are now is one very special person."

Dr. Stebbins appeared in the doorway, holding a big cardboard box in his hands.

"You ready?" he asked Alexa with an encouraging smile.

"I guess," she replied.

Tearfully, she hugged Jo and told her goodbye. Then she walked out of the door between her new foster parents. Nicole reached out and took Alexa's hand, and even though she was too old for that, it felt nice.

As they walked toward the car, Alexa couldn't help but wonder if Nicole really did have any secret family recipes.

Dear Jo,

I'm writing this from a holding cell at the police station, dictated through the deputy here. Seeing as how I'm the only person in custody and he's kind of bored, he said it would be okay. (He doesn't want to write this part but I insisted: They must not get a lot of crime out here because the place feels like Mayberry or something. Anyway, it's a lot different than the police stations in Newark!)

Now that you know everything, I guess all I can do is apologize. I should have been more aggressive about protecting you, either by calling the police directly or at least letting you know the name of the person who wanted you dead. Sorry about that.

Misty was here, in the other cell, for a while, but they've already taken her over to the county jail. I guess they'll be doing the same with me in just a bit. I'll get to meet my court-appointed attorney in the morning and probably go before the judge after that. The cops here say that besides our other crimes, Misty and Bradford and I will all probably have the book thrown at us for coordinating the sale of the Trephedine because the courts are really cracking down on that sort of thing.

So it may be a while before I ever get to use that sparkling new toaster oven I bought. It was one of the first things I moved into Misty's place when we decided to get back together. Now it'll probably be put in storage along with the rest of our stuff until we've done our time.

At least that's one way to keep it clean, right?

Listen, thanks for being so nice to Alexa. She really looks up to you. Give her my love and tell her that despite everything, I'll still keep working those 12 steps. Thanks again for everything, and, again, I'm so sorry for what almost happened. I'm just glad it didn't.

Sincerely,

Rick

28

Jo stood at the back of the church, listening to the music and wondering how they had ever managed to pull this off. A full church wedding in Mulberry Glenn, coordinated in little more than twenty-four hours? They had done it only through the grace of God and the help of countless family and friends, especially Chief Cooper, who had somehow pulled strings in Pennsylvania and obtained them a legal marriage license in record time, much as her grandmother had done in New York. It seemed that everyone wanted Jo and Danny together, and they were willing to do what they could to help make that happen as soon as possible.

Even Danny's mother, who had probably dreamed of a big church wedding for her only son his whole life, had finally acquiesced and gone along with everyone's enthusiasm. She had made it her personal mission to find Jo a wedding dress, and by the time she was done calling her friends and scouring the local consignment shops, she had managed to collect five different choices all in Jo's size. The one Jo picked, a circa-1948 duchess satin with a flared skirt and fitted waist, turned out to be a loaner from Jo's very own across-the-street neighbor, Jean White, which made it even more special to her.

Jo couldn't believe that, just a little more than one day ago, she had fought off her attempted murderer and knocked her into the old well. It had taken a while for the police to get Misty out of there, take her into custody, and finish all of their business at the estate. Misty confessed to everything almost right away, including the train incident and the toaster, and she incriminated Rick and Bradford in a shocking drug ring besides.

As it turned out, once Winnie had been told that Jo's pursuer had been arrested and that it had turned out to be Alexa's mother, Misty,

Winnie had finally revealed her own motive for what she had done with her mother's thyroid pills.

According to Winnie, when she first learned that someone was trying to kill Jo and that it probably had to do with the family trust and the announcement about Fibrin-X, Winnie had concluded that the person most likely responsible was her own son, Ian. In an attempt to protect him from himself, Winnie had decided to do something that would cause her mother to become incapacitated, as quickly as possible, so that there would no longer be any reason for Ian to kill Jo.

Jo couldn't imagine how Ian must feel now, knowing that his own mother thought he was a murderer. No doubt Winnie's suspicions were going to affect their relationship, but at least Winnie had cared less about the division of shares than she cared about her own son.

Jo couldn't say the same for her parents. Throughout this whole mess, Kent and Helen had consistently acted out of their own best interests. Last night, after Alexa was gone, Jo and Danny had made the decision to pull together a quick church wedding the very next day. They had gathered their stuff, locked up the empty estate, and driven all the way to Mulberry Glen. On the way, after calling friends and family to enlist their help in pulling together a ceremony, Jo had called her parents and told them that she wanted them to know about the wedding. She said that they were welcome to come if they so desired, but that their relationship from here on out would be greatly modified.

"I know where I stand in your priorities," Jo had told them before hanging up. "Maybe I should have figured that out a long time ago."

Now in her own church, as the music started and Marie and Anna stood poised to head down the aisle in matching dresses that they had somehow managed to scrounge up in such a short time, Jo was grateful that Chief Cooper had volunteered to give her away. He'd been making plans to get married soon himself, and he joked that he needed the practice.

Then Jo heard her father's voice behind her.

Jo and her friends turned to see both Kent and Helen standing in the doorway, all dressed up and looking strangely subdued.

"Can we talk to you for a minute?" Kent asked Jo.

Jo told Marie to motion to the organist that they weren't quite ready to start. Then she stepped outside of church with her parents, letting the heavy doors fall shut behind her.

"What?" she asked, ignoring her mother's exclamations about how beautiful Jo looked.

Without speaking, Kent handed over a piece of paper to Jo, some sort of legal document.

"What's this?"

"Your wedding present."

Jo unfolded it and started reading, realizing right away that it was notarized statement from Kent Tulip to the board of directors of Bosworth Industries, stating that he had reconsidered his position on the matter of the Fibrin-X and he was now fully supporting the announcement of information at the symposium.

"I don't understand," Jo said, looking up at them.

"It was what you said last night about priorities," Helen told her, and Jo was shocked to see that there were actual tears in the woman's eyes. "We knew the only way we could make up for what we did was by proving to you how sorry we were. About everything. This was the grandest gesture we knew how to make."

"And trust me," Kent added, "it was pretty grand. That promise right there is going to cost us millions, if not billions, in the long run."

"Maybe not," Jo replied. "If I know you, Daddy, you'll find a way to make it work. Besides, cost effective or not, this is the *right* thing to do. People with ADD and ADHD need that cure."

Jo knew that she held in her hand proof that her father had chosen her over the company and his money. Considering that the Fibrin-X could help millions of people for many years to come, she thought it was a fair price to pay.

It was also a strange way for a parent to show love to a child, but then her parents had always been strange. She nodded finally, tucking the paper into her bouquet and thanking them both for what they had done.

"So may we walk you down the aisle?" Kent asked.

Jo looked at her father, thinking of all the hurt and pain his greed had caused her. She said no thanks, that she already had someone to do that, but she would like it if they'd take a seat in the front row, in the place of honor reserved for the bride's parents. As they went, obviously humbled, Jo was glad that eventually they would be able to put this entire episode behind them and move forward.

Full forgiveness might take a while, but at least this was a start.

"Are you ready?" the pastor asked Danny and his groomsmen.

"More than you can imagine."

The pastor led the way out of the antechamber and into the church. Danny took his place up front, astounded at the number of people who had shown up considering the amount of notice they'd given. It looked like half of the congregation was there, along with Danny's entire extended family, and even a handful of Jo's relatives as well—including her Uncle Neil and cousin Ian. (Winnie was now out on bail, but apparently she had chosen not to come. Danny didn't blame her.) The biggest surprise was to see Helen and Kent Tulip sitting in the front row. Danny was glad. That must mean that somehow Jo's parents had made an effort to heal the rift been them and their daughter.

Anna and then Marie started down the aisle, and Danny could see Jo moving into position in the doorway, her hand linked in Chief Cooper's arm.

Danny focused on his bride, his heart swelling with a greater depth of love than he had ever known. Then the music shifted, the Wedding March began, and the congregation stood and turned.

Thank You, God, for this wonderful woman, Danny prayed as Jo started up the aisle. *Make me a husband worthy of her.*

Jo walked down the aisle, her eyes locked on Danny, her heart so full she thought it might burst. What a different experience this was, to be walking toward the man she knew God wanted her to be with forever.

Thank You, Lord, for Danny. Help me to be the wife he deserves.

As she got closer, Jo took a moment to look around at all of the people who had come here to share in this last-minute affair. Jo knew that she and Danny were blessed to have so many people who loved them and wished them well. Her only regrets were that her grandmother was still in the hospital and that Alexa wasn't there. But Danny's sister Denise was videotaping everything, so later, at the reception, Jo and Danny planned to record special hellos to them both and send them copies of the tape.

For now, Jo wanted to focus on her surroundings and enjoy the moment. The church looked amazing. Anna and Marie had decorated the sanctuary with hundreds of white flowers and candles, and now that the sun had set, the room glowed with warmth.

Jo and the Chief reached the altar and stopped there as the pastor welcomed the guests and opened the ceremony with prayer. After that, Jo was given away and then found herself standing face-to-face with her beloved, holding his hands in hers.

She thought about how silly she had been to let her dislike of travel be the thing that might keep them separated for the next seven weeks—or cause Danny to give up his internship completely. Late last night, after the police were gone and she and Danny had been talking about what might happen next, Jo had realized that maybe her desire to hole up at home where it was warm and cozy and safe was more about leftover baggage from her childhood than any personal preference she might have. She decided that maybe she needed to see the world again, this time not by being dragged by her parents against her will, but hand in hand with the man she loved. When she suggested that they get married right away and get themselves back to Paris by Wednesday, so he wouldn't lose the internship after all, the look on Danny's face told her all she needed to know. After that, he had surprised her by pulling a small velvet box from his pocket, opening it up, and sliding the most beautiful ring she'd ever seen onto her finger.

Now, here she was, at the altar. Looking into Danny's eyes, she savored his very strong and absolute "I do." When she said her "I do" too, there was a ripple of relief through the congregation, followed by laughter. Jo and Danny laughed too, as did the pastor. This time, the wedding was actually going to go through.

The pastor did a beautiful job, talking about the gifts of friendship and faith and their place as the foundation of a solid marriage. At the end of the ceremony, after lighting a candle together and making their vows and exchanging wedding rings, the pastor spoke the final words they had all been waiting to hear.

"And now, Danny Watkins and Josephine Tulip, by the grace of God and the authority vested in me, I pronounce you husband and wife. You may kiss the bride."

Danny took his time about it. As the congregation was hushed behind them, Danny tenderly placed a hand on each side of Jo's face and looked into her eyes. He leaned forward and brought his mouth toward hers.

Their lips met, their kiss containing every treasure of their past, every promise of their future.

When they finally pulled apart, the congregation and the attendants all burst into applause.

"How did I manage to end up with the blessing of you as my wife?" Danny asked Jo over the din, wrapping her into a tight embrace.

"Elementary, my dear Watkins," she told him in return, her eyes glowing with happy tears. "Because from the very moment that we met, it was God's plan. He knew all along, even if we didn't."

Sharing a smile, Jo and Danny joined hands, the sound of trumpets pealed from the organ, and they started down the aisle together. As they went, Jo sent up one final prayer of thanks.

Then she looked over at the man by her side, knowing that he wasn't just her husband now, or the future father of their children, or the man of her biggest dreams.

He was, and always had been, her very best friend.

EPILOGUE

Four Months Later

Jo stood far back from the yellow line as the train pulled into the station. Once the train came to a complete stop, Danny squeezed her hand, flashed her a smile, and then they both stepped forward and climbed on board.

After doing so much travel throughout Europe, they had gotten the whole train thing down to a science. This was the last leg of their European tour before they would return to Mulberry Glenn and normal life. While Jo was eager to get back home, she would also miss the excitement of life on the road. She couldn't believe she had ever hated travel, because the past few months had been a dream come true.

They found their compartment, settled in, and then pulled out the map to see the route the train would be taking. They'd be rattling through some gorgeous countryside today, as their final stop was Salzburg, Austria. There, they would be meeting up with Kalunga Bashiri, who was in town for a photo shoot about Mozart's birthplace. Danny and Mr. Bashiri had had a lot of conversations in the last few weeks and had come up with an exciting new arrangement. Rather than allow various magazines to send liaisons of their own choosing on assignments, Mr. Bashiri had simply hired Danny to fill the permanent position as his Travel Liaison/ Photography Assistant. With the older man's health as it was, he would only be taking on two or three one-week assignments per year, which sounded just about perfect to Jo and Danny. That way, Danny could have the best of both worlds without having to sacrifice much time away from his family. Sometimes Jo would even be coming along too, just for fun.

She looked over at Danny, who was still studying the map, and she couldn't help but smile to herself. She had two secrets to tell him, one of which she had learned from Mr. Bashiri over the phone last night. It seemed that the decisions had been made by *Scene It* magazine for the photo spread of the refugees. One of Danny's pictures, snapped from atop a ladder in the GMM warehouse, was going to be included in the piece. Danny would get his first photo credit in a major magazine. Seeing as how the magazine would be coming out around the same time as the movie poster, Jo knew that his career was finally coming together just as he'd always dreamed.

As for her career, surprisingly, she had managed to tap into a whole new market for household hints. With her agent's help back home, Jo had created a new "sister" column called "Travel with Tulip." From tips on packing a suitcase to doing laundry on the road to choosing accommodations wisely, the column was rapidly gaining in popularity and had just been sold as a package deal on alternating days with Tips from Tulip for syndication. Finally, Jo had taken the legacy of her grandmother and built it back up to the market share it deserved.

Not only were things going well in both of their careers, but Jo and Danny had already begun to get involved with the Bosworth Charitable Trust on the side. They had managed to secure one large grant already, to apply toward the study of pharmaceutical solutions for certain orphan diseases. Danny had found a top-notch medical team working to find a cure for Buruli ulcers, and he had convinced Jo that the best way they could help was by providing research dollars. All in all, Jo thought she was really going to enjoy being a philanthropist.

"What are you smiling about?" Danny asked, glancing up to catch her looking at him.

"I have two secrets for you," she replied, and then she went on to tell him about the photograph in *Scene It*. He was ecstatic, pulling her in for a lengthy kiss and promising her they would celebrate tonight in the fanciest restaurant in Salzburg.

"What's the other secret?" he asked, entwining his fingers with hers, his blue eyes sparkling.

She looked at him for a long moment, thinking how very right they had both been when they thought that friendship would make a good foundation for a marriage. Truly, having Danny as a husband had exceeded her every expectation. He was fun and funny and smart and passionate and loving and tender and in every way so much more than she'd ever dreamed. She spent a lot of time these days feeling grateful to God for His wisdom and blessings.

"Well?" Danny prodded. "Was it something from your conversation last night with Alexa?"

The girl was doing very well, living with the Stebbins and going to the newly renamed Bosworth School for the Gifted. Alexa had said that she might not know as much as her peers, but she was catching up by leaps and bounds. Her favorite class was science, and she'd been thinking about becoming a doctor when she grew up. She wanted to impact lives much as her foster father had.

According to Eleanor, who had fully recovered from her thyroid scare, the announcement at the symposium about Fibrin-X had gone over better than anyone had expected, and the drug was already in what they called "Phase 3B" trials. The financial impact on the pharmaceutical company had yet to be seen, but if Jo knew her father, she knew he'd find a way to make it work out. According to all reports, Ian had received the Fibrin-X himself and was doing wonderfully. He was working with a behavioral therapist to change a lifetime of compensating habits now that his ADHD had been cured.

"Well?" Danny prodded.

"Nope. It has nothing to do with Alexa."

"Is it about Chewie?"

Oh, how she missed Chewie! He was living with Harv and doing fine, but Jo would be so glad when they were finally reunited. The whole arrangement had worked out perfectly, because at the end of the year Harv would be moving into a retirement village that didn't allow pets, and he said that this gave him one last chance to have a dog before then.

"Okay, then what's your secret about?" Danny asked. "From the look on your face, it's a big one."

Jo was unable to keep from grinning.

"Yes, it's a big one," she said. "It's about the new construction on the house."

"Did you make a decision on a contractor?" he asked, as he knew that Jo wanted to get the work for their home expansion planned out and started as soon as they got back.

"Yes," she said, "but I think we'll have to change the timetable a little bit."

Jo thought of the errand she had run yesterday evening while Danny was busy on the phone with Mr. Bashiri. Fortunately, the pharmacies in Europe carried pregnancy testing kits, complete with instructions in English.

"Oh?" he asked. "How's that?"

"We need to make that extra bedroom a priority."

"Why?"

"Because by my calculations," Jo said tenderly, reaching out to touch his face, "we're going to need it in about eight months for a nursery. The only question is whether we should paint it pink or blue."

Question for www.tipsfromtulip.com

Send   Chat   Attach   Address   Fonts   Colors   Save As Draft

To: tulipfan@mailnet.com

From: JoTulip@tipsfromtulip.com

Date: Sunday, May 18, 7:43 PM

Subject: About the Author

About the Author

Elementary, My Dear Watkins is Mindy's eighth novel for Harvest House Publishers. Previous books include the Million Dollar Mysteries: *A Penny for Your Thoughts, Don't Take Any Wooden Nickels, A Dime A Dozen, A Quarter for a Kiss,* and *The Buck Stops Here.* The Smart Chick Mystery series includes *The Trouble with Tulip* and *Blind Dates Can Be Murder.*

Mindy is also a playwright, a singer, and a former stand-up comedian. A popular speaker at churches, libraries, and civic groups, Mindy lives with her husband and two daughters near Valley Forge, Pennsylvania. Visit Mindy's website at www.mindystarnsclark.com or drop her a note at

MindyStarnsClark@aol.com

Also, just for fun, check out www.TipsfromTulip.com. The story may be fictional, but the website is real.

THE TROUBLE WITH TULIP

"I have a solution for every situation...
Except my own love life and, oh yeah,
the dead body next door."

Helpful Hints and Homicides

Meet Josephine Tulip—definitely a smart chick. She's a twenty-first century female MacGyver who writes a helpful hints column and stumbles on dead bodies in her spare time.

Meet Danny Watkins, Jo's best friend. He's a talented photographer who longs to have his work appear on a cover of *National Geographic* but finds himself taking prom photos and pet portraits instead.

Together, this mismatched duo works to solve a local murder—much to the dismay of the police, who are hoping for an open-and-shut case. But there's something not quite right about the evidence. Jo knows it and Danny believes her.

Turns out, sleuthing brings out the best...and the worst...in their relationship. As Jo tries to solve the mystery in her neighborhood, she realizes she's facing an even bigger mystery—what's going on in her heart?

BLIND DATES CAN BE MURDER

*"Simple solutions are my specialty...
So why is my love life so complicated?"*

Blind Dates Give Everyone the Shivers

Poor Jo Tulip. She's a sassy single woman full of household hints and handy advice for every situation...except matters of her heart. Her first romantic outing in months is a blind date—okay, the Hall of Fame of Awful Blind Dates—but things go from bad to worse when the date drops dead and Jo finds herself smack in the middle of a murder investigation.

Poor Danny Watkins. He loves Jo but doesn't know how to tell her. They have been best friends since childhood, and Jo considers him only a pal. As Danny helps Jo with the investigation, he waits for the perfect moment to tell her how he feels about her. When that moment arrives, however, Danny is surprised to find that the outcome isn't at all what he expected.

With Danny's help, Jo attempts to solve one complicated mystery while trying to figure out another—what on earth is going on with her love life?